Praise for Isabel Cooper's
Legend of the Highland Dragon

RT Book Reviews Top Pick
Barnes and Noble Review
Best Romance of 2013
Library Journal Starred Review
Booklist Starred Review

"The mix of hardheaded realism and fantasy in this novel is enchanting... Victorian mores and melodrama are cast in sharp relief when dragons and fantastical quests are thrown into the plot."

—*Barnes and Noble Review*,
A B&N Best Romance of 2013

"An outstanding read! A fast-paced, smartly written plot—fraught with danger and brimming with surprises—makes it impossible to put down."

—*RT Book Reviews* Top Pick, 4.5 Stars

"Mesmerizing, ingenious, slyly humorous, and wonderfully romantic, this unusual charmer is a winner for fans of paranormals. A Highland dragon? How can it miss?"

—*Library Journal* Starred Review

"A light romance with strong character development and a plot rich with supernatural themes... Comical and genuine."

—*Booklist* Starred Review

Praise for Isabel Cooper's
No Proper Lady

Publishers Weekly Best Book of the Year
RT Book Reviews Seal of Excellence
RT Reviewers' Choice Finalist,
Best Book of the Year
RT Reviewers' Choice Finalist,
Best First Historical Novel

"A genre-bending, fast-paced whirl with fantastic characters, a deftly drawn plot, and sizzling attraction…"

—*RT Book Reviews* Top Pick, 4.5 Stars

"Sexy, edgy, and stunningly inventive…will have readers begging for more."

—*Library Journal* Starred Review

"A compelling debut that smartly mixes history, action, romance, and magic."

—*Publishers Weekly*

"High-stakes, world-saving magical adventure with wonderful characters and a sexy romance."

—Susanna Fraser, author of
An Infamous Marriage

"Sensational!"

—*Fresh Fiction*

the HIGHLAND DRAGON'S LADY

ISABEL COOPER

sourcebooks
casablanca

Published by Sourcebooks Casablanca, an imprint of Sourcebooks, Inc.
P.O. Box 4410, Naperville, Illinois 60567-4410
(630) 961-3900
Fax: (630) 961-2168
www.sourcebooks.com

Printed and bound in Canada
MBP 10 9 8 7 6 5 4 3 2 1

To my late grandmother, Helen Virginia (Myers) Kunkle, a truly great lady.

One

SOMEONE WAS CLIMBING UP TO COLIN MACALASDAIR'S room.

The plum tree below the balcony where he stood was moving, first lower branches shaking, then higher ones. The night was windless, and neither a bird nor a squirrel would cause quite that much disturbance. Not even the stable cats of Whitehill Abbey, overfed as they were, could manage it.

So, then: a human being, and probably a live one, despite the abbey's reputation for ghosts. Ghosts generally didn't bother climbing trees, in Colin's limited experience.

He didn't think Whitehill housed any mortals who wanted him dead. When the eldest son of the house asked a chap to pay a visit, the locals weren't generally disposed toward assassination, at least outside of novels. Edmund Talbot-Jones and his parents seemed harmless enough, and the other houseguests would be more likely to drive a man to suicide than kill him outright, although Colin thought Mrs. Osbourne wouldn't be above a discreet bit of arsenic in the teacup if she thought the situation required it.

Of course, he could be wrong.

The leaves were rustling just above the edge of the balcony now. Colin stepped back into the shadows and waited. One way or another, he suspected he'd be enjoying himself immensely over the next few minutes.

The intruder shimmied off a branch, grabbed the edge of the balcony, and swung herself up to sit on the railing. *Herself* was the definitive pronoun: the girl in question was wearing a man's shirt and a pair of trousers, but both were rather small even for the average stable boy, and she...wasn't. Athletic and limber, yes; boyish, definitely not.

This evening was definitely looking more interesting.

Nonchalantly, with the air of having regularly occupied exactly such a seat, Colin's visitor slid forward on the railing, twined her legs around the marble bars below her, and made herself comfortable. In the darkness, from Colin's distance, a mortal man would have seen only her figure and the braid of dark hair trailing behind her.

Not being mortal, Colin saw that her face was long and delicate-looking, with big brown eyes and a turned-up nose with a spray of freckles across it.

That was as far as observation took him before the girl started to speak.

"You really are a prize idiot, you know that?"

Other people, most notably Colin's siblings, had made similar observations, but they hadn't prepared him to receive such comments with perfect equanimity, particularly coming from the small mouth of a girl he'd never met in his life.

Words didn't precisely fail him. He could think of quite a few. But the process of choice stumped him just then and created a receptive silence, which the girl clearly read as a request for more on the same theme.

"*If* you don't like a girl, you poor dumb fish," she went on, "the thing to do is to avoid her, and possibly to talk about other women whenever you can. You do *not* have long, vague conversations with her in gardens at twilight, and you certainly don't jump into lakes after her hat. And you needn't tell me that you do like her, because this is me talking to you, and I know perfectly well that you don't. It doesn't seem likely that anyone could."

Hat? Lake? Gardens? Colin would have admitted, under very little pressure, to having walked in any number of gardens with any number of women. He couldn't precisely swear that, over the course of three hundred years, he'd never rescued a hat from a watery grave. None of the above, however, had happened over the course of his time at Whitehill.

He cleared his throat.

"Which brings me to point two," said the girl, sensing that the moment was right to press forward like the proverbial wolf on the fold, "which is that, if you think you're going to marry her, I'll throw you into the lake myself. There are *plenty* of perfectly nice girls in England who'd be glad to marry anybody. Even if you've given in to Pater at last, you've got no need to choose some"—she waved one white-clad arm in a vigorous manner, causing Colin to shift his weight forward in case she fell from the railing—"some mad scientist's cross between a toffee pudding and a Salvation Army captain."

"Ah—"

The girl slid down from the railing. Her tone softened. Having gotten the initial message across, she clearly felt that she could now show some mercy. "Don't fret," she said. "I'll get you out of it this time, and I'll have a word with Pater about the sort he keeps pushing on you. But *do* be careful, won't you? Leave the Heselton filly to that dancing-master-looking Scottish chap you brought down. *He* knows how to handle a girl, if you believe Bettina. And Lily. And—"

"My dear lady," said Colin, stepping forward and bowing before she could continue the list. Housemaids were clearly creatures of little discretion and a great deal of trouble. "I'm afraid you've been laboring under a case of mistaken identity."

At this point, the situation could have gone a number of ways. The girl might have screamed. She might have fainted, although your modern girl, in Colin's experience, was rather beyond fainting, particularly the specimen of modern girl who climbed up to balconies in the dead of night. She might have thrown a small but tasteful potted geranium at Colin's head, or she might have slapped him.

Instead, she laughed.

Respecting the hour, she laughed quietly, but she didn't otherwise bother to restrain herself. She leaned against the railing, tilted her head back, and broke into a cascade of giggles that made her shoulders shake and let Colin see that her breasts were clearly unbound beneath her shirt. The night air, even in July, had a certain chill, but heat welled up between his legs nonetheless. He adjusted his dressing gown to provide a little more discretion.

"Well, I'll be damned," she said eventually. "You're—"

"The dancing-master-looking Scottish chap. Colin MacAlasdair, at your service."

"Reggie Talbot-Jones. Er, Regina. Miss Talbot-Jones." She made a face. "Doesn't seem like I can stand on propriety, though, considering the circumstances. And I've known plenty of dancing masters in my life, all of them very handsome and, um, respectable."

"Good Lord, I hope not."

Reggie giggled again. "You really ought to have let me know sooner," she said.

"Oh, aye, probably. But you didn't really give me much chance to think, you know. Poor Edmund."

"Poor Edmund, my foot. You don't know half the trouble he'd have gotten into if I wasn't his sister. And why are you in his room, anyhow?"

"Ultimately, because Mr. Heselton broke his ankle," Colin said and remembered that Reggie was a daughter of Whitehill. "Have any of the steps on the front stairway ever broken before?"

"Not since we've been here," said Reggie, "but that'll only be two years at Candlemas." She lifted her eyebrows. "If you're asking whether I think the ghost could be responsible, the answer is yes. But you knew it would be. You're here because of the ghost, aren't you?"

"I'm here because your brother invited me. And because I was curious," Colin admitted.

Mr. Talbot-Jones had not invited public scrutiny of his house's less material inhabitants. His guest list, though comprised of a number of people versed in the occult, included nobody as well-known as Blavatsky had been or Besant still was, and he was clearly trying his hardest to seem as if he'd simply decided to host the indefinite houseguests that any wealthy man might welcome in summer. They'd all played croquet the day before, and there'd been sundry talk of shooting and boating among those assembled.

Edmund had put the invitation in almost those terms. "It'll be a lark," he'd said. "Even if they don't manifest more than a bit of gauze. And I could use a bit of friendly company."

"You do seem like a *curious* sort of man," said Reggie, giving him a once-over. "Since Edmund invited you and not Pater, does that mean you've no idea what to do with a ghost?"

"Depends on the ghost, I should think."

"Ha," said Reggie, her suspicions clearly confirmed. "Well, if you're just up to gawk, at least you won't be drifting around being mystic at everyone. We had a girl in over the winter who kept lecturing me on the spiritual properties of my food. I think I lost two stone before I fled back to London."

"I'd imagine you'd find that helpful, considering your hobbies." Colin gestured toward the tree.

"One, climbing trees isn't a hobby; two, I wasn't that heavy to start with—so chivalrous of you to mention that, by the way—and three, that plum is very sturdy."

"Not as sturdy as the floor, I'd think. Do you always take the arboreal route?"

"It's easier than sneaking through the house," said Reggie, shrugging. "Even when I was a child and we didn't have ghosts, we had vases. And ornamental tables. And hat stands. Do you know how much damage the average hat stand can do to a growing girl?"

Colin laughed. "I can't say I've ever made a study. But why sneak at all?"

"When I was young, because of"—she waved a hand—"nannies and governesses and housemistresses and things. They disapprove of nighttime excursions. I can't imagine why. I've always found them awfully broadening to the mind."

"That's probably why," said Colin.

"And now I don't want to wake the place. The maids talk, and then Mater frets—and if I want to air certain frank views about certain houseguests, it's dashed hard to find a time to do so during the day. Especially with those houseguests languishing around the place all the time, pouting soulfully."

The air of scorn about Reggie was too thick, in fact, to cut with the proverbial knife. A kukri might have done the job, or a machete.

Out of a mingled sense of helpfulness and devilment, Colin pointed out, "Such sisterly honesty isn't likely to do very much in the way of changing Edmund's mind, you know. Not if he's in love with the girl."

He knew that much from experience. Over the last few hundred years, he, Stephen, and Judith had all waxed fairly frank with each other on the subject of romantic connections, and all three had failed to make much impression—though Colin did give himself credit for pushing along his brother's romance with the woman who was now his wife.

"He's not," said Reggie.

"Are you certain? Miss Heselton isn't to everyone's tastes when it comes to personality, but there are men who like that sort of thing, and she's certainly up to the mark physically, if you'll forgive my bluntness."

"I will," said Reggie, perhaps feeling once again that a woman who vaulted onto balconies in the dead of night couldn't stick strictly to the approved rules of conversation. "But Edmund doesn't care about that, and he doesn't want to marry her."

She spoke quickly and clearly impulsively, but there was no idealism in her voice, no suggestion that she was a high-minded young woman who expected her brother to care only for the heart and soul or other such sentimental rubbish. No, Reggie spoke as one who knew facts that she wasn't telling.

"He must confide in you a great deal," said Colin, meaningfully.

"He does," said Reggie, with a sudden look of realization and alarm, "and I shouldn't be discussing him with a stranger. A pleasure to meet you, I'm sure, but—"

She turned toward the balcony.

"No, wait a bit!" Colin said. Reggie was the best

bit of entertainment he'd had all day, and he hated to lose her to a sudden attack of scruples. When she didn't turn at his voice, he darted forward and caught her by the wrist.

She did turn then, her eyes wide with fear, but it didn't matter. At the touch of skin on skin, Colin felt a presence in his mind, a brush of warm contact that came, in the strange way that mental contact some-times worked, with the smell of oranges.

He thought of flying on a summer's day, wings open to the updrafts, in southern climates where he hadn't been for decades.

Then he heard Reggie's shocked voice: "You're a *dragon?*"

Two

REGGIE KNEW SHE SHOULDN'T HAVE SAID IT, NOT ALOUD.

Since the age of thirteen, when her strange power had started expressing itself, she'd begun to learn the art of a closed mouth and a good poker face, as hard as both were for her. At eighteen, after an evening that still hurt to remember, she'd doubled her efforts. Now she considered herself very good when she wanted to be.

Most people didn't grab her. Most people wore gloves, and so, most of the time, did Reggie. Society made her situation a little easier that way. And most people didn't remember flying on great leathery wings or the glint of sunlight off midnight-blue scales.

Under the circumstances, Reggie really couldn't kick herself too hard for anything she blurted out.

She did wish she hadn't said it when Colin's hand was around her wrist, though. He was a dragon. He was also tall as a man, and despite his slim body, he'd caught her with considerable strength; and from what Reggie could make out in the moonlight, he was staring at her like he'd been poleaxed.

People could get damned angry when one found

out their secrets. Colin's secret was more shattering than most.

Taking advantage of his distraction, Reggie yanked her wrist away and stepped backward, trying not to stumble. Dignity: that was the ticket. Her backside hit the balcony railing and she yelped.

Dignity. Right ho.

"And what on earth," Colin asked, tilting his head to the side and staring at her, "are *you*?"

He hadn't pulled the sinisterly curved knife that books said was generally inevitable in these situations. He hadn't tried to throttle her—which was an acceptable alternative from the perspective of your average faceless fiend or ax-wielding maniac—and he didn't sound angry. Speculative might end up being just as bad, in the end, but Reggie could at least play for time.

"Just a girl," she said, "as far as I've ever been able to tell."

"A girl who can read minds," said Colin, "from a family whose house is haunted."

"We only moved in two years ago. They're not *our* ghosts," said Reggie, for all the good that correcting him was likely to do her, "and I can't exactly read minds. And I won't tell anyone, I promise."

Colin chuckled. "Of course you won't. Who'd believe you? You can put *your* mind at ease," he added, with a graceful wave of one hand. "I've no ill intentions toward you. I'm only curious."

"You mentioned that," said Reggie.

Now that she could breathe normally again, and the balcony felt more solid underneath her feet, she had to fight the urge to be surly. Her temper had been the subject of several tedious governess lectures when she was growing up. In this instance, she couldn't help feeling some justification for it.

While she was trying to adjust her view of the world, Colin was standing there, his hands in his smoking jacket, looking down at her without any apparent care. It was quite possible that the next word out of his mouth was going to be "fascinating," and it was quite possible that Reggie would push him off the balcony if it was.

To add insult to injury, he was also handsome: tall and slim, with high cheekbones and a pointed chin, large silver-gray eyes, and thick dark hair that blew picturesquely in the faint breeze. Reggie didn't doubt that he knew it.

She threw back her shoulders, raised her head, and asked, "Do I get to be curious too? It's not as if you're an ordinary sort of fellow."

"Oh," said Colin, his voice dropping and taking on a caressing tone, "I'd be glad to gratify *any* curiosity you're having, I'm sure."

Years had passed since Reggie had left the schoolroom, and she'd run with a bohemian crowd in the meantime. She'd heard her share of suggestive comments. Most of the time, she didn't even blush. When warmth spread across her face as Colin spoke, it was due to the uncomfortable knowledge that other parts of her body were responding as well.

She crossed her arms over her chest and cursed the thin fabric of her shirt.

"I should've expected that," she said, trying to sound world-weary. She really *should* have too, except—well, he was a friend of Edmund's, and many of them weren't very interested in women.

Reggie, of course, wasn't supposed to know about such things, but there were many things she wasn't supposed to know about, and yet there was very little of the world with which she wasn't familiar by now.

So she'd thought, anyhow. She was revising that opinion at full speed.

"I didn't even know your sort *enjoyed* young women," she said, by way of firing a further shot across his bow, "at least not in any way but dinner."

"Myth and fable, I assure you," said Colin. He shrugged. "Oh, there's a villain in every family, if you look hard enough. A great-great-great-uncle might have breakfasted on the occasional peasant, and I believe an ancestor on my grandfather's side swallowed up most of a Russian regiment, but that was the spoils of war. I wouldn't dream of eating anything with a mind. Besides, it's hard enough to get a cook who won't spoil *beef*."

"That's a weight off my mind," said Reggie, laughing despite herself.

"Glad to oblige. And speaking of minds—what exactly do you do, if you don't read them?"

"I get impressions. Thoughts. Memories, sometimes. I don't do it on purpose, and I can't control it very well. It's more like being shouted at than reading."

"Sounds unpleasant," Colin said, with a refreshingly matter-of-fact sympathy. "Do either of your parents have the same power? I'm sure I'd have noticed by now if Edmund had."

"Are you?" Reggie asked, but she didn't wait for an

answer. Gentlemen did take off their gloves to shake hands; she didn't want to think there was anything more involved, not when Colin had been flirting with her a minute ago. "But no, he doesn't. Neither does anyone living in the family, as far as I've ever been able to tell. Mater's grandfather was supposed to have been 'odd,' but she wouldn't ever give me details, and Uncle Lewis went a sort of puce color when I asked him."

"That's a bad habit. Doubtless highly destructive to all sorts of circulatory systems and limbic whatnot. You shouldn't encourage him in it."

"I try not to encourage that side of the family in anything much. They're the sort that need sitting at regular intervals. But it was when I first started to read people," she said, "and I was—well, curious. What about you? Great-great-grandfathers and so on aside."

"While I'd quite like to believe myself unique in many ways," Colin said, smiling, "my powers aren't one of them. Not that England is festooned with dragons, you understand, but there are a few of us, even as late as my generation. Perhaps there are more than that, only the blood runs too thin for them to change shapes. Talents like mine—and yours—do generally pass on down the family line."

"You would say that, wouldn't you?"

Colin blinked at her, satisfyingly surprised by the change in direction. "How do you mean?"

"I do pay some attention when Pater talks. You're a lord's son, aren't you?" Memories from finishing school were always at her fingertips somehow, even when more practical things slipped her mind. "The Honorable Colin MacAlasdair?"

"As a matter of formality, yes," he said, and his eyes glinted silver in the moonlight. He took a step toward Reggie. "In actuality, I'm honorable only when I can't find any way 'round it."

Once again, Reggie was glad the railing was there to support her. This time, the weakness in her knees was more pleasant, but no less dangerous.

"I can believe that easily enough," she said and didn't even try very hard to sound disapproving. "Even without my power."

"In all justice," Colin said, "you have to admit I've not done anything particularly scandalous tonight. I was simply admiring the view, and I'll presume so far as to think your father wouldn't have given me this room if he'd minded the use of the balcony."

"But he didn't," said Reggie, finding a point of challenge and grabbing for it. "It's Edmund's room. You're just here because the vicar broke his ankle— and I'm not quite sure how that means you get Edmund's room, come to think of it."

"He was going to switch with Mrs. Osbourne, but she likes an eastern view," Colin said, and his brow crinkled slightly as he thought. "So she traded with Miss Browne, but Miss Browne is allergic to the lilacs on this side of the house, and I believe she—"

"Oh, no more." Reggie stopped him with an upraised hand. "Or at least have the grace to work it out with a blackboard and a bit of chalk. I'm sure the right angle of a parallelogram comes into it somewhere."

An owl flew by as they laughed together, its call echoing across the garden below. It was the first moving thing Reggie had seen, other than her and Colin, since she'd landed on the balcony. They might have been the only two people in the world. They were, she thought, the only two people in *a* world, at least as far as Whitehill's residents were concerned.

"How long have you been reading people?" Colin asked.

"Since I was thirteen. Edmund had just come back from school. That's why he knows. He's the only other one who really does."

"But you go about in society and everything? It must be rather hard on you."

"Not as bad as all that. It only works by touching bare skin." Reggie took a step forward, looked up into his eyes, and smiled. "And that doesn't happen very often."

Fluid, laughing, Colin held up his hands. "A point to the lady," he said. "I shouldn't have grabbed at you. But surely your maid—"

"Doesn't touch me as much as you might imagine," said Reggie. "I don't get anything through hairpins or corset strings. Besides, I can generally control myself if I know in advance that someone's going to touch me."

In moonlit silence, her words sounded like the most blatant of innuendo. From Colin's slow smile, Reggie knew that he hadn't missed the implications, either. She looked between the smile and his heavy-lidded eyes and felt her heart start beating faster.

Reggie couldn't think of anything to say that would cut the tension between them. She couldn't think of much to say in general. Any minute *Colin* was going to say something, and it would be urbane and witty and put her even more off her footing than she was now—or he'd be one of those horrid skillful men who could put her at ease, and they'd both know that he was doing so.

So Reggie stepped forward and kissed him.

Scandalous as many found her life, Reggie knew that certain things were appropriate and others were not. Rules governed the universe, as strong as the laws of gravity or Mater's fussing about seating arrangements. One of those rules was that, when throwing oneself into the arms of a strange man whose balcony one has invaded in the middle of the night, one does not kiss him with maidenly or timorous forbearance.

She'd never sat down and thought about that particular rule, but it seemed obvious now.

It seemed imperative, in fact, that she grasp Colin by the shoulders so that she could feel the muscles beneath the dark velvet of his dressing gown and the way that they flexed as he wrapped his arms around her. A sense of the appropriate also dictated that she open her mouth beneath his, caressing his lips with her tongue until they parted, and that she not simply melt bonelessly into his embrace but mold her body against his.

One had to enter into things with the proper spirit.

Also, dear God, the man could kiss. After the first few seconds, Reggie stopped thinking about technique and tactics and appropriateness; there was too much sensation to enjoy. Colin's tongue stroking against hers, for instance, teasing and suggestive, or the way his hands grazed over her back. She'd never thought of her spine as a particularly sensual place, for heaven's sake, but he trailed his fingers up from her waist to the back of her neck, and Reggie felt the touch throughout her whole body.

She did manage not to moan. The man was far too smug already.

At least she was also having an effect on him. That was very definite: she felt his rod rubbing against her thigh and felt as well as heard his sudden intake of breath when she writhed in response. Either he was very large, she thought hazily, or dressing gowns and breeches provided considerably more information on that score than more proper clothing. She wasn't complaining.

She wasn't complaining about the clothing at all. The shirt, small and thin as it was, let her feel Colin's hands on her back much more and also let her press her aching breasts against his chest. Furthermore, when Colin slid one hand down to cup her backside, she thought she felt every nerve where he touched spring to life. It was almost as good as being naked.

Before very long, she would be: naked, in her parents' house, with a man she'd met not twenty minutes before, while two floors of guests slumbered around them.

The risks crashed down on her head with the weight of a small mountain.

Reggie pulled away and stepped back. "Well," she said, breathless. "You see? I didn't learn anything about you at all."

Before Colin could reply, she leaped to the balcony, grabbed hold of a tree branch, and scrambled back to safety.

Three

"ROTTEN OLD PILE, ISN'T IT?" SPRAWLED ON A VIO-lently green plush sofa, Edmund Talbot-Jones flung out a hand, gesturing to the study and the window beyond it, where darker green drapes framed a gray, rainy landscape. "This isn't the worst of it. Mater's done one of the drawing rooms in an exotic theme. There's a stuffed lion's head that'll give even you nightmares."

"It can't be *that* ferocious, surely," said Colin, eyeing his friend with amusement and propping his feet up on an oversized black-and-gilt desk. Edmund wasn't the sort to find a dead lion particularly frightening. His mortal comrades still talked about the Rowing Blue he'd earned at Oxford, and Colin had seen himself that the man knew his way around a gun.

"No," said Edmund. "It's that badly stuffed. When Uncle Gordon gave it to us, Reggie said it looked like he'd glued a bad wig on a stray dog. Not in front of him."

"Of course," said Colin, though he suspected it was a near thing, even having known Reggie as briefly as he had. Remembering their first and last encounter, he crossed his legs and reached for his glass of brandy. Best not to let his thoughts go too far down certain paths while he was talking with the girl's brother.

At least they didn't look very much alike. They had the same dark hair, but Edmund's eyes were pale blue-gray, and his features were much broader and spread across a square face. His body was square, too, and muscular.

Colin himself was stronger than he looked, even in human form. It had been a long time since a mortal, particularly a mortal with no magical skill, had worried him.

Nonetheless, he didn't think he wanted to tell Edmund about his encounter with Reggie.

"How did you get it?" he asked, by way of a change of subject.

"Uncle Gordon. The man's actually gone on a safari. He just has no taste in gifts or taxidermists—oh, you mean Whitehill?" Edmund lit a cigarette and leaned his head back on the couch, blowing smoke toward the ceiling. "Came up for sale three years ago. The last of the family has a flat in London and couldn't be bothered with the expenses. He didn't even know he was in line to inherit until he got the letter. Not a man who wanted to be a landowner. But Pater was, so here we are."

"Here we are," Colin echoed. "Who did he inherit from?"

"Oh, you mean Old Morgan?" Edmund laughed. "That's what they called him in the village, I hear. Did you ever hear anything so gothic?"

"Not in a while," said Colin, which was true. It had been at least a hundred years.

"He was a bit of a local legend, as I recall. Shut himself up in here with his books, never went down to the village, kept barely any servants. Died aged ninety-something, with no teeth and a beard down to his knees. One hesitates to inquire about his fingernails."

"Could he be the ghost?"

"Do I look like Madam Blavatsky to you?" Holding his cigarette lazily in one hand, Edmund took a sip of his brandy. "I doubt it, though. From what Pater tells me, the place was odd even before Old Morgan fell off the twig. Nothing dramatic, but plenty of the old tricks: strange noises, cold spots, faces at the window. Old Morgan had a terrible time keeping the few servants he did have, they say. Of course, I haven't really made a study of it—by the time we bought the place, Reggie and I were full-grown. I don't know that either of us has stayed here for more than a month at a time."

"Really? I would've thought it would be just your sort of place—pastoral beauty, woods and streams, plenty of hunting. And you said that your sister was an athletic sort of girl."

"Did I?" Edmund blinked, then shrugged. "Well, I might have, and she is."

"Then—" Colin gestured questioningly, the motion sending waves of brandy against the sides of his glass. "Is it the ghosts?"

"Not hardly, though I'll own some of the things I've heard about—the shrieking and that—could wear on the nerves. No, Reggie and I know that ghosts have nothing to do with the real curse of Whitehill."

"What's that?"

Edmund grinned wryly. "Its new owners."

"Ah," Colin said, laughing. "That bad, are they?"

What acquaintance he'd had with the senior Talbot-Joneses hadn't been arduous. Then again, he wasn't related to them. He remembered a childhood friend, the son of his father's falconer, asking what was so bad about Judith. After a list of successively less convincing statements, twelve-year-old Colin had finally settled on "...and she's my *sister*."

That had said it all, at the time.

Exhaling another cloud of smoke, Edmund shrugged again. "The Aged Parents are good sorts at heart," he said carefully. "For me, it's only that they have their hearts set on marrying me off soon. Particularly Pater. Now that he owns land, he's as concerned about the succession as if our line went back as far as yours did."

"It does, in its way," said Colin.

"Yes, but it goes back to a lot of fishermen in Leeds."

"So do most people's, if you look far enough," said Colin.

"To fishermen in Leeds? They must have been a randy lot—"

"You know well enough what I mean," said Colin. Of course, *his* bloodlines had stranger things in them than a hint of blue, but the principle applied. He could very well be descended, on one side, from a Chinese milkmaid or an Indian farmer's daughter.

"Yes, but I also know you're a radical," Edmund said.

"Of course. How else would we have met?"

"At some thoroughly respectable club, perhaps. I think Pater's signed me up for two or three." Edmund sighed. "He does mean well. And it's not unreasonable to want an heir, I know."

"You're not the only child."

"But I'm the son, and that counts for more here than in your homeland, barbarian." Edmund pretended to wince as Colin pretended to glare. "And Reggie's not…that is, they think she's less likely to produce a son than I am."

"Oh? Stops clocks with her face, does she?" Colin asked, glancing casually down at his glass.

Edmund shook his head. "Rather pretty, at least as far as I'm any judge of women. But she doesn't much care for their sort of society, hasn't since she was young, and said so around the wrong company. Those people have very long memories."

"Ah," said Colin.

"Besides," Edmund said, smiling again, "they don't generally dare throw men at her, and most men wouldn't dare be thrown."

"Perhaps that's your problem," Colin offered. Wind gusted past the windows, and suddenly the room was chilly; there was probably a draft somewhere. In old houses like Whitehill, there nearly always was. He tugged his coat a little more firmly around his shoulders. "You need to be more intimidating."

"And how would I manage that, pray?"

"It shouldn't take much. You're a brawny lad, so you start with an advantage already. Scowl more, look out the window and brood on occasion, and be as terse as you can. My brother, Stephen, could give you a lesson or three."

"Isn't your brother married?"

"Yes," said Colin, "but his wife's a rare sort of creature. I suspect it'd take the better part of an army to frighten *her* off once she's got her teeth into something." Thinking of Mina MacAlasdair, he smiled and raised his glass again.

This time, with no need to conceal his thoughts, he didn't look down. The rim of the glass had nearly touched Colin's lips when he heard Edmund's wordless exclamation of horror.

Instincts centuries old froze his body into tense alertness, ready to move at any second but completely still just then. Colin's perception widened and sharpened at the same time. He saw Edmund's face, wide-eyed and openmouthed, staring at the glass Colin held.

He saw the wasps on the rim.

Four clustered there: bloated things that moved without purpose or intent, buzzing mindlessly. The sound was not faint; Colin would have heard it before, if the wasps had been in the room. He would have seen the insects if they'd been in the room.

The chill from before returned, and this time Colin knew it had nothing to do with wind or drafts. He felt the hair lift on his arms and the back of his neck. Inwardly, he felt his other shape stir, then subside as his human mind rejected that option. Slowly, with utmost care, he put the glass down.

The desk buzzed underneath his feet.

"Colin?" Edmund had turned toward the desk, his eyes taking up most of his face. He began to rise.

"Be still," said Colin, lifting a hand.

He stood up. The buzzing was louder now, growing

by the second. The brandy glass was trembling by the time his feet hit the ground.

He breathed a word in Latin, transferring his vision to a different level of reality, and saw the pulsing yellow-black blotch where the desk had been. He had time to do that much.

Then the desk split apart.

Mahogany split apart in a series of jagged-edged cracks, too quiet and easy a succession of sounds to have come from such a sturdy wood. Wasps poured out in a seething cloud. Colin glimpsed a few of them, enough to see that they were as overgrown as the ones on his glass, but he couldn't make out any more details. There was only the cloud, buzzing and furious.

"Oh bloody goddamn *hell*," said Edmund, sounding half-strangled. Colin didn't turn around, but he could hear the other man's feet hit the floor. "Come on, old man, we've got to—"

He was running toward Colin as he spoke. Colin didn't know why; it seemed a damned stupid thing to do, and he was about to tell Edmund as much.

That was when the cloud of wasps dove.

Colin raised his hand again, a swift, sharp motion like the slash of a blade. He focused his will and his vital energy outward through his palm; force flowed down his arm with a faint glassy pain he'd mostly learned to ignore. The air around his hand crackled with blue sparks.

He lifted his gaze to the oncoming wasps. The power went with it, not traveling through the air as lightning did, but leaving his hand and coalescing in a spinning, hissing sphere around the cloud of insects.

Colin focused his eyes, breathed out—and the sphere flashed once, painfully bright.

A bitter, burnt smell filled the room, and so did the sound of a heavy rain: the bodies of the wasps dropping to the floor. Colin stepped forward, reaching for one of them, and saw it vanish just ahead of his fingers. He touched the rug where the insect had lain and saw a faint silver sheen on his fingers.

"Ectoplasm," he said, as much to himself as to Edmund. "That's what the spiritualists are calling it, no? Mrs. Osbourne might know a bit more."

"What are you talking about?"

Colin turned, holding his hand out. "This. Our wee friends aren't much for staying around, clearly, but they do leave some residue."

"Wonderful," said Edmund flatly. "What were those? And what—what *was* that you did to them?"

"A little trick I picked up about five years ago—there's a chap in Ireland who's doing some interesting research into what he calls 'vital magnetic force.'" Colin waved a hand. "But I expect the details aren't very interesting to you at the moment."

"I really can't say I give a damn."

Mortals. Colin stifled a sigh.

"Magic, then," he said with a shrug. "You know I've an interest in it."

"Oh, theosophy and the Golden Dawn and that, yes," said Edmund, dismissing the various schools of mysticism with a vague gesture that would've sent many of their followers into an hour-long fit of pique, "but none of those sorts ever mentioned calling *lightning*."

"Most of them probably can't," said Colin. He hadn't tried to sound humble in several decades; he didn't bother now. "It's a new sort of technique, and it takes a fair amount of practice. And it works better if you've a great deal of experience with other magic."

"Hark to the great scholar," said Edmund.

He found his seat on the couch again. Watching him, Colin observed that the man, though certainly startled, didn't seem as shocked as he would have expected from a mortal without any magic in his bloodlines.

Then again, there was *something* in the Talbot-Jones family, even if the power had come down only to one of its daughters, and growing up with a sister like Reggie was bound to broaden the mind.

"I'd appreciate it if you didn't tell anyone," said Colin. "The chap I mentioned wants his research kept quiet for a while yet."

"No fear!" said Edmund, shaking his head. "The last thing I want to do is draw attention to myself. Especially here." He glanced back to the ruins of the desk. "Though I think it might be a bit late for that."

"I hope it wasn't a sentimental piece," said Colin. "Your house doesn't appear to like me very much."

"I don't think it likes anyone," said Edmund.

Four

HOUSEGUESTS ASIDE, WHITEHILL WAS MUCH THE same as it had always been, at least if "always" meant "on any given month over the last two years." Oh, there were changes—a new portrait in the hall, a temperamental hunter in the stables, red roses in the garden rather than pink ones, and crisp pink paper in the drawing room where the ladies were having tea—but nothing particularly stood out to Reggie.

If the house had been home, she might have felt the differences more. Emotionally, home for her was still instinctively the upper floors of a London town house, crammed with toys and schoolbooks. Practically, it was the flat she and Jane shared on Percy Street, with the composer upstairs playing his piano day and night. Whitehill was her parents' home.

Thinking as much made Reggie's insides twitch with guilt. She looked hastily over the tea table at her mother and focused once more on the conversation.

"...such arguments with the under-gardeners as you wouldn't believe. He's not a local man, you understand, and they're all from the village. Clashing philosophies, one might say."

"Flowers can inspire *such* violence," said Mrs. Osbourne.

"If you make a joke about the Wars of the Roses," said Miss Browne, eyeing her employer over horn-rimmed glasses and trying not to smile, "I'll give notice on the spot."

The two of them made quite the pair: Mrs. Osbourne, tall and statuesque, looked like one of the lesser-known Roman goddesses. Even before noon, she wore green and silver silk—it did go well with her gray-streaked auburn hair—and enough rings that the mere act of reaching for a scone was apt to blind onlookers, even on a rainy day like this. In contrast, her assistant was a fair-haired elfin creature in blue muslin and a modest string of pearls.

Ten years earlier, Reggie would have been happy to follow either of them around and try to ape their looks. She wasn't sure she *still* didn't want to, but the whole affair would be far less dignified at twenty-six than at sixteen.

"Tyrannical creature," said Mrs. Osbourne, beaming at Miss Browne. "And dreadfully overeducated. I'll have you know I was thinking of my friend Diana—she had an argument over lilies with her husband once. Pushed him into a river."

"How dreadful!" Miss Heselton, sister to the local vicar, gasped with artfully wide eyes.

Reggie suppressed a strong impulse to overturn the teapot into her lap. In the day and a half that she'd known the Heselton woman, the aforementioned had gasped in shock at various types of dreadfulness at least once an hour, simpered regularly on the quarter hour, and had tried three times to make inspiring speeches about the natural purity of the countryside, particularly in relation to how late Reggie had slept in and the number of cigarettes the footmen smoked.

Granted, Miss Heselton went about her various exhortations very picturesquely. Like Browne, she was short, slender, and fair, and gave the general impression of having stepped out of an advertisement for soap. Colin had been accurate enough about her physical appeal.

What was *he* doing now? Reggie hadn't seen him at breakfast—part of the reason she'd contrived to sleep late, though that had never been difficult for her—and the men had taken themselves off early in the day. Pater was sitting with Mr. Heselton, talking spirits and broken ankles, which meant Edmund and Colin were probably shooting or drinking, or both.

Colin hadn't seemed the sort to go and blab to a girl's brother about a stolen kiss or two—and Edmund, thank the Lord, wasn't the sort of brother to come over all medieval if he did hear. All the same, Reggie wondered if Colin had asked about her, if he'd been thinking about her.

It had been a rather splendid kiss.

She shifted in her seat, schooled her face into a calm expression, and sent her thoughts along less provocative lines. Hopefully her mother hadn't been looking.

"Depends on the lilies, I'd say," Reggie drawled, settling for her third most disreputable impulse. "And probably on the husband too."

Miss Heselton's blue eyes and rosebud mouth formed three O's of shocked reproof. "You can't mean that," she said, "not really."

"I don't see why not," said Reggie, despite her mother's glare.

"I just don't see how any woman could be so awful!" said Miss Heselton.

"Neither did Cecil," said Mrs. Osbourne. "He'd been about to go shooting. The whole incident quite ruined his tweeds, not to mention his gun."

"*You're* awful," said Miss Browne, shaking her head. "That was a stream, not a river—"

"Life is very rarely as interesting if one's completely honest about it," said Mrs. Osbourne, and she stirred her tea.

"It's still a horrible display of temper," said Miss Heselton.

"Oh, quite," said Mrs. Osbourne. "Diana always *was* a bit of a volcano. There was a time—" She broke off, clicking her tongue. "But I shouldn't carry away the conversation. Mrs. Talbot-Jones, you were discussing your own difficulties over the local blossoms, weren't you?"

"Not blossoms precisely," said Mrs. Talbot-Jones. "Trees. Simpson decided that the big hawthorn on the north lawn had to come out last year. Quite right, of course: it had flowered very prettily in May, but the leaves were getting horribly blighted."

She spoke like a general reviewing a battle, and Reggie grinned around her muffin. Mater, in a pale pink tea gown with her silver hair curling gently around her face, looked and acted every bit the gentle, fluttery matron, but get her in old clothing and out into the garden, and she could be a holy terror.

"What was the difficulty?" Miss Browne asked.

"A sentimental attachment, I'm sure," said Mrs. Talbot-Jones, making a swift and dismissive gesture. "I didn't inquire too closely. It doesn't do, in cases like these. Simpson's planned a row of maples, and the effect will be stunning come autumn. In a year, everyone will have forgotten the old tree ever was there."

Mrs. Osbourne's coppery eyebrows drew together, and she tapped a tapered fingernail against her lips. Whatever destination her train of thought might have had, it was never reached—Miss Heselton spoke instead.

"For my part," she said, "I'm always overjoyed simply to be around trees of any sort. You must feel similarly, Miss Talbot-Jones, especially after having to spend so much time in London."

"I was raised there," said Reggie, wondering if Miss Heselton had put extra emphasis on that *having* or if it was just her general irritation with the woman manufacturing it, "and the city does have parks. Known for them, in fact."

"Parks!" Miss Heselton tossed her golden curls. "Cultivated, manicured little places. They bear no comparison to the real heart of nature, the wild *soul* of the countryside."

"Do you mean like the garden of a country house?" Reggie asked. Under the table, Mater proved that her matronly appearance didn't prevent a swift kick to the ankle of an erring daughter. "But there's certainly more room out here, and a few more wild places," she added, both honestly and by way of avoiding further damage. She was going to bruise, she knew. Wasn't a woman in her sixties supposed to be physically feeble? "Makes a nice change. Once in a while."

"I find that it does one good to get a regular change of scene," said Miss Browne.

"And I'm glad of it," said Mrs. Osbourne, "or I'd lead a lonely and disorganized sort of existence. I'm surprised not to have met *you* before, Miss Talbot-Jones, if you're in London most of the year. I try to go there regularly. I have the honor to have one or two other patrons in polite society, after all."

Any other time, in any other company, Reggie would have been able to answer easily enough. Mrs. Osbourne's tone had no archness to it, no suggestion of knowing more than had been discussed already or meaning more than light conversation. At a stranger's table, she would have laughed and responded quickly.

Here and now, she felt her mother very carefully not looking at her and not saying anything. Words stuck in her throat. Once more she was eighteen, standing on a balcony and facing a ring of hostile and curious eyes.

Damn Edmund and his denseness about women. Damn Pater and his inclination to push potential brides at his son, as if Grandfather had been descended from kings rather than making his fortune in cod. Damn Miss Heselton for being so willing to be pushed. And damn herself, too, for being so easily worked on.

She could have been in London now. She could have been many places, full of many people who'd never met her before she'd turned twenty.

Reggie cleared her throat. "Big city," she said, roughly at first. Then she managed a smile. "And I've not had much time for parties. I'm always haring off on some ridiculous notion or other. Just ask my maid."

"Ridiculous notions like séances, perhaps?" Miss Browne asked, smiling.

"How could I miss it? Spirits called from the other side, right in my own drawing room. Perhaps we should put down paper before tonight's adventure— I'm not sure what ectoplasm will do to the carpets."

Laughter rippled around the table. In its wake, Reggie reached for her teacup and held it like an anchor.

Five

JUST HOW ONE WENT ABOUT EXPLAINING MAGIC TO THE uninitiated had varied considerably over the course of Colin's life. He'd spoken variously of alchemy and natural philosophy, of conversations with angels and bargains with spirits. His explanations usually had some measure of truth. He could count on one hand the number of humans who, over two hundred years, had heard the entire story from him. Advances in science and mysticism had meant that he'd told more and more of the truth over time, though, and that those he did tell were often better prepared to hear it.

Taking those changes in philosophy and science into account, Colin had decided to let Edmund tell the elder Talbot-Joneses about the wasps. Breaking the news about phantom murderous insects was really the sort of conversation a young man should have with his own parents.

Therefore, when Colin took Mrs. Talbot-Jones's arm to go in to dinner, he wasn't surprised to see her looking pensive, though she tried to hide it with a smile. He *was* surprised that she was still smiling and

hosting dinner parties, but only a bit. In his experience, one could never tell with mortals. They tended
to fling themselves onto ships and climb up the sides of
volcanoes without any occult assistance at all.

So, when Mrs. Talbot-Jones said, "I hear you and
Edmund had some excitement this afternoon," as if
they'd gotten lost riding, Colin smiled in response.

Across the room, his hand on Miss Heselton's
elbow, Edmund shot him a look: *Talk some sense into
the woman, will you?*

Colin, who had never been inclined to talk sense
into anyone, put forth the best effort that he thought
his friendship with Edmund merited. "I thought
you might find it more alarming," he said. "I'd half
expected us all to be catching the next train and you
to be selling the place."

"Oh, no," said Mrs. Talbot-Jones, and she patted
his arm in a disconcertingly maternal fashion. "It's like
I told Edmund: you mustn't take on over these things.
It was *very* sweet of you to intervene, but the wasps
would have disappeared before they could really hurt
you. Everything uncanny does."

"Edmund hadn't told me that," said Colin, not sure
that she was entirely correct—the wasps hadn't looked
about to disappear any time in the near future—and
less sure how he felt about being called *sweet*.

"He didn't know himself, poor dear. He's been
away a great deal, and the showier…manifestations,
Mrs. Osbourne calls them?…have only been going
on for the last year. Before that, it was only what you
might expect, spots of cold and crying in the night.
Every old house has *that* sort of thing, I hear."

"Aye," said Colin, "but in mine it was generally to do with my sister."

Judith would have hit him for that, and it *wasn't* strictly true—their undeclared wars in childhood had been more likely to result in howls of outrage than fits of sobbing—but Judith wasn't there and the comment made Mrs. Talbot-Jones laugh, so Colin felt no guilt.

"No wonder you and Edmund get on so well," she said, finding her place at the foot of the table. "Commonality of experience, I shouldn't wonder—and on that subject, may I introduce my daughter? Regina, this is the Honorable Mr. MacAlasdair."

Colin's first thought, when he looked at the woman next to him, was something incoherent about masks and butterflies and buried treasure. Met—well-met, he would say—by moonlight on a balcony, in a stable boy's clothing and with braided hair, Reggie Talbot-Jones had struck him as a pretty girl, more so because of her obvious daring and the unconventional way she spoke.

Now she stood a few feet from him, glowing in peach satin and gold net, slim arms emerging from fashionably puffed sleeves, panels of gold flowing up over her hips to wrap around her waist. Gold combs gleamed in her dark hair, which had been gathered into a soft knot. She wore it low, but still showed plenty of both her graceful neck and the gold and amber necklace encircling it. The central stone, a large amber oval, rested just above her breasts.

"Miss Talbot-Jones," he said and met her eyes for a long moment when he smiled. "A pleasure."

"Mr. MacAlasdair." Some slight tension, though

Colin couldn't have named its source, went out of her at his greeting, and the smile she gave him in return was the free, warm grin of the girl on the balcony. "I've heard quite a lot about *you*."

"And I you," said Colin. "I feel as if we know each other already."

"I was telling Mr. MacAlasdair," said Mrs. Talbot-Jones, seating herself and watching her guests follow her lead, "about some of the earlier incidents here. At first, you know, I didn't believe that there was anything to them."

"And now you're certain that there was?" asked Mr. Heselton from across the table. He was a short, sandy-haired man with wire-rimmed glasses, a gentle face, and an unimposing manner, but his eyes were sharp and clear when he spoke. "That there's no natural explanation? A draft, perhaps, or the wind across a chimney?"

"If drafts and chimneys can produce a human face and form," said Mrs. Talbot-Jones, "it'll be as marvelous as any ghost."

"Optical illusion, then," said the vicar. "The reflection of one of the maids, perhaps—distorted, as such things often are. The refractive properties of light are very strange, you know. We're only just now beginning to discover the possibilities."

"I saw the kinetoscope pictures last winter," said Reggie, her eyes lighting. "They really do move like everyone says. I would've thought I was really at a fight, except for the colors and the sound. It's amazing. You *could* make a person seem to walk about with that sort of thing, I'd think," she added, returning half reluctantly to the subject at hand, "but why would anyone want to?"

Mr. Heselton shrugged. "An angry servant, perhaps?"

"If one of our servants had the money to buy that sort of device," said Mrs. Talbot-Jones, "I can't imagine what he'd be angry about. Besides, there were other incidents. But I shan't describe them at dinner."

That, her tone said, was the final word.

"You'll be the skeptic among us, then?" Colin asked the vicar. "It's a bit of a surprise, considering your profession."

Far from being offended, or concealing it well if he was, Heselton smiled. "I only believe in one man coming back from death," he said, "and I believe that God's laws are comprehensible."

"Are you sure ghosts aren't following them?" Reggie asked. "We're discovering new laws every day, and new ways to apply them: moving pictures and electrons that whiz through the air. I hear men will even be flying before too long," she added, smiling a shade too innocently.

"Do you?" Colin asked.

"Well, who wouldn't? There's a Prussian making gliders right now, and an Australian who got twenty feet up using kites." She looked up through her thick, dark lashes at Colin. "I wouldn't be surprised if you yourself were in the air someday soon."

"One never knows," said Colin, carefully casual. He took a sip of wine to hide his smile.

Turning back to Heselton, Reggie spread her hands. "So," she said, "perhaps there are perfectly simple laws to explain ghosts. We just haven't found them yet. Do you think that's possible?"

"If I didn't," said Heselton, "I wouldn't have imposed myself on your home."

"Imposition, nothing," said Mrs. Talbot-Jones. "You know Philip and I are always glad to have you, supernatural excursions or no."

"You're very kind. But I am prepared to change my mind if I see anything that merits as much. I simply think we should exhaust all logical explanations before bringing the restless dead into the picture."

"Your ankle doesn't weigh in the matter, I take it?" Colin asked. He was beginning to like the man. Heselton reminded him a little of an astronomer he'd met in Italy once, a priest named Boskovic. He'd found that religious men could go either way, and was generally happy when, as now, they weren't accusing him of having the Adversary in his direct ancestry.

Of course, Heselton didn't know the truth about Colin. There was always the chance that his good nature would reverse itself in that case. Colin didn't plan to test the principle.

"With all respect to our hosts and their house-keeping," said Heselton, making a deferential gesture toward Mrs. Talbot-Jones, "stairs have been known to give way for entirely natural reasons. Particularly the stairs in older houses."

"And it *is* old," said Mrs. Talbot-Jones. "The main building dates from Elizabeth's reign, or so our agent assured me. I really should have had the stairs redone before, but one wants to preserve some sense of history."

"One wants hot water more," said Reggie, shaking her head. She glanced down the table to where Edmund was sitting between Miss Browne and Miss Heselton—no doubt some parental machinations were behind that—and at least keeping up his end of the conversation, whatever his actual feelings in the matter. Turning back, she caught Colin's eye and shrugged. She couldn't help the situation, nor could she help looking.

Instead, she focused on him. "Do you believe in ghosts, Mr. MacAlasdair? Or do you just like asking questions?"

"Yes," said Colin. He waited a few seconds, just long enough for Reggie to think he would really be so succinct, and then shrugged. "I believe in a great many things, on principle. In any particular case, I can't be sure. Here? A swarm of insects is fairly convincing."

"A *what*?" Reggie asked. Mr. Heselton leaned forward, and farther down the table, conversation stopped.

Thus, Colin ended up telling the story of the wasps, eliding his magic away as "a trick of magnetism." Depending on who one believed, it might well have been. He'd read a few books that claimed everything was. Osbourne and Browne seemed familiar enough with the concept too, though surprised to hear of such practical application.

The others were silent and still as they listened, uneasy. For the first time that evening, the haunting seemed like a potential menace rather than a joke. Even if the wasps had been as ultimately harmless as Mrs. Talbot-Jones had said, they were still a tangible and unsettling indication of a hostile force. For Mr.

Heselton, they were a challenge to his beliefs; for the Talbot-Joneses, a sign of the challenge they'd taken up.

Dinner only broke the mood a little. Footmen took away soup and brought turbot; candlelight and gaslight shone off silver plates and gold jewelry. In appearance the party could have been any other vaguely fashionable country dinner. The conversation moved on, touching on decoration, politics, and cricket. There was tension in everyone's way of moving, though, and it ran as an undertone to the light chatter. More than eating, they were waiting—preparing, if they could.

Colin had never seen humans like this. It reminded him of the stories Stephen, Judith, and his father had told, the ones about war and the moments before battle. It was rather fascinating.

He listened to them talk, trying to assure each other with every casual word: *You see? We can talk about inconsequential things. We don't have to think about what happens later. Everything is going to be all right.*

Mortals spent a lot of time reassuring each other, he thought, and on very limited grounds. All the same, everything probably *would* be all right. Séances generally ended peacefully enough, even in the most haunted of houses. They'd scare each other and then go home.

Meanwhile, he could chop logic with a vicar and a pretty girl. Even with the wasps, coming to Whitehill still felt like a good decision.

Six

"I REALIZE," SAID MR. TALBOT-JONES, AFTER TAPPING on his glass a few times with his knife to get the table's silence, "that custom dictates we allow the ladies to withdraw to the drawing room at this point, but this gathering is hardly customary."

Custom also would let Edmund escape the company of two eligible young women. Pater probably wouldn't have violated it for that reason alone, but Reggie, watching him speak, had no doubt that he was glad of the opportunity. Even as he spoke, Pater's eyes kept darting to Edmund, looking for any sign of interest in Miss Heselton. Even Mrs. Osbourne or Miss Browne might have done in a pinch, though one was a paid companion and the other was old enough to make the heir-and-a-spare business chancy.

"Instead," Pater went on, "we will *all* repair to the drawing room, where Mrs. Osbourne has graciously offered to lead us in a séance. Naturally, any who feel uneasy about such activities may make use of my library, or indeed any other part of the house that they wish."

Now he glanced toward Mr. Heselton, who smiled and shook his head. "I should be glad to observe," he said, pleasant and firm.

"Yes. Good. Very well, then." At a loss now that the pressing business was concluded, Pater cleared his throat and looked down the table. The wife traditionally led the charge away from dinner. He stroked his beard and waited.

More gray stippled that beard than had been there the last time Reggie visited. Pater's hair was lighter too, and rapidly receding from his brow. An acquaintance, even a friend like Heselton, wouldn't have been able to tell, but she noticed in her parents the change she didn't see in their house, no matter how much she wished otherwise.

Standing up on her mother's cue, she couldn't help sighing.

"Don't worry," said Colin as they came around the table, "I'll stand between you and any vengeful spirits."

His voice drew Reggie out of her thoughts, and her smile had more warmth than teasing in it as a result. "How chivalrous of you."

"One does one's best. Like Lancelot or Percival or one of those other chaps, though I could do with fewer gory deaths at the end of the saga and altogether less charging about looking for Holy Grails and things."

"Only rescuing maidens, then?" Heselton asked.

"Or slaying dragons?" Reggie put in, unable to resist the urge.

"That depends on the dragon," Colin said, his eyes bright with knowing amusement, "and the maiden."

For as long as Reggie had been at Whitehill, the right-hand drawing room had been a place of spotless, formal respectability. Done in pink and white, with flowered paper, low sofas, and a crystal chandelier hanging low from the center of the ceiling, it was very different from the dark parlor in the London house of Reggie's youth, but there had always been a stiffness about it, a sense that this was a place for Following Rules and Best Behavior.

With the drapes drawn, the gas lamps blazing, and the furnishings pushed off to the sides, the drawing room gave the impression of some grand dowager shocked by a piece of modern impertinence. Stepping inside, Reggie half expected to hear a phantom voice launch into a speech that began with "Young lady, are you aware…" and lasted for five minutes.

She hoped any actual ghosts would be a little less proper.

In the middle of the room sat a vast round table made of polished dark oak. The footmen must have moved it in during dinner, Reggie thought, and grimaced in sympathy. She'd have to remind Pater about this event come Boxing Day; it was a wonder nobody had broken any bones setting the room in order.

"Make yourselves comfortable as far as you can," said Mrs. Osbourne. "Men and women alternating is best, but"—she did a quick count of the room, minus the Heseltons—"I'm afraid we're off by one. It's not likely to make much difference."

"You should've brought down another friend," Reggie told her brother.

"I prefer to limit the number of people who think I'm mad, thank you," he said. "Besides, the house couldn't support half of 'em. They'd eat everything in the larder by the end of the day."

"Do you know human beings or hordes of locusts?" Miss Browne asked. She'd been lighting a pair of candles in crystal holders, but she looked up with a grin, match in one hand.

"I've wondered that sometimes myself," said Edmund.

The Heseltons perched on one of the couches in the corner, and everyone else settled into a circle around the table. Reggie dropped into an empty chair, then looked to her right and found Colin taking a seat next to her. Immaculate and slim in black and white evening dress, he could have been a newspaper sketch: Today's Young Society Man. His skin lent some color to the picture, though, and his hair, up close and in decent light, had a blue tone to its blackness. Perhaps that was a dragon thing.

"Turn down the lamps," said Mrs. Osbourne. Seated at the head of the table, she surveyed the room with narrow eyes. An air of authority hung about her, of being quite aware of her surroundings and yet attuned at the same time to events and forces that nobody else could see. Reggie never would have associated such an attitude with the genial, humorous woman she'd sat near at dinner, but now it felt natural. If Mrs. Osbourne was a fraud, she was a very good one.

Reggie's skin prickled with tension, but Colin was at her side and Miss Heselton was watching from the couch. She wouldn't flinch before those two pairs of eyes. She watched Lily, the housemaid, turn down the gas, saw the candlelight throw everyone's face into weird relief, and tried to act as if she were watching an interesting new play.

"Take hands," said Mrs. Osbourne, and Reggie surreptitiously pressed her palms against her skirt first, certain they'd be damp.

Colin's wasn't. His skin was warm and dry, his grip firm. The fingers that folded over Reggie's were long and slender, and her skin tingled anew where they touched. Almost absently, Colin slid his fingertips down to her wrist and back: a light caress, but enough, even through satin gloves, to make Reggie catch her breath.

"Nervous?" On her other side, her father spoke, and Reggie snapped her head around to face him, trying not to look guilty. Pater wasn't the horsewhip-and-shotgun sort where young men were concerned, any more than Edmund was, but it still wouldn't do to flirt so blatantly while he was standing nearby.

She shook her head. "Should be fun. I've never been to a séance before." She squeezed Colin's fingers in a signal he seemed to understand, since he resumed a still and decorous grip. Reggie smiled her thanks back over her shoulder.

"I would have thought that your crowd had them often," said Miss Heselton from her couch. "One hears a great deal about spiritualism and the artistic set."

"One does," said Reggie, "but it's never been my cup of tea. Had a lady read the crystal ball for me once, on a lark."

"Hush now," said Mrs. Osbourne as Lily left the room on tiptoe and with wide eyes. "Fix your minds on the candles. Let your spirits travel through the flame and into the World Beyond."

Flames danced in Reggie's vision, blurred when she focused her eyes too much, and showed no real indication of any world other than the one where she sat. Either she was going about the whole business the wrong way or Mrs. Osbourne didn't intend this step to do anything but shut her audience up.

On the latter point, it worked well. Silence spread outward from the candle flame, thick and soft. Reggie could hear everyone else breathing. When a rhythm developed in their breaths, Mrs. Osbourne spoke again, and not to them.

"The door is open," she said. "I seek beyond it. Abhimanyu, are you there? Will you aid me tonight?"

For a few more breaths, the room kept its silence. Reggie bit her lip to hold back her questions. Who was "Abhimanyu"? Why was Mrs. Osbourne calling on him? Reggie was fairly sure there'd never been anyone by that name living in Whitehill.

Then Mrs. Osbourne spoke, but her voice was an Indian-accented baritone.

"You have brought me to a fell place, Daughter of the West. What would you have of me?"

Fell place—well, Mrs. Osbourne had known the house was haunted. They all did. It was just different to hear as much in "Abhimanyu's" voice and in the dark, still room. Reggie suppressed a shudder.

"Find the spirit that haunts this house," said Mrs. Osbourne in her own voice. Looking away from the candles, Reggie saw that her eyes were closed, and her lips moved only very slightly. "We would speak with it."

"Are you certain?" The voice came again, but Reggie couldn't see Mrs. Osbourne's lips move at all. "It has no love for the living, this spirit. I know as much even now, though I have not seen it."

Mrs. Osbourne opened her eyes—were they glowing, or was that the reflection of the candle flames?—and sent a questioning look toward Mr. Talbot-Jones. He nodded.

Away from the warmth and wine of the dining room, Reggie began to wish she'd brought a wrap with her. The night air was cold on her shoulders and neck, and her gloves didn't do nearly enough to keep her arms warm. She leaned toward Colin, who gave off more warmth than a normal man would have done. She would have tightened her grip on his hand, but he would think she was scared.

In the depths of her mind, she had to admit that her nerves *were* playing up. Séances acted that way on plenty of people, even people who didn't live in haunted houses.

Nonetheless, she held still and steady, waiting.

"I ask once more," said the man's voice, "is this truly your will?"

"A third time I tell you," said Mrs. Osbourne. "Do as I bid you, pray, and with all due speed."

"Powers light and dark guard you, then," said Abhimanyu.

The temperature in the room plummeted. Within a second, Reggie might have been standing outdoors in December. She heard Pater gasp. More alarmingly, she heard Miss Browne's voice, faint and uncertain, and she didn't think it was an act. "Helen?"

Mrs. Osbourne didn't respond. Under her closed lids, her eyes rolled rapidly back and forth. Small half syllables came from her mouth, but nothing coherent.

Then her head fell back and blood began to run from her nose.

"Helen!" cried Miss Browne. She dropped Edmund's hand and turned to her employer, seizing Mrs. Osbourne's arm.

The candles went out.

Reggie was across the table from Mrs. Osbourne, too far to do anything directly for the woman. She could at least get some light into the room. Dropping her father's hand gently, and Colin's with unexpected reluctance, she stepped back. One of the gas lamps was only a few feet away, and if she didn't run into an end table and break her leg—

"*Mine*," said a voice from where Mrs. Osbourne had been sitting. It might have been human once, this voice. Now it was thin and shrill, the malicious whine of the wind during a blizzard, and the only thing that kept Reggie from screaming was that it didn't sound entirely conscious. "Mine. You. You'll…you have… you…won't…"

And then, rising to a shriek: "*BLOOD.*"

A glowing face stretched itself across the darkness, a human face with the eyes black holes and the mouth opened in an impossibly wide scream. Reggie screamed too, adding her voice to a panicked chorus, and felt a wave of some force, like wind but not, slam through the room, lifting the table off the floor and hurling it toward Mrs. Osbourne.

Colin leaped forward. Reggie felt his body brush against hers in a lightning-quick motion. It wasn't quick enough, whatever he was trying to do. Even over the screaming, Reggie heard the next few sounds clearly as they all happened together.

The table hit the wall with a crash.

Crystal shattered and fell with a series of tinkling sounds.

Mrs. Osbourne cried out. She didn't do it very loudly, though. She didn't sound as though she could.

Seven

AH, DAMN, COLIN THOUGHT, AND DROPPED HIS HANDS from the table's center support. He'd managed to hold it back a bit—which was why Mrs. Osbourne still had lungs to scream with—but he hadn't been quick enough or strong enough to prevent all of the damage, and he wasn't doing any good now.

He'd felt power building throughout the séance, though he hadn't been able to sense its source or its form. As soon as the table hit Mrs. Osbourne, that power had vanished. The spirit, having done its malign work, was either exhausted or satisfied for the time being. Colin wasn't sure which to hope for. Was it better if the phantom could kill them all but didn't want to, or the other way around?

After that first scream, Mrs. Osbourne went silent, sagging downward from where the table had crushed her against the wall. Colin's human eyes weren't much better than a normal mortal's in darkness, but he could just make out the shallow rise and fall of her chest. She'd probably fainted from shock and pain.

He didn't know what to do next.

Moving the table might be helpful, or it might kill the woman; he didn't know more than the very basics of medicine. He'd never learned magic to deal with hostile ghosts, and physical battle would have been impossible, even if he'd wanted to change shape in front of an audience and had known where the spirit had gone.

"Helen?" Colin recognized Miss Browne's voice, desperately struggling for calm. "Helen, are you there? What's wrong?" The woman stumbled forward and then crashed into a bookcase with a small cry of pain.

Belatedly, he remembered just *how* bad mortals' vision was in the dark.

Now he heard other noises as well: Miss Heselton's sharp, quick breathing and her brother's low and urgent repetition of the Lord's Prayer. In ironic counterpoint, Edmund was swearing steadily. Mr. Talbot-Jones was simply moaning, his hand over his eyes, and his wife sat where she had been, frozen and silent.

Colin turned to look for Reggie.

Light flooded the room from behind him. Objectively, it wasn't very bright at all. A single gas lamp never would be, no matter how high one turned it up. Coming unexpectedly out of the darkness, though, it made Colin wince and close his eyes.

"Oh," said Reggie, dropping her hand from the lamp. It was more of a sound than a word, really: a dismayed little exhalation full of confusion and alarm. Through half-shut eyelids, Colin saw her clap a hand to her mouth. He took a step toward her. He could handle damsels in distress.

Just before he reached out, she shook her head,

swallowed, and said clearly, "Someone had better go for the doctor. Is it still Brant, Mater?"

"I—yes," said Mrs. Talbot-Jones.

"Then you'd best do it, Edmund. My motorcar will never manage the roads, a carriage won't get here anything like soon enough, and you're the only one who could ride double with the doctor on a fast horse."

Thus galvanized, Edmund was on his feet even before Reggie had finished speaking, and the room came back to life in his wake.

"Anyone else badly hurt?" Reggie asked and then looked absently down at her hand. Now that the light was on, Colin could see a shallow but long cut on the back of it. Mrs. Talbot-Jones was pressing a handkerchief to her cheek, and Colin, seeing both wounds, noticed a dim pain in his own forehead. Putting a hand up, he was unsurprised to feel blood.

"I'm afraid the chandelier's a lost cause," said Mrs. Talbot-Jones. "Pity: I always liked it. Other than that, no. Just…" Her voice died away and she looked back to Mrs. Osbourne.

"Should we move the table?" Mr. Talbot-Jones asked. "I know one isn't supposed to remove a knife, but I'm not sure—"

To widespread surprise—or at least to Colin's astonishment, and he rather assumed to Reggie's and Edmund's as well—it was Miss Heselton who answered, shaky but coherent. "Yes. Crushing is different. If some of you gentlemen could assist?"

All of the gentlemen assisted. Colin's chief effort lay in holding back and letting the other two think that he was no more than a wiry young man. The table tilted back and away in a matter of seconds, and gasps of horror went around the room when it did.

The front of Mrs. Osbourne's body, from her forehead to her waist, was a pool of blood. Colin couldn't even see her clothing beneath it. One arm hung limply in front of her, also covered in blood, and with a white glimmer of bone protruding above the elbow. Even he had to wince, and he'd seen plenty of human death over his lifetime, much of it nasty.

"Oh God," said Miss Browne. "She's dying, isn't she?"

"We don't know that," said Mr. Heselton. He'd already been on his way to Mrs. Osbourne's side. Now he stood there beside Miss Browne, face pale and rather green. "It may not be as bad as it looks. We'll just have to hope—and pray."

He knelt in the classic pose of bowed head and clasped hands, and Miss Browne knelt beside him. She took Mrs. Osbourne's limp hand between hers, and her lips moved as well, though even Colin, who could faintly make out Heselton's quiet prayer, couldn't tell if she was joining him or saying something else altogether. He turned away.

"We could at least try to stop the bleeding," said Reggie. She looked at Mrs. Osbourne and chewed pensively at her lower lip. "I'd never make a nurse, but—"

"I did, or nearly," said Miss Heselton. She turned to Mrs. Talbot-Jones. "Have one of your maids bring us some clean sheets and towels, and boil some water."

"Good thought, that," said their hostess, rising and assuming command with a single tug of the bellpull. "It'll keep the girls occupied too. They'll have vapors otherwise."

Colin thought of how his sister-in-law—who'd been a scholar's secretary before marrying Stephen, and whose sister was in service herself—would have reacted to *that* comment, and bit the inside of his cheek to stifle a smile. "You might ask if any of the servants can help us," he said. "They might know a thing or two themselves."

"Most of them *were* local girls," Mr. Talbot-Jones said, nodding slowly. "Farmers' daughters. Practical wenches, I'd think."

"Someone around here has to be," said Reggie.

The next few minutes became as frenzied as those just after the séance had been frozen. Mrs. Talbot-Jones gave orders with a speed and decisiveness that Wellington might have envied. A variety of maids came in and variously looked faint and left, brought supplies, stayed and rolled up their sleeves, or went to fetch steadying beverages. Miss Heselton and Emma— the maid who'd pitched in—sponged, pressed, and wrapped, taking care not to move Mrs. Osbourne too much. The medium's eyes opened a few times during the process, and once she regained consciousness long enough to make a feeble sound of alarm.

"Helen, we're here," said Miss Browne. She choked up then, unable to continue, and simply squeezed the hand she held.

Mr. Heselton took over. "The doctor's on his way," he said in a low soothing voice. "Amelia and Emma are seeing to you in the meantime. Just lie as still as you can," he said, "and drink this if the pain is bad."

Calmed by sentiment or laudanum, or both, Mrs. Osbourne closed her eyes again. Activity went on—and left Colin standing in the corner of the room, a glass of brandy in his hand.

Reggie drifted to his side, her elaborate hairdo collapsed into a straggling fall down her neck, her satin gown crumpled and ripped at the hem, and her dark eyes half-glazed. She held a cup of tea, and the fingers of one glove showed that she hadn't entirely been holding it steady.

"Be a gentleman and trade, will you?" she asked, after a quick glance around. "Mrs. Kelly doesn't approve of spirits for women unless we've fainted in the last minute or two."

"Mrs. Kelly?" he asked, passing over his glass but waving off the offered tea.

Reggie gulped brandy and handed the glass back. "Housekeeper. She brought in the, er, refreshments."

"Ah," said Colin. "Old-fashioned sort?"

"Very. And I don't feel like an argument tonight."

"I'd rather think not," said Colin. "How are you faring?"

"Bloody useless, just now," said Reggie, looking back over her shoulder. "Nothing like a disaster for showing the value of a classical education, what?"

"I was thinking something of the sort myself," Colin replied. "About me, that was, not you."

"*Your* education," she said, with another look around to make sure nobody else was in earshot, "might be helpful here, at least in the long term."

"Only so helpful. I haven't generally had much to do with ghosts. We have a few back home, but they just appear"—Colin held a hand out and then flipped it over—"and then disappear again. No phantom wasps. No flung tables. And magic, as such, hasn't had a great deal to do with them, either."

"Really?" Reggie put her free hand on one shapely hip and peered up at him. "How can ghosts not have much to do with magic?"

"Easily enough. Magic involves finding secret rules to this world, often rules that break the ones we already know. Sometimes it involves creatures or forces from other worlds that don't have the same rules, but all of them are alive—for some value of life. Ghosts aren't. By definition, rather. You can use magic to talk with them, but it's a chancy business."

"Then what about séances? What would you call them?" Reggie asked. Her eyes were brighter now, more alert.

"A radical new development. It might be magical. It might be scientific. There might not be much difference. We're finding out new things every day. You said as much at dinner."

Dinner seemed like a year ago to Colin, and Reggie clearly felt the same. She had to pause and blink several times before she smiled uncertainly. "Oh—so I did. Never thought of mediums as the frontier of knowledge before."

"Some aren't. Most, I'd say," said Colin. "Like most magicians. But there are more and more of the genuine article these days. That's one of the reasons why I wanted to be present tonight."

"I'm glad you were," said Reggie, and before he could ascribe any meaning to that, she added, "and so should Mrs. Osbourne be, though of course I won't tell her. You caught that table, didn't you?"

"Not fast enough," said Colin, "or with enough force."

"You're not blaming yourself, are you?" Reggie's eyes widened and she stepped toward him. "Listen, there's not a man in the world—"

Normally, he wouldn't have disillusioned a woman who was about to offer comfort and praise. This was different—or maybe Reggie was, because she knew more. Either way, he couldn't help speaking. "That's what's worrying me. And I'm not blaming myself." It was Colin's turn to look around for witnesses. The room was safe, though it wouldn't be soon. Edmund and the doctor would be arriving any minute, if the heavy footsteps in the hall meant anything. "If any single man had thrown that table, even the strongest and fastest man in the world, I would've been able to keep Mrs. Osbourne from getting more than bruised. If two or three men had been behind it, perhaps she'd have cracked some ribs."

Comprehension left Reggie very still for a minute, then she drew a long, dismayed "Ohh" from her mouth.

"Aye," said Colin in the last moments he knew he had before Edmund and Brant came through the door. "I'm not blaming myself. I'm thinking that we're in the house with a very strong creature."

Eight

BED WAS A MIXED BLESSING.

Reggie was glad to be alone. Rather, she was glad to get away from the scene downstairs. After the first rush of action and catastrophe, waiting had kept everyone's nerves trembling on edge. When Dr. Brant had emerged from the drawing room, wiping off arms that were bloody to the elbow, and announced that Mrs. Osbourne should be all right with time and care, the frail structure of calm had collapsed. So had Miss Heselton, literally, falling into the nearest set of male arms and having hysterics.

In deference to the woman's surprising competence and the events of the evening, Reggie made herself consider it possible that the hysterics were real and that Edmund being the first man at hand was sheer coincidence. Mr. Heselton, after all, had been engaged in comforting Miss Browne, who'd been looking all of three steps from the grave herself, and Colin was not the sort of chap who made one think of comfort.

Nonetheless, for a moment their eyes had met, and

Reggie had considered going over to him, as little as they knew each other. His presence had been calming and refreshing earlier, unless that had just been the brandy. For a moment, she'd thought he might come to her.

But she didn't know him, she didn't want to presume that one rash act on a balcony and his unthinking response gave her the right to drape herself over the man whenever she pleased, and she had things to do. There were servants to talk to, while Pater paid the doctor and Mater got the guests off to bed. There were orders to give about breakfast the next day and trays to be taken up to Mrs. Osbourne and Miss Browne. Emma was to come off her general housemaid's duties and keep an eye on the night's casualty, and someone had to clean up the ruins of the chandelier. Moreover, Reggie had to explain what had happened, and sound calm and unconcerned when she talked about the "accident."

She thought she managed all right. Woefully inadequate as she might be in society, she was her mother's daughter in some ways. She answered questions, neither lying nor giving too much information. She smiled, she said that she was certain everything would be all right, and she didn't think the servants looked too worried.

Then again, they hadn't been at the séance, and they hadn't heard Colin talk about the ghost's possible power.

If the spirit had wanted to kill her, Reggie told herself as she went upstairs, it could have done so any time in the last two years. It hadn't hung about in the drawing room and done more damage, so either it didn't want to or, for some reason, it couldn't. She was very probably safe that night.

"Very probably" and "safe" were not words that went well together, but she didn't have the energy to worry. Talking to the servants had used the last of her strength. She practically pulled herself up the stairs, careless of the damage to her gown, and let Jane undress her in numb almost-silence.

"Your hand," the other woman said as Reggie raised it to push back the heavy mass of her hair. She'd sponged the cut off, and it really wasn't bad enough to need a bandage—not much more than a scratch, but obvious. "What happened?"

"Chandelier."

"I'd heard," said Jane, and she fixed Reggie with a knowing look and a thin smile. "At least you're tired enough to stay in tonight."

"It could be worse," said Reggie, managing a smile of her own. "We could be in London. I get less sleep there."

"Don't I know it? This was supposed to be a *rest* for you, Miss Regina."

"The world is so infrequently what it should be," Reggie said. She slipped between her sheets, feeling her body sink into the mattress. A yawn cracked her face. "Ask Mr. Heselton about it sometime. I think the subject's in his line of work."

Sleep claimed her almost as soon as Jane left. Even as she slid down into darkness, though, Reggie felt a sense of unease, as if she already knew that the night to come would bring anything but peace and calm.

❧

The dream began with screaming.

There was no beginning to it, no end, no words: only endless sound and the rage behind it, coming at Reggie in high, piercing waves. Only she and the sound existed at first.

Then she could see again, though not well and not steadily. The small space around her was featureless and blurred, and she couldn't make out what was shadow and what was casting it. The walls came together in odd ways, bulging and squashing and not quite meeting up properly—or the same way every time she looked. Her vision was wrong somehow.

Or was her eyesight to blame?

The thought that she might be seeing just fine, that the blurring shiftiness of the room might just be how things were, gave Reggie a dull, nauseous feeling. She closed her eyes to get away from it, and the screaming around her grew louder, angrier.

About to snap her eyes open again, she stopped.

Did she really want to make a disembodied screaming thing happier? It might have been the one to put her in this…place?…or it might not, but it didn't sound like a gentle and considerate host. Dashed if making it angry might not be the way forward, assuming that "forward" had any meaning here.

Still, she'd open diplomatic relations.

"Now I say," she began, shouting so that she could hear herself, "what's the point of all this noise?"

She got no answer except for more screaming. Reggie hugged herself and tried again. "I don't suppose we could talk about this? You quiet down a bit, and I'll take the thorn out of your paw or your beard out of the stump or whatnot?"

After another moment of shrieking, she decided that diplomacy was a wash. Unfolding her arms, she stepped forward and reached out toward one of the walls. There had to be a door *somewhere*, and maybe her vision really was to blame. Her fingers touched nothing, so she took another step forward.

What she touched was not a wall.

Skin stretched beneath her fingertips: warm, living skin. Reggie could feel it moving too, although she couldn't feel bones or muscles, only a rippling half-solid mass.

She couldn't help opening her eyes, and when she did, a face stared back from the wall. It was gray and vaguely human-shaped, but more like a tragedy mask than anything with features. A vague rise in the middle of its face roughly indicated where a nose should be, and instead of eyes, it had oversized gray pits, completely blank and yet angry at the same time. As Reggie watched, the mouth opened, wider and wider, far beyond what a human's could have managed.

"*MINE!*" it shrieked, and Reggie screamed and stumbled backward into the center of the "room." Now she could see other faces, copies of the first, bubbling out of the walls all around her. They shrieked in chorus from the lipless black voids of their mouths.

She flung up her hands to guard herself and saw blood running down from her nails, or from where her nails should have been. There were no nails now. Her fingers had no tips to them, only blood and the ends of bone.

She didn't feel pain.

She didn't feel anything.

Reggie stared from the mutilated ends of her fingers to the faces protruding from the walls. The muscles in her mouth and throat worked, but nothing happened. The strength had all vanished from her arms and legs. It was as though her muscles themselves knew that there was nothing further to be done here, that fighting was useless and talking worse, that there was nowhere for her even to run or to hide. Her mind could not accept any of those things. Her body already had.

She slumped to the floor and felt nothing against her legs or her buttocks, any more than she felt pain from her hands. She'd touched the face; maybe that was all she could manage. It didn't make any sense, but what did?

Perhaps she should try to figure that out.

Carefully, leading with her palm, she reached down toward her leg. She saw her hand come to rest against the white cotton of her nightgown, but she felt neither cloth nor the body beneath it.

Out of the corner of her eye, Reggie saw a flicker. It wasn't quite movement, but more as if something had snapped into place, though when she looked up, she couldn't tell what.

Behind the screaming, dimly, she heard another noise.

It might have been flowing water.

It might have been someone sobbing.

"Who are you?" she asked, but the screaming faces drowned her out.

"*Who are you?*" she yelled, and the force of it sent unexpected pain down her throat and through her whole chest. She doubled over, coughing, and heard the screaming around her take on a new tone, a mocking note. Reggie would have said a few words about that, but she was coughing too hard, and she kept coughing harder and harder, until blood sprayed from her mouth and stippled her nightgown.

She tried to push herself up but her legs gave out under her, spilling her back to the floor. This time it hurt. Everything hurt, intensely and all at once. If Reggie could have drawn breath without coughing, she'd have screamed.

"No," she said, looking up. "No, please."

The faces only shrieked down at her. Reggie shut her eyes and twisted helplessly away—and then woke in her own bed, gasping for breath, her nightgown soaked with sweat.

At first the dream still lay firmly over reality. Reggie touched her own face, then grasped the rungs of the bed frame. She could still feel. She was in her own room, where nothing was screaming at her and the darkness held no threat.

"Nightmare," she said to the air, as if by speaking the word, by naming what had frightened her, she could push it away and lock some door behind it. "Small wonder. Oof."

Now the bed was too hot and her nightgown unpleasantly clammy. Reggie sat up, swung her feet over the edge of the bed, and crossed over to her window. Some air would do her a world of good, she thought as she drew back the drapes.

There she stopped, hand outstretched, and stared.

After that first second, there was nothing out of the

ordinary about the view. A waning moon still bathed the back lawn in plenty of light. The grass was a sea of silver; the hedges and trees were dark shadows above it. The whole effect was very pretty, and Reggie had seen it a dozen times before.

And yet…

In the second when the curtains had parted, Reggie had seen—or thought she'd seen—a glimpse of something else: something very pale and shaped vaguely like a human face.

It might have been nothing. It might have been the reflection of the moonlight or a passing owl or a leaf blowing by on the night breeze. After a dream like Reggie'd had, she knew she'd be likely to turn anything she saw sinister, no matter how innocent its origins.

She stood for a few more seconds, staring out the window. Whatever had been there was gone now.

Still, she thought perhaps she wouldn't open the window after all.

Nine

COME BREAKFAST TIME, THE ASSEMBLED COMPANY WAS still dazed. The Browne-Osbourne contingent, of course, remained above stairs, under the ministrations of Emma the maid. Everyone else confronted the silver breakfast trays as if they were complicated new mechanisms from some inventor's mad dreams, and once they'd managed to reach the food, most of the guests were singularly unenthused about it.

Colin, more ravenous than troubled, made himself go along for the sake of appearances, but felt like the proverbial toad beneath the harrow. Poking at eggs he would rather have savored, he sighed. When faced with the prospect of acting listless over a rather remarkable kipper, he silently cursed mortals and gave up the pretense.

Mrs. Osbourne was alive. *He* was alive. That was enough to be going on with, and as for danger, the world was full of that. Brooding over it would scarcely lessen the risk.

Humans rarely grasped that fact—even more rarely these days than they had in his youth, which Colin had always thought strange. The world held much more danger for them, and even the most fortunate was a century or two closer to death than he was. And yet, because of an angry ghost and a hurled table, they moped and picked at their food.

He didn't understand. Some decades ago, he'd given up trying.

Now he poured another cup of tea, glanced out the window at the pouring rain, and then looked back to see Reggie come through the door, wearing rose-colored muslin that she'd probably picked to make her look more awake. It didn't work, not when she moved like she still wasn't sure what purpose feet served, or when she swallowed an entire cup of tea before trusting herself with a knife and fork.

Like those around her, she might have been brooding—but given the symptoms, Colin thought it likely that she was also used to city hours, or possibly that she'd settled her nerves the night before with something stronger than tea and more substantial than the few sips she'd had of his brandy.

When Mr. Talbot-Jones cleared his throat, Colin saw Reggie wince.

"I spoke to Emma this morning," said Mr. Talbot-Jones, "and she told me that Mrs. Osbourne is recovering as well as we might expect. She has no fever, and she evidently passed the night peacefully enough."

Laudanum probably had a fair bit to do with the latter, Colin thought. Still, he joined the rest of the table in smiling. There was no harm in optimism, and the woman's injuries were the sort that responded well to rest and time: sundry cuts, three broken ribs, and an arm that had fractured in several places. Nasty stuff, true, but not likely to be permanent or fatal—not in this time.

In his youth, there had been no such guarantees.

"The doctor will look in again after lunch," Mr. Talbot-Jones added. "Meanwhile, we'll do everything in our power to make her comfortable. As for"—he glanced around, saw that the servants were out of the room, and continued—"the events of last night, I confess that they caught me very much off guard. You all have my most sincere apologies."

More murmurs went around the room. These were of the pray-don't-mention-it and quite-all-right variety, enthusiastic whatever their degree of sincerity might really have been.

Mr. Talbot-Jones smiled. "Quite kind of you all. I admit, as well, that I have no solid notion of how to proceed."

"I do," said Mr. Heselton, flushing even as he spoke. "Though I'm not certain how it will be received. Last night convinced me. Whether a ghost or not, there's certainly a presence here that belongs to no living man. That makes my duty clear. After breakfast, I'll be posting a letter to my bishop, and I'll ask him to send me a rite of exorcism."

Awkward silence descended, and Mrs. Talbot-Jones stepped forward to meet it like a good hostess. "I didn't know there was one," she said conversationally.

"It's not at all commonly used," said Mr. Heselton. "For obvious reasons. I'd only heard of it in pass-ing before."

"Good show, then," said Edmund, surfacing from

his toast. "Anything we can get for you? Bell, book, candle? We've got plenty of 'em around."

"I don't know. I can only assume that my superiors will tell me—or they'll send someone more senior to perform the rite who will bring the necessary implements himself. If they approve the process at all, that is."

"And if they don't?" Colin asked.

Mr. Heselton straightened his shoulders. "Then I'll try again to convince them." With less conviction, he added, "Or perhaps we'll find another way to lay the spirit, or whatever it is, to rest."

"Perhaps if we could talk to it," said Mr. Talbot-Jones. "I know we tried last night, and that went... well, *very* badly"—he tugged at his beard—"but the ghost might not be as wholly opposed to us as it seems."

"It tried to kill us, sir," said Miss Heselton. "I was never so frightened in all my life," she added, pressing a slim hand to her white throat and widening her eyes. She glanced toward Edmund, but he'd turned back to his breakfast. "Even thinking of it now—"

"She has a point, Pater," said Reggie, a weary and amused counterpoint to Miss Heselton's fluttering. "As a rule, when a fellow tries to hit me with a table, I take it that he doesn't want a deeper acquaintance."

"'As a rule'?" Colin asked.

"I live a very exciting life," she said with a grin and then, at her mother's alarmed look, added, "No, not really. But trying to kill Mrs. Osbourne is a fair sign of hostility."

"I don't know about that," said Edmund. "A

trapped animal, or a hurt one, might bite you out of fear and be quite loyal with the proper care."

"A ghost's not an animal," said Reggie.

"We don't know what a ghost is, really," Mrs. Talbot-Jones said and frowned, tapping one finger against her teacup. "And last night was the first real act of violence we've seen, or we never would have stayed here, much less invited all of you. Perhaps we did disturb or frighten it, and it wouldn't have wanted to hurt us otherwise."

"Or perhaps it just *couldn't*," said Colin, "until we opened a clear path between its world and ours."

Miss Heselton gasped.

"Would that path still be there now? If we did?" Reggie asked.

"I don't know," said Colin. He would probably have to get used to saying that. "There must be an obstacle or two to harming us, if only in the creature's own mind. If it had no limits on either means or motive, we'd not be sitting here now. But as for what those obstacles are, or whether the séance last night lessened them at all, I could say no more than any of you."

Reggie closed her eyes. "And the only person who *might* be able to say is upstairs and in no condition to talk. I could almost be jealous," she added under her breath. "Due respect, Pater, but I don't think we should try striking up a conversation with the ghost on our own. Wouldn't even know how to start, for one."

"Neither would I, Regina," said Mr. Talbot-Jones, and gave his daughter a mildly reproving scholar's look, as if she'd flubbed her French lesson. "But while we wait for more skilled authorities, we can perform our own sort of investigation. There are many stories where simply finding out who a ghost is and what it wants will solve the problem quite handily."

"Blood, it said," Reggie pointed out. "If it wants a virgin sacrifice—"

"Regina Elizabeth!" said Mrs. Talbot-Jones in a voice like very quiet thunder.

"Sorry, Mater. Classical allusion." Reggie smiled an apology, though not a very downcast one. Watching the curve of her lower lip, Colin wondered if she'd been about to speak to her own qualifications—and what those might be.

"I don't propose sacrificing anyone," said Mr. Talbot-Jones, interrupting this promising train of thought, "or anything. The ghost didn't speak clearly. It might have been referring to blood spilled in the past—"

"Or bloodlines," said Edmund. "We're not its relations."

"And we've arrived nicely at my point: we can't know unless we learn more," said Mr. Talbot-Jones.

"Even if the spirit's hostile," Colin said, reluctantly pulling his mind further away from Reggie's possible past, "knowing more about it might help. If we could find something it owned in life, that might give us power over it. Or its name."

"Like Rumpelstiltskin?" Mrs. Talbot-Jones asked, smiling.

"Aye, in a way. There's truth in a lot of those old tales, if you know how to look for it. Names are magic. And the more you know about something, the more you can make it do as you wish." He took a sip of his tea and glanced over toward Reggie. "Something—or someone."

By the abrupt way Reggie gulped her tea, Colin knew he'd hit a target.

"You know a dashed lot about magic, from the way you talk," she replied, recovering enough to sound casually curious. "Merlin in disguise, what?"

"Oh, I take a bit of an interest between fits of idleness, but that's neither here nor there. The real question is this: if we wanted to learn more about this ghost, how would we do it?"

"We could talk to the servants," said Mrs. Talbot-Jones. "At least the ones who didn't come from London with us."

"We could ask in the village too," said Mr. Heselton, and he glanced toward the window, where the rain continued unabated. "Though that might wait a day."

"And there are the attics," said Reggie, grinning suddenly. "Miles of 'em, and I don't think anyone's been there in years. A little exploring sounds like it might be just the thing for a rainy afternoon."

Ten

As far as Reggie knew, nobody had *really* been in
the attics since Pater had bought Whitehill. A few
servants had gone up to make a cursory inspection and
set rattraps, but her parents hadn't had generations of
clutter to store, and they'd been content to leave the
existing detritus shrouded and mysterious.

Now, outfitted with lamps and chattering brightly,
the party split up and—except for Heselton, nursing
his broken ankle, and Mr. Talbot-Jones, who stayed
to keep him company—headed for various sets of
stairs. In addition to the main house, Whitehill had an
eastern wing with its own set of attics.

"It's probably terribly cold," said Mrs. Talbot-
Jones, "and a bit dusty, though Mrs. Kelly does send
girls in regularly, and of course we did have the rooms
opened up when we decided to have guests. We just
never use it very much, you see. Mr. Talbot-Jones
doesn't play at billiards himself, and we don't have the
large parties that some do."

"Not with only the two of you out here, no," said
Miss Heselton, and she shook her head. "I confess,

Edmund, you and your sister are a complete mystery to me. I can't imagine what keeps you in London for so much of the year."

This time, there was no question that she'd looked at Reggie when she spoke, or that the innocent wonderment in her voice was false.

"Not always London," said Reggie. "Edmund goes to Scotland for shooting parties." Behind Miss Heselton's back, Edmund sent a brief glare Reggie's way. She couldn't blame him, but the conversation was quickly descending into every-man-for-himself territory. "Mater, why don't you and Miss Heselton take the main attics? Edmund and Colin and I are fairly hardy souls."

"Well—" said Mater, frowning slightly as she weighed chills and dust against her husband's plans for Edmund, then the aforementioned plans against the likely volleys back and forth from Reggie and Miss Heselton.

"Wouldn't want either of you ladies to catch a chill," Edmund said heartily, with a smile that Reggie absolutely knew Miss Heselton was going to take the wrong way. "House is full of invalids as things stand, you know."

"It's so very sweet of you to be concerned," said Miss Heselton. "But aren't you worried about Miss Talbot-Jones's health too? She *seems* very sturdy, I'm sure…"

Edmund, in the way of men in general and himself in particular, noticed none of what "sturdy" meant in this context. "Oh, Reggie's a fine strapping girl," he said, and as Reggie considered proving as much by kicking him in the shin, he went on, "but we'll send her in your direction if she starts to have the vapors. Good hunting!"

"Yoiks and away," said Mater, more than a touch sarcastic.

One reached the east wing proper, and thus the stairs to the attic, through a long stone hallway whose high ceilings and dim light made Reggie feel that she and her companions were sneaking into a giant's castle. She wasn't the only one. Colin took a slow look around as they walked, then whistled. "Medieval sort of place, this."

"It *was* an abbey once," said Edmund. "An actual one, with monks and…bees? Wine? Whatever monks use to occupy themselves. The main house is really the new bit."

"One modern family naturally needs more room than a whole abbey full of monks," said Colin.

Since he sounded amused rather than disapproving, Reggie didn't bristle. "Monks were short fellows, I hear," she said, "like everyone back then. Besides, would you care to live in a cell? And have one robe to your name?"

"I'd go a long way to avoid it," said Colin, and Reggie wondered if he *had*. He was a younger son; would he have gone army or church? She couldn't ask, so she just listened, and caught his eye and his lazy smile when he added, "Even without those rather troublesome vows."

"I can't say I'm surprised," said Reggie, smiling back. Feeling rippled across her skin, like faint electricity, but she tried not to pay too much attention. Edmund was walking on her other side.

The stairs up began grandly enough, a sweep of polished stone to which successive owners had added a wooden banister and a thick blue rug. At each floor, though, the staircase became smaller and plainer, until at last they were climbing a set of narrow wooden steps that was barely more than a ladder.

"Pity we're not doing this three years from now," said Edmund, "when they've redone the whole place."

Reggie shrugged. "They might keep the stairs. Pater's traditional."

"I'd think so," said Colin from behind her. "*Regina Elizabeth*?"

"And here I'd been hoping you hadn't paid attention to that," said Reggie.

"A vain hope, I fear. Though a very impressive name."

"I think it's only the threat of treason," said Edmund, "that kept 'em from going the other way 'round. Reggie here was the first child. Spoiled, naturally."

Walking single file as they were, it was a trivially easy matter for Reggie to lean forward and flick Edmund in the back of the neck with her thumb. "No such thing, Edmund St. John."

"Ouch," he said, though Reggie knew it was mostly for show.

Colin laughed. "I should have known. Though you're not much like the oldest of my family."

"Well, you're not much like Edmund. You dress too well, for one thing."

"I have better things to think about," said Edmund.

At the same time, Colin said, "I'd been hoping you'd notice," and Reggie felt his breath on the back of her neck with each word. She almost stumbled.

"What, um, what is your older brother like?" she asked, trying to compose herself at least enough to walk smoothly. "Or sister, I suppose."

"One of each. Judith was wild when she was young, but she's settled down now. Takes an interest in farming and such, though I can't imagine why. Stephen's a good man, but rather tiresomely responsible at times. And fairly respectable too."

"You're right. Nobody'd ever say that I was either," said Reggie cheerfully. "Quite the opposite, usually."

"Here now," said Edmund, "don't sell yourself short, Reggie. You haven't lost the family fortunes gaming, spent them all on clothes, or given 'em all to some harebrained sect. Comparatively, I'd say you're doing jolly well."

"Mostly so you can say that *you're* doing jolly well," said Reggie, but she smiled. "Oh well. Neither of us is dead or bankrupt yet. And here we are."

Edmund opened the attic door. Around him, Reggie could see a dimly lit world of huge trunks and shrouded furniture. A wooden rocking horse peered back at them from one button eye, the yarn of its mane tangled and mouse-eaten.

"Well," said Colin, "I doubt that it'll get *more* inviting. Shall we?"

"Gladly," said Reggie in her best garden-party voice, and they stepped into the attic.

Dust was everywhere. It settled on their clothes; it clung to their hands when they opened boxes or removed cloths; and it had all three of them sneezing regularly before long. Dragons, Reggie was pleased to see for the sake of the house, did not breathe fire when they sneezed, or at least not when they walked as men.

"I'm amazed Mater hasn't gone through these things by now," Reggie said, opening one drawer after another of an old armoire. "There's enough here to fit out a house or two, and I'm sure there are people in the village who could make use of a bit of furniture."

"There are people in London who'd pay a fair amount for some of it, I'd wager. At least for the smaller pieces and the books," said Edmund.

"Books?"

"Mm-hmm. Over here." Edmund was kneeling by an old trunk, one of a group of five. He held up a largish volume bound in red leather. "Homer. It's not pristine, but the mice haven't gotten to it, and the date on the flyleaf says seventeen eighty."

"Is there a name inside?" Colin asked, turning from a chest full of old clothes.

"Not in this one. Maybe in some of the others. I'll bring the trunk down and we can have a look once we've finished up here. What exactly *are* we looking for, by the way?"

"A body in a trunk would be ideal," said Reggie. "Or bloodstains."

"Long knives with serpents carved into the hilt," Colin volunteered. "Evil symbols scratched in the wall."

Reggie laughed and then shrugged as she tried to come up with a serious answer. "Anything with a name on it that we don't recognize, I suppose. Or pictures or maps. I hadn't really thought about it."

"Shocking," said Edmund, rolling his eyes.

Stepping past him, Reggie toed him in the side with one booted foot. "A little less sarcasm there, if you please."

"Watch out, Reggie—if I fall over, this whole place could come down."

"Quite likely," said Colin, looking up at the rafters. He raised a hand and tapped one of his long fingers against the wood. "Nobody breathe too hard, hmm?"

"I'll do my best," Reggie said and plucked the dust cloth off of a picture. She eyed it, blinked, then stepped back and studied it a little more. Without thinking, she crossed her arms over her chest, protecting herself.

She couldn't have said exactly why. The portrait showed a young woman in a wide-panniered dress: green silk with a white lace kerchief, and a stomacher frothing with white ribbons. A small spaniel sat in her lap. The background was dark and featureless.

The woman didn't look at all unusual. She was smiling and mildly pretty, with powdered brown hair and large blue eyes that balanced out her soft mouth and weak chin. From what little Reggie knew of the fashions a hundred years and more in the past, the dress was ordinary enough for formal wear, and the spaniel was rather cute. Yet a sharpness in the woman's eyes, and the way her hand rested on the dog's neck, suggested that she was less pleasant than she appeared and far less kind.

At the bottom of the portrait, a brass plate had tarnished so badly as to be illegible, at least in the attic's dim light.

"Quite a lady you've found," said Colin, coming

up behind her. "I hope the painter escaped with his head."

Reggie laughed and let her arms fall back to her sides. "Let's be fair," she said. "If I had to sit for a portrait, I'd have looked a dashed sight crosser by the end."

"You haven't heard the plans?" Edmund asked. "Next Christmas, they're thinking."

Just as Reggie groaned, a voice called up from below, and all three of them turned.

"Mr. Edmund?" It was one of the maids. "There's a telegram for you. A Mr. Meadows?"

Edmund sighed and struck his palm with his head. "Harry," he muttered. "I wonder who it is *this* time. Excuse me," he said and headed toward the stairs.

"Harry?" Reggie asked.

"Chap with a taste for opera singers. Rather heartless ones too, if I'm thinking of the right gentleman— although his expectations are largely to blame," said Colin.

"And Edmund's his shoulder to cry on," said Reggie, and shook her head. She couldn't say anything more. She didn't know how much Colin knew, and there was nothing to say in any case. She stepped away from the portrait and opened one of the other trunks. "At least he gets out of some dusty work."

"Leaving the burden to the two of us," said Colin.

"I'll pay him back for it later," Reggie said.

She tried to sound casual, but her senses had come to full attention when Colin had said "the two of us" in his silky, accented voice.

It was true. They were alone in the attic.

Eleven

REGGIE WAS NERVOUS.

Colin could see it in the way she kept glancing toward him and then away, in the swift movement of her hands as she sorted through a box of old clothes. When she spoke, he could hear tension beneath the laughter in her voice.

"We ought to bring all of these rags downstairs," she said. "Have a fancy dress party." She held up a red velvet doublet, considerably moth-eaten. "Can you picture yourself in this?"

"Red was never my color," he said. "And besides, I'd have to powder my hair and wear knee breeches. No thank you."

"You've studied those fashions more than I ever did."

"Experience, not study. I managed to avoid portraits."

"My God," said Reggie, going still and staring at him.

"Not last I was aware. Although if you feel like making an offering—"

Reggie laughed unsteadily, pushing loosened hair away from her face. "How old *are* you?"

"That's hardly a polite sort of question, is it?" Colin asked, because joking felt familiar and safe. He wished he knew why she was nervous—whether she worried that he'd try to take some advantage now, whether she regretted kissing him two nights before, or whether she simply felt awkward about the whole situation.

Such wishing was new. Women weren't usually much of a mystery to him—he'd learned to read those particular tea leaves when Regina Talbot-Jones's great-grandmother was a girl—but this one was harder to interpret, and Colin wasn't certain whether that was her doing or his.

As he watched her laugh, he discovered that he was more than a little on edge himself.

He'd never had anyone discover his real identity. He'd told a few people over the course of his life—he'd traveled far and wide, and mixed with a number of strange folk, and he wasn't as twitchy about secrecy and reputation as Stephen was—but it had always been his choice, and he'd always known them quite well.

Now Reggie knew.

And as lovely as she was, as much as his eyes kept drifting to her neck, her breasts, or the curve of her derriere, Colin couldn't think of her as lightly as he did other attractive and potentially interested women. He kept rethinking what he was going to say, wondering what she'd truly meant when *she* spoke, stopping before he reached for her—in other words, overthinking as he hadn't done since he'd been a spotty youth.

He knew what she could do, and she knew what he was, and he knew that *she* knew and she knew that *he* knew…and Colin was giving himself a damned headache.

"A hundred and thirtysomething," he said.

"Hmm?" Reggie, who had turned back to the clothing, lifted her head again and blinked.

"You asked how old I was."

"And you said it wasn't polite," she said, smiling.

"Many very enjoyable things aren't."

He caught Reggie's eyes and grinned, and saw a slight flush rise over her cheeks. It probably wasn't embarrassment. She met his eyes too squarely and smiled back too readily. Not for the first time that day or that hour, he felt arousal tighten his skin.

"You seem very…well-preserved," said Reggie, and her eyes traveled down his chest for a teasing second before rising back up to his face. "For a man of your advanced years."

"Not all that advanced, relatively speaking," said Colin. "I expect to see four centuries and still be…vigorous."

Reggie was facing him completely now, forgetting for a moment the trunk and its contents. Her lips pursed into a very tempting O as she heard his response, and she whistled. "Not bad innings, I'd say. Doesn't that depend on you staying out of trouble, though?"

"Are you implying that I don't?"

"I'd bet all of Whitehill on it. Though I'm not sure I'd find anyone to take that wager," she added.

"Nobody who knows me, at any rate."

"I was thinking more that nobody'd want to take the chance of winning this place now."

"Not at all," Colin said. "Ghosts add interest."

"They've certainly gotten all sorts of exciting people to come out here," said Reggie, and she grinned up at him again.

Over the course of his life, Colin had been alone with young ladies in a variety of places: featherbeds, haystacks, and even the occasional riverbank in pleasant weather. Dusty attics had never featured. Yet these places also had never featured Reggie, with her dancing eyes and her hair falling down around her shoulders.

"You've got a bit of cobweb," he said, noticing the strands at her temple. He knelt down and reached out. "Hold still. And, er, brace yourself."

She closed her eyes and waited, patient for once in their brief acquaintance. Colin brushed his fingers over her temple, lifting the spider's web away. Beneath it, the edge of her face was warm and soft, and her hair was like heavy silk. He swallowed, brushed his hand off on his trousers, and noticed that Reggie hadn't yet moved.

Mostly, at least. Her breasts were rising and falling rapidly, and he could see the quick pulse in the hollow of her neck.

Colin touched his fingers to that spot, lightly, and felt the speed of her heartbeat. Desire was coursing through his own veins, collecting warm and heavy in his groin, but he kept his voice quiet. He could be playful for the moment. He could be human, as she was.

If she let him, at least.

"'Exciting people,' is it?" he asked. "You certainly don't seem calm."

Without opening her eyes, Reggie shook her head slightly. "No," she said, drawing the word out.

Colin traced a finger along her collarbone, just above the neckline of her dress. "Are you afraid of me, then?"

Her eyes snapped open at the question. "No," said Reggie, very definitely. Then she gave him an impish smile, one that went straight to his swelling cock. "Should I be?"

"That depends verra much on who you ask," he said and leaned forward to kiss her.

At first, Colin did no more than brush his lips against Reggie's. His touch was light, but not tentative: the card that led the trick, the advance of the first pawn. He felt her mouth soft below his, her quick inhalation, and the way she leaned toward him. Then, hands on her shoulders, he pulled back just enough to look into her eyes.

"How about now?"

She shook her head, smiling and biting her lip. "I hope that doesn't disappoint you."

"I doubt there's a man on earth who'd find you disappointing," he said and leaned forward again.

This time, the kiss was deep and lingering. Colin took his time, savoring the building tension between them, nibbling at Reggie's lips and stroking his hands down her sides. He only let his fingertips skim the sides of her breasts, and even that through the rigid casing of her corset, but she still gasped at the contact and wriggled closer to him.

By the time he broke off the kiss, they both lay on the floor facing each other, Reggie's breasts just grazing Colin's chest, and both of them breathing hard. Circling the rise of her hip with one hand, Colin used the other to brush her hair back again. He studied her face, her swollen lips and dazed eyes.

She let him look for about three seconds. Then she ducked her head and bit him lightly on the neck.

It wasn't so much the bite itself that made him go cross-eyed with lust, although God knew the sensation of her warm lips and sharp teeth against his skin was maddening enough. It was the surprise of it, the daring playfulness, and also the way it brought Reggie's whole form against his. His hips jerked, thrusting his erection pleasurably and frustratingly against her stomach, and without thinking, he tightened his hands in her hair and on her hip.

She made a strangled noise, too low to exactly be a whimper, against the hollow of his neck.

"Good?" he asked, mastering himself enough to speak. He knew already—she was trailing kisses down his throat now, and her fingers were digging into his back—but he wanted to hear her say it.

Wanted, in fact, to make her say it.

She hesitated a moment. Then she raised her head and flashed him a grin. "I like to think so. Although a good girl wouldn't be doing this." Momentarily, she went still, just long enough for Colin to wonder whether she'd call a halt to their play. Then she shifted the angle of her body, just enough to wrap one leg around his waist, her skirts falling around them in a tangle of muslin and silk. "Or this."

The feeling as she pressed against him was amazing, was wonderful. It was not yet what his straining body was coming desperately to need, but Colin could wait. He would be glad to wait, would cheerfully give up everything he had for the waiting alone. He groaned and kissed Reggie again, this time cupping one of her breasts, or at least doing the best job he could, given the impediments of wardrobe.

"You're very pretty like this," he muttered as he nibbled at her earlobe, "but I'd prefer the shirt and trousers just now."

"Me too," said Reggie, breathless. Then, at another motion of Colin's hand, she closed her eyes and bit her lip, silent for a second before managing, "Though I'm…I mean, this is still very…"

"Very?" Turnabout being fair play, he bit gently at her neck. She arched against him, which had the useful effects of pushing her breast further into his hand and of sliding her thighs against his cock. Colin stifled a groan. "Don't leave me in suspense," he said.

"There aren't…mmm…there aren't really *words*. 'I like it' is…" She swallowed as Colin cupped her calf and slid his hand upward. Taking off the corset was probably impractical, he'd decided regretfully, but other regions were at least a little less guarded. And the lady seemed to like that decision. "Inadequate. As a description."

She wore silk stockings, he discovered, and silk drawers as well, and her legs were long and shapely, firm under his fingers. Colin was vaguely aware of a cracking sound nearby, but it didn't come from the stairs, so it was probably mice or the house settling, and he ignored it in favor of stroking Reggie's thigh and making her moan. "Fortunately," he said, "there are less verbal demonstrations."

"O-oh?"

He wasn't sure whether she was urging him to elaborate or honestly uncertain what he meant. He didn't know how far her experience had gone, either with others or alone. He didn't ask, preferring to skim his fingers upward and over as she shook beneath his hand, to trace the seam of her drawers and find it as intoxicatingly wet as he'd hoped. "Yes," he said, confirmation and arousal at the same time. She did whimper this time, and thrust her sex against his fingers. "Yes, sweetheart, like that."

Another series of sharp cracks reached his ears, this time getting through his desire. What the hell *was* that?

As he heard the first rumble, he realized that the temperature had dropped.

Lust vanished. The need for action took over. With no time to get to his feet, Colin wrapped his arms around Reggie and rolled, shoving them past the trunks and farther into the attic. As his shoulder collided painfully with the edge of a cupboard, he heard another rumble from above.

Then the roof parted and a cloud of rubble poured in, just over the place where he and Reggie had been.

Twelve

"WHAT—WHAT—"

Reggie needed to stop stammering. She needed to catch her breath. She needed to remember how to say more than one word. Her brain was not cooperating on any of the above, her corsets were stabbing her in the ribs, and she understood for the first time why people fainted. She felt numb and light, about to crack down the middle.

She focused and pulled in air. "What in the name of God *was* that?"

Not much of an improvement, that question. *That* was the ceiling falling in, *idiot*, and Colin was looking down at her, frowning with concern, probably over her physical welfare but quite possibly because she sounded completely dense.

He could have his wits about him. He'd lived more than a hundred years, which was bound to give a man some experience with both lust and danger. She had comparatively little of either. Also, perhaps dragon minds could handle going from exquisite torment to stunned terror in a matter of seconds. The human brain was not built for it.

Damned if she wouldn't try and rise to the occasion, though.

Before Colin could answer her, Reggie summoned what remained of her self-possession. "I mean, was that magic? Did you sense anything this time?"

"No," he said. His lips quirked upward, and he added, "But then, I wasna' in much of a condition to notice."

Even now, the husky tone that crept into his voice made Reggie's insides melt a little—and even now, she was satisfied to hear Colin say it first. That probably betrayed a sad lack of perspective on her part, but she was a flawed creature. She'd accepted that much years ago.

She did wonder if he was sincere, or if some version of "Oh, I was carried away by lust, of course" was simply what one said to women after. Not that this was really *after*, since they'd still been in *before* when the ceiling had fallen in, or possibly *during*, but she thought the reassuring phrases would be the same either way.

She didn't know, and that didn't sit much easier with her than the collapsed ceiling did.

"Are you all right?" Colin asked.

"Ye-es," she said, taking a moment to be certain of it. "Well done. You move very fast."

Fast wasn't half of it. She remembered a flash of movement and that was all, except that remembering made her conscious that she was still lying underneath Colin, his body solid and warm against hers. He was still aroused too. She felt the evidence pressing into her thigh. Her own body throbbed in response, but now was very much not the time to act on it.

Colin seemed to realize that when she did. He got to his feet in one graceful motion, then offered her a hand.

Reggie took it and pulled herself to her feet, aware of how much more awkward skirts and corsets and being human made her. Beneath Colin's gaze, she flushed with embarrassment and unreasonable anger. Did he have to *watch* her? Was he hiding a smirk?

Yes, he did, or at least it was easier to help someone up when you were looking at her, and no, he probably wasn't. Reggie knew these things, and still she wanted to slap him.

Reaction, said the sensible part of her. You want to slap *someone* and he's what's around.

She sighed. "We'd better go down," she said, pulling her mind toward organization and reaction, toward things that had to be done. "Otherwise—"

"Good God, what *happened*?" Edmund asked, stepping through the attic door. Mouth hanging open, he looked from Reggie and Colin to the pile of rubble in the middle of the room and the hole that gaped just above it, rain falling steadily through. "Are the two of you all right? Anything broken?"

"Master Edmund?" one of the maids said from below. "I heard a crash."

Reggie closed her eyes and watched pink and green blobs collide in front of her vision.

Suddenly, fainting seemed not just understandable but perhaps the best option going.

She didn't faint. It wasn't the sort of thing one could honestly do on command. Pretending was a gambit the Miss Heseltons of the world practiced, and Reggie wasn't a wonderful actress. Also, it was a safe bet that fainting would have just brought on more hysterics.

"I'm sending for workmen," said Mater, pacing the upstairs drawing room. Her skirt swirled out behind her at every turn, adding to the theatrical effect. Reggie decided that it wasn't the time to tell her about the painting they'd found. "We should've had that roof redone long ago. I don't *care* whether they preserve the original character of the house," she added, with a sharp look at her husband.

"The workmen might be in just as much danger," said Mr. Talbot-Jones. "Perhaps more, if they're unprepared."

"As far as we know, it was only a bad roof. I'm certain they'd be prepared for *that*," said Mrs. Talbot-Jones. "And we've had men in before without much trouble. Drink the rest of your tea, Reggie. How are you feeling?"

Slightly homicidal, she thought.

"I'm fine," she said for approximately the fiftieth time in the last quarter hour. "Not injured at all. Mr. MacAlasdair was very alert."

Unable to help herself, she glanced over at Colin, who was lounging in an armchair by the hearth—and out of the line of fire. He looked slightly amused and perfectly composed, as if he spent half his life pulling girls out of the way of collapsing ceilings. Maybe he did; he probably spent enough time seducing them.

That wasn't entirely fair. She'd been enthusiastic. And she wasn't jealous—at least, she didn't think so. Of course Colin had been with other women. He was male, and more than a hundred years old, and she had no claim on him, nor did she want one. It was just…it had been so easy for him to make her beg and squirm. He'd kept so much of his own self-control. Reggie was a worldly girl and could meet his eyes without blushing even now, but remembering the noises she'd made and the way she'd moved against him was not comfortable, and not just for pleasant physical reasons.

She looked away, down at her teacup. Miss Heselton was having the vapors now, talking about how awful it would have been and how she didn't think she could have endured it. Mater was demanding to know why Edmund had left Reggie and Colin up there in the first place, and while seeing the future was *not* one of Reggie's freakish talents, she knew that the conversation would not take any pleasant paths.

"We found that portrait," she said, speaking loudly enough to interrupt the others and gesturing to the corner, where the eighteenth-century lady smiled her thin smile from the painting propped against the wall. Edmund had brought it down, but everyone had been too busy fussing to discuss it yet. In Reggie's opinion, the time had most definitely come. "I don't know if it's important, but she's the first face or name we encountered up there. And it wasn't hung up like the rest, though it's no worse than most of them."

The walls of Whitehill had come complete with sundry portraits of its previous owners. A lady from

Regency times looked soulfully out from between the dining-room windows, and a bilious Tudor lord glowered on the wall opposite Reggie's room. As surly as that gentleman seemed, she'd never gotten the sense of cruelty and even danger from him that she'd felt from the woman in the attic portrait.

She didn't mention that. Talking about vague feelings that she "just had" didn't usually help a situation.

"Bring it over into the light," said Pater. When Edmund had obliged him, he squinted down at the nameplate. "There's certainly a *J* here, and an *M* for the last name—though that's no surprise. She'd be a Morgan, at least by marriage."

"That might be a place to start," said Mr. Heselton, speaking up for the first time since they'd gathered in the drawing room. "The church records don't go back more than a hundred years or so—there was a fire—but we could look in the village cemetery. She was one of the family, and the gravestones were good quality. Hers would probably have lasted."

"I'll have one of the girls polish the nameplate," said Mrs. Talbot-Jones, "and we'll see what's to be seen. Reggie, do you think you should lie down?"

"No," said Reggie decisively. "Did you and Miss Heselton find anything?"

"A book," said Mater, her mouth tightening at the memory. "Or part of one. Evidently it'd been in a fire, like your records," she added, glancing at Mr. Heselton. "However, it looks to be a journal, and a rather old one at that, and the remaining pages might well be useful. It's mostly in French, though, and I think some Latin as well."

"I don't think any of the family came from France," said Mr. Heselton, frowning as he tried to remember.

"Wouldn't have to be French themselves," said Reggie. "You write foreign when you want to make it harder for people to snoop." The others turned to her, curious, and she shrugged. "Girls' school. Six years."

"Can you read it, then?" Pater asked.

Reggie shook her head. "I never bothered keeping a journal. Or reading other people's."

"That speaks very well of you," said Miss Heselton. "So many girls these days are furtive and dishonest."

Making rude noises probably wouldn't pass, even if Mater was inclined to be sympathetic right now, and Reggie couldn't explain that she'd merely had her fill of other people's heads by the time she'd started school. She sought refuge in her tea.

It was only a brief respite. "But you *took* French," said Mater.

"I can order off a menu and buy a hat," said Reggie. "I'm lost at reading."

"George can read both," said Miss Heselton, gesturing to her brother, "but it's quite a daunting job for one person, and we might not have very much time. I thought that, perhaps..." She trailed off, looking at Edmund. "Your father says you went to Eton and Oxford."

"Went, yes. But it's been years, and I only passed Latin by the skin of my teeth."

"And the cuffs of your sleeves," said Reggie.

"I'm glad to hear your time—and school fees— were so well-spent," said Pater, but he was grinning just a shade less obviously than Edmund. "And I'm afraid too much time might have passed for me as well, though I'd certainly be glad to make the attempt."

"Halves, then," said Colin, "as I'm a fair hand with both. At least until we're more certain about the book. Unless the ladies upstairs can assist us."

"Mrs. Osbourne won't be well enough to help," said Mr. Heselton, "and I wouldn't want to tax Miss Browne further. Thirds it is—assigned as you like, Mr. MacAlasdair, once we see the book. At least we've profited by the afternoon's...adventures."

"We might have," said Mrs. Talbot-Jones. "It could be that neither of the things we found has anything to do with the ghost. Let's not get our hopes up too quickly."

Growing up, Reggie had heard *that* warning more times than she could count. Mater had cautioned her against expecting too much from the weather, from new horses, from balls and friends and men. More often than Reggie would have preferred, she'd been right.

"It's our only place to start right now," she said. "Going forward is better than doing nothing."

Thirteen

His actions are a disgrace to our blood and our name. As undutiful as it may be, I cannot but blame Father, at least in part, for failing to correct such tendencies before they became truly and indelibly marked. Now it is left to me to deal with their repercussions. Sarah will certainly be of no use—she's never had a strong will where our family is concerned.

Colin put his pen down and lifted his head, not sure whether to rub his eyes or his wrist first. He did, as he'd said, know both French and Latin, but the French in the journal had been old when he was born. The writer's hand was graceful enough but small, and neither age nor fire had made his task any easier.

In his progress through the first few intact pages, he'd read a great deal of frustration. The writer clearly felt that he or she was the only moral and responsible person for at least fifty miles. Over centuries of undeath, that could well have turned into the rage that had ended the séance. The writer talked about family blood too. As Edmund had said, the ghost could have been speaking of that.

Colin had found no name, though, and no identifying details, and the whole project was slow going. It was easy to let his mind wander.

Dinner that night had been a quiet affair, though it had lacked the morning's unease. With a clear plan of action before them, however ineffective it might prove to be, everyone had eaten a little heartier, and their silence had been as much planning as brooding.

Mrs. Talbot-Jones had placed Reggie between her and Edmund, perhaps surrounding her daughter with people who would spot any signs of infirmity. Colin, at the other end of the table, had shot a few glances her way, but had been looking for other signs entirely, though he couldn't have said exactly what.

He hadn't been expecting a nocturnal invitation from her. He wouldn't have accepted one. The rest of the household was bound to watch Reggie's movements especially carefully that night. Delightful as Reggie was, no woman was worth the likelihood of getting thrown out on his ear and missing further events at the house thereby. Girls—even pretty, bright, daring girls—came along often enough in a man's lifetime. Genuinely haunted houses were far rarer.

He still wished she'd look back at him more, and for longer. Instead she'd seemed very intent on her dinner, and on the conversation with her mother and brother. The one time Colin had managed to catch her eye, she had flashed him a grin of unusual and, he thought, unwarranted fierceness, as if she was daring him to do something.

Or perhaps to think something.

As dearly as he would have liked to investigate the subject, Colin had managed no chance to do so. Reggie's parents had, through a variety of not-very-subtle hints, hustled her off to bed shortly after dinner. Miss Browne's genuine weariness had provided an excellent opportunity to begin the suggestions. Reggie had waited until Edmund had retired, though. If the events of the day had troubled her, they hadn't done so badly enough for her to forget that she was trying to be her brother's chaperone.

The memory made Colin smile.

Now he was at his desk with a cup of tea at his left hand, and the journal and an almost-blank copybook at his right. The situation inspired much less good humor than his memory of Reggie. He wasn't surprised that his mind roamed back to her whenever he allowed it to stray from the work at hand.

There wouldn't be too much more work for him tonight, Colin knew. Already the words in the journal were starting to blur in front of his eyes. His dragon side gave him night vision and other forms of perception, but it had no facility for words, nor for close-up sight. If he tried to push himself harder, he'd begin to make mistakes—possibly fatal ones, given the forces he was dealing with.

After another paragraph in which the writer railed against his or her brother for what sounded like an unfortunate liaison, Colin shut the journal. The footman who was serving as his valet—Loch Arach had yet to send him a suitable replacement, and he didn't like traveling with strangers—had long since gone to bed, and Colin didn't have the heart to wake him. He'd undressed himself before; he could do it again. He turned to leave his desk.

A face peered in at him through the window.

He only got a momentary glimpse before the figure saw him and vanished. He saw that the face was the color of raw dough and almost as formless. The mouth was a lipless gash, the eyes indentations, the nose non-existent. It was a sketch of a human shape, done by a not-too-bright child.

When the figure vanished, it *vanished*. One second it was there; the next, as Colin choked out a low Gaelic curse, it was gone. He dashed to the window, but the landscape that met his eyes was as still and empty as any other country night would have been.

It was empty to human sight, anyhow. But he knew a trick or two.

He spoke a quick stream of Latin, triggering one of the universe's hidden rules, and the world around him changed. Now the bedroom was full of gray mist, turning faintly rose around the bed and blue by the desk. Outside, faint shades of green and brown rippled through the gray—and by the window, traces of putrid green lingered. The color was fading quickly, but now it was still sharp.

Reggie wasn't the only one who could climb out windows.

Colin spent a moment to make sure that the green residue *was* just residue, leftover aura from whatever the figure had been, and not hostile in itself. He spent another second checking for other traps. Seeing none, he wrenched open the window and sprang out onto the balcony.

From his new perspective, the green traces trailed away into midair. Nothing had climbed up to the balcony. The tree from which Reggie had entered bore no tracks, and neither did either of the walls beside the balcony. Colin leaned over the iron railing, looked out across the lawns of Whitehill, and saw no figures, human or eldritch. There were only the trees, the hedges, and a few swooping owls and bats silhouetted against the sky.

He could almost have thought that he'd imagined the shape outside his window—but he'd never been particularly given to hallucinations, and the traces of its rotting aura *did* hang in the air, even now.

With the night air cool against his face and the balcony cold beneath his feet, he tapped his fingers on the rail and thought of possibilities. He'd been sincere in telling Reggie that he didn't have much experience with ghosts, and he didn't think that the creature stalking Whitehill was anything else—he'd have been able to sense much more about a demon. Colin had lived long enough to know when he was over his head, and even to admit it sometimes, particularly to himself.

A few basic principles should still apply.

To wit: the creature had been at his window. He couldn't see where it had gone or how. Thus, either it could transport itself instantly elsewhere or it had moved up—though one might as well say down or sideways or *blue*, since human directions didn't really apply in these circumstances—to a different level of existence. Neither course would have left traces that Colin could perceive, even with magic.

Not in human form.

Responding to his thoughts, his fingers stretched out, reaching to their full length and then longer than any man's would have been. Silver claws and blue scales glimmered in the moonlight, and Colin heard iron bending beneath his grip.

No. Not yet. Think first. He pulled his human shape back around him like a man adjusting a coat and looked down at his hands in what he wouldn't allow to be alarm. Such lapses in self-control were rare, at least for him.

It was the prospect of a hunt that provoked him, maybe, such as he hadn't truly had in decades: a hunt beneath the open sky with an enemy who deserved no mercy. He had never thrown himself into such matters as his father had, or as Judith and Stephen did, but the instincts of his blood were still there and evidently still clamored to be heard.

Old, hostile magic almost certainly didn't help, and neither did rolling around on the floor with Reggie, though none of the dancers or maids or other women in Colin's past had brought his other self so close to the skin. Then again, few of them had made him so dizzy with lust, either.

He shook his head, tossing hair out of his eyes, and made himself let go of the railing.

What his dragon side wanted didn't matter. The reasons for it didn't signify, either. It was time to be practical, recognizing that the dragon had talents the man didn't. The dragon was also not a shape to assume on the second-story balcony of an old house, and even if he went to the ground to transform, he would be… deeply conspicuous, to say the least.

Colin couldn't see anyone on the lawn. That didn't mean everyone was asleep—looking to either side, he could see light shining through the windows nearby, tinted red and blue by various sets of curtains—or even inclined to stay indoors. Nor did he know where chasing the ghost would take him and who he might encounter there.

He turned his face to the sky where a crescent moon hung in the velvet darkness. It was waning, thinner than it had been the night before, but it still cast too much light.

In a day or two, changing his shape would be far less of a risk.

If, in a day or two, the ghost had vanished, or if it no longer came around his window, Colin was certain he'd regret the decision to wait—but he couldn't worry much about those possibilities. The figure had come that night. Whether the magic of Colin's dual nature drew it or it was simply curious about one of the new arrivals, he doubted that it had gotten what it wanted. It would be back.

Turning from the balcony railing, Colin saw the door leading back to his room. A moment or two of thought, and he could have spared himself the climb out the window. He could have spared himself the climb back in too—he was certain that the door was locked from the inside.

He couldn't regret much, though. There were times for haste—if that Ecclesiastes verse didn't say as much, it should have—and besides, a man who always went by safe paths grew old before his time.

Colin didn't exactly know what his time was, but he was in no hurry. Placing one hand on the window-sill, he swung himself up and in, and landed lightly on the floor of his room.

Sleep would be a long time coming. The shock of the figure and the excursion out-of-doors had gotten his blood up, and he paced the floor a few times but knew that he would never tire himself that way.

He didn't think it likely that Reggie would climb up to his window again, either, but he wished otherwise—strongly enough to surprise him and impractically enough too. Mortal girls were out of their depth in this business—but she hadn't seemed out of her depth at the séance, or no more than he'd been. Colin didn't think she'd have screamed or fainted at the sight of the ghost, and he did wonder what she would have said about it.

Miss Talbot-Jones, he was beginning to think, was no more ordinary than her house.

Fourteen

A BOILED EGG CRACKED UNDER REGGIE'S SPOON, AND she began to peel away the splintered shell, always a satisfying process, not least because it gave her an excuse to ignore the conversation around her. Eight hours of dreamless sleep had done her good— "knit up the raveled sleeve of care," if she recalled her Shakespeare by way of a nervous second-form mistress—but she'd never really felt up to company before noon. She certainly didn't think she could manage to talk about—she raised her head and listened to Mr. Heselton for a second—German theology. Oof. How had *that* happened?

Pater had thrown himself into the discussion, so there was some balm in Gilead. The aged parents had calmed themselves considerably after an evening without casualties, but Mater had still turned a gimlet eye on Reggie that morning and had listened with considerably more attention than usual after asking if she'd slept well.

Colin hadn't asked. Dimly, Reggie was aware that other girls might have found that insulting. She didn't think she could claim any grounds for the insult, and anyhow his silence came as a relief. She thought he knew as much, which *wasn't* a relief. Just how transparent did the man find her? More or less so than the average mortal mayfly?

Sitting at the other end of the table from him, she could hardly bait him with words. All the same, she caught his eye and smiled, lifting her eyebrows in what *generally* came off as cool and composed regard, and what she intended as a challenge. She was still here, and she was as serene as he was about yesterday's events.

Since it was nine damn thirty in the morning, Reggie didn't know that she succeeded. She *did* know that Colin looked far too cheerful and relaxed for the hour. Dragons didn't get shadows under their eyes, maybe, or maybe they didn't need sleep.

There were no words for what she thought of *that*.

German theology continued as Reggie applied herself to her tea. Then, abruptly, it didn't. Mr. Heselton's flow of speech cut off mid-sentence, and Reggie heard rustling as the gentlemen stood. She looked up to see Miss Browne standing on the threshold, pale and neat.

"Good morning," she said, bearing up very well under seven pairs of eyes, in Reggie's opinion. "I hope you're all well. Mrs. Osbourne is awake and having her own breakfast, and she sends her regards—and her thanks."

Not everyone let out their breath at the same moment, but the relief around the table was audible all the same. Mater was the first to speak.

"That's wonderful news," she said. "You must

come have some tea and some breakfast, and then tell us all about it." Her voice was heavy on the "and then," her gaze keen as she swept it around the room. Having spent years with the woman, Reggie picked up the message at once, but even the others weren't long in realizing her meaning: don't bother the girl before she's gotten some food inside her.

A small whirlwind of solicitude resulted. Mr. Heselton served food; Mater poured tea; Edmund pulled out a chair for Miss Browne; the others, bound by manners and distance, offered compliments and good wishes as audibility allowed. Even with Mater's warning, Miss Browne might have been quite over-whelmed, save that Watkins entered just then with the mail, and the ensuing bustle enabled her to eat at least a few slices of toast and jam.

Nothing came Reggie's way, which didn't surprise her. She couldn't think of one of her friends in London who was a good correspondent. She was sure that half of them didn't remember where she was at the moment, and she would have bet that half of those didn't quite know where *they* were. She leaned back in her chair, sipped her tea, and tried to wake up.

"Oh," said Mater, looking up from a letter and smiling faintly. "It seems that we have more good news this morning."

"The more the better," said Edmund, looking up from his bacon. "Someone sending you a new gardener or three?"

"Not quite *that* good. Your Aunt Claire is giving a ball in a few days—a small affair, she says, but she'd be glad to have us and our guests."

"Quite decent of her," said Pater, and he added, by way of explanation, "My wife's brother Lewis and his family have lived around here since before our marriage, you understand. Perhaps an hour away—no time at all on a pleasant evening. They're very hospitable."

"And," said Edmund, directing a prophecy-of-doom look toward Colin and then Mr. Heselton, "they have three single daughters."

"Don't be ungracious, Edmund," said Mater, "and don't exaggerate, either. Cynthia's as good as engaged to…oh, that young man in the Navy, the one with the beard…and Minerva's only eighteen."

Edmund made a skeptical noise into his tea.

To Reggie, sitting still with her hands wrapped around her teacup, the exchange drew itself out over about a day. She heard it from far off and felt the knotting of her stomach just as remotely. A ball at Aunt Claire's: wonderful. That was exactly what she needed. After all, it had worked out so bloody well last time.

Don't have hysterics, for God's sake, she scolded herself, hoping the thought would stick. *It's been years. Nobody will remember you.*

Swallowing tea still took more effort than it should have.

"As I said," Mr. Talbot-Jones continued, "quite the decent thing of Claire. But would it be wise, considering everything?"

"I think it would, actually," said Miss Browne. "It's fairly common that negative emotions will excite a spirit—fear and tension can make a ghost antagonistic even if it wasn't before."

"And if it already was?" Colin asked.

"I don't really know." Miss Browne looked down at her hands. "I've never encountered such an angry spirit before. But emotions do affect all of them. I'd imagine that a hostile spirit would grow bolder. Perhaps stronger."

"Sounds like dogs," said Edmund. "Or horses."

"Spirits are, in a way. Death"—she frowned over the words—"simplifies things, it seems, and intensifies them at the same time. Particularly feelings—a ghost's own or those of others. They sense them more deeply than what you or I could observe."

Remembering the mental tumult the first time her power had woken, Reggie fought the urge to shudder. That moment had been bad enough. If she'd been reading other people without even having to touch them, she thought she might well have ended up in an asylum—or dead, as little as that apparently solved the problem. For the first time, she felt some sympathy for the ghost, and a good deal of fear along with that.

On the other hand, there were those at the house for whom a ball at Claire and Lewis Stafford's would do absolutely nothing to banish negative emotions. Reggie thought she'd be first among them, but she doubted that Edmund would be far behind, particularly with the way Miss Heselton was eyeing him.

"Well, I would love above all things to accept such generous hospitality," she was cooing, even as Reggie watched. Miss Heselton's eyes grew wide, and her bow-shaped mouth formed just the beginning of a pout. "I just hope that I'll have enough partners. I don't know *anyone* here, and with James injured as he is, I'm a little scared that I'll be a wallflower."

"I shouldn't worry over it," said Reggie. "Country's absolutely infested with young men this time of year—up for the shooting."

"Oh, but strange men?" Further widening of the eyes hadn't seemed possible, and yet there Miss Heselton was, accomplishing just that. She shook her head slowly, the picture of demure propriety. "I'm not at all sure it would be right—"

"You needn't worry about *that*," said Mr. Talbot-Jones, shaking his own head but smiling with approval. "Claire's sure to have gone through her guests with a fine-tooth comb. *She* won't let anyone put a foot wrong. Never has. And a young lady like you will never lack for partners—don't you agree, Edmund?"

Thus cornered, Edmund nodded. "Oh, yes, rather," he said, but even if he hadn't sounded a little too hearty for perfect sincerity, Reggie knew the uneasy look in his eyes well enough. "Might be better if I stayed home, actually," he said. "Wouldn't want to unbalance things. Aunt Claire hates superfluous men."

With three debatably single daughters, Reggie didn't think Aunt Claire would find any man—even a relation—all that superfluous, but she didn't say anything, and neither did Colin, although she saw him hide a smile behind a slice of toast.

It was Pater who made the correction, of course. "Don't be idiotic, Edmund," he said, though cheerfully enough, "and don't slight your aunt like that. She'd be glad to see you."

"But he does have a point," Reggie put in, seeing

her brother begin to founder and searching for nearby ropes. "In a way, I mean. About staying home. Not all of us, of course, but—well, we've got two injured people here, not to mention an angry ghost."

"Don't worry on my account," said Mr. Heselton quickly. "I've every intention of going. I won't be able to do any good as a dancing partner—but then, I never really could. I'll enjoy the dinner and the company, at any rate. And I think it would do the rest of us good," he added, looking across the table and smiling at Miss Browne. "Including, as the lady says, the spirit."

Mater nodded. "And I'm sure Emma and Mrs. Kelly will take excellent care of our remaining patient. Of course, Regina, you're quite welcome to stay behind if you think it's best. I'm sure it would be very generous of you."

She didn't even look over at Reggie, but she didn't need to. Both of their memories were as sharp as ever.

"Maybe," she said, not wanting to seem too eager—and not wanting to leave Edmund in the lurch. She cast a glance his way, trying to think of a means for pulling him into her excuse.

"I understand," said Miss Heselton, with a syrupy smile in Reggie's direction. "I'm nervous myself. Society at these country parties can be *so* overwhelming at times, particularly to people who haven't been…able…to be part of it for a while."

She sounded completely innocent. If asked, she would surely reply that she'd meant nothing but a remark about how busy Reggie must have been in London. There was real venom beneath the sugar this time, though, and Reggie didn't mistake her meaning for a second. Her hands tightened on the edge of the table, and she knew that her face had gone very still.

"Quite overwhelming indeed," said Colin. "As a matter of fact, there are some parts of society I'd consider it a privilege to avoid." He spoke lightly, even carelessly, but the edge to his voice was like a blade against silk.

Reggie turned to look at him. Why was he defending her? Why did he think she *needed* defending? How much had he heard? She saw no answers in his face, just his usual faintly amused expression.

Before *that*, she wouldn't back down.

"Well," she said, smiling back at Miss Heselton, "it's sweet of you to worry, but I think I'll be fine. Mater's right—the servants can handle things for one night."

So could she.

She'd just have to keep from strangling anyone for the next few days.

Fifteen

THE TREES AROUND THE WHITEHILL VILLAGE GRAVE-
yard still shone lush and green in the late-morning
sunlight. The cemetery was a well-kept little place, the
stone walls neat and the grass well-tended. A lark was
singing somewhere above, and only consideration for
his companions kept Colin from whistling himself, at
first. A moment's thought convinced him that it was
best to keep silent regardless. Places of the dead had
never been as solemn to him as they were to modern
mortals, but he and the Talbot-Jones men had come
here with a purpose, and not a merry one.

Many more ghostly tricks, and Colin thought he
might become a sight more solemn around grave-
yards himself.

Still, he stood for a moment and took in the view,
admiring the way the old stone church beckoned
from among the trees a short distance away. It made
him think of his own youth, though the MacAlasdairs
had only showed up at chapel often enough to keep
suspicion down.

"Young Heselton's kept the place very well," said

Mr. Talbot-Jones, coming up a little ways behind Colin and Edmund. "They say the last man who held his place wasn't half as diligent. Older chap, of course, and only had a housekeeper."

"Heaven forbid," said Edmund.

"It's quite a scenic little place, at that," Colin offered. "And Heselton seems a sensible fellow, as vicars go. I'm not terribly well-acquainted with the species myself, you understand."

Although the comment had passed only idly from his lips, he saw Mr. Talbot-Jones frown and his bushy gray eyebrows draw together with concern. "Ah. Yes, quite—I'd forgotten that religion's a bit different in Scotland. I do hope you've taken no offense. I assure you I intended none."

"No, no, not at all," Colin said, holding up his hands and smiling reassuringly once he'd realized what his host was talking about. The Church of Scotland was not the Church of England, nor could a man translate between the two as easily as taking a train across the border. He dimly recalled some controversy about the matter perhaps fifty years ago, though he'd mostly been in Italy at the time. "As much as I'm sure it would scandalize some on both sides to hear it, the difference is mostly an academic one with me."

"Oh, yes," said Edmund, sitting down on the wall. "Colin's wish to sleep in on a Sunday knows no nation or creed."

Hearing Mr. Talbot-Jones chuckle, Colin allowed himself to laugh as well. One never knew how men would take such matters. He'd seen religion turn deadly often enough, in Ireland and elsewhere, and he understood the man's caution. "I think," he said, "as long as a man tries to live well, it's probably no great matter. And Heselton's certainly been fine company, and helpful as well."

"His sister's been more helpful, I should say," said Mr. Talbot-Jones. "Rather something, the way she stepped in to take care of poor Mrs. Osbourne like that. I'd no idea she'd been trained as a nurse."

"I'd think her brother's parishioners couldn't do without her," said Edmund.

"Yes," said Mr. Talbot-Jones. "It'd be best for them if she settled down with some local fellow."

"Plenty of those around, aren't there?" Edmund asked. Hands in his pockets, he inspected the marble angel in front of him. "Plenty of chaps in London who'd be glad to settle down in the country too. I'd imagine she's had quite a few proposals already, a girl like that."

Mr. Talbot-Jones nodded. "I shouldn't wonder if she's engaged before the year's out. On the other hand, she might still be waiting for the right young man to make an appearance. One who could support her comfortably, perhaps."

"I'd hope she wasn't the mercenary sort," said Edmund.

"No, of course not. But there's nothing mercenary about a girl who wants to see herself provided for, and her children. She comes from a large family, you know."

"For the love of God." Edmund sighed. "Don't go any further with this line of discussion. I've no wish to hear about the suitability of her hips."

Mr. Talbot-Jones scowled. "Really, Edmund, I fail to understand why you take such a—" he began, at which point Colin felt that he'd best remind both men of his presence and coughed politely. His host flushed and cleared his throat; they sounded briefly like an outing of consumptives.

"Well," said Mr. Talbot-Jones, recovering himself, "quite so. It's a shame Heselton himself couldn't accompany us today. I'd imagine he knows the place better than any of us, and I'd, ah, rather not disturb the sexton if we have a choice."

"By which he means," said Edmund, drawing up to Colin's side for a moment as the three of them began to walk about the graveyard, "that Mater doesn't want word of what we're doing getting about too quickly."

"And he's not concerned?" Colin asked.

"Less so. Shortsighted of the old man. The son of an eccentric might be less of a catch, regardless of his wealth." His smile was thin and bitter.

Looking back and forth between Edmund and Mr. Talbot-Jones, short and straight-backed as he peered at gravestones, Colin shook his head. "You'll have to marry sometime, you know. You said so yourself. Unless you've a cousin you truly want to see inherit."

"Or unless Reggie produces a husband and heir," Edmund said and snorted.

"Not such a ludicrous prospect," said Colin, more warmly than he'd intended. After watching the morning's quiet storm, he found himself inclined to come to the lady's defense, whether or not she needed it.

"Is if she's not inclined, and she's fended off all comers—at least as far as I can tell—for ten years or so." Edmund sighed again. "No, I'll step up to the block in time—but I'd like to find a woman who understood, if you catch my meaning. One who was as happy to be left alone and could tend to her own affairs."

"Miss Heselton isn't that," Colin said. It was a bad time to inquire about the man or men who Reggie *hadn't* fended off, and he couldn't think of a way to do it subtly, not now that Edmund had moved on. "To say the least."

"Neither are the other women Pater thinks would be good for me. Sweet, romantic creatures, all of them." Edmund frowned down at one of the tombstones they passed. "And marrying a girl like that... well, it'd be a cruel trick. I can try to be decent in some ways, at least."

In his long life, Colin had rarely been at a loss for words, but now all that he could think of were the things that he couldn't say: that times changed and changed back again, that the standards of England and of humanity were not the only ones by which a man could be judged, that he'd known plenty of lawbreakers in his time and would have trusted many of them more than their respectable counterparts. To speak too freely along those lines would have invited questions he didn't want to answer.

He clapped Edmund on the shoulder, a light and friendly gesture. "I've always thought you decent enough. Except for your ties."

That got an honest grin out of the other man. "Have a word with Perkins, then. He's always having hysterics at me about 'em."

"And you scorn his advice. The man might just as well work in a factory, you know that?" Choice bits of Reggie's conversation on the balcony came to mind then, and Colin began to ask, "Does your sister—"

"Over here," called Mr. Talbot-Jones from the other end of the graveyard. "All the Morgans, from the look of things."

As Edmund turned, Colin saw the expression on his face. In sharp contrast to the way he'd looked before, he now seemed relieved to hear his father's voice.

Under the shade of a leafy chestnut tree, in the corner of the graveyard where the land began to slope upward into a hill, generations of Morgans lay beneath the earth. Limestone vaults, carved with figures and stained with moss and rain, stood next to simple worn markers, and a plain granite stone in the center crowned the only newish grave of the lot. *James Edward Morgan*, the carving said, and the dates suggested that this was the "Old Morgan" Edmund had mentioned.

The others were the usual mix that one found in family plots: old and young, alone or surrounded by family, and one small marker to commemorate a lad who'd been lost at sea in the days when Napoleon had loomed great and villainous in the English mind. Colin looked down at the small polished marker and shook his head, remembering how perilous the ocean had been in those days—perilous even for him. The breadth of the Pacific was too far for flight, and a dragon needed even more food and water than a man.

"Fifteen," said Mr. Talbot-Jones, regarding the

same gravestone. "Poor boy. If the modern world has anything to recommend it, Mr. MacAlasdair, it's that war on such a vast and brutal scale is far behind us."

"I wouldn't say that's the only advantage," said Colin, who'd been thinking of steamships himself, "but it's certainly one of the foremost. I don't see any women named *J*-anything about, do you?"

"No, not at all." Mr. Talbot-Jones frowned and stroked his beard. "Men—there are about five Jameses and a number of Josephs, and I believe a Julian somewhere—but no women. Unless she's under one of those terribly worn stones, and I think those are too old for the woman in the picture."

"There's another possibility," said Edmund, walking up to them. He gestured over the wall to a smaller and much humbler plot.

Mr. Talbot-Jones's eyes widened. "Unconsecrated ground?"

"It might explain why she's a ghost," said Colin. Before he thought of either reverence or concealment, he vaulted easily over the wall, a possible stunt for a mortal young man, but one that made Edmund whistle and Mr. Talbot-Jones cough.

Devil take it: they could think what they liked.

Leaves and sticks crunched beneath Colin's boots as he wandered, inspecting the markers. Most of these were plain, carved with businesslike starkness: a name, two dates, and nothing more. Against the wall, though, a neighbor with the respectable Morgans, stood another stone, overgrown but sturdy. Colin knelt and tugged away ivy until he could read the inscription.

"Janet Morgan," he said aloud. "1700–1750. May God Let Her Rest."

"I suppose He didn't oblige," said Edmund, and he chuckled hollowly. "Or she chose not to take Him up on the invitation."

"If she's our ghost," said Mr. Talbot-Jones.

His protest was obviously formal, though. The cruel cast to the woman's face in the portrait, the lady's grave in the midst of thieves and suicides, and the inscription—so close to a normal platitude, yet just far enough away in phrasing to be significant—might not have been an airtight case in a court of law, but it was enough evidence for Colin.

He didn't fear the dead. He didn't fear very much, as a rule. Mortal weapons could kill one of the MacAlasdairs, but it took considerable doing, and he'd spent a long time learning the ways of magic. Yet, kneeling by Janet Morgan's forgotten grave, he felt a chill run through his body.

Sixteen

"YOUR BROTHER SAID YOU'D PROBABLY BE IN HERE."
Reggie stepped into the blue drawing room and
shut the door behind her. Belatedly, she caught Miss
Heselton's startled expression as the other woman
looked up from the book she'd been reading and
added, "I hope I'm not disturbing you."

"No, not at all."

That was the only polite response that she could
have given, sincere or not, but Reggie didn't feel too
guilty. It really wouldn't have mattered what Miss
Heselton had said, even though she wanted to start on
something approaching the right foot.

"I'll send for some tea if you want," she said to
that end as she took a seat in one of the delicate chairs
opposite Miss Heselton. "I think there should be a
batch of muffins ready soon too. The cooking here
always brings me back, you know, no matter how
much time I spend in London."

"Food always tastes better in the fresh air," said
Miss Heselton, with a condescending smile, "and
surrounded by wholesome company."

"Yes, rather," said Reggie. "So, er, tea?"

"I'm not sure I could eat just now. But you're welcome to, if you wish." Miss Heselton closed her book. Glancing at the spine, Reggie saw that it was poetry, the author someone named Patmore. "Will your mother be joining us? Or the other ladies?"

"Browne's upstairs with Osbourne again," Reggie said. Unable to see any gradual path to her destination, she thought it was past time to forge ahead. "And I told Mater that one of the gardeners wanted to talk to her."

Miss Heselton blinked. "Did he?"

"Probably. They always do in the end. It'll keep her busy for a little while, at any rate. I wanted to have a word with you in private."

"Oh?" Miss Heselton tilted her head to one side and smiled again, outwardly the picture of welcoming innocence. Reggie didn't miss the way her eyes narrowed at the corners, though. She'd already been curious; now she was suspicious. Since Reggie had been bracing herself since breakfast for this conversation, that at least put them on more equal ground. "If there's anything I can help you with, please do let me know."

Reggie took as deep a breath as her corsets would allow. "Well," she started, "you were dashed helpful with Mrs. Osbourne. Thank you for that."

"Oh," said Miss Heselton again. "Well, it was nothing more than my duty."

"The rest of us couldn't have done it. I know that much. You're a smart girl." Reggie fought the urge to look away from Miss Heselton's smiling face. She twisted the cuff of one sleeve, steeled herself, and finally brought out the most awkward sentence she'd ever given thought to beforehand. "So you should know that—well, that you and Edmund won't suit."

Silence descended: a horrible hot silence during which both women looked at each other, and Reggie, at least, wished they were anywhere else, ideally a thousand miles or so apart. Then Miss Heselton drew herself up, widened her eyes, and said, "I'm sure I have no idea what you mean."

"Oh, have done," Reggie said, as kindly as she could manage. "I'm not saying it's your fault. I know damned well"—she ignored the little gasp at her profanity—"that Pater's been encouraging you, and I know Edmund's twelve different kinds of dunce when it comes to women. Nobody could blame you for getting the wrong idea. I just want to give you the right one."

"Which is," said Miss Heselton, "that we 'won't suit.'"

"Er. Yes. Nothing to do with you, of course." When Edmund came back, Reggie vowed, she was going to throw him into the pond. Never mind that he couldn't have this conversation himself—no gentleman could—but he could have done *something*. "You're a good sort. Very pretty. I'm sure you could have your pick of men, as a general rule."

Miss Heselton's lips pressed together. "I'm not shameless, thank you."

"I didn't say you were. I'm sure you're modest and virtuous, and men chase you. From afar. Politely." Unable to sit still any longer, Reggie rose from her chair. "It's just that Edmund isn't. Even if you think it looks that way."

"Oh?" The third time, the word had ice in it. "Because I'm a clergyman's sister? Because my father was a major instead of a lord? Because I don't have a great house and spend most of my time at London parties?"

"That's got nothing to do with it," Reggie snapped back, her face hot. "Our blood isn't any bluer than yours, and we don't need to marry for money. Edmund just—well, he isn't—he doesn't want to get married. Not to anyone."

Miss Heselton blinked again. Then she laughed, light and airy, and almost all of the tension seemed to leave her body. "Is that what's been worrying you? Oh, dear. It's very loyal of you, I'm sure," she said, as if Reggie were a child and not five years her senior, "but you know, gentlemen never do want to get married. And then, when they meet the right woman, they *do*—if they're truly gentlemen, that is, and that's certainly true of your brother."

"Yes," said Reggie, "Edmund's a gentleman."

She walked a few paces and studied the mantel, wishing that she could rest her head on it or kick it, or perhaps throw one of the china shepherdesses on top of it against the wall.

In all justice, she couldn't fault Miss Heselton for not understanding. A vicar's sister, gently reared and clearly innocent, despite both medical knowledge and a certain amount of cattiness, *wouldn't* understand. Most people wouldn't—certainly Reggie's parents didn't, and had never guessed where their son's reluctance to marry came from.

Neither could Reggie explain in any great detail. Her own knowledge of Edmund's nature had come through her gift—by the grace of God, without any more explicit longing or experience than the desire to kiss one of the footmen. She had accepted it, after a few months of wrestling, as a fifteen-year-old who'd adored her younger brother and who'd known herself, by that time, to be something of an aberration. It had helped, too, that Edmund had been the only one who knew and accepted her power.

These days, she read the papers as they covered Oscar Wilde's trial, and she thought of the crowds Edmund moved in, and she worried. The two of them had only mentioned the subject in the vaguest of terms. If she told the unvarnished truth to Miss Heselton—

God, no. The *best* result for Edmund there would be revulsion, scandal, and disinheritance and pain. The worst didn't bear thinking about.

"I don't think he's going to meet the right woman," Reggie tried, feeling her way along. "And if he ever does, she'll be the sort who—who doesn't want her husband to pay very much attention to her. Edmund's very fond of his clubs and his friends, I mean to say, and of riding and shooting and sport, and he doesn't want to spend his time at home with a wife. Or out at parties. And he's not at all romantic."

She turned and looked once again at Miss Heselton, on whose clear white brow a few lines of worry had appeared. As Reggie watched, though, they vanished, and Miss Heselton shook her head. "But he'd change," she said. "Of course he would, if he truly loved a girl. That's what love is *for*."

For the most part, Reggie had stayed out of any real gambling. Such games as she'd played in or witnessed had largely been between friends. Even there she'd seen men—often drunk or drugged and just as often riding high on pride—who realized that they held a bad hand through luck or their own bad gamesmanship, but stiffened their backs and doubled their bets.

She saw the same impulse in Miss Heselton now.

Reggie tried once more. "Maybe," she said, "but if I were you, I wouldn't hold my breath waiting. You're young. Go and find another nice young man. Your brother's probably got loads of friends who'd do—or you could go to London for a season or two. They're thick enough on the ground there."

"Thank you," said Miss Heselton, "but I don't think I need advice from you on matrimony." Then she stood and put a hand on Reggie's arm. She smiled sweetly, and when she spoke, the edge was gone from her voice once more. Every word left a sticky trail in the air. "After all, he is a grown man—you can't keep him at home forever. And you couldn't *really* want to prevent your brother's happiness, could you?"

Reggie could have been outside at that moment. She could have been walking around the churchyard with Edmund and Pater and Colin. The summer day was beautiful, and even the most macabre of outings had to be a dashed sight better than this. "Of course not," Reggie said and even managed not to grit her teeth.

"I didn't think so." Miss Heselton stroked Reggie's arm as if she were a restless cat. "I know it must be *very* hard for you, Regina. But we mustn't let our regrets make us bitter or spiteful, must we? The past is over and done, and we must all move forward."

"Exactly what," Regina Elizabeth Talbot-Jones, Louisa's daughter, asked, "do you mean by that?" Taking a step back, she threw off the intrusive hand.

"Why, nothing, dear, I'm sure." Miss Heselton looked down at her hands, then back up, all earnestness and sympathy. "And I'm certain that you haven't spoiled your own chances quite as much as you must suppose. After all, forgiveness is so important. I'm sure that if you came back home and lived quietly and modestly, you'd do quite well. Plenty of young—well, *relatively* young men—"

Absurdly, Reggie's first thought was to wonder if "a hundred and thirtysomething" counted as *relatively young*. When her self-control finally snapped, she knew that was at least one of the straws.

"You can marry them, then," she said, feeling red heat rush to her face, "or you and they can all go to the devil together. I've tried being civil, and I've tried warning you, but if your heart's desire is to make a damned fool of yourself over a man who hasn't given you a second thought except as a sentimental young nuisance, then I promise I won't stand in your way any longer."

"Oh!" Miss Heselton sprang to her feet. "I shouldn't imagine you *could* stand in my way, Miss Talbot-Jones. You're wrong about Edmund—you simply imagine everyone to be as heartless and rootless as you are. And your parents would love to have me as a daughter-in-law. After all, I'd imagine they want at least *one* young woman in their family who can move in polite circles."

Being back home clearly took a dozen years from

Reggie's mind. The only thing that kept her from boxing Miss Heselton's ears was the conflicting impulse to take hold of those golden curls and start pulling. With her baser instincts warring, she was able to remind herself that she was twenty-seven and that Miss Heselton was a guest.

"I don't think we have anything else to say to each other," she said, conscious that her voice was lower than normal, and that she was baring more of her teeth than each word really required. "Good afternoon, Miss Heselton."

Reggie did slam the door behind her. She was only human.

After striding halfway down the hall, face flaming and hands clenched at her sides, she grew calm enough to chide herself. Losing her temper hadn't done any good. Maybe even having the conversation had been a poor idea. She couldn't tell Edmund or her parents, of course—nor any of the other guests. It would only make dinners awkward, and eventually they'd all have to be on hand for an exorcism.

Colin was very good at not being awkward, and he already knew that she disliked Miss Heselton.

Reggie stopped short in the middle of the hallway. Where had *that* idea come from? It was ridiculous. She barely knew the man, carnal impulses aside. He couldn't mend the situation; she would have to explain the events of ten years before in order for him to understand properly; and she didn't want his pity anyhow.

Of course she wouldn't tell him.

All the same, she wondered when he'd get back.

Seventeen

Having come to Whitehill for novelty, Colin couldn't have said he was disappointed. The house and the company had provided any number of fascinating new experiences within the last few days. The latest was trying to figure out how to open a conversation with the sexton. "Excuse me, do you know anything about a vengeful ghost?" perhaps, or "Good day, sir. Did a woman named Janet by any chance commit particularly foul acts here a century and a half ago?"

Neither of those seemed likely to do the job.

Colin agreed with Edmund that they needed to investigate further and concurred with Mr. Talbot-Jones that he, Colin, was the best choice to go around asking the villagers questions. Since he was clearly an outsider, nobody would expect him to know old stories or wonder why he was suddenly asking about the former owners of a house that had been in his family's possession for years.

He was just having a bit of difficulty starting out.

He began by walking away from the graveyard and around toward the front of the church. Hands behind his back, he whistled a few bars of "The Sidewalks of New York," trying to clear his mind. It was a merry little song and very modern, yet whistling made him think of far older verses that he'd heard in his youth.

> *Oft in the lone churchyard at night I've seen,*
> *By glimpse of moonshine chequering thro' the trees,*
> *The schoolboy, with his satchel in his hand,*
> *Whistling aloud to bear his courage up.*

Centuries had passed since anyone could have called Colin a schoolboy, and he wouldn't have said his courage needed bearing up, but when he rounded the corner and a dog flew barking to the church fence, he welcomed the sign that he wasn't alone. It helped that the dog was no great black beast or thin white hound with red ears, but rather a young, golden-brown spaniel with flopping ears and boundless energy.

The pup's owner wasn't nearly so reassuring in appearance: tall and gaunt, with a jutting nose and a fringe of gray hair. When he turned from cutting the hedges, shears in hand, his eyes fixed immediately and sharply on Colin, and he bobbed his head with curt politeness.

"Friendly little creature," Colin said, by way of breaking the ice. He knelt and extended a hand through the bars of the fence, allowing some enthusiastic sniffing. "Hello there."

"Granddaughter gave 'im to me," said the sexton. "For Christmas, it was. He's a spry fellow, though giddy. But he's young yet."

"It's one of our faults," Colin agreed and scratched

the spaniel absently behind the ears. "Some of us settle down more rapidly than others."

The sexton chuckled, cut a few more branches, and then asked, "You're up at th' manor, then?"

"For a few days. I'm one of their son's friends."

"Ah." A particularly stubborn branch finally cracked with a sharp sound that sent the puppy bouncing back to investigate. "Good rider," said the sexton. "Good hunter too. He taken you out on the grounds yet?"

"A little," said Colin. "I get the impression they're rather extensive…" He let himself trail off, dangling that sentence like a baited hook.

"Oh, they are that. More than most people know—there's a river somewhere back there, and some caves, though I'd think the paths are all overgrown by now. Old Morgan wasn't much for riding himself. A man could break his neck out there these days, I'd imagine."

"I'll try and avoid it," said Colin.

"You young men never truly do." The sexton closed up his shears, bent down, and tossed one of the smaller sticks for the spaniel to chase. As the dog bounded away across the church lawn, the man came up to the gate. "But you're not from London, at least. Or you don't sound it."

"Not originally. Scotland."

"Well, that's something."

"Thank you," said Colin, allowing himself a smile. He cleared his throat. "I've mostly seen the house so far. It seems like a place with a long history."

"It is that," said the sexton. "And showed every year of it before the current lot bought it. I'd a niece in service under Old Morgan toward his end, and—well, if they've made it a place fit to live in again, they've done small miracles, and no mistaking it."

"Was he that bad?"

The sexton shook his head. "Not a bad man. An odd one. Didn't entertain, closed up most of the rooms, did Lord-knows-what with himself all day. Mary Ann was just in to work in the kitchens. She said you couldn't have caught her near the rest of the place. And—but she was a young thing then and got carried away with fancies."

Colin tried not to look too interested. "Fancies?"

"Oh, shapes in the window and sounds in the night. Nothing to it, of course, but girls are what they are. Unsteady creatures."

"Ah," said Colin, and he chuckled. "Very dramatic, I'm sure."

"Oh, aye. And I'll say this for her: the house was a gloomy place back then. Made it easy to imagine things, I don't doubt."

The spaniel came back, having thoroughly subdued the stick, and dropped it at its master's feet. The sexton patted the beast a few times with an offhand sort of gentleness.

"I was wondering, actually," Colin said, "if you'd heard any stories about one of the family—the Morgans, I mean. Janet?"

Lightning did not flash, nor did the sexton fork the evil eye and turn away. His face grew still for a moment, but it was a face that would show soul-deep trouble when its owner was trying to calculate train fare or considering dinner, so Colin tried not to take any omen from it.

"Might have heard a few things," the old man said at last. "Why do you want to know?"

"I think there might have been some connection between our families," said Colin. "I saw her portrait and—well, she looks a bit like one of my cousins."

"Could be," said the sexton, shrugging one shoulder, "but I'd not look too deeply into it if I was you. There's not many families would want to be connected with the Morgans, not now."

"Family curse?" Colin asked lightly. "Or just a scandal?"

"Neither. But—" The sexton looked uneasily to either side. "Well, take Old Morgan. Never married. Died alone and half-mad. 'Is father got himself shot in London before the son could walk—cards or a woman, I've heard both—and before that... You hear rumors."

"So you've said. What sort of stories?"

"They say the grandmother was a witch," the sexton said flatly. "Your Janet."

"And do you believe them?"

"Don't know what I believe. It was a long time ago. There's her stone outside the family plot, right enough, so she can't have been a good woman."

Colin nodded. No objection he could make would alter the man's mind; no story he could tell would disprove his convictions. Mortals were often like that. "What do they mean, a witch?"

"In league with Old Nick. When I was a boy, we used to dare each other to pick a flower from her grave after dark."

"Did you?"

A brief smile, full of dry and withered humor, crossed the sexton's face. "A time or two. Joe Wilson sat all night on the grave once, when we were a bit older. I suspect he took a bit of his old dad's liquor to help him along. He's in London now," he added, by way of implying the grave fate that came to all such incautious men.

"A rite of passage, I suppose. But you never saw her."

"Not a trace. And I can't remember much of the stories now, save that she was bad."

"Is there anyone in the village who might?"

"Gammy Jones, maybe. She's old enough. Not to have met the woman, of course—" he said, just as Colin was beginning to wonder if Whitehill was even more than it had seemed, "but to have heard from people who did. Can't promise anything," he added, picking up another stick. He turned this one over, but didn't throw it. "Not sure why you want to know. It's a nasty business, whatever's at its root."

"Oh," said Colin, "I just think perhaps I should find out before anyone else does. The best response to scandal is to be forearmed, after all."

⁂

He'd just stepped back out onto the main street of the village when he saw a familiar figure approaching: Reggie, her head up, striding along as quickly as tweed skirts and women's boots would permit. She saw Colin at the same moment, visibly hesitated, but then slowed down enough to let him reach her side.

"Have you found a country in need of conquering?"

he asked. "Or simply remembered a letter you'd meant to post yesterday?"

"No," she said. Her eyes were glittering, hard and fierce, her face tight even when she smiled. But she did smile, and a trace sheepishly at that. "The sweet-shop. I want to eat something that never dreamed of being wholesome."

"A noble ambition."

"I'd buy a bottle of gin if I thought they'd sell it to me."

"Probably not in a sweetshop. People talk. They'd get letters." Colin studied her flushed cheeks, charming but as much a warning sign as the proverbial red sky at dawn. "I'd buy one for you, if I knew where one managed that sort of thing in a village like this. And if the ground's done anything to offend you, do say the word and I'll call it out like a gentleman. It's a rather vast foe to take on alone, though you seem to be making a good start," he added, waving his hand toward where her boots were clicking on the cobblestones.

Reggie opened her mouth, stopped, and then surrendered to a laugh. "I'm sorry," she said. "I'm in a wretched mood. Been trying to talk sense into people who won't hear it."

"Doing three impossible things before breakfast, aye?" He considered telling Reggie that there were more enjoyable things to do with her mouth, but he didn't think she was in the right mood. "I wouldn't have recommended that one."

"You don't have to try much, do you? Just wait a few decades and the problem takes care of itself."

"Mostly," said Colin, though he had the momentary and foreign urge to deny the accusation. "Though we're not the only long-lived creatures in the world. And we've been known to be fond of human beings from time to time—*very* fond, in some cases, or I'd not be here now."

"Seems odd to me," said Reggie, looking off past a town square full of marigolds and a statue of a squat man in a feathered hat. "You'd think you—or they—would find us all small and pink and squishy and hairy. Like me suddenly having a mad passion for a lapdog."

"Some people do that too."

"Ugh," said Reggie, wrinkling her nose.

Colin shrugged. "If you spent a few years as a lapdog yourself, perhaps you'd feel differently. The shape has a mind of its own. And the Old Ones were gods, and—well, 'tis always different for them. Zeus, for instance."

Anger forgotten, she stared at him. "Your ancestors were *gods*?"

Colin laughed. "And so were yours, somewhere along the line, or you'd not have the talents you do. Gods or fairies or fallen angels. Things from outside the world."

"Don't tell Pater that," said Reggie, and she grinned more happily this time. "I don't know whether he'd be too ashamed to show his face again or too proud to live with." She looked up at Colin. "*You're* not a god, though."

"You probably wouldn't let me claim as much," he said. At first perplexed, he quickly realized what she was hinting at and drew closer to her, almost by magnetic force. "But even if we don't have the Old Ones' way of looking at things, we do spend most of our early lives as squishy, pink, hairy things. We've... human attractions, generally speaking."

Reggie stopped walking. Looking up at Colin, she took a breath, which expanded her bosom nicely even beneath a layer of tweed. "Then—" she began.

"Bloody hell," said Edmund, coming up behind her, "has Mater turned everyone out of the house today? I always suspected she might."

"You're certainly enough to drive anyone to it," said Reggie.

Under the sisterly mockery, Colin was sure he caught a strain of real frustration. Good: he wasn't alone.

Eighteen

REGGIE LET GO OF THE LAST BRANCH AND THUMPED TO the ground beneath the elm tree. The moonless night welcomed her. The wind was warm, and the stars shone down through the branches like the eyes of old friends.

She took a look around her just in case. No outcry went up from the house; she couldn't see light in any of the windows above her; Pater didn't keep dogs; and they had no neighbors within half a mile or more. The country did have advantages. Reggie knew she could never have gotten away with such a midnight excursion in London.

Then again, in London, she'd never felt such a strong impulse to wander after dark.

She struck off across the lawn with no real plan, only some idea of heading toward the lake. She could watch the stars in the water, listen to the bullfrogs and the owls, and be alone for once in what felt like a hundred years. Odd how six people could be a crowd when she lived daily among millions.

The grass rustled beneath her feet. It was still green,

or would be in the sunlight, but it was drying out now. Autumn was coming. Soon the leaves would turn, and the chestnuts would fall; already most of society was out shooting in country houses like Whitehill.

Well, probably not *exactly* like Whitehill.

Reggie glanced back at the house over her shoulder. It looked normal enough: the long, low building of the original abbey, with the new portion rising to one side, a red brick Palladian square that managed by the grace of trees and gardens not to look utterly awkward. One wouldn't have looked at it and thought of ghosts.

One wouldn't have looked at Colin and thought of dragons, or at Reggie and of…whatever was in her bloodline. *Gods or fairies or fallen angels.* That was a revelation to spring on a girl. She wondered if things would have been easier in her youth if she'd known where her talent had come from.

Probably not. History rarely made anything easier.

Besides, nobody needed a thirteen-year-old to think she was descended from Titania or Zeus, let alone anyone more Miltonian. Reggie had been bad enough at that age already.

She followed a path through the gardens, absently trailing a hand across the leaves of the hedges while listening to her own steps and the call of night birds. She recognized owls; the others were a mystery, and so were the dark shapes that flew above her head.

Then a white shape moved on the ground, at the edge of her vision. Reggie spun to look.

She saw a sexless human figure standing near one of the riding paths, completely white and slightly

translucent around the edges. Shapeless robes, also
white, wound around it. The face above them was
masklike in its regularity, but Reggie could make out
no edges to it, and none of the stiffness a real mask
would have.

The figure stared at her. She stared back at it.

Then it vanished.

All of a sudden, the night air was much colder.
Reggie sucked in a long, unsteady breath. Even after
the past few days, even after growing up with her
power, she still had to tell herself that she really *had*
seen what she'd thought she had. She pinched herself
to make sure she wasn't dreaming.

Then she took off down the path where the figure
had been.

For all that Mater complained about the gardeners,
the path was well-kept. The ground under Reggie's
feet was smooth and uncluttered, and no low
branches or wayward briars got in her way. Without
corsets or skirts, wearing a pair of flat-heeled boots,
she ran lightly and well. There was joy in the motion,
in the world streaming silently around her, even in
the thrill of pursuit itself. She'd known similar thrills
when she'd gone hunting, but never anything quite
so visceral.

She could see no trace of the white figure, though.

That didn't surprise her. Clearly it hadn't been a
person—or wasn't a person now, even if it had been
Janet Morgan once—and it didn't have to follow
the rules that people did. She ran thinking that there
might have been some significance in the place where
it had been standing, that there might be a sign at

the end of the path: buried treasure, maybe, or Janet Morgan's *real* grave.

Mostly, she just ran to be running.

Athletic as she was, she was a woman, not a horse or a dragon, and she couldn't keep up her speed forever. Half a mile down the path, she slowed up enough to catch her breath and to let her vision clear.

When it did, she saw a small clearing ahead of her. The trees were young, not very tall or very wide, and Reggie could see the stars between them.

She saw more than that when her eyes focused. Something moved within the clearing. It wasn't the white figure. This was dark, blending with the shadows except for the motion Reggie had seen and a faint suggestion that it shone in the starlight.

It was very large.

Another movement brought a glimmer of silver to her attention. It took Reggie a moment before she recognized it as an eye, about twice the size of her hand, with a slit pupil and no white around it. In the darkness, it shone like a fallen star.

It was looking toward her.

Reggie leaped backward, which might have allowed her a graceful escape—she wasn't sure whether the shape had seen her yet—except that fear had narrowed her perception and skewed her sense of direction. In short, she ran into a tree. Her head hit the bark with an audible *whack* and a jolt of dull pain. She bit back a curse, then froze as the creature, alert now, turned to take another look at her.

Hitting one's head was not a recipe for improved vision. She saw a dark shape, blurred around the edges, with those huge silver eyes. She managed not to shriek when it moved closer. Then she saw a hint of blue in the eyes, and the outlines of the creature became clearer. Reggie saw a long neck—curved horns—wings—

Fairy tales had been long ago for her, but a few images had stuck. She thought *dragon* with, possibly, the first sense of relief any human being had ever felt on making that identification.

"Colin?"

She whispered the name, partly because she wanted to be discreet but mostly because she didn't think she had enough air in her lungs to speak louder.

Even as the massive head moved in what she could only assume was a dragonish attempt to nod, Reggie squirmed inwardly, embarrassed to have asked. As though there were many dragons around Whitehill—as though any sinister third cousin of Colin's would actually bother to correct any mistaken identity.

"What are you *doing* out here?"

The mouth began to open, disclosing extremely large, extremely sharp teeth. Then Colin stopped and looked down at Reggie. She wasn't sure what his expression meant—not until he sighed and lowered his head toward her.

Ah. He couldn't speak English in this form. She couldn't speak Dragon, if that was even a language. There was only one avenue of communication open to them.

Still, she hesitated with her hand half an inch away from his jaw. "Are you sure?"

In answer, he raised his head. Reggie had a moment

to feel scales beneath her hand, metal-smooth and slightly chilly to the touch. Then a stream of images entered her mind: not a flood, as with most people on whom she'd ended up using her power, but a steady march of pictures and feelings.

She was Colin, looking out the window of his room and seeing, close up, the figure she'd seen from a distance. She knew that this wasn't the first time he'd glimpsed whatever-it-was. Together, they remembered a much less human, much less *finished* form.

In their memory, Colin spoke a phrase in what sounded like Latin. Reggie thought one of the words might have been *sight*, but she wouldn't have put money on it. She'd always been more interested in languages that living people spoke. (Although Latin might actually be one of those, depending on how one defined "people." Quite a thought.) She saw the world blur into a mass of shifting colors and saw the figure's gray-green trail.

The moment of shifting was a blur, whether because her human mind was too small and fragile to take all of it in or because even Colin felt it that way. Then she was flying, as she'd flown once before inside Colin's memory, looking at Whitehill from above and feeling the ground fall away from her. He had been more businesslike on this flight than on the first one she'd called forth from his memory, but the sensations were still there, even if he'd paid less attention to them.

As him, Reggie saw the trail of the figure grow fainter, and then fainter still, and felt the dragon's body dive to pick it up again, peering closer and closer to the ground until here, in this clearing, the trail stopped. It had been sudden. Colin hadn't meant for that to get through, but Reggie felt it all the same. His landing had been clumsy, and he'd known he was lucky not to have injured himself.

And then—a human shape in the darkness.

Reggie stepped back. Colin wouldn't want her seeing herself through his eyes—indeed, the memories were growing less orderly now—and she didn't think she wanted to get that perspective herself.

Not really.

Not when she was being sensible, anyhow, and Reggie thought that this was one of the times when being sensible really was the best course.

Back in her own body, catching her breath and once more getting used to the feeling of human-sized lungs and human proximity to the ground, Reggie just stared for a bit. "I…" she managed eventually. "Well. Right." She gave herself the best mental shake she could manage. "I think I'm rather jealous. Men might not ever fly like *that*, whatever they do on the Continent. But—"

Colin froze. Reggie stopped talking and listened. Footsteps were approaching, heavy ones, and bodies were coming through the brush.

Nineteen

KEEN SMELL AND HEARING TOLD COLIN THAT THE approaching forms were a man and a large dog. Experience suggested *gamekeeper*, given the evidence at hand. Probably looking for poachers. Damn. The dog would probably run—there had once been dogs, or beasts very like them, trained to attack dragons, but that knowledge was probably centuries old and certainly miles from Whitehill—but men were tricky when they were frightened. Some of them ran. Some cowered. Some went berserk, a more intimidating prospect in modern times. Two barrels from a shotgun would not leave Colin in an enviable condition, and would at the very least be the devil to explain in the morning.

He took a quick look at his surroundings. Hiding was impossible. Running along the ground would only result in a long chase through the woods. Changing back into human form would mean a long chase through the woods while naked, which would also be hard to explain, not to mention painful, between the cold and the likelihood of briars. Flight was the best way out. This close at hand, with the lantern that even now bobbed closer, the gamekeeper might well spot him, but Colin would simply have to take that chance.

In the trees beyond, not at all far away, the dog started to whine. Colin heard a man trying to keep his voice low even while he cursed at the animal, and he heard the puzzlement and fear beneath those curses as well. He gathered his body, preparing to spring into the air.

"Wait," Reggie hissed. She held up one hand, the sleeves of her shirt flashing white. "I'll handle it."

Without another word, she headed into the trees. As she walked, Colin heard her start humming. A short distance away, her footsteps stopped, and Reggie raised her voice. "Good God!"

The man choked off a curse. The dog's whining didn't change. Colin could almost see it straining at its leash, desperate to get away from the smell up ahead. Humans might have spun legends about his people, animals knew them as large predators that stunk of magic.

The man spoke, hesitant this time. "Miss Talbot-Jones?"

"Hobb, isn't it? Didn't know anyone else was awake at this hour."

"Well, miss, Rex was nervous. And I thought—it might do to check, that's all."

Even without Reggie's power, Colin knew what the man had thought and not said: guests were trouble, or brought trouble with them. You couldn't accuse an official visitor at Whitehill of poaching—even if you caught him with a trap on a moonless night, most likely—but most of them had brought servants, and catching a few unauthorized rabbits wasn't the worst thing a man could get up to in the dark woods.

The thought of rabbits, authorized or not, had a visceral appeal. Not that they'd make more than a mouthful, but they would be prey, and that was rare enough in these lands. He thought of chasing deer back at Loch Arach, and the memory was vivid enough to make his stomach growl.

The dog yelped.

"Have you found anything?" Reggie asked, a little louder than conversation would have called for. "He does seem out of sorts."

"Nothing so far, miss."

Reggie made a small noncommittal noise. "Well," she said, and Colin could see her now, shifting from foot to foot, her hands in the pockets of her trousers. "I thought maybe I saw a light near here. A little ways west." She'd be pointing now, off to the side and away from Colin. "I, um, couldn't sleep, you understand."

"Of course, miss. A light, you said?"

"I thought so. But—I mean, it's awfully dark out here, and I might have gotten the direction wrong too." She gave a self-deprecating giggle, quite different from anything Colin had heard out of her before. "Actually, if you don't mind—I'd really rather an escort back to the house. I don't think I can find my way—got all turned around."

"Oh," said the gamekeeper. Obviously, he was suspicious. Just as obviously, he couldn't ask the daughter of the house what she was trying to hide. Colin would have felt pity for the man, had his own thoughts not been rather thoroughly occupied. "Well—of course, miss."

"Much obliged. And, you know," Reggie said, "I don't see any reason why anyone else needs to hear about this, do you?"

Her voice faded as their footsteps began again, moving farther and farther away. When they were out of earshot, Colin spread his wings and launched himself skyward, moving out of sight as fast as he could.

༄

"Much obliged," Colin said to her the next afternoon, when Edmund had briefly excused himself from the card table. The rain had returned, but this time nobody had suggested exploring the house. The "young people" sat in one of the drawing rooms instead. He and Reggie played cards with Edmund, while Miss Heselton produced some rather nice music from the piano and her brother talked books with Miss Browne. "For the rescue last night, that is."

"Not at all," Reggie said, not looking up from her cards. "He might not have noticed anything amiss if I hadn't been out there talking to you."

"All the same, I hope you didn't have to go to very much trouble."

"I gave him a tenner this morning. And I'm sure he thinks I have—" She bit her lip. Beneath violet-striped cotton, her breasts rose with a quick inhalation. "Some kind of secret."

She still didn't look at him.

"A lover out there, maybe?" Colin said, dropping his voice and coming closer to the truth than she'd managed. Reggie sat very still, except to swallow, and he watched the motion of her neck. There was color creeping up from the edge of her bodice, and he didn't think it was all embarrassment. He laid down a card, remembered that they were surrounded, and asked more lightly, "Smuggler or poacher or wandering minstrel?"

"It's several hundred years too late for that the last one," Reggie said. She glanced toward the king Colin had played, then back to her hand. "And I'm not nearly romantic enough for any of the other options."

"But your man Hobb doesn't know that, I'd wager."

"Probably not. No matter." She shrugged, and then did lift her gaze. Now there was a hard edge to her smile, and her brown eyes flickered with challenge, though to what opponent Colin didn't know. Despite her mortality, he was relieved not to think it was him. "Every village has to have its rumors, you know. Having me around might be doing them quite the service."

He wanted to ask. He wanted, more than that, to put a hand over hers or an arm around her shoulders, but surrounded by people, and with her looking so spiky, he decided on discretion.

"For a time, perhaps," he said lightly, "until the baker's son gets himself called out for pistols at dawn."

"People don't duel these days," said Reggie, and then she tilted her head to study Colin's face, her own expression softened now by amusement and surprise. "And you know that."

"It's possible that I do." Colin rearranged his hand, watching Reggie over the edge of the cards.

"Laws change so quickly, you know. And I've never really bothered."

"With dueling? I'm surprised."

"Do you really think I'm the sort to go around calling men out?"

"No." She dimpled. "I think you're the sort to *get* a challenge every day or two, if people let you into polite company."

"Hardly," said Colin. "One only got called out, you understand, if one got *caught*. Credit me with some grace, at least."

Hearing her fake laughter the night before gave the real thing that much more clarity and warmth. "Do you generally tell that to young women?"

"They generally don't ask."

"Fair." Reggie put her cards down and leaned back. "Not even once? Really? The dueling, I mean, not the—er—asking."

"I wouldn't go that far. Usually I refused. It didn't seem precisely fair to the other fellows." Nobody could ever have credited him with Stephen's sense of honor, but there was such a thing as sportsmanship. "There were one or two exceptions over the years. Nasty sorts."

"Oh," said Reggie. He could see the curiosity on her face, and then her decision. Colin hadn't pried earlier, and she wouldn't do it now.

He smiled at her, unspoken thanks.

"How's the translation coming along?" she asked.

"I truly wish that someone two hundred years ago had been bright enough to invent the typewriter," said Colin. "Or longer-lasting ink, at the very least. Then

again, perhaps it's best that I only read this journal a
bit at a time."

"Is it that dire?"

"In a way. The author—and there are a few bits
that make me think it's Janet, offhand references and
that—hasn't mentioned anything very classically occult
just yet. No arrangements, no sacrifices, not even any
contacts. But"—he rubbed at the bridge of his nose
with his free hand—"she's very angry. Angry with
everything and everyone who doesn't come up to her
standards, and I don't think she's mentioned anyone
who *does*. I've met men like that a time or two."

"And women?"

"Oh. Aye. Though fewer of them—or perhaps I
just saw it less. When I noticed, it was because the
men in question had power," he said, thinking back to
some very unpleasant years, "and it made their anger
a formidable thing."

"She wouldn't have had much," Reggie said
slowly. Her fingers stroked the back of the cards while
she thought. "Not the normal sort of power anyhow.
Money, yes, and position, but that's not power."

"You should talk to my brother's wife," said Colin.
"She'd have a bit to say about that theory."

"Is she—"

"A typewriter girl. Or was. I'd pay red gold to hear
the two of you thrash this one out."

That drew a laugh, but Reggie went on. "Power's
not a constant, though. You have it depending on
how much other people have. You know that—the
Honorable Mr. MacAlasdair." This time the challenge
in her eyes *was* for him.

Before it, Colin bent his head. "It's been a long
time since I worried overmuch about titles and
inheritance—but then, she wouldn't have had that
time to get used to the state of things, would she?"

"No. And she wouldn't have been a man, and able
to run off to London and not think about it, and she
wouldn't have been—well." Reggie waved a hand at
Colin, presumably indicating a dragon or a freakishly
powerful immortal or a god's bastard spawn. "It's
much easier not to be angry when you can get away.
Not that it excuses hitting people with tables, or whatever she got up to before she died. Do you know?"

"The book hasn't said yet, and I've not been able to
meet with 'Gammy Jones.'"

"The woman the sexton mentioned?"

Colin nodded. "I don't suppose you've encountered her?"

"No. We've only been here a few years, if you'll
recall—and I've spent most of that time in London."
Reggie picked up her cards again and studied them,
although Edmund had shown no signs of walking
back into the room. "And I don't spend much time
gossiping when I am in the country. Usually, I just
catch up on sleep."

"Then this trip must be going sadly awry for you,"
said Colin, "at least if last night is any indication."

"It hasn't been as restful as usual," said Reggie,
"but I can sleep in London. Or the grave. I'll take
excitement any day."

She stopped pretending to look at the cards when
she said that, and her eyes lingered on Colin's—
playfully, but play that was quite enough to make his

body react. "I'm glad to hear it," he said. "I'd much rather provide adventure than rest, myself."

"I'm sure," said Reggie, and then she laughed. "Though I can't say you're the person who causes the *most* excitement around here. Hope you're not too disappointed."

"No," said Colin. He knew that Edmund had to come back soon, that the room was full of onlookers, and that one had to seize certain moments even if there was no hope of an immediate conclusion. He smiled at Reggie, letting himself feel the charge between them, letting it show on his face. "Most people like my sort of excitement better."

Twenty

OTHER THAN ACCIDENTALLY CLIMBING UP TO THEIR balconies, Reggie had never had much to do with the guest bedrooms at Whitehill. She'd seen the maids keeping them cleaned and turned; she'd heard Mater fuss over new paper and curtains; and she'd paid no more attention to anything else that had gone on in the background of the house.

Standing near the foot of Mrs. Osbourne's bed, she noticed only how normal the room looked: white paper with pink roses, pale bedclothes and curtains, a small desk and chair in one corner and a dressing table in another. To the eye, the only incongruities were the bandages Mrs. Osbourne still wore and the small crowd of worried-looking people standing between the bed and the door.

Hearing what Mrs. Osbourne said took the whole scene out of "a bit odd" and several miles into the country of "damned uncanny."

"I'll make no claims to vast experience now," Mrs. Osbourne had begun, once everyone had been notified and had assembled. "I have no means of supporting them, and they're not very relevant regardless. The power I felt on the night of the séance was more than I've ever encountered. Almost any medium would say the same. There may be those who've faced and fought greater threats, but I've never heard of any—and we do talk among ourselves now and again."

She smiled, but faintly. She spoke quietly, too, and paused every sentence or so to take a breath, and her face was nearly as white as her dressing gown. Standing at her side, Miss Browne watched her with the intent gaze of a man tamping down a gunpowder charge, heedless of anyone else in the room—even of Mr. Heselton, who was watching *her* rather closely, to Reggie's mind.

"Who is it?" Pater asked.

At the same moment, Mater gave voice to her own questions: "What does it want? How, in heaven's name, do we get rid of it?"

Mrs. Osbourne sighed. "The simple answer," she said, "is that I don't know. Hosting a spirit doesn't let me know its mind. The vessel never has much awareness. I sensed that it was a woman. I sensed that she was grown, though I had no further notion of her age. And I sensed her wrath."

"Why was she angry?" asked Mr. Heselton.

"I couldn't really tell. It may not even matter." Mrs. Osbourne closed her eyes. "Ghosts aren't precisely people any longer. They don't act the same. They don't *feel* the same."

Mr. Heselton nodded. "Miss Browne told us how death is a simplification for…those who remain, and how emotions can lead them out of balance." He touched his collar, frowning. "I don't know why it should be so—"

"Neither does anyone else," said Mrs. Osbourne. "There are theories and theories. If we have time and leisure, we can discuss them in the future. For the moment: she is, or was, angry. Whatever caused that anger in the first place, it's very likely that the ghost let it consume her. Now she is angry because"—she spread her hands—"because anger is what exists for her."

"Oh, how *horrible*," said Miss Heselton, and Reggie couldn't exactly disagree with the sentiment, much as it went without saying, or should have done. She watched Miss Heselton shrink back against the mantel and direct wide eyes toward Edmund. She saw Edmund pat her reassuringly on the shoulder, and she saw Pater, even worried as he was, smile for a second.

Angry ghosts were more important than rescuing her brother. Still, it was time to change the conversation. "What do we *do*, then?" Reggie asked. "Take rooms at a hotel and burn the place down?"

"I'm not sure even that would help," said Mrs. Osbourne, though she did smile. So did Colin, Reggie noticed out of the corner of her eye. "Spirits have been known to haunt the land when the building is gone."

"And we have a long way to go," Mater said, "before arson becomes a solution to our problems, Regina."

"Just skipping to the end," said Reggie. "Figured someone might as well ask. If it *was* the only solution, we'd feel dashed silly mucking around here for days beforehand, wouldn't we?"

"Some people might say 'thorough,' dear," said Mater.

Mrs. Osbourne chuckled, which was a short and dreadfully raspy sound. "There are other avenues, or should be. Have your exorcism," she said with a gesture in Mr. Heselton's direction. "I can only invite and suggest, for the most part. I have not the Lord's power to command"—she blinked suddenly and made a thoughtful little *hmm* sound before going on—"and a man may have more influence in this case."

"Oh?" Pater asked.

"It's only a supposition, but"—Mrs. Osbourne shrugged—"now that I think of it, I got the feeling she grew angrier when she realized I was female."

"Jealousy?" Colin asked.

"It could be," said Mrs. Osbourne. "Or it could not. I'd have to speak with her again to know more, and"—she touched her side gingerly—"I think perhaps that should be a last resort. Preferably in a room without any heavy objects."

"I'll second that," said Miss Heselton. "I have no doubt that I need more practice as a nurse, but I have no wish to acquire it in such a dramatic manner."

Mrs. Osbourne smiled. "I couldn't have wished for anyone more skilled," she said and turned toward Reggie's parents. "I do regret imposing myself on your hospitality for so long. Dr. Brant says that I should be quite capable of travel within a few more days."

"Capable or not," Mater said, "you'll stay here as long as you wish—and at least until you can walk again. We *had* anticipated having guests until the, ah, process was completed, and it's hardly your fault that it's taking a while. Besides, we have company so rarely, other than my sister and her family."

"Yes," said Mrs. Osbourne. "I'd heard something about a ball? I'm afraid I won't be able to attend, of course—" She gestured to the bandages again. "It sounds like an excellent distraction, though."

"And Miss Browne assures us that distraction will be helpful," said Mr. Heselton, with a quick glance toward the lady in question.

"Oh, yes. Particularly now. You'll have to wait on your bishop, yes?" Mrs. Osbourne nodded without waiting for a reply. "There's nothing so distressing to the mind as a prolonged wait, and nothing so disastrous in dealing with spirits as a distressed mind. Putting the whole matter aside for the evening can only help you."

"And you won't be bored to death here alone?" Edmund asked, though he didn't sound hopeful.

Sure enough, Mrs. Osbourne shook her head. "I'll most likely be asleep the whole time," she said. "And in case I'm not, I'm certain that your mother can find me a good book beforehand."

Reggie considered mentioning the potential danger of leaving a woman on her own, then discarded it. Her mother would only mention that they *did* have footmen, Regina dear, and a gamekeeper as well. Miss Heselton would talk about the country being much less dangerous than London, and there would be no escape for Edmund, let alone for her. She couldn't escape now, at any rate, without the Heselton girl thinking that she was hiding. There came a time when a brother, no matter how well-loved, would just have to sink or swim on his own. Heselton didn't seem like the type to engineer her own compromise, at least, and there was nothing more Reggie could do about her delusions.

"Speaking of books," she said, "we've found one. And a painting. And a grave."

"So Miss Browne mentioned. It seems…a likely start." Mrs. Osbourne looked from Colin to Mr. Heselton, and the corners of her mouth turned up. Without needing to touch her, Reggie knew that she was considering the two men as a pair: the one slight, sandy haired, and respectable, the other tall, serpent-slim, and just on the decadent side of fashion. All they needed, going by appearances, was a soul to fight over. "How has the translation been coming along, gentlemen?"

"Not so badly, once I got accustomed to the lady's writing," said Colin. "And the writer is a lady—she finally said as much. She's talked of finding a book in London, and of 'experiments,' but I haven't gotten much further than that."

"She burned the book," Mr. Heselton said, his face grim. "After her experiments were successful. She transcribed notes about the hours and the phases of the moon and other things—she uses some sort of code that I can't make out—and then she burned the book itself. She'd gotten all she wanted from it."

The room went still. Colin's eyes narrowed; Mrs. Osbourne and Miss Browne glanced at each other in alarm. Even the Talbot-Joneses and Miss Heselton, less familiar with the occult, felt the weight of this latest development, and the unease of knowing that Whitehill had hosted darker things than an unquiet spirit.

Reggie wanted to wrap her arms around herself, for what little protection that could provide, but she forced herself to stand still and keep her face relatively impassive. From what she could tell, Colin and Miss Heselton were both looking elsewhere, but one never knew—and she'd be damned if she'd act like just another mortal in past her depth.

Therefore, she let Edmund ask the question that she was sure everyone was thinking: "What *did* she want?"

"She hasn't made that clear just yet," said Mr. Heselton. "Nothing concrete. But she speaks of the right times and places for conversation, and that suggests an unfortunate conclusion—though I really couldn't speak with any authority on the matter."

"It would ha' been contact, at first," said Colin, his accent deeper than Reggie had ever heard it. "She'd have been after summoning a…being"—he dismissed the question of further identification with a flick of his long fingers—"and striking a bargain with it."

"You," said Mrs. Osbourne, "sound like you *can* speak with authority."

Or think you can, she wasn't saying, and everyone in the room knew it. Reggie had used that tone of voice herself a time or two. It tended to work fairly well on overstuffed young men, as long as the object was to make them sputter and go away. She wasn't sure how it would work on a dragon—even one in disguise— when magic was the subject at hand. Part of her tensed for an explosion.

Colin chuckled, though it wasn't a particularly pleasant

sound. "More theoretical than practical in this specific matter, I assure you," he said, "but aye, I've a bit of knowledge on the score."

Seven pairs of speculative eyes focused on him. Unperturbed by the attention, Colin just smiled and then shrugged, as if he'd admitted to collecting butterflies or breeding Persian cats.

"Will knowing all of this help in any way?" Mater asked. "I'm not certain what an exorcism involves, but—is knowledge of the spirit necessary?"

"It can only help, I'm sure," said Mr. Heselton.

He sounded confident. Reggie was glad of it. Although she couldn't speak for the others, she knew that the exorcism wasn't the only reason she was trying to find out more. One route to getting rid of the spirit had already failed. The second might prove fruitless as well.

For once in her life, she wanted to be prepared.

Twenty-one

THE ENGLISH, TO COLIN'S MIND, HAD A DAMNED PECU-
liar sort of affection for the trappings of their conquered
subjects. Half the drawing rooms in Mayfair had statues
of Bubastis on the mantel or paisley paper on the walls.
He'd seen more than a dozen pendants or pairs of
earrings that were supposed to be "authentic Chinese
jade," and the current queen had followed her uncle's
example in waxing romantic about tartans and kilts.

Perhaps all empires behaved so once they'd established themselves, the lure of the exotic serving as
a way to reassure themselves that all that effort and
death had produced something of value. Or perhaps
the act of conquering was simply a penny dreadful writ
large, with one nation as the dashing highwayman and
another as the abducted maiden. First one ravished,
then one loved.

Philosophy aside, the result was that Colin's valet,
temporarily elevated though he might be, knew what
to do with a kilt. The pleats of the green-and-gold
tartan fabric were crisp, the buckle polished, and
the shirt above it was flawlessly starched and white.

Helping Colin into a dark green jacket, Hill nodded his approval perhaps a shade more than professionally.

"Obliged," said Colin. "I think I'll do."

He *didn't* think he had any need of assistance putting on a jacket, but *when in Rome* and all that. Looking into the mirror to tie his ascot, though, he had to smile and shake his head. When he'd first become a man, or at least old enough to attend parties rather than sneaking down to pinch sweets and watch the guests, formal dress had been velvet knee breeches and matching coats. Tartan had just become *legal* again—and his father had said a few sarcastic things about that development.

His smile softened at the edges. He still missed the old dragon at times. Andrew MacAlasdair would have said a few more choice words about the image his son currently presented—probably ending with a sigh and a comment about "pleasing the wenches"—but they would have been affectionate underneath, an affection all the more meaningful because it wasn't easy for the untrained to hear.

Colin cleared his throat and returned to the present. The house had ghosts enough. "You're from the village, Hill?" he asked.

Hill, a blond young man who looked fully capable of wrestling an ox, nodded. "All my life, sir."

"Ever heard of a woman called 'Gammy Jones'? I'm guessing from the name that she's not a recent arrival."

Hill laughed. "Not at all, sir. I mean, no, she's not recent, and yes, I've heard of her. Know her a bit. She was a great one for telling stories, even when I was young."

In the way that mortals of twenty-odd years had, he spoke of his childhood as if it had happened before the Flood. By now, Colin was too accustomed to laugh.

"Could you tell me where to find her? In a day or two, of course—tonight I hear I'm going to meet every eligible lady in fifty miles." He suspected he'd also meet a few technically ineligible ones, but he hadn't known Hill long enough to make such a comment. He didn't want a disapproving valet. "Hopefully I won't have any shoes to track to their owners in the morning."

"I shouldn't think you'd have much trouble in that area, sir," Hill said.

Colin raised his eyebrows. "Not the local girls' sort?"

"Oh, no, sir." Hill laughed again, glancing up to Colin's face to see if he'd given real insult and almost hiding his relief when he found otherwise. "I mean to say, the lady in that story lost a shoe running away, didn't she? I don't think you'll have to chase anyone tonight."

"I'm not in the habit of running after women," Colin agreed. "It's been a long time since I bothered."

He would have sprinted a fair distance after Reggie, though, if he'd thought that would avail him of much. When he stepped outside with the rest of the party to be sorted into various carriages, she was standing on the steps and looking out over the gardens. The last rays of the setting sun cast a gloss over her dark hair and made her skin glow almost as golden as the shawl around her shoulders or the ribbons on the ball gown she wore.

There were quite a number of gold ribbons, wound into elaborate patterns against sea blue silk. On a smaller woman, or one with less vivid coloring, the effect would have been overwhelming and fussy. On Reggie, the ornaments seemed only appropriate. The gown flowed over her legs, then clung to her slim waist and her breasts, which the low-cut bodice showed off to what Colin dimly thought was a very fashionable effect. It damned well was a good effect for *him*. Looking at her, he had to remember that he wore a kilt that evening and exercise all his self-control accordingly.

When the footman gestured for Colin to enter the carriage with her, he sent a silent prayer of thanks to Fortuna. Not that they were unchaperoned—Miss Browne came along with them—but that was just as well. Unchaperoned, Colin might have lost control of himself, and there was really only so much one could do to rearrange formal clothing.

As the carriage left the drive of Whitehill, he had to reconsider. Lovely as Reggie looked, there was nothing about her tonight that suggested she'd welcome his attentions. She gave him a smile and a polite greeting, but her eyes lacked the playfulness and the warmth that had been there on other occasions. She sat beside Miss Browne, upright as any soldier under parade inspection.

Seeking to lighten the mood, Colin looked from her to Miss Browne, all curls and rose-colored taffeta. "The two of you," he said, "look like sunset over the Caribbean. Did you plan that? I'm afraid I ruin the theme."

Both women laughed. Reggie's laughter didn't last as long, though, and her gloved hands clasped and unclasped in her lap.

Now Colin wished that the two of them were alone, and not so that he could tumble her. He wanted to put a hand on her shoulder, or to take her hands in his, and ask her what was wrong. She might tell him, of all people. He knew himself enough outside of her world to be safe. He could have pointed that out, given a chance. Men and women had sensed that much about him before and been drawn to it.

Never before had he thought to offer himself as a confidante.

"Make it the Mediterranean," said Miss Browne, "and you'll do fine for a grove of pine trees. In Cypress, perhaps, around some ancient temple."

"Either I'm flattered to be thought stately," Colin said, trying to keep his gaze from sliding back to Reggie, "or I'm dismayed that you associate me with great age. I'm not sure I can decide which."

"Oh, be dismayed, by all means. If you're wrong, it's much better to be relieved than disappointed." Reggie looked at him when she spoke, but her smile was brittle and her eyes distant. "And men never have to worry about being old."

"No?" *Colin* didn't, not for a century or more yet, but he'd never thought that his sex had much to do with that freedom.

She shook her head, sapphire earrings swinging with the motion and brushing against the firm line of her jaw. "Women are old. Men are distinguished. Wealthy men, at least."

"Wealthy women aren't old, either," said Miss Browne. "I'm not sure what they are."

"We'd better find out sometime in the next twenty years," said Reggie. "Not knowing what you are sounds much better suited to the young."

"It takes energy to be enigmatic, does it?" Colin asked.

Miss Browne laughed. "Oh, it does indeed. Just ask Mrs. Osbourne. There was one party in London—" She unfolded a story that kept them all occupied through the journey, though she glossed over what Colin suspected were highly indelicate parts.

Reggie smiled and laughed at the right places, but she never lost her air of tension—as if bracing herself for some unpredictable blow—and though he tried to give his full attention to the story, Colin was all too aware that he was, well, all too aware that Reggie was distracted.

He wondered if his company made her uneasy now, if he'd caused offense in an obscure way since they'd flirted over cards, or if she'd simply reconsidered the flirting and the kissing and decided that she wanted no part of him. It wouldn't be an unreasonable decision for a young lady of good character, even if the prospect did make Colin's heart sink. He wondered if she was worried that he'd reveal how far they'd gone together, or her power, and wished that he had the privacy to reassure her.

Then they pulled up in front of Damarel Hall, a redbrick Gothic house crawling with spires and arches, and Colin revised his opinion. Far from being eager to get out of the carriage, as Colin would have expected had he been the problem, Reggie swallowed, took a breath, and stiffened her shoulders even more. Most humans wouldn't have noticed the change. Colin knew that even he might not have, had Reggie been a stranger, but he did now. She was bracing herself.

Walking toward the doors, she suggested—only slightly, and to a very observant eye—a prisoner approaching the bar.

For the first part of the ball, Colin didn't know why. Claire Stafford, a woman whose fair and immaculate good looks greatly resembled her sister's, was warm bordering on effusive as she greeted Reggie. The puffily respectable Lewis was prim but pleasant. Colin wasn't close enough to catch all of what they said to their niece, but at least from a distance, they seemed no worse than any other set of relations.

The ball, too, had nothing so dire about it at first glance. It might have been any of a thousand Colin had attended over the years: bright silk and gleaming jewelry, perfume warring with the smell of many people in the same room, voices rising and falling as the guests called to their friends or whispered in groups, the orchestra tuning up in one corner. Servants in dark clothing stood by the walls, taking wraps or pouring drinks. The skirts were slimmer than they'd been twenty years ago, and he could smell the earthy scent of gas behind the perfume rather than the faint sea tang of whale oil lamps, but all such changes just floated on the surface. The world did change, often deeply, but parties were always late to show it.

As he'd expected, Colin was the focus of considerable attention when he walked into the room. Nobody had likely heard much about him, but a man in a kilt stood out. And if nobody had heard much about him—well, nobody had heard much about him. Most coins had two sides. He met a few of the curious gazes and gave them his best only slightly roguish smile.

Then he noticed who *else* was attracting attention. Reggie caught the eye—Colin would have been the last person to deny that—but it wasn't just men looking at her as she followed her family through the crowd, and the gazes weren't all admiring. Colin saw one older woman lift her eyebrows as Reggie passed, then turn and whisper to her companions, who cast theoretically subtle glances back toward the Talbot-Joneses. Not everyone seemed interested, not even half the people in the room, but he noticed the speculating minority easily enough.

He couldn't tell if Reggie did. The crowd swept both of them up in a flurry of introductions and small talk, and Colin went along, until one of the men he was talking to broke off a bad soliloquy on hunting to glance past Colin and give a low whistle. "By Jove," he said, "there's a chance tonight will shape up interesting after all."

"How do you mean?" said a third in their party, a gangly redheaded chap.

Colin turned and followed the first man's gaze. In the middle of the room, Reggie stood facing a tall, dark man. He was a little older than her, well-dressed and more than usually handsome, but there was no hint of romance between them, nor of anything tender. She stood at her most rigid, his mouth curved up in a sneer, and the air nearby suggested glaciers and icicles.

"Oh, Kimpton and the Talbot-Jones girl?" said the man who'd last spoken. "Engaged once, I'd heard."

"Or nearly," said the whistler, while Colin kept watching. Reggie's aunt was watching the pair as well, her face not quite masklike enough to hide her anxiety. "She broke things off. *After* spending some time on a balcony with the chap, you understand— and he'd never say what happened. Came in looking white as a sheet, though."

Kimpton said a few quiet words. Reggie replied. Kimpton gestured to a lady nearby, a pretty dark-haired woman in a modest silver-gray dress, who stepped forward. She and Reggie exchanged what looked like polite greetings. The idiots around Colin kept up their speculation.

"Probably earned himself a slap in the face."

"That wouldn't have thrown Kimpton. Besides, the girl came down from London for the summer, and you know that sort. If she came over maidenly, it was *very* sudden. If you ask me—I say, are you all right?"

Watching Reggie walk off through the crowd, aware of the eyes on her and knowing that she felt them too, Colin was only belatedly conscious of the question, or of what had prompted it—the dragon's growl coming from his own chest. He spun back to face the men.

"Only amazed," he said in his silkiest tones, "at how much grown men can sound like fishwives. Excuse me."

He could have said more; he could have *done* more, without even changing shape or calling on magic. What little chivalry remained in him said to teach the men a sharp lesson.

The rest of him was old enough to know that it wouldn't help—and that there were more important things to do.

Twenty-two

PUNCH, OR AT LEAST AUNT CLAIRE'S VERSION OF IT, didn't do a damned thing to soothe the mind.

The act of drinking helped: the motion of the hand, the weight of the glass, the taste of fruit, and the need to swallow all drew attention back to what one of Reggie's spiritualist friends would have called "the base material sensations." Reggie *needed* base material sensations. She needed to remind herself that she was a physical being, that she was here and now, that she wasn't eighteen. Even punch would suffice for that. All the same, she missed the parties in London like hell. She could have gotten whiskey there, though she wouldn't have needed it.

The paradox almost made her laugh, but she caught herself. She was conspicuous enough just now without laughing at nothing. She gulped punch instead, even though it hurt her throat.

Damn country parties. Damn country society and its long memory—in London, a ten-year-old scandal wouldn't even have raised an eyebrow. And damn her, too, for caring. Ten years had passed. She was far away from the debutante she'd been, the child who now seemed to have been desperately naive for all that her power had already told her. She shouldn't have cared if people stared or whispered.

Reggie certainly shouldn't care now that Jack had married.

And she didn't, or not in the way he had clearly been hoping she would. When he'd introduced his wife, Reggie had felt no pang of jealousy, no longing for the life she'd left behind ten years ago with a hard slap and a stream of half-hysterical accusations. Margaret Kimpton was pretty and pleasant, well-spoken, probably intelligent, and quite kind to those who knew her.

When she'd said hello to Reggie, she'd tried vainly to conceal pity as much as she had anger.

And why not? Reggie could guess what Jack had told his wife over the course of their courtship and marriage. Either Miss Talbot-Jones had been a heartless, spoiled city creature whose need for dramatics had led her to try and ruin his good name, or she'd been a foolish child, ready to believe any likely rumor and take it too seriously—and perhaps mentally unsound into the bargain. If Mrs. Kimpton had been charitable enough to consider the second possibility, it was more than many women in her position would have done.

Jack was a respectable man. In the years since he and Reggie had parted, he obviously hadn't gambled away the family fortunes or involved himself in any public disgrace. He was probably kind to his wife and children, perhaps even loving, in his way—as he would have been to Reggie, had fate and her power played a different hand.

To the world as it was, Jack Kimpton was a good sort, and nothing Reggie had said or could say now would change that. She'd known as much, and known what it meant, for a long time now. It shouldn't have been so much of a shock to remember.

Reggie's glass was empty. She passed it mechanically to a servant, said, "More, please," in as casual a tone as she could manage, and considered her options.

There was no cloud of silence in the room—many people had turned back to their own affairs or had never paid attention to anything else—but there were still eyes on her and still patches of whispering about what had happened once upon a time and what might happen tonight—and do you think that *she* thought that he was going to be here, and what do you reckon his wife has to say about it, and so on. Reggie could feel the gossip clinging to her skin like spiderwebs.

Strategic retreat to the cloakroom or a balcony might give her some relief from the eyes. The chatterers would use that as more fuel—but they'd talk anyhow—but Jack would know that she'd gone and know, or think he knew, what it meant. So would Miss Heselton, and though her malice now looked pale and harmless, Reggie didn't want to give any ground there, either.

Also, if she hid, Uncle Lewis would likely come and give her a solicitous moral lecture, at which point she might just stab him with a hairpin.

Lingering by the table wouldn't be much better. Reggie took her glass, smiled at the maid, and cast her eyes around until she saw her oldest cousin. "Cynthia!" she said, descending with as bright a smile and as cheerful a voice as she could manage. "Seems an age."

"Too long entirely. I feel like an absolute relic here," said good old Cynthia, who had been away at school during Reggie's disastrous summer, and who had sent Reggie a gradually less misshapen scarf every Christmas. If she knew anything about Reggie's past, she'd never said. "You look rather divine, though. I'm quite jealous."

"No reason to be," said Reggie. She paid the appropriate compliments—easy to do with Cynthia, who was round and bubbly and generally delightful—and began to catch up on news about Cynthia's young man and how Aunt Claire had taken to raising spaniels and what Uncle Lewis thought about that. The conversation steadied her, and smiling was beginning to feel almost natural. When two other women, both a little older than she was, joined in, Reggie didn't even worry.

"I don't suppose you remember me," said one of them when the conversation paused. "I'm Maria Charlton—or I used to be. I'm Maria Harlow now."

The name and the piquant face, now a trifle fuller than in the past, did call forth memories after a few seconds of thought. She'd ridden with Maria Charlton on occasion, played the piano with her at those musical evenings that had been so frequent back then, and drunk a lake or two of tea with her and other girls while the men had been out hunting.

"Oh, quite," said Reggie. "Lovely to see you again. It's a bit late for best wishes, isn't it? They look to have come true regardless."

Mrs. Harlow laughed. "Oh, yes. And you? Still Talbot-Jones?"

"Is now and ever shall be, I expect," said Reggie, laughing herself to show that she didn't mind.

"I'm surprised," said Mrs. Harlow, and she sounded flatteringly sincere. "Men in London must be blind."

"Oh, I don't know," said her companion, who seemed vaguely familiar but who Reggie couldn't place. "Perhaps the local lads simply ruined her for all other candidates."

There was nothing personal about the comment. In a way, that was the worst part. She saw Mrs. Harlow hesitate and Cynthia look away, as uncertain as she was about what the other woman might mean, all three of them knowing what it *could*, and why. Reggie felt her face freeze into immobility.

Retreat suddenly seemed like a far better option.

"I hate to separate such an artistically displayed collection," came a voice from behind her: male, light and teasing, with a faint hint of Scotland. "But I'd been wondering if Miss Talbot-Jones might do me the honor of a dance."

Colin had looked dashed well all evening. Even in her distracted mood earlier, Reggie had noticed the sleekly angular lines of his shoulders in his jacket and the way the kilt hung from his lean hips. She'd been anxious, not blind.

Now, as he offered his hand and Reggie stepped forward to meet him, she thought he might be the most beautiful thing she'd ever seen.

He danced well too, of course. She'd said at their first meeting that he looked like a dancing master, and he equaled any who'd ever taught *her*. He swept her across the floor with little apparent concentration, as if he were walking down the road, and he never lost track of the beat.

"Your cousin?" he asked, glancing back toward Cynthia.

"The almost-engaged one."

"Safe, then."

"Any of them would be," she said, looking up at the crisp blackness of his hair, the thin yet promising line of his mouth. "At least where you're concerned."

"The lady is flattering tonight."

"The lady knows you're not Edmund," said Reggie, shrugging. "If you haven't learned how to handle respectable girls in a hundred and thirty years, there's not much I can do to help you."

He laughed. "Only a hundred and eighteen, really."

"Oh?"

"Well, I was hardly thinking much about girls when I was ten or so, was I?"

"I don't know," said Reggie, and her face relaxed into a smile. "I wouldn't put it past you."

"I give you my word. The only interest I took in the fairer sex at the time concerned wheedling extra pastries out of Cook and putting ink down my sister's back."

"I don't know how you made it *past* ten, in that case."

"Neither do most of my family," said Colin. His fingers moved against her spine, an absent caress that Reggie could feel even through the layers of corset and clothing. Was his hand warmer than a normal man's would have been, or was she overly aware of his touch?

No reason both couldn't be true, of course.

"Do you go to many parties like this?" she asked, knowing that she sounded breathless and that her face was flushed. Nobody with sense would believe it was exertion, not on her first dance and that a rather slow waltz—but she didn't care.

"When the mood takes me. None in the country," said Colin. His eyes held hers, with a heat in them that she hadn't thought silver could hold. "And none with you until now."

"That makes a difference, does it?"

"Good company always does."

Colin's arms were as strong as Reggie remembered. She felt herself relaxing into the strength of that embrace, as formal as it was, found herself breathing in the pine-and-woodsmoke scent of him, and the distance between them seemed both very small and all too great.

Sensation uncurled in her lower body. Unconscious of the motion at first, she slid her tongue over suddenly dry lips and saw Colin catch his breath.

"I should have known I was entering dangerous waters," he said.

"Ha," Reggie said, though the husky tone of his voice sent thrills through her that were entirely inappropriate to the dance floor. "I wouldn't think any woman would be a danger to you these days."

"Ah, yes—you think I know how to handle respectable girls."

But I'm not respectable, Reggie almost said. *Or haven't you heard?*

That would sound bitter. That would *be* bitter. And

if he *hadn't* heard about her already, she was hardly going to tell him.

Instead, she grinned. "I said I think you should. That's different."

When he didn't mention her, Reggie wondered how much he did know, or had guessed, and whether he'd come over deliberately to rescue her.

Maybe her pride should smart at the possibility, and maybe it would later that night. Maybe she'd kick herself when she got home and bristle at Colin the next day, half angry at him for knowing too much and making her feel grateful, half angry at herself for welcoming his help.

She looked up at Colin and let the music carry them onward. For the moment, she didn't give a damn.

Twenty-three

WHILE ETIQUETTE HAD COME SOME DISTANCE FROM the days when two dances on the same night meant one was engaged to a girl, Colin knew that spending too much time with Reggie would create talk. He wouldn't have cared, but more gossip was the last thing she needed.

So he let Edmund and his hosts take him around and introduce him to other guests. He met the cousins, safe and unsafe, and found all three of them charming. He discussed art with Edmund and a small group of aesthetically dressed young men. He took the floor with other women and claimed Reggie for three more dances, judiciously spaced.

After the second, he decided that the boundaries of etiquette were probably more of a safety rail than a prison in this case. He could have spent the evening with Reggie otherwise, watching her full red lips as she talked, feeling her body move with his in the steps of many dances, finding new excuses to stand closer and touch her casually—and then they'd have still been at a party, with dozens of people around.

Afterward, they'd have gone home to Whitehill, a house populated both by numerous guests and Reggie's family, none of whom were blind or deaf. *He* might have dared social disapproval, but he didn't think Reggie would be enthusiastic about being seduced under her father's roof, and without her enthusiasm, the game wasn't worth the candle.

As Reggie had observed, he knew how to handle respectable girls.

Colin watched her, though. He stole glances across the ballroom, and he kept his eyes on hers while they talked. By the time they went home at the end of the evening, while she'd rarely seemed precisely relaxed, she'd lost the look of a convict waiting for the sentence.

Colin saw that and smiled and took the memory to bed with him, where, despite unsated lust, he slept deeply and well. If white figures appeared at the window, he wasn't awake to see them.

Philanthropic moods had come and gone in Colin's life—he'd thrown himself passionately into the Chartist cause a while back, to the extremely sarcastic amusement of his father—but this was the first time since childhood that he'd felt so satisfied after helping one single mortal. Like most new emotions, it was at least amusing—although he did wonder, as he slid down into sleep, if this was how responsibility had trapped Stephen and Judith.

The possibility didn't frighten him. He was more elusive than either of his siblings, as a number of people had learned to their distress over the years; Reggie didn't really *need* anyone looking out for her; and he'd be at Whitehill only until they settled the ghosts.

Thinking of that the next morning, he came down to breakfast to find Mr. Heselton holding an opened letter and everyone looking nervous.

"Word from on high?" Colin asked, helping himself to eggs and kippers while the footman poured his tea. "'Joy cometh in the morning,' they say—or are they wrong in this case?"

"Not precisely," said Mr. Heselton, with a faint but determined smile. "Or, not precisely right, but not precisely wrong, either. We've a rite and a man who usually performs it for this part of the country, on those rare occasions when it's been needed before, but he's come down with the influenza."

"Dashed bad luck," said Edmund, and he glanced around. "You don't think—"

"I doubt a ghost in Whitehill has power over illness in Kent," said Mr. Heselton. "Although—but it doesn't matter. The point is that nobody expects him to be up to an exorcism for a fortnight, if that."

"A fortnight?" Mrs. Talbot-Jones set down her fork, closed her eyes, and then rallied. Colin could see the lists assembling themselves in her mind: adding to the grocer's bill, taking on an extra girl from the village, and so on. "Well, I'm sure you're all welcome to stay."

Mr. Heselton shook his head. "You're very kind," he said, "but waiting a fortnight more could put us all in danger. That's why I've been sent a copy of the rite. I'll perform it myself. This evening, if it wouldn't inconvenience the rest of you."

He spoke quietly and simply, without drama, but the whole room stood still. Colin saw Miss Browne turn toward Mr. Heselton, but she didn't say anything. She just met his eyes, openmouthed. Miss Heselton also stared at her brother.

Without thinking, Colin glanced over to Reggie and found her looking back at him, her brown eyes asking silent questions with no real expectation of answers. He'd told her already that he had little experience with ghosts, and nobody would have thought he'd had much to do with the Church of England. She was mortal and her power limited. Neither of them could speak to this matter.

"Wouldn't be any trouble at all," said Mr. Talbot-Jones, breaking the silence. "Much obliged to all of you for your assistance. Just let us know what we can do to help, will you?"

"Gladly," said Mr. Heselton.

❧

If there had been an undercurrent of nervousness among Whitehill's owners and guests before Mrs. Osbourne had tried to contact the spirit, there was a positive riptide when everyone gathered for the exorcism. Standing side by side near the center of the room, Mr. and Mrs. Talbot-Jones looked completely expressionless, as sure a sign as any, with people of their age and class, that they had just about reached their breaking point inwardly.

Edmund paced. Miss Browne nibbled at her fingernails. Miss Heselton had at least temporarily abandoned her pursuit of Edmund and stood near her brother, hands clasped so tightly that the knuckles were white. Reggie, at her mother's side, had some of the same masklike quality about her face that Mrs. Talbot-Jones had, but the color was high in her cheeks and her eyes were very bright. Upstairs, Mrs. Osbourne was doubtless wearing her own nerves thin.

Even Colin, lounging against one wall in his best casual manner, couldn't deny a certain agitation. He was eager to have the whole episode over and done with, and to be sitting elsewhere with a drink.

He smiled at Reggie instead, and saw her lift her eyebrows in return. "Quite the lark, isn't it?" she asked, keeping her voice too low for Heselton, in the middle of his preparations, to hear. "I expect we'll set quite a trend for parties this autumn, assuming any of us survive."

"We'll all come out the other side intact," said Colin, and he immediately wondered if he'd jinxed the whole endeavor.

He wanted to dismiss that thought as idiotic and superstitious. On the other hand, he was a dragon, trained in magic, and he was standing here about to try and exorcise a ghost. He couldn't really afford to be secure in his judgments about idiocy or superstition. Surreptitiously, he tapped the wooden surface of the table next to him—and saw Reggie's smile flicker forth, amused and understanding.

"I, ah"—Mr. Heselton cleared his throat—"I believe I'm ready to begin."

He stood near the hearth, clerical robes a dark cloud around him. A censer in one hand sent up smoke that smelled of sage and roses. Surrounded by all the panoply of a modern drawing room and wearing an expression whose very determination spoke of his uncertainty, he should have been a ludicrous figure, or at least terribly out of place. But a sunbeam from the cloudless afternoon sky bathed him in light, his head was high, and in a way, his very uncertainty spoke of his determination.

Colin, to whom reverence toward most things had been foreign for some time and to whom awe for anything mortal had been alien for much longer, felt both emotions brush his mind as lightly as the sun itself but just as present. Mortal and unsure Heselton might be, but what he served was neither.

"If you follow me when I leave the room," Mr. Heselton said, "I think it will help. The more vessels the Lord has to work through, the better. But I would understand if you didn't want to take the risk."

Drawing a breath, the vicar turned his gaze heavenward and began to pray.

The words he used were English, not Latin, Arabic, or Enochian, but Colin recognized the same sort of rhythm in them that he'd heard in spells: the sounds of invoking and imploring, of repeating a message in order to get it through to a being or beings without mortal ears or consciousness.

Still praying, swinging the censer in rhythm with his words, Heselton paced the room—and as he moved, Colin could feel immaterial powers turning their attention on the space his steps described. One of those powers was the one Heselton invoked, and Colin would not presume to name It.

The other...had been human once.

As Heselton neared the door, the temperature in the room plummeted. Colin felt hostile eyes staring at him from every inch of the wall. He felt a power gathering itself, ready to strike.

He stepped forward to follow Heselton. Reggie walked forward as well, her pale blue dress rippling around her. She might have been a temple maiden from centuries past, the inspiration for some Roman statue of courage.

They fell into step behind Heselton and passed through the doorway together.

Twenty-four

THE HALLWAY WAS COLD, BUT NOT AS BAD AS THE drawing room had been. The chill here didn't hurt one's bones, and the sensation of being glared at by a dreadful sort of ethereal governess was less severe. The governess in question was still there and still not pleased at all, but she wasn't holding a ruler at the moment.

Reggie wasn't sure why. The hallway might have provided some protection, if only because the spirit took a little while to shift her full attention between rooms. Having everyone walking in step might have, as Mr. Heselton had said, provided additional vessels to counter the power of Janet Morgan and whatever she'd bound herself to. Also, walking by Colin might have itself made her feel better.

There were good, sound, practical reasons for that. He knew magic. He wasn't mortal. Also, he was a larger target, but thinking *that* didn't actually reassure Reggie at all. She took a look to the side just to make sure he was still there and in one piece, then snapped her gaze forward again, watching Mr. Heselton as he led them down the hallway.

It was a long walk. Reggie had thought Whitehill enormous to begin with, but she'd never fully realized how huge it was until she marched through it in careful double file with her parents and Edmund, an apprentice medium, a vicar's sister, and a handsome dragon-man, while a ghost glared at them and God—whatever that name meant—was their only real protection. They walked very slowly, step by step in time with Mr. Heselton's prayers and the constantly swinging censer.

The process felt like it took years. She knew she'd remember it for years to come.

They began in one of the first-floor drawing rooms and continued down the hallway, through the dining room and the kitchens—Mater had sent all the servants into the village for the day, thank goodness—and down around to the rest of the rooms on the first floor, then through the hallway to the older wing.

Now the cold was painful around Reggie again, and the ghost's anger hung tangibly in the air. She should have worn warmer clothing, she thought. Nobody told one how to dress for an exorcism. After this, she would write a book, or possibly a series of short columns for one of the ladies' magazines. There was a gentleman in London who she could probably get to do engravings.

She bit her lip against a giggle, knowing that it came from nerves, like the urge to whistle past the graveyard. This spirit wouldn't be deterred so easily.

Wrapping her arms around herself, she stared straight ahead and kept walking, trying to ignore the cold.

At the light touch of a hand on her shoulder, she almost jumped. She didn't, and she didn't scream— and while Reggie would have liked to credit both to excellent self-discipline, she knew that it was really because the quicker part of her mind, even through her fright, felt that the touch was not cold. Far from it: the hand was actually warmer than she'd have expected from a human.

She turned toward Colin and saw him holding out his coat.

Reggie gave him a questioning look: *Won't you be cold?*

Dragon. Remember? he mouthed back silently.

She smiled and took the coat, shrugging into it as she kept walking. It was linen, but warm with the heat of his body, and the smell that clung to it warmed her inwardly like a glass of whiskey. There was no way to really thank him without disrupting the exorcism, but she met his silver eyes and smiled again. He sketched a little bow in response.

As they went on, Reggie clung to that moment as much as to the coat itself—those few seconds of good humor and connection, of...well, "humanity" was an ironic word, considering the other party, but she couldn't think of a better one. She'd needed that. It was the last embers in a blizzard or the final gasp of air before diving.

The ghost's presence around them was like water at its worst, cold and dark and crushing. Reggie had devoured tales of polar expeditions when she'd been in school and had shuddered enjoyably to think of ice that could splinter ships like eggs and of pounding, frigid waves that sucked the life away from men. Now the force around them was the northern sea and they were the ships, a tiny fleet in the immense darkness.

They labored onward: up the stairs, through the bedrooms, through the room where Mrs. Osbourne lay, a ring of candles around her bed. She met their eyes as they passed, and Reggie felt some strength returning to her. She could go a little longer. She turned back to see her family and the other two women, white but steady. She realized that she had no doubts about Colin, but met his eyes anyhow.

Then they were in the attics, and the pressure doubled, tripled, mounted so high that breathing was an effort. Reggie thought she could feel each individual muscle in her legs and her lungs, all straining to keep her going. She wasn't sure how Mr. Heselton still managed to speak, but he did—his voice rising, becoming startlingly deep and resonant. He lifted his arms and shouted, and an answer came: a banshee shriek that sent the attic windows crashing inward in a shower of glass.

And then it was over. The pressure and the cold abruptly vanished, and they stood in a dusty attic, catching their breaths and feeling themselves for cuts. By a miracle—possibly a literal one—the flying glass hadn't hit anyone. The shards formed a neat ring around the group.

"Nicely done," said Edmund, hoarse in the silence.

"Thank you," said Mr. Heselton. He took a handkerchief from his pocket and wiped his face. "At the cost of your windows, I fear."

"I'd been meaning to replace them at any rate," said

Mater, waving one ringed hand carelessly. She glanced toward one of the frames, which still had jagged bits of glass sticking out here and there. "We'd better close the shutters, though. It looks very much like…rain."

Her voice died away, and when Reggie followed her gaze to the sky outside, she understood why.

The day had been beautiful when they'd started the exorcism; if there'd been a single cloud in the sky, Reggie hadn't seen it. Now the sky was a hideous greenish-black, and a wind was starting to whip at the trees outside, a wind that sounded like an echo of the ghostly scream they'd heard before.

Barely breathing, she turned to Colin. "That's not—that can't be—"

She wasn't sure what word she was going to use—normal or natural or right—but she never got the chance to say it. Colin caught sight of the sky, or of something beyond it. His lean body snapped to attention and his eyes blazed with silver fire.

"Get out, the lot of ye," he snarled, his accent far stronger than Reggie had ever heard it, and his voice lower than it had ever been when he was in human shape. With far more than human speed, he reached forward, grabbed Mr. Heselton by his collar, and pulled the man back toward the door. "Go now!"

From outside came another scream, but this one was from many throats: not human, but flesh and blood all the same. Underneath it, Reggie heard flapping, as of many sets of wings beating in unison.

Edmund moved first, reaching to open the door. Mater, Miss Heselton, and Miss Jones hurried through without any questions. Lightning flashed outside, a sheet of blinding radiance, and there was barely time for the thunderclap before the bolts came again and again, stabbing into the ground outside the house. At the doorway, Reggie turned back for a moment, thinking of Pater's age and Mr. Heselton's ankle, and seeing Colin silhouetted against the light. She thought that a faint blue glow rose up around him, but her eyes were dazzled, and she couldn't be sure.

Then Miss Heselton grabbed her wrist and yanked her back through the door. "The gentlemen won't leave until we're out," she said, reminding Reggie of the obvious and clearly knowing it.

As Pater escorted Mr. Heselton out, and Edmund hurried after them, another scream ripped through the room. Dark shapes dove through the windows, claws raking at Colin's face. Reggie darted forward, knowing she couldn't do much but hating to stand back helplessly. She saw Colin raise an arm and strike a large winged shape backward.

He spun and bolted for the door, stumbling through with a lack of grace that made Reggie realize how smoothly he usually moved. As he collected himself, she grabbed the door and slammed it shut with the weight of her whole body. A weight struck the other side: *THUMP.*

Thunder roared, hungry and thwarted.

"What—" Pater began.

"Birds," said Colin. One side of his face bled from a deep set of scratches reaching from forehead to jaw. The sleeve of his shirt hung in shreds, and blood welled from beneath that too. "Let's go down. She canna' strike the house directly, not after the exorcism, but it's still safest to be lower."

Nobody asked, just then, how he knew. Nobody said much until they'd retreated back down to Mrs. Osbourne's room, compromising propriety for safety. There, everyone half collapsed into seats or against walls except for Miss Heselton, who cleaned Colin's wounds.

Her brother sat on the edge of a chair, staring at his clasped hands and looking far older than he had a quarter of an hour before.

"It didn't work," he said. "I suppose I hadn't had the proper training."

"No," said Miss Browne, looking over from the edge of Mrs. Osbourne's bed. "It worked. I felt her leave the house."

"So did I," said Mrs. Osbourne, "even down here."

"Aye," said Colin. "You did precisely what you'd intended, Heselton, and you made a good job of it. She's out of the house now. I'd think she'd be gone from the world of the living, except"—he jerked his head toward the window—"I'd imagine she split herself before she died. Anchored part of her soul to a place outdoors. I wish I'd thought of it before."

"I wish one of us had," said Pater, shaking his head. "If splitting herself implies what it sounds like it does…"

Colin nodded. "The exorcism's banished her from the house," he said, "but it's also made her whole again. Wherever she is, she has all her power at once."

Twenty-five

"What do we do now?" Reggie asked.

Of course she'd be the first one to speak, Colin thought, and of course she'd ask a question like that. He smiled for the first time since they'd all fled the attics, and then hissed as the motion stretched the scratches on his face.

Damn hawks. He was lucky he'd gotten his arm up before the bird had taken an eye.

"First of all," said Edmund, "we should find out what we can do—and I mean the very basics." He looked out the window to where lightning still shredded the air. "Are we trapped here? Will all of this stop?"

"I'd think it would have to," said Mrs. Osbourne. "But we've moved outside my area of knowledge. I've heard very little of ghosts that could influence the weather, but I've never heard of one who could do this."

"I'd be surprised if any ghost, on its own, could," said Colin. "This one isn't. I don't know if she's even strictly a ghost."

"What do you mean?" asked Mr. Talbot-Jones. "What else would she be?"

"She likely bound herself to the being she summoned—or one of them," said Colin, trying to remember the journal's contents. Heselton wasn't contradicting him, which was a decent sign. "It would keep the entity on the grounds outside, but that's not the worst of our problems. A part of it merged with her soul in the process. That'd give her more power than any mere restless spirit could command. It's not infinite, though. I'm certain she'll exhaust herself before too long, and then we'll have a few days' window while she gathers her strength again."

That was true of all lesser demons that Colin had ever heard about, and of the few he'd encountered directly in his younger and more foolish days. A greater demon would never have been able to bind to a human soul without shattering it. As it was, he suspected that the creature who'd been Janet Morgan was now twisted beyond any remnant of rational humanity.

"Ah," said Mrs. Talbot-Jones. She smoothed her silver hair with one shaking hand. "I—I suppose we're back to your question, Regina."

"All right, then," said Reggie, though her eyes lingered on her mother's face before she went on. "We could leave the blasted place for good, you know. Burn it down, salt the earth, do the whole classical bit. It might have cost a pound or two, but that's not worth getting killed over. There are plenty of houses in England."

A moment passed without anyone speaking, without any noise except the thunder outside and the steady hiss of the gas lamp. Then, slowly, Mr. Talbot-Jones shook his head. "Running away never solves problems," he said and held up a hand as both Reggie and Edmund started to object. "The ghost would still be out there, wouldn't she? Somewhere on the property?"

"Yes," said Mrs. Osbourne, and Colin nodded his agreement.

"I thought as much," said Mr. Talbot-Jones. "Then I, at least, have to see this matter through. If we abandoned the land, the next person to occupy it would be her prey—and there would be an occupant before very long. Perhaps I shouldn't have tried to contact her in the first place, but I did. She's my responsibility now." He reached for his wife's hand. "But she's none of yours, and three of you have gotten hurt already. The sensible thing would be for the rest of you to leave. That includes you, Louisa, and the children as well."

Mr. Heselton smiled shakily. "I have a duty too," he said.

"And," said Mrs. Talbot-Jones, "I rather think you're my responsibility, Peter."

"I'm staying if the two of you are," said Edmund. "But maybe the ladies—"

Reggie shook back her dark hair, which had come undone during the flight downstairs, and glared at her brother. "Damned if I'll go haring back to London without the rest of you," she said. "Sorry for the language, Mater. But you?" She turned to Mrs. Osbourne. "You're in a bad way already."

"I'd like to deny that," said Mrs. Osbourne, "but

I can't." She touched her side lightly through her dressing gown and shook her head with amused resignation. "My injuries will keep me indoors, though, so I should be quite safe. Mr. MacAlasdair's right. The ghost won't be able to enter the house or do anything to it directly. I doubt she has the control to have a tree fall on the place or she'd have done it already, and thank God the beasts she can influence are all fairly small. And if my experience is ever to be of any real use, I suspect that moment is here and now. But—" She looked toward Miss Browne.

"Don't even ask," the younger woman said crisply. "I assure you that I will take offense."

"You always were a touchy girl," said Mrs. Osbourne, and she patted her hand.

Miss Heselton had been looking at the ground since Mr. Talbot-Jones spoke. Now she raised her head and looked at her brother. "I'll stay too," she said simply and quietly.

Informal as they were, the words were vows nonetheless. They dropped into place like figures in a magical circle, binding the people who spoke them— and defining them too. Colin watched and listened the way he usually did with mortal ceremonies, gazing from a great height as lights went on below him.

He hadn't expected this.

He'd seen human bravery from time to time in political movements and personal affairs. He'd heard stories of it in war, although he'd never seen a battlefield close at hand. Those men and women had faced mortal opponents, though, people and states with earthly powers. Most of them had known very well the nature of their foes, and what forces those enemies could bring to bear.

Now six people, two of them wounded, promised to face down a would-be killer that none of them fully understood—that, for all they knew, nobody did.

Colin wasn't sure he'd have had the nerve to stay, in their shoes.

Coming back from his thoughts, he realized that they were all very politely not watching him. It took a second or two for him to realize why.

"Oh," he said and cleared his throat of a sudden obstruction. "Of course I'll stay."

"Of course," said Reggie, and her full lips curved up into a slight, very kissable smile. Her eyes were what surprised Colin, though, or rather what he saw when he met them.

She sounded amused, but she was telling the truth. She'd never doubted that he'd stand with them.

❦

The decisions that came after were less heroic but just as necessary. Everyone had agreed to stay and fight. Now they needed a battle plan.

"Most spirits—the ones that linger in the material world rather than just popping by to deliver a message—are tied to a physical object," said Mrs. Osbourne. "It's often their remains, particularly if they died violently or their death was concealed."

"Ah," said Mr. Talbot-Jones, and he stroked his beard. "Well."

Reggie was more blunt. "If we've got to dig up Janet Morgan's bones," she said, "we'll have to make up a dashed good story about it, or be the talk of the county."

"And I rather think it's illegal," said Miss Browne.

"Maybe not," said Mr. Heselton, though he didn't look as though the thought gave him any pleasure. "She's been dead for a long time, and there are no immediate relations in the area. I still would rather avoid any such thing if we can. I can only imagine what my sexton would say."

Remembering the sexton, Colin could imagine too, and had to chuckle.

"It might not come to exhumation," Mrs. Osbourne said. "The spirit's mostly been in the house or on the grounds, unless there's anything you haven't told me. Nobody's seen her in town, and nothing uncanny has happened there. Unless I'm wrong." She looked to the Talbot-Joneses, who both shook their heads, and then to the Heseltons.

"I'd only heard stories about the house," said Miss Heselton. "I paid no attention at the time, of course—they were very vulgar and upsetting—but no, nothing in town."

"Then," said Mrs. Osbourne, "I would think her remains aren't what ties her to the world."

"I'd wager it's a place," Colin said. "Generally one seals an outworld bargain with blood, and the place where one sheds that blood has power."

As he spoke, he saw the others watching him, breaking down the image they'd previously carried of him in their minds and putting it back together with this new information. Oh, Edmund and his family had known for days that Colin had some facility with magic, and the others, hearing, might have believed. They'd never heard him speak about demons before, and he was no longer bothering to disguise how certain he was of his knowledge.

Miss Heselton was eyeing him like he might try to disembowel her at any minute, and her brother was frowning. Mrs. Osbourne was regarding him with professional curiosity. Colin didn't look at Reggie.

He heard her voice, though. "It'd probably be out in the woods, then." She groaned, and though he didn't look at her, Colin could see her raking her fingers through her hair and the way her mouth twisted with exasperation. "It'll only take a year or ten to turn over every rock out there."

"That book might tell us more," said Edmund. "Maybe she took some notes about how to get where she was going. I'd rather think she'd have to, unless she'd a mind like a steel trap for directions."

"And there's at least one old woman in the village who knows stories about her," said Colin. "She might cast a little more light on the subject."

Mrs. Talbot-Jones nodded. "Otherwise," she said, "there are at least five of us capable of dividing our forces and covering the ground. I've no real experience in such things. Do any of you"—she gestured to the mediums and to Colin—"know whether one of us would feel it, should we come close to the correct place?"

"I don't know for certain," said Mrs. Osbourne, "but I'd imagine so. Very haunted places, if they're small enough, are usually colder than normal, and often there's a sense of being watched as well."

"Considering what she likely bargained with," said Colin, "the spot will likely be strange in other ways. You could smell sulfur, for instance, and feel sick. The world may seem a bit out of focus."

"Sounds lovely," said Mrs. Talbot-Jones.

"Reggie and I will take most of the search," said Edmund. "You and Pater have to keep the place running, I mean to say. Might take up a bit of your time, what? Especially since you'll need to bring glaziers in for the attics."

"Well, yes," said Mr. Talbot-Jones, and he frowned over at his son. "I'm not entirely certain that Regina should be out riding with you. Those woods have been let go wild."

"I'm a decent enough rider for most occasions," said Reggie, "and it's not as if we can go at a particularly cracking pace anyhow, if we have to stop and look for haunted bits. Besides, if the woods are that wild, none of us should go off entirely alone. I don't think either of you ride much," she said to Miss Browne and Miss Heselton.

"I'm afraid not," said Miss Browne. Miss Heselton opened her mouth, looked from Edmund to Reggie's eyes to the storm outside, and shook her head.

"Might be best if you looked around the gardens, then. There might well be a hint there—God knows we had enough decorative statues and things. And Colin and Mr. Heselton will be translating that book," Reggie added, turning back to her father. "So there we are. All hands on deck, you might say. But what about the servants? Will they be in danger?"

"The evidence suggests not—or not until we're all

out of the way," said Colin after a moment's thought. "Janet's directed none of the attacks at them. Indeed, the impression I get from the journal is that she's the sort of woman who wouldn't even notice servants most of the time. If she'd been able to destroy the house, I doubt she'd have hesitated because of their presence, but I also doubt they'll be targets now."

"Good," said Reggie. "And everyone staying here can help protect them—much better than Edmund and I could."

"I suppose so," said Mr. Talbot-Jones, "but you will be careful, Regina."

"I'll go out with them sometimes," said Colin, absently examining the scratches on his arm. "Clearing my head will probably be essential, if the rest of this journal is like what I've already read."

He was being halfway honest. He suspected that he would need a distraction, and that riding through the forest with Reggie would provide that and more. Colin didn't think, though, that spending time in her company would leave his head clear.

Twenty-six

As they talked, the lightning outside slowed, then stopped. The clouds began to break up and drift away. Looking out the window, Reggie thought that they'd be gone within half an hour. The sky would be as blue as it had been in the morning, the birds would sing, and only some fallen branches would testify that anything had ever been otherwise.

She wished she could make herself calm again as quickly. Either she managed a decent bluff or everyone else was too rattled to take notice of how many times she wiped her hands on her skirt, or how often she had to lick her dry lips.

She wanted to be sick. More than that, she wanted to crawl somewhere dark, curl up, and wake when the whole damned mess was over—when the ghost had been found and put to rest and Whitehill was just Whitehill again, without mysterious white figures, sudden storms, or homicidal birds. Reggie had asked what to do now, but her first impulse had been to storm at her father: *You couldn't have left well enough alone, could you?* It would have been better, she'd thought just then, if they'd never tried to contact the ghost at all.

Of course, Janet could have turned deadly anyhow in time—or been deadly already. A broken ankle could have been a broken neck. And if Pater hadn't decided to pry, she'd never have met Colin.

Almost as soon as she thought *that*, Reggie told herself not to be revolting. No man was worth having a dozen people in danger. Besides, if she'd never met Colin, she'd never have missed him, so that line of thinking was stupid as well as horrible.

Even so, when she met his eyes, the impulse to run away faded, and she was at least glad that she hadn't stayed in London. Looking at him or hearing his voice made Reggie feel as though there was at least a chance that everything was going to turn out all right, and that she was doing some sort of good.

Also, he made a dashed pleasant distraction. Even sitting at a decorous distance from him, and watching him lean against the wall and look weary, Reggie only had to let her gaze travel the length of his sleek thighs or dwell on the thin yet sensual lines of his lips to feel her body tingle. The scratches on his face and the bandages on his arm didn't detract from the effect, oddly enough.

"Regina?"

Mater's voice pulled her, blushing again, out of her carnal reverie. "Um. Yes. Sorry. Yes?"

"Your father and I are going down to the village to see that everything's all right. Will you and Edmund be able to see to our guests?"

"Yes," Reggie said, stifling a wholly inappropriate

fit of giggles regarding which guests she'd be happy to "see to."

"Downstairs seems the ticket for most of us," said Edmund. "Our current hostess excepted, I'm afraid." He bowed a little to Mrs. Osbourne.

"I'd best clear up the candles," said Miss Browne.

"I should help," said Mr. Heselton. "The exorcism was my doing, after all."

"But your ankle—"

"I'll do it," Reggie said. "The rest of you go raid the pantry. Edmund can show you how. I don't think I'll summon anything nasty."

"Not with my guidance, at least," said Mrs. Osbourne.

There wasn't actually very much to snuffing candles, not even ones that had been lit in a mystical circle, not now that the ghost was out of the house, at least. Reggie went counterclockwise at Mrs. Osbourne's instruction, but she didn't feel any particular power leave or build as the candles went out.

"I probably shouldn't make a wish," she said, looking up from the next-to-last one.

Mrs. Osbourne laughed, though not too heartily. She was still being careful about her ribs. "You could if you wanted," she said. "I think I've already wished on these particular candles, though. Their virtue might be exhausted."

"Have you?"

"More or less. That's a substantial chunk of what magic is, you know—wishing hard enough and doing it through the appropriate channels."

"Huh," said Reggie, and she set the blown-out candle on the dresser in a neat row with the others.

They'd tell the servants that the gas had gone out, probably. Mater was decent at making up stories when she needed to be. "How long have you been doing this?" she asked, turning to look at Mrs. Osbourne.

The medium was wearing a pink dressing gown with ruffles at the sleeves and the neck. Her hair was down, the covers were pulled up to her waist, and her nightstand held a box of chocolates, two green bottles, and a half-read novel: *Cut by the County*. She didn't look like a magician, all pointy hat and star-spangled robe. Aside from being female, she didn't look like a gnarled old witch, either.

But when she smiled and said, "Most of my life— and that's a while, though I won't tell you exactly how long," Reggie believed her.

Kneeling again, she picked up the last candle. "You are the—well, the genuine article." Puff went the flame. "I always thought most mediums were fakes."

"Most of them are. Like many businessmen and not a few doctors. Even I'm not entirely honest all the time. It's a hard world, and most of us have to make a living somehow."

"And the spirits don't always answer?"

"Or they answer too well. I never wanted to tell a client that his son barely knew him when he was alive and doesn't care much now, or that her husband misses his mistress—or his card game—more than he does her. There's no comfort in it for them and no money for me." She gestured languidly toward the nightstand. "Chocolate? I should warn you, I've eaten the hazelnuts already."

"Er—"

"I find that they settle the nerves wonderfully. So much worry comes from a lack of adequate food. Particularly in young ladies."

Helpless before that line of argument, Reggie took a chocolate. It turned out to be strawberry cream. "Maybe," she said. "You seem calm enough, that's for certain."

"Oh, that's mostly the laudanum, dear."

"Right," Reggie said slowly. "I'd guess it would be."

Mrs. Osbourne chuckled again, low and throaty. "Granted, I also won't be in much danger now that Madam Morgan's out of the house. I'd be fretting more about the lot of you if I was entirely in my right mind, though, I assure you—I'm not completely callous." She leaned back against her pillows. "I should have broken bones long before this. It gives one such wonderful license."

"I'll keep that in mind," said Reggie, laughing herself this time. "I'd thought you just had too much experience to worry."

"I'm flattered. But one never has too much experience to worry in situations like this. Not that I've been involved in anything precisely like the current state of affairs. Most of the spirits I've encountered have been rather peaceful. Surly, at worst. I'd never met one who'd dabbled in the black arts, let alone one who was partly a demon." Mrs. Osbourne sighed. "I doubt anyone will believe me if I tell them what's happened here. I never quite believed the stories I heard."

"You'd heard about demons?"

"Here and there, and very vaguely. Nothing

particularly useful. It's too bad, because I rather like being the source of knowledge on these excursions. Now the Scottish young man gets to hold forth while I'm reduced to an ornament. I hope your father doesn't mind terribly."

"Not at all. Pater simply feels guilty that you got injured." Reggie picked up the candles, then stopped. "What about other things? Other beings, that is?"

Mrs. Osbourne blinked. "What about them?"

"Well—have you ever met anything that wasn't human? Alive or dead." Reggie was glad she was holding the candles. She wanted to rub the back of her neck and was sure that would give away that the question wasn't entirely offhand. "Um. Mermaids or, um, fairies, or dragons, or, I don't know, angels?"

"I've never met any such thing, no," said Mrs. Osbourne, forehead wrinkling as she thought. "I don't think I've ever been virtuous enough—or wicked enough—for angels, and I doubt I'd see a mermaid unless she took a liking to Blackpool. And I'm still alive and unburned, which would seem to let out dragons. Why?"

Reggie rearranged the candles she was holding. "Just wondering. I mean to say, if ghosts and demons and all that are real, there's nobody to say that other things from stories might not be out there somewhere."

"Quite possibly," said Mrs. Osbourne. "I doubt one would know about fairies—nobody ever seems to, in stories, unless they announce themselves as one's godmother—and there's plenty of the world that nobody's been to yet. I did meet a talking cat once, and a friend of mine knew a man who was supposed to be three hundred years old. He was human, though, or so she said."

"How would a human being live that long?"

"Oh, magic, I suppose. There are men in China who say it's all a matter of having the right sort of elemental balance. And one hears about the Philosopher's Stone and so forth. I've honestly never bothered investigating. The Other Side seems quite restful to me. Have another chocolate."

This one was coconut. Reggie chewed it thoughtfully. "You'd probably get bored," she said eventually, "and also feel superior to everyone. If you lived that long. There'd be no living with you."

Mrs. Osbourne shrugged. "With some justification. Once one sees a few hundred years, I'd imagine that neither the world nor the rest of us can be very surprising. And when one knows a pattern, the people who don't see it must seem very stupid at times. Petty and emotional. Like schoolchildren at dinnertime."

"Oh," said Reggie.

"Are you all right?"

"Chocolate," she said. "Swallowed too quickly."

Also, it felt like a large invisible hand was squeezing her rib cage, but that was probably the corset and the aftereffects of fear. Surely she couldn't be upset hearing Mrs. Osbourne confirm what Reggie had already known, or should have known, herself. If she was upset, it was only because the day had been long and unsettling. The week had been long and unsettling.

"Still and all," said Mrs. Osbourne, "I'd imagine the man would have some fascinating stories. I should write—wouldn't mind meeting him." Her voice was getting hazier. "Wouldn't object to meeting any of the beings you mentioned. Except dragons, naturally. I make"—she yawned—"a very bad Saint George. And probably a very good second course."

"We'll have to hope they're not around these days," said Reggie, managing another laugh. "Or that they've all become too civilized for that sort of thing."

"Civilized dragons? In top and tails, I suppose? I can just see it." Mrs. Osbourne shook her head. "You've got quite the imagination, Miss Talbot-Jones."

Twenty-seven

"MY GOD," SAID COLIN, STOPPING IN HIS TRACKS AND staring. "Is that yours?"

He looked back and forth between Reggie, descending the steps to the courtyard, and the machine parked there: a small automobile, black wood and brass fittings polished so that they gleamed even under a hazy sky. Colin had seen his share in France and Germany, and even ridden in one or two, but this auto, waiting in front of Whitehill's stately walls, was quite incongruous.

Reggie looked suited for it, though. A tan duster wrapped her slim form and flapped around her ankles, and she'd tied a number of veils around her large brown hat. Colin wasn't surprised when she nodded. "Quite a beauty, isn't she? I suppose autos are 'she'— like ships?"

"I don't think there's been a tradition established yet," said Colin. He stepped forward for a closer look. With a horse rather than all of the valves and wheels, the machine could almost have passed for one of the phaetons of his youth. Young men had raced those on occasion—he'd done it himself—and more than one had died as a result. "Is it—she—new?"

"A little more than a year old. Benz 'Velo'—there's nobody like the Germans for invention."

"They'd have said the same of us, from time to time," said Colin. "Where are you motoring off to?"

"Out to make sure we haven't overlooked anything," said Reggie. "I know nobody in town has seen anything strange, or not that they're talking about, but the road *to* town branches a little ways out from here, and there are some farms on the edges of the property. Some not exactly farms too. If the people there have got odd stories to tell, we might want to cast our nets further when we start hunting through the woods."

"Wise thought," said Colin.

"Thank you." Reggie looked at him, taking in coat and hat and the parcel under his arm. "And you?"

"On the directions of my valet, I'm off to see if Mrs. Jones is willing to talk to strange men bearing cake."

"I see," said Reggie. "Have you heard that there are wolves in the forest?"

"I think they died off a while back," said Colin, "but I'll not leave the path to pick flowers, I swear."

"That's what they always say."

"Fighting a wolf might be a welcome change, if it comes to that." Colin rubbed at his forehead. "I've been translating from French all morning, and I need a respite before I climb the walls. I just hope I can read my own handwriting on the directions."

"Let me see?" Reggie asked, then took the half envelope Colin proffered and glanced over it, lips pursed.

When she lifted her eyes, there was an unreadable look in them. Colin felt as if she was weighing him, or perhaps the moment, but he couldn't tell for what quality or to what end. Then the evaluation was over, and she spoke again. "This is three miles. And it's not out of my way. Care for a lift?"

"Much obliged," said Colin.

He didn't deceive himself. He wouldn't have minded walking three miles—he'd gone much farther easily in his day, and generally carrying more than a lemon cake. He accepted the offer because Reggie was making it, and the leather seat of the auto was on the small side.

And he wanted to see her drive.

Reggie produced a pair of dark goggles from the duster's pocket, handed them to Colin, and grabbed another for herself. "Good thing for you that I carry a spare," she said, pulling hers on. "Just let out the strap in the back." She mounted to the driver's seat before Colin could hand her up.

Colin took his own seat—not terrible, particularly in comparison to some of the carriages in which he'd been not so privileged to ride. Reggie's proximity, so close that he could feel the warmth of her body and smell the scent of lilac from her hair, definitely helped. He leaned back and crossed his legs, trying to look casual.

Whether she knew the source of his agitation or not, when Reggie turned to him, the smile on her lips was pure challenge. "Hang on, Mr. MacAlasdair," she said, "and don't fall out."

She hadn't spoken without reason. The road out of Whitehill was comparatively smooth. Riding in a carriage, Colin had barely felt it. Now every bump transmitted itself up through the auto and into Colin's spine, until he felt like his teeth themselves were rattling. Dust and the smell of petrol filled his nose, and the sounds of the motor and the air strove for possession of his ears.

Reggie didn't drive sedately, either. She didn't seem careless, from what little Colin could tell, but she cornered sharply and decisively and then went ahead without hesitation, braking when she needed to and not dithering at all. A grin stretched her lips, as wolfish as any Little Red Riding Hood's foe might have worn, but vastly more attractive.

"You must be a terror on horseback!" Colin shouted over the car and the wind.

Without slowing down, Reggie shook her head. "Decent. I'm better at this, though!"

"How did you get the car down here?"

"Drove down from London." Her veil whipped into her face and she shook it back impatiently.

"Alone?"

Another shake of her head. "With Jane, my maid. She's not bad, either. Thinks it's a fad, though, like Pater."

Colin's ears and voice were both adjusting, though he wasn't sure if anyone who wasn't a dragon would have been up to the task of making conversation over the noise. "Edmund?"

"Likes horses better. Horses care if you shout at 'em. That's why I like autos. They do what they do no matter how you talk. Also, it feels a bit like flying." She laughed into the wind and shot him a look out of the corner of her eyes. "Or maybe not."

"Flying doesn't rattle your teeth," said Colin.

"I'll get you an extra cushion next time. This isn't as hard on the muscles, though, I'll wager."

"There's that," Colin began, "but—"

Thunk.

Colin's side of the auto dropped an inch, and the whole mechanism lurched along for a few more seconds before jerking to a stop. Steadying himself, Colin grabbed Reggie's shoulder just in time to keep her from pitching forward or out. The smell of heated metal and petrol smoke rose up around them.

"Oh, damn," said Reggie quietly but with immense feeling. She pulled a lever, bringing the remaining mechanical sounds to a halt, and stalked out of the auto. With an irritated gesture, she yanked her goggles up onto her forehead. "Stay there, will you? I'll need the light."

They'd stopped on the side of a fairly wide road, with oak and aspen trees partly screening them from the fields of grain beyond. Colin couldn't see any human figures in those fields, even when he removed his own goggles, and there certainly wasn't anyone on the road.

"Should we stay here?" he asked. "Is it likely to explode?"

From below the automobile's front, Reggie's voice rose up. "No. And why would you care? You're immortal."

"Only long-lived and hardy, I'm afraid. An explosion might not kill me, but it wouldn't leave me feeling my best. Besides, I was concerned for you."

"Well, don't be." Reggie stood up and came

around to Colin's side. "I do well enough. Or will until Pater and Edmund hear about this and give me the devil."

She knelt again, putting the top of her head on a level with Colin's thigh. The posture stopped just short of suggestive. It would have been blatantly so if he'd turned toward her, and he badly wanted to. Her proximity, combined with the minor shock of the last few minutes, had desire pulsing through him again.

Acting on desire on a public road was unwise, Colin reminded himself. Acting on desire with Reggie in her current mood, and all her concentration on the present calamity, would probably get him slapped. She was trying to fix their current predicament, and she might actually know how.

"Do you need a hand?" he asked, talking mostly to the crown of her hat. "I could lift up the wheel if you want."

"No need," said Reggie, rising with a disgusted sigh. "I can see the problem from here—there's a part that's supposed to be down there and isn't. Probably the screw came loose and it dropped off on the road."

"Should we go and find it?"

"Yes," said Reggie, "but we should find a farmer first. One with a couple of strong horses and an hour to spare in return for a ten-bob note. I'll have to get this back to Whitehill and then have a man come out for the repairs."

The breeze gusted past them, tugging at Reggie's veils again. It was chilly at the back of Colin's neck, and he saw Reggie shiver as well. "Do you know the people who live over there?" He gestured to a house and barn, just visible beyond the waving corn.

She shook her head. "No, but they're a place to start."

They walked quickly. Overhead, the sky had gone from hazy to slate colored: not a promise of rain, but a threat. "I hadn't known how bad the roads out here were for driving," said Reggie, after a few yards. "I'm afraid this is a far cry from saving you time."

"The afternoon's young."

"I could walk this on my own, if you want to go on. We're not too very far from Mrs. Jones's house."

"Wouldn't dream of it," said Colin. "Once you offered, I also thought my visit might go better with a woman there. Old ladies are suspicious creatures on occasion."

"I suspect you'd manage to charm her," said Reggie. She stared off toward the farmhouse, and whatever had crossed her mind was clearly still on it, but she did laugh. "And this would all be rather dire without company, so thank you. I suppose horses do have some advantages, even now. Though I'd take it harder if mine broke its leg."

"Is that what this is like?"

"Hard to say. Horses don't generally have parts drop off, at least not that I've ever experienced," Reggie said, and with that, they found themselves in the yard of the farmhouse.

It did not look promising. The yard itself was a neat little place, with a swept path to the door and a red-painted chicken coop, but it was also empty. Nobody came out the door to meet them, though a large ginger tabby slunk around the corner of the house and eyed them with nonchalant suspicion. Through the curtained windows, Colin could see no light, and when they knocked, there was no response from inside.

"It's a large enough house," said Reggie. "Try again?"

He did. The cat stared at the noise, then trotted briskly off to parts unknown. Other than that, there was no reaction.

"Probably gone to the seaside for a week," said Reggie sarcastically. "Just our luck."

At that, because the universe had a sense of timing, the rain started.

It was a cold rain, which fell in big no-nonsense drops, and the wind picked up with it, making it very clear that the eaves of the farmhouse weren't likely to do him and Reggie much good. Reggie pressed herself against the side of the house regardless, swearing under her breath in terms that, while not as profane as Colin had ever heard, would probably have shocked the respectable owners of the house.

"This is going to go on for a while, isn't it?" she finally said.

"Odds are," Colin said, leaning back against the wall and trying not to anticipate wet feet. His boots would hold out until they didn't; there was nothing he could do.

"Then for the love of God, let's find the barn. I think I saw one around the back."

Running would have been pointless, since they didn't know their destination. Instead, they squelched their way around the house, determined and silent, until the great bulk of a barn came in sight and Reggie let out a small cheer.

"Hayloft," said Colin, spotting a ladder and gesturing to it. "It'll be warmer and drier."

"And have fewer cows," said Reggie, climbing in a flurry of muddy boots and skirts. The duster kept Colin, following her, from getting the sort of view he'd have killed for as a youth. The modern age had its disadvantages.

Finally they hauled themselves up into the loft, breathing the sweet smell of hay and peeling off drenched boots and coats. Another oath from Reggie made Colin look up to find her struggling with the knot of her veil, which the rain had condensed into an impenetrable soggy ball. "You don't have a knife, do you?" she asked.

"No," he said, "but stand still."

Walking over, the hay pleasantly scratchy beneath his damp feet, he stopped a few inches from Reggie. "Raise your chin," he said, and when she complied, he took the gauze between his fists and yanked. It parted easily.

"Oh, thank you." Reggie sighed, pushing off hat and veils and shaking her head so that her hair went tumbling down her back. "You've saved my sanity."

She didn't step back from him. Instead, she looked up at him, with her skin flushed from the rain and exertion, her lips red and her eyes bright. Colin had never had pretensions to sainthood.

"Only for my own purposes," he said and pulled her into his arms.

Twenty-eight

THIS TIME, REGGIE HAD NO CHANCE TO BRACE HERSELF for the contact. Her mind was open when Colin drew her close, and her power active as soon as he touched his lips to hers. She didn't get any memories, though, or even discrete thoughts. Intentionally or not, Colin's mind was very focused just then. All she received from him was desire, formless and insistent as the wind.

She opened before him, mouth and body and will.

It was too hard to resist when she could feel how much he wanted her—not just from the hard urgency of his mouth or the firm bulge that pushed against her stomach, but from the hunger all through the back of her mind. He craved her. That gave her power— not over him, since every inch of Reggie's skin was tingling with her own yearning, but power enough. Here and now, on this particular playing field, they could meet as equals.

She tested that theory with a slow, deliberate flex of her hips, forward and then back, teasing them both. Pulling away took more willpower than Reggie would have thought, but it was worth it, because

Colin actually growled a little, a low sound in his throat that might have been frightening if it hadn't been arousing.

"Wicked," he said, beginning to trail a line of kisses up her jaw. Reggie tangled her hands in his dark hair, caressing and tugging, feeling the silk of it between her fingers and the building charge of his lips against her skin. She closed her eyes, tilting her head back to give him better access, and this time when she arched her hips, she did it with no conscious thought of teasing.

"Very wicked, Miss Talbot-Jones," he muttered again, his voice thick. "Although I'll give you daring as well."

"Daring?" She trailed her fingertips down the back of his neck, as far under his collar as she could go, and then drew them back up quickly, turning her nails to his skin this time. He hissed—not in pain—and looked up. His eyes were silver fire. Reggie swallowed. "I thought," she said, breathless, "that I shouldn't be afraid of you."

Colin shook his head. "I didn't say that, did I?" He slid one hand around her waist and up the line of her blouse, skimming over the buttons, nearing but never quite touching her breasts. Reggie stared down at the blouse, captivated by the sight of his fingers against the white linen and almost surprised to see that they weren't actually trailing sparks. "Look at me."

"I am looking at you," said Reggie.

He took hold of her chin and lifted it, his fingers warm and strong. "My face, you devilish girl."

"Oh." She met his gaze and caught her breath. Lust was apparent on every angle and plane of Colin's face, showing through his features like an inner light. Before he spoke, she'd forgotten what she was waiting to hear.

"I said, as I recall"—he deftly undid the button at her collar—"that it depended on who you asked."

Corsets really were the horrible things reformers talked about, Reggie decided. For instance, if hers hadn't been in the way, she could have leaned forward just a little and felt Colin's chest against her breasts. Furthermore, she was increasingly short of breath, which was clearly the fault of her stays, although far more pleasant than such experiences usually were.

Heroically, she managed to think of a marginally witty rejoinder, even though Colin was on the second button now. "If I asked you?" she asked and smiled up at him.

He laughed, deep and unsteady. "I'd say no, of course." The third button fell away. Then the fourth. He pushed her shirt aside, baring her corset and the upper slopes of her breasts. "Whether it was the truth or not."

"I can't really be surprised," she said, laughing. She leaned forward and kissed him again, running her fingernails down his back. He was still wearing a shirt, and she really ought to do something about that, but it took her a minute to pull back to the proper distance. "And I'm not. Afraid. Of you."

"Good." He stepped forward, pushing her against a pile of hay. That was fine—scratchy, but yielding— and Reggie forgot the scratchiness when he started kissing her again. Now he was opening her corset, and even his fingers grazing over the outside were maddening. She moaned and wriggled, and Colin responded, thrusting against her through the layers of their clothing.

His rod pressed against Reggie's inner thigh now, hot and hard beneath his trousers. Feeling it, feeling the answering throb in her own sex, cleared her head abruptly. She knew where this path led, and while she wanted it, she knew what else might happen as a result.

With her remaining willpower, she pulled back enough to talk. "Are you—" She'd heard of precautions, but her memory was hazy and secondhand. "You're not going to get me in trouble, are you?"

"In—" It took a second for Colin to catch on, but when he did, he shook his head at once. "No, no risk of that. We can't interbreed without magic."

Reggie blinked, then absolutely failed to keep from giggling.

"It's true," said Colin, holding up a hand. "My word on it."

"Oh, no," said Reggie, "I didn't doubt you. I couldn't—nobody could make up a line like that!"

"You give men too little credit," he said, "but I'll not object at the present time." He kissed her quickly and reached for her corset hooks again. "Lie still, if you please. These contraptions are trouble enough without provocation."

"That sounds like a challenge," said Reggie, but she didn't move. Victory might be a thrill, but she suspected that she'd have more thrills with the corset off.

She was right. She knew she was right even before Colin touched her, because he caught his breath as she squirmed out of the corset, and then swore, quietly and almost reverently, when she impatiently rose and dispensed with her skirt and petticoat as well. His eyes went the length of her naked body, and she felt every inch of her skin tingle under their scrutiny.

"My God," he said.

Now she did blush, like a dashed milkmaid really, and shook her head at him. "I won't believe I'm the first naked woman you've seen."

"Not the first." He caught her hand and pulled her down to the hay again. "I'd make a strong case for the best, though."

"You could easily have made up *that* line," Reggie said, laughing, "but I won't argue. Not with, um, proof at hand." Hoping she moved with some degree of grace, she closed her hand over his member.

Colin groaned. He went completely still too, which gave Reggie a second of worry, though she'd felt no pain from his mind. She relaxed her grip. "Er—too hard?"

"No." He shook his head quickly. Then a wry smile rose to his lips. "Not you. Me, certainly."

Reggie hadn't known that was possible, and she thought about saying so, but in the second before she spoke, Colin ducked his head and closed his lips around one of her nipples. At that point, she lost interest in talking. She lost interest in most things, in fact—in anything unrelated to his lips, and his tongue, and the sensations they were building inside her. She closed her eyes and let her head fall back against the hay. Every stroke of Colin's tongue, every touch of his hands as he cupped her breasts and raised them to his mouth, had her writhing, yearning for more.

She was aching between her legs, conscious that she

was hot and almost embarrassingly wet—presumably that was supposed to happen, and Colin hadn't seemed to mind at all before, and she was beyond caring—and when he slid a hand down to cup her there, she made a sound that was too dashed close to a squeak.

This was getting one-sided again. Reggie couldn't think well enough to speak, but she grabbed the remnants of coherent thought and shifted her weight up and over. Dragon or not, Colin was distracted enough, and his position precarious enough, that he went with her. As she settled herself on top of him, Reggie noted with satisfaction that he didn't manage to say anything, either.

She was not good with men's trouser buttons. Her current situation wasn't ideal for learning, what with Colin hard and insistent behind the buttons in question, making more of those little growling sounds every time her fingers brushed over the fly. Reggie bit her lip and focused, glaring at the buttons until they yielded to her rather clumsy efforts.

"You could have helped, you know," she said as she undid the last.

"You seemed to—aahh—have a plan. Didn't want to—" Colin caught his breath again. His rod sprang free, large and stiff.

It was very like some scandalous pictures Reggie had seen once, but illustrations hadn't been able to show how red such an organ would be, or the moisture at the tip. She ran her fingers lightly up its length, and it jerked in response.

"*Reggie*," said Colin, sounding like she'd hit him in the stomach.

This time, though, she was quite sure he wasn't in pain—at least not that kind. She knew the urgency that made his breath ragged, that had his hands in fists at his sides. She felt his desire in her mind and her own in her sex, and the time for teasing had just about passed.

She had some idea of what to do. Life outside society was educational, at least. Reggie slid herself upward, then swung a leg over Colin's body until she was straddling him, his organ hot and smooth between her thighs. It was a bit of a puzzle, albeit a delightfully frustrating one, getting everything lined up—one shifted back, yes, and then—

—ah. She felt Colin's hand between their bodies, guiding himself into her. That worked. That worked very well, in fact. She sank downward, felt herself stretch around his shaft, felt the stretching become less comfortable, and then, as she'd half expected, a quick, sharp pain shot through her.

She felt Colin's surprise even as she bit her lip, and certainly before he opened his eyes. "Good Lord."

Reggie took a breath. In and out—that was the way to cope with pain, her sportsmistress had said. Granted, Miss Snopes had been talking about a twisted ankle on the playing fields, but the principle probably applied. "I'd hoped riding and bicycles and so forth would've taken care of that," she said. "Damned archaic things, maidenheads. No place at all in the modern world. Er. Sorry."

"Don't be," he said hoarsely, and Reggie knew that he meant it. She felt his delight in her body and his struggle for control. As the secondhand sensations entered her mind, the pain began to recede, replaced by a sense of pressure that became more enjoyable by the second. "Hold still," Colin said then, and he moved his hand to stroke her, fingers threading through the soft hair between her legs and circling over the sensitive spot there.

She didn't hold still. Gentleness felt too much like condescension just then, even if she knew Colin was enjoying the process, even if she needed it—perhaps especially if she needed it. Even as she gasped at Colin's touch, Reggie shifted her weight, an experimental motion of her hips up and down the length of his rod.

She might have spoken. She might have only moaned. Reggie wasn't sure. Pleasure swamped her mind, and if it was raw-edged with pain, she could ignore that easily enough. Colin's organ was hot and full inside her, his fingers deft between her legs. Those things mattered. Everything else was as inconsequential as the rain on the roof.

Now she *had* to move again, to repeat what she'd felt and build on it. It was easy enough to fall into a rhythm once she'd started. Need drove her and guided her, and Colin helped, cupping one of her hips with his free hand and urging her on. She didn't need much encouragement—the goal was just ahead, the charge building like the wind before a storm.

Then ecstasy.

Reggie threw her head back and screamed. Pulsing, shaking, eyes closed as the peak hit her, she felt Colin grip her hips with his hands and thrust upward, felt a rush of heat within her, and heard him cry out as well.

Twenty-nine

COLIN HAD HAY IN HIS HAIR. HE REALIZED AS MUCH AS he came slowly back down to earth: hay in his hair, no bones in his body, and a beautiful woman lying naked on top of him. The afternoon had not gone as he'd expected. Thank God for that.

Languid, letting the last lingering pulses of his climax fade away, he ran his fingers through Reggie's hair. Her dark curls were damp, probably more from their recent exertions now than from the rain earlier. Her cheeks were still flushed, and her body still quivered slightly around him.

He wanted to tell her that she was a remarkable girl, but for one of the few instances in his life, he hesitated. It sounded too light in his mind, too sporting, the sort of thing one said to a future mistress or an enthusiastic dairymaid.

Colin frowned up at the barn roof. He had been very fond of his mistresses. He'd rather cherished the memory of the girls who'd passed a night or two with him, giving no thought to the future and not pressing him to do so. Nor, in all of his dealings with Reggie, had he gotten the impression that *she'd* press him for anything, or that light speech would upset her. No, the urge away from frivolity had come from inside him, and he didn't know what part of his mind had given rise to it.

A man couldn't be expected, after all, to figure out both ghosts and the sudden vagaries of his own subconscious.

He looked down at Reggie. She was smiling in a sleepy, sated way, which boded well. Even the dim vestiges of chivalry couldn't make Colin reproach himself. She'd taken the lead quite handily when matters had come to a point, and he thought she might pinch him if he asked whether she was all right.

Startling himself for the second time in as many minutes, Colin realized that he couldn't think of anything to say. He coiled and uncoiled a strand of Reggie's hair and tried to come up with an appropriate comment: witty, yet considerate, yet not so considerate as to seem patronizing.

It had been a very long time since his last virgin, and the world had changed considerably. That, he decided, was where the trouble lay.

Knowing the source didn't particularly help.

Silence proved to be its own cure. Gradually, Colin caught on to the fact that it *was* silent in the barn, save for their breathing. He'd gotten used to the steady drumming of rain on the roof. Now it was gone.

"I think the storm's over," he said.

"Right." Reggie sat up, too quickly for Colin's taste, and moved to the side, donning her corset hastily. She left the laces loose, not asking him for aid;

from her brisk manner, he didn't think he should volunteer. "Yes. Good of you to notice. Best get going before we have to explain ourselves to the farmer."

"Could get embarrassing," said Colin. He reached for his jacket and took a handkerchief out of the pocket. "Er—"

"Oh," said Reggie, and she glanced down. "I've, um, got one. But thank you."

"Thank *you*," said Colin, and he smiled at her, then turned away so that each of them would have some privacy. "I'll admit the accommodations are a bit lacking in certain respects."

"I'll be writing a stern letter when I get home," said Reggie, laughing.

"Speaking of which," Colin said, "what should we do now?" Still fastening his jacket, he turned around in time to see Reggie shoot him a nervous glance over her bare shoulder.

"Nothing to do, really," she said. She bent and retrieved her shirt, so that he was looking at her back again. "I enjoyed myself. You enjoyed yourself. You said there wouldn't be any consequences. There's no reason to make anything of it, is there?"

Her voice, quick and fierce, brooked no argument. With her back turned, she buttoned her shirt. Colin could see the swift movements of her arms.

"I meant to ask," he said with deliberate lightness, "what we should do about the auto and getting back to Whitehill."

"Oh." Reggie's hands went still. Colin could see color rise up the back of her neck. It took a moment for her to clear her throat and go on. "Good thought. I suppose we'll just have to keep walking—there should be another farmhouse farther down the road. We might as well keep on to your Mrs. Jones's house, for that matter. We're on the way as it is, and we'll likely come across someone between here and there. Er. Or you could go back to Whitehill and send someone. Or I could."

"Best if we stay together. Two of us won't get lost as easily—and I'm less likely to get shot at if you're with me."

"I do seem to be useful that way, don't I?"

"You're a pearl beyond price, or whatever it is a woman is supposed to be."

"You might stand alone with that opinion," said Reggie, but she didn't sound bitter about it, and she smiled when she turned around.

"My powers of judgment are simply"—Colin flung one hand out in a theatrical gesture—"far beyond those of mortal men."

"Yes, *that's* how you've wound up in a houseful of ghosts and spiritualists. Superior judgment."

"Superior enough to know how boring complete safety would be. Besides," Colin said, and this time he didn't think long enough to doubt himself, "the company makes the whole experience worth it."

"Very gentlemanly. Top marks for form," said Reggie, grinning up at him.

He wanted to linger. He wanted to ask why she'd remained a virgin—whether she'd held back because of her power or the last vestiges of propriety—and why she'd chosen him. He wondered if he'd been merely the first man she'd liked whose mind had been disciplined enough to make the experience bearable. That, Colin supposed, would have been at least flattering to his powers of concentration.

Asking was likely a bad idea. Her quick dismissal earlier, even if it had been mistaken, was a sign that she wouldn't welcome personal questions, and the time for them was probably past at any rate.

At the ladder, he stood aside to let her descend first. Their eyes met as she passed, and she stopped for a second, the air between them growing thick once more. Their sport showed very clearly in Reggie's face, Colin thought. Her lips were faintly swollen, her eyes bright, and her hair considerably disarranged. In fact—he reached out, as she stood, and gently plucked a strand of hay out of her curls.

"I think this is the only one," he said, and the emptiness of the barn made him soften his voice.

"Oh. Much obliged," said Reggie. She drew a breath to speak on, then thought better of it, turned, and darted down the ladder like a small animal seeking shelter.

❧

Out on the road, the tension ebbed. It was hard to sustain any sort of awkwardness when one was tromping along the side of a country road, particularly when dodging puddles was now a significant part of the journey. By the time they'd found a farmhouse where the owner actually *was* present, Reggie and Colin had passed through a companionable silence and into an offhand conversation about dogs, the seashore, and brothers.

It was easy to talk about Stephen with Reggie—easy despite how foreign the two of them were to each other, or perhaps because of it. Explaining Loch Arach and life as a MacAlasdair was a matter of putting facts together, not much awkwardness there.

"I've generally been glad that I'm not heir to anything," Reggie said. "It sounds like even more trouble for your family."

"Self-inflicted, much of it," said Colin. "The Fabians I knew would've said we could always give it up, and thus aren't much to be pitied—although our children would have quite a time living in London. Even this"—he gestured to the fields around them—"would be a tricky situation. Too little privacy, and not enough deer."

"You could become shepherds," said Reggie. She tucked an errant lock of hair back up under her hat and asked offhandedly, "Your children?"

"The MacAlasdairs." Colin surreptitiously looked over, but couldn't make out the expression on her face. "There's only my niece just now. Stephen's the fatherly sort, though, and his wife's a healthy girl—among her other sterling qualities," he added with a wry smile. Mina MacAlasdair had been formidably practical when her last name was Seymour. Titled marriage and sharing the MacAlasdair blood had turned her into something like a force of very organized nature. "I should think they'll do very well by the line."

"Thus taking a weight off your mind," Reggie said, laughing. "Is she another dragon, or—I mean, I'd think it'd be a surprise for a human girl. Not to mention it'd be the devil to explain why you looked thirty and your wife was sixty-five."

"It would," said Colin, "but marriage helps. Children, more accurately. If a human woman does bear one of our children, she gets some of our blood."

"So she lives longer?"

"Among other things."

"I'm surprised you're not all knee-deep in women."

She was still looking for a farmhouse, and Colin couldn't tell if she was saying the prospect would appeal to her or making a statement about women in general. "The lady doesn't always survive," he said.

Their boots squished in the mud. "Not good odds, I take it?" Reggie asked.

"Worse than most women face, I hear. I like to think that they're better now—science has come a long way, no reason that magic shouldn't do likewise—but we have damned few sample cases. We live long and breed rarely. Stephen's wife took the chance and made it through." Colin shrugged. "It's not unheard of for us to marry human women, but it's not common, either. When we do, they're generally familiar with magic. Mina's the first in a while."

"Maybe that's a sign of progress," said Reggie. "I don't claim to know much about magic, but we're finding new worlds every day. Sooner or later, we'll all have to start living with each other."

Thirty

GAMMY JONES WAS *OLD*—NOT WITH THE CHEERFUL, plump old age of Pater's parents, nor the dour yet formidable state that Reggie had seen from a dozen dowagers in a hundred ballrooms over the years. The woman was skeletally thin, bent until she barely came up to Reggie's shoulder, and completely toothless. More than that, there was a sense of ethereality about her, a feeling that she didn't quite belong to the world any longer.

Once again, Reggie thought of fairy tales, but she didn't think she was seeing Red Riding Hood's grandmother. She thought of witches instead.

It wasn't Gammy Jones herself who answered the door, but a woman in her fifties, heading straight for the dour-and-formidable model. Both of them wore black, but Gammy's dress was a faded and frilled thing, probably from before Reggie had been born, while the younger woman's was more modern and quite plain. She wore it like a uniform.

"Can I help you?" she asked, eyeing Reggie and Colin with a stare about two degrees friendlier than one might have seen over a shotgun.

Reggie was glad that she'd paid the farmer and his sons—the Weatherbys, as it had turned out—to take her auto back and had come on with Colin. He'd been right. She didn't think anyone recognized her, and she didn't look much like a squire's daughter should, but a young woman was at least dimly reassuring. She doubted Colin would have gotten anything except screams and threats if he'd come alone, particularly as he'd left the cake in the auto.

"I'm Reggie Talbot-Jones," she said, stepping forward, "and this is Colin MacAlasdair. We'd come to talk to Mrs. Jones. I'm, um, not related or anything."

"I should think not," said the younger woman, and she turned back to the elder, who was sitting at the table beyond and peeling potatoes with still-quick hands. "Mum?"

Gammy Jones looked up. Her eyes were cloudy, but she seemed as if she could see at least a little. "They be the ones little Tommy Hill mentioned, likely. Sit yourself down, Sarah. And the two of you."

There were chairs enough for that purpose, though barely, and the cushions were not an improvement over bare wood. The cottage was mostly kitchen, sternly clean but still smelling of woodsmoke and onions—unsurprising, as strings of said onions hung from the ceiling, as well as garlic and other vegetables that Reggie couldn't identify offhand.

"We were going to bring a cake," said Colin, "but I'm afraid the storm ruined it rather. We'll make it up another time."

"Very nice of you," said Gammy Jones, continuing

to slice potatoes away from their peel. "I be partial to lemon. No walnuts, if you please."

"I'll be sure they don't sneak in," Colin said gravely.

The old woman smiled, a flash of bare gums and wrinkles. "You trust your cook, then. If you know baking, I be a mule." She looked back and forth between Colin and Reggie, her eyes narrowing, and Reggie fought the urge to squirm. Her hair was disarranged, but she could blame the storm for that. Surely nobody, especially a half-blind old lady, could tell what she'd just done. "Sarah, put the tea on. We've visitors."

"We don't want to put you out," said Reggie.

Gammy Jones snorted. "You want *something*, an' you might as well have tea with it, an' so might I. You, you be the gel from the big house, be you not? The new lot from up London way?"

"Yes, ma'am," said Reggie.

"Hmm. Your mum be a kindly sort of lady. An' your da' hasn't too heavy a hand with the place, from what I hear. Good folks. Not blood, but—that be just as well, mebbe. More than just as well, considerin'."

"Mum—" said Sarah, turning from a small cupboard where she was assembling a tea service.

"It's all right," said Reggie.

"We've actually come to ask about that," said Colin, "or about something related."

"Have you, now? Hmm." The old woman pushed the bowl of potatoes to one side and leaned forward. "I thought someone would, soon or late. You're not of the family, though, young man. Not of any family 'round these parts, not old nor young."

"However were you telling, lass?" Colin asked, exaggerating his accent.

Reggie giggled at that, Gammy Jones chuckled, and even Sarah cracked a smile as she put down saucers and teacups, yellowed china with faded violets around the rims. "Co—Mr. MacAlasdair's a friend of my brother," said Reggie, and she didn't meet either Colin's eyes or Gammy Jones's. "He's staying with the family for a while."

"Ha, yes," said Gammy in a knowing tone. Reggie didn't want to press her about *what* she knew or thought she did—it didn't matter, and in her experience, there was no convincing old women out of anything they'd made up their minds to believe. "And it be the Morgans you want to hear of? The madman, the rake, or the witch and her sister?"

"The madman would be Old Morgan, I'm thinking," said Colin. "I've not heard anything of the rake, though. Have you?" He looked over to Reggie, who shook her head. "And the witch would be Janet?"

"Aye, that was her. Lady Janet Morgan. Gold hair an' cold heart, they used to say when I was a gel." Gammy chuckled again, low and thick in her throat. "'Course, you bear in mind that she was considerably 'afore even *my* time. I never met the lady, but my auntie told me of her—me and the other kiddies 'round here."

She paused as her daughter poured the tea. It was very strong, and there was sugar and cream to go with it, both in the same ancient china. After a hard look from her mother, Sarah got out a packet of ginger biscuits, too, and handed them around on a plate.

Reggie took one, more to occupy her hands than for any other reason. Her fingers brushed against Colin's as she passed him the plate, and even that brief contact sent a shiver through her body.

For a moment, she was very aware of her body: an unfamiliar soreness, an equally unfamiliar satisfaction, and the potential, so soon, to surrender once again to passion. She forced all of those feelings aside, concentrated on the Jones women, and tried not even to look over at Colin.

"Lady Janet was the oldest, my auntie said," Gammy began. "The Morgans were a good family back then, a *noble* family, and they went back far. She was the oldest, an' her sister was the youngest, and their brother an' heir came between. My auntie said it might've been better had she been in her brother's place, and he hers, but 'twas nothing to be done about it—she was the eldest, and she was a gel."

"Oh," said Reggie. "Did she mind?"

Gammy shrugged. "At first? Mebbe not. She was a dutiful gel, from what my auntie says, an' a man leaves his wealth to his sons. That's right an' custom, it is. She'd have known it, Janet would, an' she was proper. Problem was—he wasn't."

"Ah," said Colin, and Reggie knew he was making an effort to sound thoughtful rather than reveal what he knew, even by the tone of his voice. "Older siblings tend to mind that, on occasion."

Edmund never had. Reggie had been lucky that way. She wondered about Stephen—the brother who was the fatherly type—and any other siblings in the MacAlasdair family, and how they'd been with Colin, who was anything but proper. But maybe he had been, earlier. More than a hundred years gave a man a lot of time to become respectable, or not, or both.

She jerked her attention back to the task at hand.

"…and finally," Gammy Jones was saying, "he took up with a gel. A farmer's daughter, they say. They also said it was the first respectable thing he ever did, and that he was in love with her. And he might have been," she added, dunking a ginger biscuit into her tea, "at least for the moment. He'd have been a romantic sort of chap, from the stories, and they fall in love easy enough. Never lasts, 'course, but the young take no heed o' that."

She paused, gummed part of the biscuit, and drank tea from the saucer. "Any rate, some say his intentions were honorable, an' some say he brought the girl up to the house without the benefit of clergy—if I be not offending either of your tender ears. And *you've* no call to look so shocked, Sarah Williams, as you've been a married woman these twenty years."

"Mum," said Sarah, a weary reproof that didn't expect any results.

Gammy shrugged. "Whether they married or no, Janet hated 'em for it, an' hated her pa for letting it happen. *She'd* never married, of course."

"Of course," said Reggie, biting back a sarcastic reply.

"Might have taken her mind off brooding if she had. Instead—well, I heard that she raged, and she screamed, and then she seemed to calm herself some. And then"—Gammy Jones leaned forward, her eyes glinting like stars through the clouds—"she made herself a pact."

"A pact?" Colin asked, still in his tone of off-hand curiosity.

"Aye. Signed in blood—and not all hers. Her brother's woman sickened and died. Her brother got more biddable. Moved around like a cow in the field, they said. And children went missing."

The tea stuck in Reggie's throat momentarily, in a way no liquid should have been able to do. She swallowed several times before it went down. "How many?" she asked.

"It's a story. I couldn't say. Even those who lived in her shadow couldn't say, mebbe—the world was wilder when I was a gel, and wilder still in Janet Morgan's time. There are bogs in the woods and there were men on the roads. But they say she killed at least three before the end."

Silence was thick in the room. Now Reggie did look to Colin—a brief glance, just to make sure he was still there and still hearing what she was. The day was warm, now that the storm had passed, and the cottage was close, but she felt an echo of the cold that had surrounded her during the exorcism and knew that, if she pushed her sleeves up, she'd see every hair on her arm standing on end.

At the same time, a small voice inside her said that she should have known, that she couldn't be surprised. Colin and Edmund had told her about the grave. They didn't bury someone outside church grounds for rumors or for being a priggish sort of harridan, not even in the bad old days. Not if you were *Lady* Janet Morgan, from a good family and an old one.

Not being surprised didn't make the information

go down any easier. She almost reached for Colin's hand, and only the gimlet eyes of Mrs. Williams made her draw back. Either unseeing or uncaring, Gammy went on.

"Her sister found her out, they said. Some said she found Janet's book of spells, an' some say she found bones or a bloody knife. One I heard said 'twas a room like that Bluebeard chap in the stories, but I never counted that for much. Too many people up at the house, even then. But Lisbet found it, whatever it was, an' she followed her sister out to where she met with Old Scratch, and nary a one ever saw them again."

"Where did she go?" Colin asked.

Gammy Jones shrugged. "Couldn't say. Off in the forest, most like. An' most of it may have been a story—though the two of 'em disappeared right enough. Their brother, Michael it was, had the men searching for days, and nobody found a sign of 'em. There's graves in the village, but nowt in either one."

"And—Michael? Did he get better?"

The old woman raised a hand, the knuckles swollen and the nails long, and waggled it back and forth in the air. "Better. Never good again. He took himself off to London a bit after. Folks said, when I was young, that he drank like a fish and he babbled to himself, an' his man said he screamed in the night often, but his bride was dead and his sisters were gone. It's enough to drive a man mad, that. He married again, in time. There's plenty of gels willing to look past a bit o' madness for such as him. His son was worse than him, and *his* son worse than that. Old Morgan, that was. Last of the line."

There was that third cousin in London, Reggie thought, but he wasn't worth bringing up. He had no part in this, whatever *this* turned out to be.

She made herself drink more tea and, despite her earlier resolve, watched Colin as he spoke again. "We're quite obliged for your time, Mrs. Jones," he said, "and your hospitality."

"It makes a change, having visitors," she said. "Mind you take care, though, boy. They say Janet Morgan's spirit rests unquiet—and if she did half of what the stories say, 'tis no wonder at that. Take good care."

"For once in my life," said Reggie, "I think I will."

Thirty-one

"I'D SAY IT'S SPREAD A BIT THICK, EVEN WITH ALL we've seen," said Edmund, perched atop his bay gelding and looking like one of his hounds had gone astray. "The devil? Really?"

"*A* devil," said Colin. "'Tis as fitting a name as anything else for the creature she would have been bargaining with. There are things outside the world, things inimical to it and all dwelling there. They've been known to deal with us from time to time, though never honestly nor with good grace. What else would you be calling them?"

That sent Edmund into silent thought. Horses and riders continued down the trail toward the forest: Edmund on his tall bay, Reggie crisp and sportive on a chestnut, and Colin on a gray gelding, old and plump and docile. Even in human form, men of his bloodline didn't get on particularly well with horses, other than those bred and trained to the MacAlasdairs' service. Some clump of the beasts' little minds was likely to speak up and say *predator*.

He'd chosen a mount that he doubted would be

perturbed by firecrackers going off under its nose. If Reggie hadn't known his true identity, it would have been rather embarrassing.

Now she was turning to look at him, her own seat and her grip on the reins careless with experience, her gaze speculative. "Does *the* devil exist?"

Colin had given some thought to the question before. He considered his answer again before speaking, though. A man's views bore contemplation, especially on such issues as this. "A greater creature might spawn the things I've seen, or lead them. They'd not be easily led, though." He shrugged. "In the end, I don't know much more than you do."

"That's rather a relief," said Reggie, laughing.

They rode onward. The trail took them under pines and oaks, and for the first part of the journey the road was broad and well kept. The sky overhead was clear, and various birds sang in the trees. The whole scene was very pastoral, very wholesome—as long as nobody was listening to their conversation.

"The two of you didn't meet at a séance, did you?" Reggie went on, turning from Colin to Edmund with the same deliberately joking air. "Never took you for the levitation and tea leaves sort, Edmund."

"Not directly," said Colin.

"Literary types, mostly," said Edmund. "I told you about a few of 'em. Bright chaps and quite willing to let me lurk round the edges, though I've no talent myself."

"As a fellow lurker," said Colin, "I've found that they generally prefer a man who can listen to and applaud a fellow artist. One only wants so many rivals, you know."

Before them, the road forked, and the three of them paused to look at each other for direction. "Don't ask me," said Reggie. "I told you—I'm not up here very often. At least Edmund comes up for the hunting."

"And nobody I've ridden out with has stumbled over anything suspicious as yet. Might as well go left—it looks more overgrown."

Colin couldn't see much difference himself, but left made sense. One took the left-hand path, were one inclined as Janet Morgan had been. Left was *sinister*, in the Latin. The left path was certainly as good as the other.

They turned, and now they kept a lookout as they rode, scrutinizing the trees and undergrowth to either side of them, searching their own senses for a hint of unusual cold or a trace of nausea. "One day," Colin said, half to himself, "I'm going to try and develop a manner of tracking magical trails."

"Like a compass," said Reggie, "or a bloodhound, if you could get one to pick up that scent. I've a friend in London who breeds dogs—I'd introduce the two of you, if I thought she'd believe a word of what you wanted."

She sounded as she always had: straightforward and friendly, with her mind on the problem in front of her. Colin kept trying to hear something in the way she spoke or see something in her face that had changed since their time together in the hayloft. So far he'd found nothing. As he'd thought before, that should have been a relief, but he simply couldn't believe she really had taken their passion so lightly, that she wanted nothing more from him than that afternoon.

Judith would have said more than a few words about vanity and might have boxed his ears into the bargain.

"Is that Louisa?" Edmund asked.

"Mm-hmm. Lovely girl, though I'll never know what she sees in such a messy business." Reggie frowned over at the trees to her side, then shook her head, dismissing whatever she thought she'd seen. "Asked after you when I was leaving, actually. I'd forgotten in all the trouble. She said she had a setter pup she'd like your opinion on, when you're in Devon next."

"Did she? That's good." Edmund rubbed his chin. "That's jolly good," he said and then added quickly, "I don't guess Janet Morgan would've gone off cross-country. Even to meet with Lucifer himself."

"Doubtful," said Colin, remembering the woman in the portrait and the journal. "She'd have wanted a fairly remote place to conduct her rites, but she'd have looked for a path there, even a small one."

"Any path might have grown over in the last century or so," said Reggie, sighing.

"Aye," said Colin, "but—well, give me a moment. And your discretion, of course."

"Of course," Reggie said and lifted her eyebrows.

Colin wasn't a blushing man, but he was glad to have the spell as a distraction just then, even if it didn't do very much. Whatever magic Janet Morgan had performed once upon a time, it either hadn't been nearby or hadn't left a trail. The forest swarmed with the sort of auras he saw anywhere full of life: the solid green and gold of the trees, the bright sparks of animal life, and the more complex clouds around his companions. Edmund's was a deep navy blue, he noticed, while Reggie's was a lighter color, shot through with gray like the sea during a storm.

He didn't see the rotting greenish-gray that he'd spotted when he'd sought the white figure, nor the swirling radiance he associated with magic. Still, he kept the veil of the world parted. He could manage a docile horse well enough in such a condition, particularly when Reggie and Edmund were with him.

"Nothing," he said. "Or nothing yet. Let's press on—I'll try to keep my seat."

Without seeing her face clearly, he felt Reggie's attention. It appeared in her aura in a pattern of light and movement that Colin hadn't yet learned to translate into words. "…miss the branches…" she said, her voice faintly muffled. "Rocks too."

They started forward again. The landscape went by in shifting kaleidoscopic waves. When they grew too confusing, Colin looked to Reggie without thinking about it.

After the third time, she turned to him. "Anything wrong with me?"

"Not at all. You clear my head. Steadying."

Her laughter came to him as through water. "First time for everything…"

"…more responsible than most…" said Edmund.

"In comparison. You…" Reggie said and went on. She was joking, or trying to. She was also worried, and about more than their immediate threat. "…tired."

Edmund's sigh went out from him in a cloud of blue-tinged gray. "I am. My own damned fault, isn't it?"

Worry became sorrow, which Reggie immediately translated to sharp-edged impatience. "...be completely gormless, Ed. You know——"

On the edge of Colin's vision, the gray-green hue he was looking for flickered through the trees. He glimpsed it just as he heard Reggie, though he saw her surprise first.

"——the hell is she? Hello?" She raised her voice. "Didn't mean to intrude——is anyone out there?"

Suddenly the world around them went rotten: putrid green lay over the trees, the ground, even the sky. Reggie and Edmund stood out against it, untouched. The horses were less clouded, but even they took on a sickly, greenish cast. The color seemed thickest around Reggie's, even seeping into the whites of its eyes.

Before Colin could truly register what he was seeing, much less work out what it meant, Reggie's gelding threw its head up and screamed.

It was a terrifyingly human sound. Colin knew it of old, from fields and lonely highways where human screams had usually played a grisly accompaniment. His own horse shied in response, and he snapped his attention unwillingly away from Reggie as the gray fought him with a strength and violence he'd never have expected.

"Easy there——" Edmund was saying, sounding outwardly calm but doing a bad job of disguising both alarm and bewilderment. "Easy——what the devil?"

A devil, Colin heard himself say. This was Janet Morgan's doing——hers and her ally's——whether it was her will striking at them deliberately or simply natural creatures panicking at her unnatural presence. For the present, the difference didn't matter.

"Turn around!" he yelled, having to raise his voice because all three of the horses were screaming now. He heard hooves hit the ground as one of them reared and plunged. "We'll have to go back!"

Turning, he discovered even as he shouted, was all well and good in theory. His horse snaked his head around and snapped at Colin's leg when Colin tried, then suddenly bucked like an unbroken colt. Janet or the gelding's own fear was using the horse's body unmercifully. If he'd had a moment to spare, he would have felt sorry for the beast.

On his other side, Reggie was cursing, low and hopeless. Colin saw her in flashes: the iridescent blue feather in her hat, the dark lines of her arms as she pulled on the reins, and the desperately clenched muscles of her legs as her struggle yanked her skirt tightly over them. He caught his breath at the sight, and stamped on the urge to reach for her, knowing it would do no good. If he could only get his own damned horse to settle—

"Jump off!" he heard Edmund say. "No calming them—jump and let 'em run!"

Not needing to be told twice, Colin kicked his feet out of the stirrups, let go of the reins, and all but launched himself from the gray's back. He hit the ground with none of his usual balance, coming up beside Edmund.

As Edmund had said they would, their two horses dashed off, saddles on and reins dangling. Reggie's chestnut didn't. She was still mounted, trying to disentangle herself from the sidesaddle, while her horse screamed and reared up, hooves lashing at the trees in front of it. Branches broke beneath the blows. Colin saw foam around its mouth, and wide rings of white around its dark eyes.

Years around horses told Colin that his presence would frighten the creature still more. Only that held him in place.

Edmund stepped forward. "Good old fellow," he said, voice low. He and Colin both knew it was hopeless, even as he spoke. "Nothing to worry about..."

Once more the chestnut reared, with Reggie leaning forward on its back. This time, its downward plunge took it just under a tree branch—to Colin, it looked the size of a whole tree itself. He saw Reggie duck at the last minute, then heard the sickening dull *crack* that meant she hadn't ducked fast or far enough. He saw her body topple out of the saddle.

She fell into the undergrowth, where the brush grew too high for Colin to see whether she was breathing or not. Her horse didn't run like the others had, but stood over her, snorting and pawing at the ground. When Edmund started forward, it flattened its ears and snapped at him, blank murder in its eyes.

"*No*," Colin said from deep in his rapidly expanding chest. He felt fangs lengthen in his mouth, knew when his feet had split his boots, and didn't care. Meeting the horse's eyes with his own, knowing that his gaze was no longer human, he addressed it and the beings behind it both. "Leave. NOW."

He roared the last word. Edmund turned to gape at him, seeing a monster and not his friend. The horse saw a monster too, and its instincts overpowered any control the ghost-witch had over its mind. It turned tail and fled, leaving the path clear so that he could sprint to where Reggie lay.

Thirty-two

THERE WAS DARKNESS—JUST DARKNESS. NO FACE OF the deep here; no heavens, no earth; certainly no light, good or otherwise. Only darkness. For a long time that was all.

Or was it a long time? It felt that way, but she had no way of measuring. Everything was dark; then both pain and memory unfolded like the sudden snapping open of an umbrella. Reggie remembered who she was, the past few days—ghosts and dancing and dragon-men—and her stupid horse's sudden stupid panic. She must have hit her head, she thought. It felt awful: swollen to three times its size, oddly numb at the same time that it throbbed with pain, and sticky on one side. She was lying on a field of rocks, by the way her left side felt, and it almost didn't matter compared to her damn head.

Reggie opened her eyes a slit and immediately regretted it. The light seemed to be made of long needles that went right in through her eyes to her bruised brain. She groaned and snapped her lids shut, throwing her arm up over her face to be sure.

In that instant of vision, she did glimpse silhouettes: legs, hurrying toward her. She could hear voices too, above the sound of footsteps in the grass. They were male, and she didn't need to concentrate very hard to recognize them. Colin and Edmund were here. How embarrassing.

"She's alive. Conscious too," Edmund said in the bluff pretend-nothing's-really-wrong tone she'd only heard him take about horses and hounds before.

Colin said something rough. He said it in a foreign tongue—not French or German—and it had a number of syllables, but Reggie knew an oath when she heard one.

"...gonna hope," she managed, though her tongue was as swollen as her brain from the feel of it, "you're not mad 'm alive."

"For the love of God, woman," said Colin, "don't *talk*."

Close up—and he was close up now—his voice didn't sound normal. His accent was very thick now. More to the point, his voice had dropped at least an octave, and it sounded almost sibilant. Reggie heard more swishing grass and felt a shadow fall over her, then a hand on her arm. It was Colin's, she thought, but even hotter than he normally was.

"...'s wrong w' you?" she asked. She didn't want to open her eyes to find out, because of the light needles.

"A damned fine question," he said. "Do *not* move. Do what I say this time."

As Reggie wasn't inclined to move anyhow, she held still while an equally warm set of fingers traveled gently but urgently over her head, at first avoiding the sticky place on one side and then probing lightly around its edges. No amount of gentleness could have made that not hurt, and she couldn't manage to control herself. She cried out and batted at Colin's arm. "Stoppit. Go 'way."

"Damned if I will." He caught her fingers in his free hand. "There's a bloody great lump here," he said, not to her, "but nothing feels broken. But she's bleeding. Quite a bit, and would you for the love of God go get a doctor? Make yourself useful, man!"

"I—" Edmund started to retort angrily, and Reggie wondered if she'd have to get up and deal with the two of them, because she'd quite cheerfully kill them both if so. Moving hurt. Thinking hurt. Edmund and Colin shouting hurt. Luckily for everyone, she heard Edmund take a long breath. "I'll go down to the village and get Dr. Brant if you take Reggie back to the house. We can't bring him out here, and I don't want to leave you both waiting—not when *she* might come back."

She? Reggie was puzzled for a moment, then remembered: Janet Morgan. Ghost, witch, and generally unpleasant person. Quite possibly the reason she was lying on the ground with spikes in her brain.

"Stupid cow," she said.

"Stupid? I'd love it if she were," said Edmund. "Reggie, do what he says. And don't try to do anything yourself. Colin—I'll be as quick as I can."

He started off at a run. Listening to him go, Reggie felt a wave of affection. How many times had she gotten him in trouble? And he'd always covered for her.

"Poor bastard," she muttered.

"Aye, well, he's not the one with a head wound." Colin's fingers held hers tightly, and his other hand rested on her head, but either he was controlling his feelings or her pain and dizziness were blocking her abilities. "Reggie, sweetheart, I'll need you to open your eyes. Just for a bit."

"Ugh," she said and sighed. "All right."

The light still hurt. She was staring into Colin's eyes now, though. They were the same metallic silver that they'd been in his dragon form, with serpentine vertical pupils. "You…" She waved a hand, trying to think of words. "You changed."

"It seemed wise at the moment. And you can shut your eyes again. What's your name?"

"Regina Talbot-Jones. Typical of a man to forget, after," she said, laughing as the idea struck her.

Colin's hand tightened on hers. "And what year is it?"

"Eighteen ninety-five."

He sighed. "All right. I'll be picking you up now. Put your arms around my neck, aye? And hold tight. This will take a while."

"I guess you can't fly me," she said with a sigh of her own, "in the middle of the day."

"For sixpence I would," he said curtly, "and damn the daylight. But I'd not be able to carry you without hurting you, and you can't hang on like this. Brace yourself."

Then his arms were around her, beneath her knees and her neck. Colin lifted her and held her, her head against his hard chest. It would have been very pleasant to lie that way if the motion hadn't sent her brain bouncing against the inside of her skull. She bit her lip. She would not cry out, because Colin was doing the best he could, and she would certainly not be sick, because it was disgusting and would just make her head hurt more.

Nonetheless, she heard him draw a sharp breath, and now she did feel a little of his emotions around her own pain—mostly remorse, at the moment, and worry. "None of this will be pleasant for you. I'm sorry," he said.

"Not your fault."

She settled her face against the hollow of his neck, smelling smoke and clean linen. She focused on that smell when Colin started to walk. It helped the nausea.

Even so, it was a very long journey.

She knew, from both his body and his mind, that Colin was going as carefully as he could, but every step still jarred her head and her stomach. When they walked out of the shade, the sunlight hurt even through her closed eyelids. She didn't dare to open her eyes again. Reggie didn't talk, either. The effort to hold on physically and mentally, not to scream or vomit or black out again, was taking every atom of concentration she had.

Colin was silent too, and for the most part, all of his mind that she could read was concentrating on walking. Memories crept in around the edges, though—most alarmingly, that of a stable boy who'd been kicked in the head, seemed fine, and fell over dead two days later.

She did speak then. "Horse didn't kick me. Did he?"

"What?" Colin looked down, realized who he was talking to and why she was asking, and shook his head quickly. "It was only a branch. And on the side of your head, not the front. You'll likely be fine."

He was telling himself that just as much as he was reassuring her, Reggie knew, but he mostly believed it, and that made her feel better. After that, his concentration deepened, and she could sense less of his mind. She still picked up that he was angry at Janet Morgan, for obvious reasons, and at himself, for reasons she couldn't make out, and that he was desperately worried about her.

Most of his emotions, she thought blurrily, felt rather close to human—or maybe those were the only ones *she* could feel. Dogs couldn't see color. Humans couldn't hear certain sounds. She'd gone to a lecture on that in London. Louisa had been there. Edmund was suddenly more interested in Louisa than Reggie would have thought.

Briefly, she forgot whose arms she was in and why, and muttered a profane question up at the man— handsome enough, but dashed impertinent to be toting her about like this.

"You hit your head, Reggie," he said, and his voice reminded her that he was Colin.

"But you *are* a dragon," she said, frowning up at him.

"You're not imagining that part," he said, his mouth twitching.

"And we—"

"We did."

"Oh. Jolly good," she said and let her head fall back against his shoulder.

The flickering pattern of darkness and light outside

her closed eyelids became all light, and Reggie knew they'd come out of the forest even before she heard more voices, and then running footsteps. Mater was trying to keep everyone calm, including herself; Pater was talking of mad horses and getting the gamekeeper with his gun; the others were harder to make out, because she couldn't read them as well. Edmund wasn't there. Where was he? Ah. Gone to get the doctor.

Inside, then. Stairs. A bed. It was good to lie down, but she felt cold without Colin's arms around her. He wasn't in the room anymore, either—it was Mater, saying calming things, and women who were taking off her clothes and bathing her. Breathing helped her head, and she didn't want to be sick any longer.

She opened her eyes. That wasn't quite so painful, either. Miss Heselton was bending over her, washing the cut on her head with sure, gentle hands. Her lips were thin, but she didn't look rigid or disapproving, just concerned.

"You should be this way," Reggie told her. "Don't—don't make yourself less. It's not worth it."

Miss Heselton gave her a glance that said at first *What?* and then *Head wound, I won't pay attention,* so Reggie didn't know that Miss Heselton had gotten the message. That was all right. Everything was all right. Life was like a dream, as the song said.

Dreamlike, Dr. Brant came in and examined her. He bandaged the cut, palpated her skull, shone a bright light into each of her eyes, and asked her a number of questions, then had her touch her nose with each hand. "She should be all right," he told

Mater, and then turned to Reggie and spoke firmly, as if she were still ten. "You're going to sleep for the rest of the day, and you're not to do anything strenuous tomorrow. Do you understand?"

"Mm-hmm," said Reggie. Sleep sounded pleasant, and she was glad to close her eyes and slip down into darkness.

She had no dreams, thank God, and when she woke, her head only ached a little in a bruised sort of way. The room was dark, except for where moonlight spilled through a crack in the curtains. At first, she thought she was alone. Then she heard breathing.

In a chair in the corner, the shadows were thicker than normal: too thick and man-shaped. Momentary panic froze her where she lay.

She saw the figure's moonlight-colored eyes just before he whispered. "Oh, damn—I didn't mean to frighten you. Terribly sorry. I didn't think you'd wake up."

"Colin?" she whispered back. "What are you doing here?"

He shrugged. "Head injuries are tricky things. I'm not a medical man, but one never can tell. I thought it might be best if one of us kept watch. If I'd asked your mother or one of the maids to do it, they'd have just been nervous all evening."

"Oh," she said, thinking of the stable boy, the one Colin hadn't meant to tell her about. He'd probably seen others: a long lifetime of unexpected deaths.

"I couldn't heal you, not really," he went on. "We can't, as a rule, just as we're not very good with animals—well, Judith is, but more from a distance.

Healing magic takes a body like the one being healed, and ours are close, but not close enough. But I thought, if something did go wrong, I could probably manage a botch job and keep you alive until—until the doctor got here, I suppose. Or until I thought of something more useful to do."

Helplessness must have been very new to him. Reggie smiled into the darkness and wished he'd been close enough to kiss—not out of passion, though she suspected that would happen regardless, but because he was dashed sweet at times.

Shadowed, he rose. "Regardless, you're awake now. I should stop intruding on your privacy."

No sound came from the hallway outside. No shape peered in at the window. They were alone, and his voice was low and warm in the darkness.

Reggie found that she could sit up without pain. She turned back the covers. "You," she said, "should stay."

Thirty-three

THE WORLD AROUND COLIN SCREECHED TO A STOP. IF the crickets still sang outside or the grandfather clock still ticked in the hall, he couldn't hear them. He wasn't even sure that he breathed. He heard only Reggie's voice, telling him to stay. He saw her turning back the covers with one hand, and the moonlight shining through the flimsy nightgown she wore, exposing the dark shadows of her nipples and the darker patch between her legs.

Yes, said his mind, almost hissing it. *Yess, pleasse*.

"That might not be the best idea," he managed. His voice was thick, but he was proud that he'd gotten the words out at all.

The impact on Reggie was negligible. She shrugged and pointed out, "You must have had some way to get out of here tomorrow morning before anyone saw you. You can still use that. And you'll be able to lie down and get warm, and maybe even get some sleep this way. Unless you sleep better on your own."

"I don't," he said, caught off guard. In fact, he wasn't sure how well he'd sleep with Reggie curled up mostly naked next to him, but he *was* sure he didn't give a damn.

"Well," she said, as if the one word indicated everything needful, and patted the bed next to her.

Colin braced his mind, braced his body even more, and settled himself onto the mattress.

The bed smelled of her: lilac and linen and woman. He sighed, both because he couldn't avoid it and because he didn't wish to.

"How did you get in here, anyhow?" Reggie asked, shifting her body to accommodate his. She was turned away from him, at least.

"Climbed down the tree," he said.

"The window was locked."

"Locks generally aren't a great problem for me."

"Oh."

Satisfied, she snuggled back against him, tucking her head beneath his chin. Colin wrapped his arms around her, luxuriating in the warmth of her body, the firm curves that pressed against him through the nightgown, the little contented noises she made as she shifted to get comfortable. Disciplined as he was, he had to control both body and mind now, and one inevitably slipped his grasp.

"Colin," she said, her voice low and amused. Lithely, she turned in his arms, so that her breasts were full and soft against his chest, and the juncture of her thighs pressed against his persistent and obvious erection. Dressing gowns did not hide a great deal. Neither did nightgowns. "Colin," she said again, this time with a hint of a question.

Flushing for the first time in God knew how long, he

cleared his throat. "Can't really be helped, I'm afraid. Not now, not most of the time when I'm around you. Doesn't mean I've got to do anything with it, either just now or in general." Not with Reggie, at any rate. His rigid cock would demand some kind of satisfaction, sooner or later, but he thought it was best to stick to chivalry and reassurance just then.

Of course, then Reggie flexed the muscles of her thighs, which was a test of his honesty. Colin sucked in a long breath and reminded himself that he was more than a century old.

"What?" she asked into his neck, so that he didn't understand her at first. When her hand slid over his thigh and inward, though, he became amazingly more adept at translation. "What would you like to do with it now?"

"Reggie."

"I'm not naive," she said, "but you may have figured out that I don't have much experience in propositioning men. This is me trying, in case you haven't caught on."

Awareness was rapidly leaving his head and traveling south, to where he could only ache and hope for her touch. A small sliver of gentlemanly behavior still governed the mouth, though, and one hand. Colin put it over Reggie's before she could achieve her goal. "You're not well. You could barely talk this afternoon."

"That was this afternoon. I feel much better now." When Colin lifted his head to look at her skeptically, Reggie shrugged. "I'm not saying you should bend me over the nightstand and yank up my skirts—"

They both went still. Colin wondered if a man could go blind with lust. Certainly all he could see was the image—Reggie's face in the mirror, mouth open in ecstasy, her hair tumbled down her back and her skirts around her waist, revealing all the hot loveliness of her sex—and all the air had left the room.

"I should take more care with my phrasing," she said unsteadily.

"Oh, yes. You should."

With effort, she cleared her throat. "It's only, I get the impression there are a number of different ways to bed a girl. And that one can do it, at times, more gently. Though I hate to say it that way. Sounds like such a whimpering request. But I'll do the wide-eyed begging act if it'll get you to touch me."

Between her thighs, his rod pulsed at almost every word. He wanted to move—to take those few thrusts that would likely bring him to climax even outside Reggie's body. Colin held himself completely still from the hips down and lowered his head until he just breathed the words across Reggie's lips. "You promise not to move."

"Cross my heart," she whispered back and directed his hand to the appropriate place. Her breast welled into his hand, soft and smooth, and he could feel the rapid beat of the pulse beneath it. He circled the nipple with his thumb, slow and gentle, until it tightened and pushed at him through the thin cotton of her nightgown. After a few moments of him touching both breasts in that fashion, Reggie, true to her word, hadn't moved. She was simply panting and making little whimpering noises in her throat.

"I'll let you sit up," he said, trying to sound stern through his haze of lust, "but just to take this off, ye ken?"

"I...ken," she said, mocking his accent in her own throaty voice.

That earned her a pinch on the backside, once the nightgown was off and Colin could slide down her body to suck at her nipples. He stroked her legs, first soothing the spot where he'd pinched, then running his fingers up and down the muscular curves of her thighs. She shifted, then caught herself, and he chuckled against one breast. .

Such lovely legs she had: long and strong, silver and shadowed. More enticing still was the place between them, the nest of soft dark curls that Colin began to tease, brushing his fingers forward and back. He could feel heat there, and he swallowed when his fingertips grew damp. Patience, he told himself. Patience. Calmness. Caution.

He'd never been very good at any of the above.

When he lifted his head from her breasts, Reggie raised a hand as if to pull him back, then remembered her promise and dropped it to her side. Colin smiled at her. "Very good. Besides," he added, shifting so that he lay between her legs, "you'll like this."

"Will I?" she asked, raising an eyebrow in pretend skepticism.

"Oh, yes. Open your legs for me, sweetheart."

She complied instantly and unhesitatingly, and the trust of it made Colin's heart skip a beat—as did the final revelation of her sex. He worshipped it with his mouth: the warmth, the wetness, the rigid little bud that made Reggie moan when he circled it with his tongue. Pressed against the mattress, his cock was torturously hard, sweet agony with every movement, but he held on to his self-control just as he held on to Reggie's hips as she neared the end.

It wasn't very long before she convulsed under his tongue, a rush of sound and motion and moisture that damn near sent Colin over the edge himself. When she lay quiet beneath him, he rested his head on her thigh, breathed in the scent of her, and tried to figure out what to do next.

Reggie, typically, addressed the issue.

"I could do that to you," she said, still breathless. "Take you in my mouth. I've—heard how. I think I'd like it." As Colin's mind struggled to make sense of basic words, she began to sit up.

The motion helped. Or, at least, it pulled Colin's attention away from the weight between his legs and back to Reggie's condition. Willing or not, *passionate* or not, she'd taken a blow to her head earlier. Some activities went even worse with head injuries than what they'd already done.

"Later," he managed, rasping the words. "I promise. I might demand. But not tonight. Lie back."

She didn't, but she paused. "But you—" Her gaze went to his trousers, which were barely containing a rather significant bulge. "You deserve—release, is it? And I want to touch you."

"You will. I do." Colin let out a long, shaky breath, his fists clenched at his sides. A better man—Stephen, perhaps—would have showed her how to bring him to climax with her hand, or done it himself, or gone away altogether and left her in satiated peace. Reggie was not an inch away from him, her smell surrounded him, and Colin had never been a particularly good man. "Lie back. Turn on your side."

He was moving as he spoke, taking off dressing gown and trousers, so that he could stretch naked beside her and pull her into his arms. Sensitized from her earlier climax, Reggie caught her breath at the first touch of bare skin to bare skin, and when he ran his fingers down her spine, she wiggled against him in a way that could drive a man mad.

"I think," she said, pressing her breasts against his chest, "that I might be insatiable. Dreadful sort of thing in a woman, I hear."

From the sound of her voice, she was joking, but Colin responded emphatically anyhow. "You didn't hear it from me. Or from any other man with sense." He slid an exploratory hand between her thighs and found her wet and ready again. "Ahh. No. Certainly nobody would complain. Now—your leg, Miss Talbot-Jones."

He helped her wrap her leg around his waist as she giggled, then guided himself smoothly inside her so that the giggle turned to a gasp. "Oh. *Oh*. I didn't know—"

"The theory," said Colin, already beginning to breathe raggedly, "neglects some possibilities. I'll show you."

It *was* gentle, what they did. He couldn't drive himself into her; she couldn't ride him, or buck beneath him and send him to greater frenzies. Instead, there was sweet tension, and a smooth rocking with his hand cupping one of her buttocks, guiding her in the unhurried motion that built until both of them hung on the edge. Then Colin slid his hand between them, circled, and felt Reggie's climax grip him like an electrical current, blinding and binding. He couldn't have stopped if his life depended on it. He couldn't have moved, other than to spend himself inside her in burst after burst that made his whole world go blank.

Thirty-four

AFTER, THEY DIDN'T HAVE TO MOVE THIS TIME. IT WAS one of many advantages to an actual bed. Another was that Reggie didn't have hay in unmentionable places. When numb arms made it necessary to disentangle themselves, she stretched slowly, relishing the traces of sensation that still lingered in her body, and then rested her head on Colin's chest. He didn't make a bad pillow at all.

"I assume," he said dryly, "that you're feeling quite well."

"Are you asking for medical reasons or looking for a compliment?"

He laughed, his chest vibrating beneath her cheek. "Well, yes."

Reggie had thrown an arm across him, which put her in an excellent position to administer a pinch. "You know perfectly well I enjoyed myself. If you want more than that, I'm afraid I can't help you. No basis for comparison, you know."

"I suppose one could find that reassuring."

"Do you?"

"It's been over a century since I felt any need for reassurance," said Colin. He stroked up and down her back, the touch of his fingers soothing now, rather than arousing. Reggie knew that she wasn't keeping his mind out completely, but all the contact gave her was hazy satisfaction, almost an echo of her own emotions. "I wasn't sure you *were* a virgin," he said, "until the, ah, crucial moment."

From a man of her time, that might have been insulting, but Reggie knew he didn't mean it that way. Besides, he did have some justification. "The London crowd's fast," she said. "And I can't pretend I've exactly been sheltered."

"Yes," Colin said slowly, "and—I had heard you were nearly engaged." He hesitated, waiting for anger or at least for Reggie to pull away, but she didn't. She waited. "You wouldn't have been the first girl to anticipate a proposal or believe promises, and then find you'd set your hopes on a rotter. I've seen it happen more than a few times."

"It wasn't that," said Reggie, and then she laughed. "Obviously."

"Obviously."

She could feel nothing from Colin now, which meant that he'd clamped down on some emotion, most likely curiosity. He didn't ask, either. The room was dark, he was warm, and every muscle in Reggie's body felt loose in the aftermath of pleasure. Besides, Colin was ancient and inhuman, both of which were bound to make his point of view different. She couldn't imagine him gossiping. She wasn't sure she could imagine him caring very much.

"When I was seventeen, I came out here to stay with Uncle Lewis. Well—I say Uncle Lewis, and he's my blood relation, but mostly it was to stay with Aunt Claire and the other girls. Mater thought I could go to a few country parties, you understand, as a way to get my footing before I really came out. Might have been a good idea, at that—I liked the country, and I was enjoying myself. And then I met Jack. I suppose Mr. Kimpton now."

Colin said nothing. The hand on her spine continued its steady sweep up and down. Reggie thought of the way one might gentle a horse or a dog, considered being insulted, and decided that it was too much trouble.

"He was—is—the son of a friend of Uncle Lewis. That's how things work out here. He'd come back from university a year before, and he was a nice, respectable young man. Also handsome, especially when I was seventeen," she added, shaking her head as she remembered her young self and the raptures she'd gone into. "There were calls and picnics and dances. We went riding quite a lot. He was a good rider. A good dancer too, and his conversation was interesting. I liked him."

"Did you love him?" Colin asked, only curious as far as Reggie could tell.

She shrugged. "I was under that impression. Maybe it was even true. Love at seventeen's a queer beast, though—quite different, I'd think, from love at thirty or sixty. Or a hundred and ten," she added, looking up at Colin and smiling.

"I'd not know," he said and shrugged at her frankly

incredulous look. "Oh, I was infatuated quite a few times when I was younger—but as you say, that was infatuation. If age and a certain cynicism have any advantage there, it lies in knowing the true metal from the dross."

"Why not?" She blushed a minute after she asked the question. It was hardly tactful—perhaps even inappropriate here in this most intimate of settings. Perhaps that was why her heart had started hammering. "I mean, you must have known enough women."

"Not many who thought I was anything but human," Colin said. "Love may not demand honesty about all things—I haven't given it much study—but I think my nature would be too large a lie to ignore. With the women who do know...it simply never happened. The heart's difficult to explain. I've never tried."

"Wise of you," said Reggie. "No dark secrets, then?"

"Only myself."

"You're not even dark enough to hide from a gamekeeper properly," she said. As she spoke, she began to feel as if she approached a precipice, and backed hastily away. "I don't really have any, either. Not the sort you were thinking of. Jack and I never really did anything much. He certainly never pressed me. He didn't even kiss me until he proposed."

"Quite the gentleman."

"So I thought." Reggie closed her eyes. It was late, she was tired, and she didn't want to watch Colin when she kept talking. She didn't even want to be tempted. "My aunt gave a party. We danced. It was all very nice. When he asked me to come out onto the balcony, I didn't even hesitate."

"And then?"

"He asked me to marry him. I said yes, of course." Reggie sighed. "And then he kissed me."

"I've heard that some men aren't very skilled at that," said Colin, a gentle joke that made Reggie laugh despite her memories.

"No, he was fine—or he wasn't so bad that I noticed. I hadn't kissed anyone before. I wouldn't say that was the problem, exactly, but the rest probably wouldn't have happened if I'd had more experience. It rather overwhelmed me, you see."

"*Not* bad, then," Colin said. He didn't feel jealous, which was a relief. Possessiveness, particularly over a kiss years in the past, was the last thing Reggie needed. "I take it the problem was with your abilities?"

Reggie nodded, relishing, even now, the feel of his skin beneath her cheek. "I thought I was good at putting up barriers, but I didn't know how much more effort it would take. And Jack didn't control his thoughts as much as you do. Or he wasn't as single-minded." She managed a grin. "Don't tell me which. I'd prefer to flatter myself."

Colin tweaked her ear. "I'll just say, then, that I'm a fair hand at living in the moment. And that you furnish some very easy moments to live in."

"Thank you," she said and then sobered. "I saw some of his memories. I've never been sure why I see what I see, but sometimes there's a connection. There might have been this time. He was kissing me, he'd just proposed, and so he thought of, well"—she searched through the terms she knew, decided against both vulgarity and sentimentality, and went with the clinical—"sex. Only he was remembering it. With one of his housemaids."

When Colin didn't respond, she would have known what he was thinking even without her power. He was trying to find a diplomatic manner to phrase certain home truths that he was surprised she didn't know.

Before he could embarrass them both, Reggie flicked her fingers outward, dismissively, and went on. "Oh, I know men do that sort of thing. I had guessed, even then. Maybe it would have upset me without everything else, but that wasn't all. He wasn't remembering the act. That had been months ago. She'd come to him a fortnight before that party, though, and told him she was in trouble."

"Like I said," she went on, "I'd guessed about that sort of thing even then. And I'd overheard bits, either physically or not. I knew nobody could expect him to marry her, and I don't think she was even asking for that—she was just hoping he'd provide for her and the child. I don't know how much. I know he was angry at her, angry that she'd even dared bring the matter up with him. He talked about impertinence and he said he doubted it was even his, that she'd likely opened her legs for everyone from the butler to the boot boy. And he had her turned out. Without money, without even a character."

"What happened then?" Colin asked. His hand had stopped moving in the course of Reggie's story, and his arms were very tight around her.

Within the circle of their warmth, she shrugged. "I

don't know. The workhouse—the streets—dying in some back alley when she tried to get herself out of the fix she was in. The world doesn't much like women in her situation. Jack didn't care—he was just relieved she hadn't shown up again, and thinking about how she might have spoiled everything if he hadn't taken care of her."

Colin kissed the top of her head. "I mean," he said, "what happened to you?"

"Oh. I didn't scream, I don't think—nobody came out to get us, so I must not have—but I slapped him. And then I started talking about it: how could he have been so heartless, didn't he care about the child at all, plenty of melodramatic claptrap," she said and forced another laugh from her throat. "Stupid too. I'd mostly gotten past the babbling-everything-I-saw stage when I was thirteen. There's just been that one time. And with you, I suppose."

"Dragons," said Colin, "are also quite startling. Though I hope not as appalling."

"No. Not at all." Reggie drew a deep breath and went on. "Jack went absolutely white, as I suppose one would rather expect, asked what kind of a creature I was, and fled the scene. Good riddance, really."

"I was going to say something of the sort myself," said Colin. "But it must have been hard on you at the time."

"The scandal was. Young girls acting freakishly are always good for entertainment, and God knows the country needs that. I couldn't explain my side of things at all, which probably made everything better for the gossips. The truth is never nearly as fun as speculation. Jack didn't make up any stories to ruin my good name. He didn't have to."

"And your family?"

"I told Aunt Claire that night, when she asked. Not about my powers—that was a bit too far—but that I'd heard the story." Reggie laughed again, although there was little humor in it even to her own ears. "She couldn't deny it, not entirely—the girl in question *had* been turned off in what she called 'a disgraceful state'—but she said that one couldn't believe servants. And after all," Reggie went on, falling into an imitation of Aunt Claire's calm, sweet, poisonously reasonable tones, "even if it was true, it was nothing to get upset about. The girl was obviously no better than she should be. She was just sorry that I'd had to hear about such unpleasantness."

"It's not an uncommon way to think."

"I know," said Reggie. "She touched my hand when she was trying to comfort me. She believed everything she said. She was sure her friends did too—everyone worth knowing. *That's* mostly why I stopped bothering with society. I could have lived with the scandal, but if everyone thought like my aunt did, then following the rules and marrying well and all of that…it didn't seem worth the effort anymore. It had always been a trial, anyhow."

Now that most of the story was out, it was better to get the rest over with before Colin could ask any more questions. "I didn't tell my parents. I didn't want to know how they'd react—or what they'd think—and they've always known just enough of my power to ignore it. I liked things that way. Edmund wanted to blacken everyone's eye when he found out, but I was back in London by then. Thank God."

"I'm surprised you came back," said Colin.

"I do love my parents. And this visit was the first time the old business has ever come up quite so... vividly." She chuckled, shaking her head. "Ghosts and ghosts."

"Aye," said Colin. "The past clings, no matter how much we'd like to shake it off. I've regretted that at times myself. In some ways, the world never moves quite fast enough."

"Imagine how we feel," said Reggie.

Thirty-five

"BLOODY ROTTEN LUCK ABOUT THE HORSES," SAID Edmund, glancing over his shoulder for one last glare in the direction of the forest. "Quincy was a top-notch jumper too."

Hobb had found the bay the night before, after the doctor had come for Reggie and the household had mostly settled down. The horse had been in such condition that the gamekeeper had been forced to put him down. From what few tracks Colin, Edmund, and his father had been able to make out that day, one of the other horses had fled for the road, where its hoofprints had vanished into the general mass of traffic. Some farmer's son a few miles off might have had a nice surprise.

Three hours of searching had shown no sign of the third horse. Either it had gone through thick enough undergrowth to hide its tracks, or the three men had simply been looking in the wrong places. Either way, the clouds overhead were closing in, and none of them had wanted to risk being in the forest during a storm. Janet Morgan might have temporarily expended all of her power in the previous day's attack, but one didn't gamble on lightning. By mutual agreement, they'd started back toward the house, Edmund looking uncommonly glum until he'd finally spoken.

Mr. Talbot-Jones shook his head. "Rotten luck about your sister, I should say, Edmund," he chided his son, but his voice was mild and even amused, as if he knew what Edmund's reply was going to be.

Sure enough, Edmund grinned sheepishly. "Oh, but Reggie's got a skull like a block of marble. I could've told you that when I was ten. And she *is* fine now, you know—though I'm not sure it was a good idea to leave her in La Heselton's capable hands."

"Miss Heselton *is* a very skilled nurse," said Mr. Talbot-Jones, though Edmund's warning glance stopped him from pressing further.

"Yes, that's what I mean," Edmund went on quickly. "It'll deprive the local populace of a great force for good if Reggie buries an egg spoon in the back of Miss Heselton's neck."

Almost hidden by his beard, Mr. Jones's mouth twitched at the corners. "I doubt we have to worry much about that."

"*You* weren't around the nursery when she was getting over measles," said Edmund, shaking his head. "This fortnight's been a seaside holiday in comparison."

"She may have learned some patience over the years," said Colin. He flattered himself, too, that maybe his visit the night before had left Reggie less restless than she might have been otherwise. She'd been half dozing when he'd slipped out, her only response a sleepy complaint at losing the warmth of his body and an equally incoherent assent when he'd said he didn't want to drive anyone into hysterics in the morning.

He hoped he hadn't set her recovery back. She'd certainly seemed confident at the time, not to mention enthusiastic, and he trusted her judgment—but he'd been vastly relieved when Dr. Brant reported in that morning and said that she was progressing nicely.

"Stranger things have happened," said Edmund, though he didn't sound convinced, and he looked at Colin for a moment longer than necessary. He cleared his throat. "Any more progress on that translation?"

"Some," said Colin. He bent and picked up a branch that had fallen across the path, then tossed it into the undergrowth. "Mostly, it only confirms what Mrs. Jones said. The brother was a spoiled wastrel—at least, Janet thought as much—and the girl he chose was common. And," he added, tightening his lips, "the bargains she made would have called for human blood."

"She truly was a witch, then," said Mr. Talbot-Jones. "I'd thought that had all been hysteria and superstition—and the odd misunderstanding."

"It was, mostly," said Colin. He'd been too young to see most of the trials for himself, but he'd heard plenty from his family. Mortal mobs could be dangerous even to them, if they were unprepared and outnumbered. "Old women with bad luck. Young women who caught the wrong eye. That was lucky for the witch finders—something like Janet Morgan could have cut a bloody swath through most of them, and she was a rank amateur."

Crows called to each other overhead, finding roosts before the storm hit. Colin realized that the other two were staring at him. He shrugged. "My brother's interested in history," he said, which was true enough. "It rubs off now and again."

"Helpful in situations like these, perhaps," said Mr. Talbot-Jones, Britishly polite even if he didn't believe a word of Colin's explanation. "Though hardly cheerful, considering that we—fairly rank amateurs ourselves—have her on our hands now."

"Oh, chin up, Pater," said Edmund. "Her sister very likely managed to put her down, since she vanished about when Janet stopped causing trouble in this life, and she was one woman. And we've got more assets than the old Puritans dreamed of," he added, with another significant glance toward Colin.

"Oh?"

"Modern thinking, for one," Colin put in, seeing that Edmund hadn't expected his father to ask for specifics. "It's the age of reason and discovery. I'm sure human innovation can come to our aid here."

"Hmm," said Mr. Talbot-Jones. They stepped out of the last clump of trees and began to head up a much broader and better-rolled path. "I wish I were as optimistic as you young men—and I hope you're right."

"So do we," said Edmund. "Colin, could I have a word back at the house?"

"I'll go talk to Boone about the horses," said Mr. Talbot-Jones, politely stepping away. He didn't ask what the prospective word would be about, because one didn't, and neither did Colin, because he already knew.

◆

The two of them went into the study, where Edmund sat down on the couch, stood up, poured two large brandies, and sat back down, while Colin seated himself in a chair, leaned back with his drink, and waited.

None of this was entirely new. Few mortals had learned his real identity, but there *had* been those few. Whether they'd been fawning, hostile, or simply curious, he knew roughly what steps to take. Still, he was glad of the brandy.

Edmund probably was, too, as he polished off half the glass with a swiftness that would have made a connoisseur wince. He set the glass on a nearby table and leaned forward, elbows on his knees, to look at Colin. "Yesterday," he finally said. "With the horses."

"Yes?"

"First off, we're all very much obliged, you know," Edmund said stiffly. "I'm sure Reggie will tell you herself, once she's feeling more the thing."

"I'm sure," said Colin, waving a hand negligently. The brandy sloshed against the sides of the glass. He watched it, wondering momentarily how much gratitude had played a part in Reggie's invitation the night before.

Surely not—he didn't have her powers, but he could tell genuine female pleasure from an act, generally speaking. She'd come to him before too, or at least she'd been seemingly enthusiastic when he'd taken her in the hayloft.

He looked over at Edmund. "I'm glad I was able to be of assistance," he said to move the conversation along.

"Yes. Well. Jolly good." Edmund squared his shoulders. "Look here, there's no delicate way to put this. What exactly *are* you?"

Pretending innocence was pointless, particularly with everything that had happened since Colin's arrival. He *might* have been able to explain the whole thing away—the excitement of the moment, a trick of the light, even one of the ghost's illusions. He could have kept Edmund from trusting his own perceptions. He'd done it before, with other men.

The thought made him feel grimy.

"Dragon," said Colin, and he took a drink. "Partly, at least."

"I—well, I'd thought *something* serpentine, at least—I suppose it stands to—" Edmund shook his head, cut off the flow of words, and then blinked at Colin. "*What?*"

So Colin explained. Leaving out specific names and details, he told Edmund as much as he knew of his history and his nature, keeping his voice matter-of-fact and his face composed. As he went on, the other man went from stunned disbelief to confused acceptance, which Colin supposed was the best he could expect under the circumstances.

Reggie had been much easier, but Reggie was one in a million.

"I'd transform here," Colin said, winding his discourse up, "but I'd make rather a mess of the place."

"I'd rather not answer to Mater for that, thank you," said Edmund with a trace of his old humor, "and neither would you, dragon or not."

"No, not at all," Colin replied. "I like to think I was properly brought up."

Edmund leaned his head back and closed his eyes. "A devil of a lot makes more sense now," he admitted, "and I can't really blame you for keeping mum, considering. It does upset one's notions of the world, though. Even for me, and I'm used to a bit of strangeness now and again."

"So I'd imagine," said Colin, thinking of the crowds they'd moved in and then of Reggie.

As if he had his sister's power to read thoughts, Edmund opened his eyes, looked straight at Colin, and asked, "I'm not the first one in this family to know, am I?"

"No," said Colin. "Though Reggie found out rather by accident."

"She would, poor girl."

Changing topics before Edmund could ask about the exact circumstances of the accident, Colin said, "She tells me you know about her gift."

"Oh, yes. Though I'd not call it a gift"—Edmund made a face—"except of the sort one gets from a tasteless great-aunt. I suppose she could make quite a go of detective work, if she was a chap. Or if the parents wouldn't keel over at the thought of it. Otherwise, I don't see much use in it. Life's mostly trying *not* to know too much about others."

Colin laughed. "Here and now, aye."

"I'm glad she does know," said Edmund. "I'd have wanted you to tell her, otherwise."

"Oh?" asked Colin, lifting his eyebrows and trying to sound casual.

Edmund shook his head. "It won't do, that face. Reggie may think I'm an idiot about women, and she might be right—but I'm not about her. Or you, I think." Although his posture didn't change, his eyes narrowed, and he spoke with a quiet and complete seriousness. "I don't inquire much into her personal life and she doesn't into mine—and I know neither of us runs with a very polite crowd—but she *is* my sister, Colin. I'd be obliged if you kept that in mind."

"I've no intention," Colin said, "of treating her shabbily."

"I didn't think you did," Edmund said, and his face eased back into a smile, "but one does like to drop the word, you know. Reggie's a sensible girl. She's not the sort to expect anything grand just because a chap has a few dances with her. Just don't offer more than you want to give her. She's done a lot for me. I won't see her hurt and take it lightly."

Despite the smile, the warning in Edmund's voice might have suggested that he'd forgotten what Colin had just told him and what he'd seen the day before. Looking into his friend's face, though, Colin thought Edmund knew perfectly well who and what he was threatening.

Thirty-six

Even the cloudy day seemed bright and lovely. The air was warm and smelled of roses and fresh-cut grass, while overhead, the birds trilled beautifully.

Being finally allowed out of bed was a wonderful lift to one's outlook. Walking about outdoors, without any trace of a headache, and with the prospect of tea with cream and buns after a day of broth and toast, was enough to make one start writing sickening poetry for women's magazines and burbling at animals and small children.

"I should probably hit my head more often," Reggie therefore said in response to Miss Browne's query as she sat down at the table. "Perspective and all that."

"Or," said Mater, pouring tea with a slight smile, "you *could* simply try and learn from the experience, Regina. It would be so much easier on everyone."

"Would if I could as I'd love to oblige you," Reggie said cheerfully, "but it doesn't seem very likely. Human nature. And me."

Perspective wasn't the only source of her good

mood, either, but she didn't think she could get away with mentioning the other two contributions in company, even if the only man around was the footman. One element was that, by dint of injury, she could get away with wearing a tea gown with no corsets underneath and leaving her hair in a loose braid. She'd have to change for dinner, of course, but a few more hours of liberty were nothing to sneeze at.

The other factor was Colin.

He wasn't around—Mater would have absolutely drawn the line at her mode of dress then—but he'd left what one might call a vivid impression on Reggie's memory. On her linen too. When she'd woken up in the morning, her pillowcase still smelled like him. The aroma would doubtless be gone by evening, but right then it had made her whole body tingle in an utterly ludicrous, thoroughly enjoyable way.

She realized that Miss Heselton hadn't responded to her comment as Reggie would have expected—prating something about human nature and the need to strive ever upward—and hadn't, in fact, said anything at all. She was spreading butter on a scone, calm and silent.

Really, if the day got any better, it was going to make Reggie nervous.

"Awfully nice of you," she said to Miss Heselton, feeling that she owed a debt to both the woman and the universe at large, "to take care of the lot of us like this. I know you didn't come up here to dash between two sickbeds at once."

"It's quite all right," said Miss Heselton. She looked up and smiled sweetly. "Really, I find it quite fulfilling. Taking care of others gratifies something essentially tender and feminine in a woman. And it's such good preparation for family life."

Metaphysically, hearing that little speech was reassuring. Reggie wasn't dreaming. Heselton hadn't been possessed by anything, nor was she under a spell. On a more mundane level, Reggie reached for the jam, made a noncommittal noise, and exercised her own restraint. Heselton had nursed her competently and well—none of the fluttering Reggie had dreaded— and didn't the Arabs put a flaw in every carpet so that they wouldn't offend God with their presumption?

"Although," Mater said, "it's to be hoped that Regina didn't give you nearly as much trouble as when she was younger. We never had much doubt that she'd come through illness, as a girl," she said to the table, shaking her head and smiling affectionately at Reggie, "but we often wondered whether the household would survive."

"Slander," said Reggie, after swallowing a bite of muffin. "Slander and calumny. I shall file a suit directly. And Edmund was a hundred times worse. *I* didn't have friends smuggle reptiles into my room."

These days, the reptiles in her bed did their own smuggling. Reggie tried to stifle a laugh when she thought of that and nearly choked on her tea as a result.

"Are you all right?" Miss Heselton asked. "If you're feeling unwell—"

"She'll be fine," Mater said as Reggie finished her coughing fit. "Too easily amused, but fine. I recognize that expression."

"I've always wondered what it would be like to have a brother," said Miss Browne, looking rather wistfully back and forth between Reggie and Miss Heselton. "Although in your case, Reggie, it seems life-threatening at times."

"Only the memories," said Reggie, "and only when I'm eating. And I suppose it depends on the brother. Edmund's too dashed fond of leaving London to shoot things for months on end, but he makes for jolly good company when he's in town, and his clubs give good suppers generally."

Miss Browne smiled. "A most useful quality in a male relation. You see a great deal of each other, I'd imagine, if you both live in town."

"Oh, somewhat," said Reggie. "He likes most of my friends and I like most of his, which helps tremendously."

She didn't watch for Miss Heselton's reaction. She did think of Louisa, who, despite the exterior, was more of a romantic than Edmund was thinking, and rather fond of men; of Cora, who was the latter but not the former; of the small parade of feminine faces that made up most of her friends in London. The thought, and its necessity, made her weary despite her good cheer.

Edmund had been tired when he brought up the idea—not physically so, but worn out with Pater, with secrecy, with the parade of hopeful young ladies, of whom Miss Heselton was but the most recent and irritating. Marriage to one of Reggie's friends, or to another worldly and understanding woman, would at least remove the first and the last thorn from his side, and perhaps would make concealment easier. Marriage and children was the proper form of things too, and it certainly was his duty to Pater, and many would say to God.

It just felt so much like giving up. She couldn't come up with a good reason why.

Best not to think too much, she decided. It was probably against doctor's orders anyhow. And Mater was looking at her expectantly, so she'd probably missed something.

"Sorry? Head wound, you know."

"I asked," Mater said, "if you'd seen Mr. MacAlasdair in London before—with Edmund's friends, I mean."

"I might have"—although Reggie thought she'd have remembered any man who'd looked like Colin— "but not to speak to. I'd have said something when you introduced us, otherwise," she added, by way of reminding her mother that she wasn't a complete barbarian. "Edmund had mentioned him a few times. That's all."

"Ah," said Mrs. Talbot-Jones. "For such an unusual young man, he's managed to stay out of the public eye. It's rather surprising. I had thought perhaps your father and I simply didn't hear very much about London life, but if you hadn't heard much more about him…" She trailed off, glancing toward Miss Browne as well.

The medium shook her head. "Then again," she said, "this is a rather unusual situation. Most circumstances don't lend themselves to revealing—or discussing—the sort of powers with which we've been dealing here."

"True," said Mater, smiling. "Demons and ghosts

weren't at all polite conversation when we were in London."

"Almost as bad as politics," said Reggie. That took them onto the subject of a friend of Miss Heselton's whose brother was running for a district seat, and thence onward, and a stranger to the Talbot-Jones household could have thought the whole exchange only a commonplace interlude in the conversation.

Twenty-seven years had taught Reggie better.

When they left the table, she fell back under the pretext of wanting a word with her mother about the menus for that night. Mater agreed with reluctance—the kitchen, like the gardens, was a topic generally not open to discussion—and seemed, by comparison, pleased when Reggie said, "You must have known *enough* about Mr. MacAlasdair to let Edmund bring him, especially when you had guests already."

"Try to sound a little more like a lady in your insinuations, Regina dear," Mater said, examining a late-blooming yellow rose, "and a little less like a Scotland Yard constable."

"I think they're inspectors, Mater."

"I'm sure I wouldn't know. Do you think this bud will ever open? I begin to despair."

"So do I," said Reggie dryly. "If you're worried about Mr. MacAlasdair, you should probably say so. And why. It's probably best not to bottle things up with ghosts about."

"I'm not worried at all," said Mater, turning an apparently sincere smile on Reggie. "I'd simply prefer to know more about the gentleman and his family—although Edmund does say they're respectable enough. An old Scottish line, and his brother's a lord. But I'm sure you knew that already."

"Being Scottish is obvious," said Reggie, blinking, "and you introduced him as 'the Honorable,' so I could guess the bit about his brother. I'd worked out that his family was old too," she added as a diplomatic truth.

"I thought so. I—I have always been glad, Regina," Mater said, looking back at the rose and then swiftly at Reggie's face, "that you're such an…extraordinarily good judge of character. You remind me very much of my father that way."

"Oh?" Mentions of Reggie's grandfather had been few and far between, so she eagerly discarded one form of curiosity in favor of the other. "How so?"

"He was very kind, but I don't believe that anyone ever took advantage of him. Certainly not anyone he spent any length of time around." Mater patted Reggie on the arm and smiled. "So I'll be very modern and not ask any more questions about Mr. MacAlasdair. I'm certain that he'll answer any that really matter before very long."

Her meaning broke upon Reggie like the first rays of sun when one had spent the night before surrounded by music and suspiciously green drinks.

Mater was talking about marriage. Whatever she'd noticed, whatever she'd worked out, Mater *expected* marriage, or at least expected Colin to propose. He, Reggie was damned sure, had no idea of doing any such thing.

She would have put a hand out to steady herself, but the only objects nearby were Mater herself and the rosebush, thick with thorns.

How bloody appropriate.

Thirty-seven

THIS TIME, REGGIE CAUGHT HIM BY SURPRISE.

More precisely, she climbed up to his balcony again and knocked at his window while he was trying to translate another page of Janet's diary. Colin snapped his head around and saw a white human form. He was on his feet in an instant, knocking the chair over and then kicking it out of the way, feeling the energy of transformation begin to crackle along his bones.

Then he saw Reggie's face.

When he opened the door to the balcony, any impulse to leave human form had subsided, but his heart was still pounding away in his throat. He was leaning against the balcony in an outwardly casual pose, but Reggie nonetheless looked back at him with her dark eyes wide. "Maybe I shouldn't surprise you, in the future," she said.

"Not in this house," said Colin. "I'm a terribly placid chap under most circumstances, I assure you."

"Ha," said Reggie, and she stepped inside at his gesture of invitation.

She was dressed as she'd been the first time they'd

met: Edmund's old clothes, or a groom's, with her hair braided and hanging down her back. The breeches still outlined the curve of her rear and the length of her muscular legs admirably. Through the thin shirt, Colin could see that her nipples had tightened to dark rose points.

He'd had worse surprises in his life.

Looking at her, and remembering the night before, transmuted alarm to lust within a matter of seconds. He saw the same energy flicker in Reggie's face as her gaze lingered on the open neck of his dressing gown and the expanse of chest thus displayed, then dropped to where his change of mood was beginning to make itself clear. She didn't come to him, though. She stayed standing against the window, hands thrust into her pockets.

"Have a seat?" Colin asked, picking up the fallen chair. "I think it's still in one piece."

"No, thank you." She glanced over her shoulder, then back at him. She smiled, but it was thin and nervous. For the first time since the hayloft, Colin felt the distance between them as a deliberate thing and longed, with an almost physical force, to close it.

He tried humor first. "Most people manage these affairs with a discreet note. Not by climbing trees with a day-old head wound," he added, giving voice to the other subject of his concern.

Predictably, Reggie waved that off. "I'm fine. I promise. I didn't want to expose you—" She bit her lower lip and sighed. "People might notice. And that wasn't my—although you—it wasn't like I—oh, *hell*."

Red-faced, she slumped and studied her feet.

"My reputation's survived more than a bit of gossip," Colin said, trying to be soothing without patronizing her. "And I've heard much worse scandal than anything that's happened here. Whatever you have to tell me canna' be as bad as all that, Reggie."

The hands in her pockets turned into fists. She straightened her shoulders and looked up with a clenched jaw. "They think you're going to propose to me," she said in a flat voice. "Mater does, at least."

"Ah," said Colin. Evidently it was the hour for surprises, although this one shouldn't have come as that much of a shock. He could already hear Judith making one of her half-amused speeches and using the word "reckless" about ten times, as if she'd been any better at his age.

Reggie's eyes held his. "I came to warn you about that. And to say you don't have to. Regardless." She cleared her throat. "I told you there was no reason to make more of—of whatever this was—and you never led me down any garden path. My reputation wasn't any prize before, and I stopped caring long ago."

She swallowed, and Colin saw the strung-wire tension of her throat, her shoulders. He wondered what she was thinking: worry over her parents, and how deep their disappointment might go this time; dread of being trapped in a marriage she'd never chosen; or simple embarrassment at her own recklessness? Her face wasn't calm, but the anxiety there could have been any or all of the three.

"I don't *think* they know about anything we've done," Reggie went on. "Or, if they suspect, they don't have any real grounds for it. If you start ignoring me, and we're not alone together after this, it should all blow over. They'll probably assume you heard about Jack and changed your mind. A man might."

Moonlight from the window flowed over her as she spoke. The edges of her white clothing almost blended into it, while her hair and eyes were deep shadows. Colin listened to her, began to think over their situation—and then, as he often did, spoke on the impulse which immediately arose.

"Or I *could* ask for your hand. It might be an unexpectedly fortunate circumstance."

Colin hadn't had a mirror at hand when Reggie had knocked at his window, but he still thought her expression now was very like what his had been. Her mouth opened. She started to say something, or at least a sound came from her throat. She closed her mouth, closed her eyes, and took a deep breath.

"You're not serious," she said.

"Rarely," said Colin, "but in this case, yes. Or no. Yes, I am serious, and no, you're wrong." He pretended to frown at her. "You could make this easier."

"Both etiquette and fairy tales say otherwise," said Reggie, her lips turning up at the corners.

"Aye, well," said Colin, "I warn you, a glass mountain isn't likely to give me much of a challenge. And I won't slay a dragon for you, although there are a few cousins you could persuade me to drop in a river."

Reggie laughed. "I think I could manage that without marriage," she said, and then the laughter turned incredulous. "We haven't known each other more than a fortnight."

"Many quite happy couples had less introduction. And we've spent more real time together than most do," he added, thinking of the patterned steps of courtship, the chaperoned hour in the parlor, and the odd few dances at large parties. "I'm well able to support a wife, by the way, even without my family's money."

"I hadn't thought of that," said Reggie. "I've got an independence. Though it'd set my parents' mind at ease, I should think, and Pater might stop hounding Edmund. But"—she frowned at Colin—"what would *you* gain from the arrangement? You've already gotten me into bed. We could probably keep on as we are once I'm back in London, if that was any consideration. People do. What good would I be to you as a wife?"

He hadn't expected that. He hadn't had time to expect *anything*, but the possibility of marriage had occurred, both to Colin and to those around him, a few times in his life. Vicarious experience, too, had given him an idea of how women normally responded to proposals. The man sometimes had to argue his own case, but he'd never heard of anyone having to argue the woman's.

Yet Reggie had asked. Nothing about the set of her chin or the flash in her eyes suggested that the request had come from modesty, false or real.

"I wouldn't have to sneak into your room, for one thing," Colin began. It wasn't the most courtly of opening arguments, but it was the most obvious, particularly when the moonlight was practically shining through her clothes. He went on, as brisk and businesslike as the situation permitted. "I do like a companion when I travel, if I can find the right sort. You know about me, you know about magic, and your power's useful. You're good company too: bright, funny, not given to fainting or tantrums."

Colin stopped himself. If he went on listing Reggie's good qualities, he'd sound idiotic and she'd grow skeptical—more skeptical than she was already. He cleared his throat. "And I really *should* marry. It'll keep some of the more predatory sorts away, and it's not as though the line's any too populated as is, even with Stephen breeding away."

"Ah," said Reggie. She thought about his arguments, chewing on her lip lightly. "I don't know if I want children," she finally said. "I thought I did, when I was younger, but—it hasn't seemed like a possibility for years. I don't know how I'd feel. And I damned well don't know that I want to risk my life carrying them, or not more than any woman does already. Even if I could double or triple the length of my life in the bargain."

I don't know that I'd want you to. Colin closed his mouth over the words. They'd sound absurd, when he'd just mentioned his reproductive duties. But an image had flashed in his head as Reggie spoke—of her mobile, cheerful face still and gray-pale in death—and it had felt like lead in his heart.

During Mina's pregnancy, Stephen had lost three stone, and the walls at Loch Arach still bore the imprint of his fists. But Stephen had been and still was in love, whereas Colin—wasn't sure what he felt. It wasn't anything like his first dogged romances had been. That was a sign in itself.

Reggie was watching him; he had been silent for too long. Colin put aside his confusion for the moment and focused on facts. "Medicine's going forward all the time," he said, as he had when they'd been walking the lanes, "and magic does likewise—or should. We'll find a way to lessen the risk. And if we don't, or you'd rather not, it's not the end of the world."

"Easy for you to say." Reggie smiled again, but thinly. "If you're unhappy with me, you can always wait a few decades. No time at all, hmm?"

"No," said Colin roughly. That picture, of death in its natural time, wasn't as bad as the first image had been, but he still shoved it away. "I mean, I hadn't intended any inequality." Stepping forward, he took her shoulders in his hands. "If you're unhappy wi' me, I'll disappear for a while. I'll have to do it anyhow, in the course of things. You'd have money, and I'd not interfere with your life."

"Very neat," said Reggie, and she didn't sound entirely happy. "How do I know you'd do that? Lots of men forget their word when they're angry—or think they know best—and I couldn't do a bloody thing to make you keep it."

She didn't pull away, though, which gave Colin hope.

"There are spells. *Geasa*. And you could make allies of your own."

"Who I'd meet through you," Reggie said, but her voice warmed, and she chuckled. "Not too much worse than it'd be with any other man, though, the courts being what they are. Marriage is always rather a leap into the abyss for a woman."

"For anyone," Colin said. "Though I'll admit your point. Bonds...well, they *bind*, to be dreadfully obvious about it. Takes a bit of nerve to hold out your hands that way."

Reggie's eyebrows went up, and a sudden smile flashed in the moonlight. "Colin MacAlasdair," she said, "are you *daring* me to marry you?"

"Of course," he said, though he hadn't thought of it before.

Her laughter rippled through the darkness. "Well, God knows I'm not much for backing down," she said.

"Is that a yes?" He tried to sound casual, but his throat was tight.

"Provisionally. Don't talk to Pater until we've wound this mess up," she said with a vague gesture at the house around her. "I don't want to distract him, and I don't want to tempt fate. And I want a few days in case I figure out another objection."

"I'll have to remember not to eat peas with my knife," said Colin. For the first time, he felt in human form as he did the moment before flight: muscles tensed and ready, preparing for a great effort, anticipating a greater thrill.

"I'll see if I can find a glass mountain," said Reggie. "And now, since we've worked that out, I think we can stop worrying about scandal."

She stepped forward, wound her arms around his neck, and kissed him.

Thirty-eight

KISSING COLIN, REGGIE COULD ALMOST HAVE FORGOT-
ten everything else: the ghosts, Edmund and Miss
Heselton, her parents' expectations, and even her
sudden engagement to a man who wasn't entirely
human. He'd said he was good at living in the
moment. In his embrace, with his mouth hot on hers
and his hands cupping her backside, Reggie wasn't bad
at it herself.

It helped that she could feel his desire—pressed
rigid against her stomach and also as a constant, rising
pulse in the back of her mind, echoing her own
longing. When she nipped gently at his lower lip, he
shuddered. When she kissed the hollow of his neck,
he sucked in a breath, and Reggie shared the spark of
lust that leaped within him each time.

She thought he'd been telling the truth about his
reasons for proposing. She couldn't have made herself
accept otherwise—the idea of marriage to Colin had
sent a stupidly girlish tingle of excitement through
her, but it had been, and still was, terrifying. She
wouldn't try and touch his mind more deeply, to find

out if he truly thought she'd be more than a pretty girl who'd needed a favor at a convenient time. Her ethics forbade it. Her pride forbade asking more than she already had.

Touching Colin, kissing him, she could be certain of his reaction. She didn't come to the table entirely empty-handed.

As he stroked her breasts, she thought of the previous evening: of what he'd done and what he'd said, of what she'd offered at the time. Reggie caught her breath and stepped back, taking hold of Colin's hand as he reached for her.

Caught off guard, he tilted his head to the side and regarded her, puzzled. Reggie smiled at him. "Don't move," she said and carefully put his hand back at his side.

Oh, he liked that. Reggie wasn't touching him anymore, but she saw the way his whole body went rigid when she spoke and his pupils widened, almost eclipsing the silver-blue of his eyes. "Your servant, madam," he said thickly, not entirely joking.

She began kissing him again, slowly and lightly, but without the gentleness he'd shown her. Every twitch of his body, every swallowed oath made her smile against his neck. She didn't know how good his control was, but the idea of testing it made her own heart race. So did being pressed up against him. She'd thought leaving her shirt on would keep her own desires in check. Instead, it was one more source of friction, tormenting her breasts in the best way possible. When she undid the knot of Colin's dressing gown, her hands shook—but she got it open without his help, and if he noticed any unsteadiness about those same hands as she ran them up his chest, he didn't say anything.

Beneath the heavy brocade, his body was slim and firm, his skin pale and silk-smooth except for a small patch of dark hair between his tawny nipples. Reggie knew that the usual metaphor for handsome men was marble statues, but touching him, she thought of some great metal machine: smooth and hard, warm and thrumming with energy just under the surface. She stroked his nipples and grinned again as his hands clenched at his sides, then traced a line down his flat stomach to the waistband of his trousers.

He held very still. Reggie wasn't even completely sure he was breathing.

At first she touched him very softly through his trousers, the barest brush of her fingertips up and down his shaft. Then she slid her palm over his length and squeezed lightly. He made a sound. If it was a word, it was all vowels.

"I take it that's good," she said, because she didn't want to ask. Not here, not like this. She wanted to know, but she wouldn't ask.

"Very good. Too good. You shouldn't—"

"I don't take instruction well," she said, rubbing her hand slowly back and forth. "Ask anyone."

"Don't think I will," he said hoarsely.

Reggie chuckled. "Unless you were going to say I shouldn't stop. Except I have to," she added and started to unfasten his trousers.

Buttons were slightly easier the second time, or maybe just with concentration. She then discovered that no man on earth, mortal or not, looked anything remotely close to dignified with his trousers around his ankles, even if looking at the rest of him did make her sex ache with longing. "I should have seduced you at the ball," she said. "Kilts are probably much more convenient."

"Oh, aye," said Colin, and his smile was full of light. "But you'll get another chance or ten, I promise."

"Good," said Reggie, sincerely. She eyed Colin, trying to put aside lust long enough to work out logistics. "Lie down on the bed," she said finally.

Complying, he reached for her, and Reggie shook her head. "You still don't get to move," she said, grinning at him. "That was just a temporary exception."

"Oh?"

Reggie took a long look at him: his lean body framed by the dark sheets, his organ jutting up, long and proud, against his flat stomach, the look of sheer lust in his silver eyes, and the inviting smile on his lips. "I don't want to kneel tonight," she said and climbed onto the bed beside him.

Evidently, it took Colin a second or two to realize what she'd meant. When Reggie bent her head and ran her tongue down the length of his rod, his groan sounded a trifle surprised. Mentally, Reggie took back her earlier statement. She liked surprising him, she was discovering—at least in certain ways.

The male body presented its own set of surprises and was generally more complicated than the vague stories she'd heard. Supplementing her own sketchy knowledge with her power and the sounds Colin made helped considerably. The first time Reggie closed her lips around his rod, she felt a burst of sensation that made her press her legs together and whimper.

Later, she told herself, and concentrated. It was a pleasant puzzle to solve, this way of pleasing a man. There were angles to try, and experiments involving her tongue and her hand, and a whole assortment of new sensations. Reggie took her time as long as she could, until she found a rhythm that made Colin throw his head back and groan, until she felt from his mind the inescapable desire for *faster* and *more*.

"Reggie," he managed, and she knew it was half a protest, felt him trying to make himself pull away. Then he couldn't. Caught up in the shadow of his climax, she tasted him in her mouth and heard him cry out, and she smiled to herself once again.

"Can I move now?" he asked afterward, opening one eye.

Reggie laughed. "I think you already did. A few times."

"Involuntary. Doesn't count. Can I touch you, or would you like me to beg? I never did get down on one knee," he added, looking down at her thoughtfully.

"Both, sometime," said Reggie, and she stretched herself out beside him. "And yes."

She didn't ask. He didn't wait for her to. With a speed she wouldn't have expected from a man so recently sated—"and then they generally fall asleep and snore dreadfully" had figured in the stories she'd heard—Colin was kissing her, hard and eager, calling all of her own desire to the forefront of her mind. She'd held those impulses in check for what seemed like hours. Now they left her aware of only sensation. As Colin ran his hands down her back and over her derriere, she was already circling her hips against him, desperate for his touch.

Even as preoccupied as Reggie was, she felt quite smug when Colin fumbled with the fastenings on her trousers. "Not as easy from that angle, is it?" she asked in between kisses.

"No' as easy under these circumstances, I should say."

"Hah," said Reggie, except that Colin took her nipple into his mouth then, lashing it with his tongue through the worn linen of her shirt, and it was very difficult to sound skeptical when one was moaning.

Whether sensing Reggie's mood or acting on his own urgency, Colin didn't tease her that night. He jerked her trousers off roughly—Reggie heard a seam rip and didn't care—and then slid one hand between her legs: deft, considerate, but not lingering. He didn't make her ask, not even silently. He gave without prompting, and the motions of his fingers, inside and over her sex, sent Reggie soaring quickly to the peak where she'd brought him only minutes ago.

Reggie had enough composure to sigh at the end instead of screaming, but only just. "I really don't know," she said, floating and giddy in the aftermath, "how people manage this sort of thing most of the time."

"Not sharing a house with their parents, I should think," said Colin, draping an arm around her. "And counting on everyone else to ignore them, or pretend to. At least there's more privacy now than when I was a boy—wooden walls don't block as much sound as you'd hope, and it wasna' as common to have your own room."

"No wonder you know so much," Reggie said, laughing.

"An early education, but not a comprehensive one. I'm not certain any living man has *that*."

"'Nothing new under the sun'?"

"I've never believed that." Colin leaned over and kissed her lightly. "I've not met anyone like you before, for instance."

"You're supposed to flatter a girl before you take her to bed, not after," said Reggie, but she was aware that she was smiling idiotically. She wasn't sure it was a bad development, but it was one she'd have to think about, and her present position didn't really encourage thought. She sat up and reached for her trousers. "And I'd better get back to my own room. We're not free from scandal yet, you know."

Thirty-nine

"I DO WISH WE COULD BRING DOGS," SAID MR. Talbot-Jones, looking around the game trail with a great deal of attention and no certainty at all. "I see the danger after what happened with the horses, of course—but I'd like a better way to track than my own intuition. I don't trust it at all on business like this."

"I see what you mean," said Colin. "I've been thinking something similar myself."

To wit: they were supposed to know whether they were on the right track by the air getting colder or by feelings of unease. The human mind—even a mind that was only part human—was very good at manufacturing sensations for itself, and tracking a murderous ghost would have anyone feeling uneasy right from the start.

He wished that his magical skills could tell him more. The life of the forest was still enough to drown out any trails. They'd started at the point where he, Reggie, and Edmund had lost the horses, on the basis that they must have been getting close to something, but Colin hadn't yet seen any trace of magic.

As he and Mr. Talbot-Jones walked, Colin kept glancing at the sky overhead, looking for signs of impending storms, but none showed. The air was warm and clear, and with any luck, Janet Morgan still couldn't manage such a dramatic attack again—at least not when she'd spent more of her strength controlling the horses.

"Thank God we're not in America," Mr. Talbot-Jones said, as if following Colin's thoughts, "or anywhere else where the local wildlife's larger than a few squirrels."

"There are always hawks," said Colin, giving the sky another look for good measure. He could probably scare a hawk away magically—he could certainly kill it, one way or another, if the situation so demanded—but that required him to be prepared.

"Hawks are intimidating, I'll grant you," said Mr. Talbot-Jones, looking farther down the road, "but mountain lions and grizzly bears outdo them handily."

"Yes," said Colin, grimacing at the thought. A full-grown grizzly bear could have given him a hard time, even in dragon form. One possessed strongly enough to be heedless of its own life and limb could very possibly kill him. He'd heard, in generations before his father's, of dragons who could have made two minutes' work of such a creature, but the world was fallen and his blood was thin and all that. "Count our blessings, eh?"

"I try, even in situations like these. Perhaps particularly in situations like these." Mr. Talbot-Jones sighed into his beard. "Not that I've encountered very many of those in my life. Do you know, I honestly thought myself fairly knowledgeable about the Other Side before all of this unpleasantness." He shook his head. "Hubris, I suppose."

"Human nature, I'd say," said Colin. Thinking, he peered off to the side of the road, trying to make out anything unusual—dead trees or clumps of standing stones. Summoning demons wasn't the sort of thing one did just anywhere, but whatever spot Janet Morgan had picked, he couldn't make it out. "There's a certain comfort in believing that we know everything about this world or the next one. Or our fellow man, for that matter."

He glanced back to see how Mr. Talbot-Jones took that line of philosophy. They'd been wandering the forest for the better part of an hour, and in all that time, Colin had been acutely aware that he was going to be asking the man for his daughter's hand before very many more days had passed.

That interview was *likely* to go well. As Colin himself had said, he had money independent from the MacAlasdair fortunes. Although he was two steps removed from the inheritance now, he was nobility, and of a decent vintage. And there were no current scandals about him in England, Scotland, or even Ireland, where he'd been living for the better part of two decades before Stephen's recent troubles had brought him to London.

Poking around Loch Arach might reveal a few odd rumors, but he didn't think any of the tenants there could complain about him. Mr. Talbot-Jones might not be a magician himself, but he believed—all the more strongly now—so the truth, eventually, might actually go over better than with most mortals.

Then again, it might not. Whatever his openness to new theories, Mr. Talbot-Jones could easily be far less open to his daughter marrying a man who could turn into a whacking great lizard. He might investigate Colin's past thoroughly, even if Colin didn't tell him, and a few of the names and dates that turned up might raise his suspicion. Colin thought he'd done a decent job of covering his tracks, but he hadn't cared, until now, nearly as much as Stephen had said he should.

He hated it when his brother was right.

If her father did object, what then? Reggie might be open to elopement—she was an unconventional girl and might figure that her family would come around later. On the other hand, she'd already weathered one scandal. And she'd only said yes provisionally: hardly Juliet, there. Colin would have liked her better for her sensibility, most of the time, but at the moment it was doing nothing for his case of nerves.

Because he had a case of nerves. Over a mortal. Over, specifically, whether a mortal actually found the prospect of being married to him pleasant, or whether she'd been lured into it by Colin's skills in bed or driven there by desperation and her family, or indeed both. If she changed her mind, or if another obstacle came up, Colin thought he actually might rather fight a bear.

Judith would make fun of him for years if she ever found out. Stephen would just smile knowingly. He could see them both, and the desire to bang their heads together was almost as great as if they'd actually been present.

Perhaps he should just concentrate on the ghost. That was less complicated.

"I don't know what we would have done without Regina here," said Mr. Talbot-Jones, helpfully. "She's a tremendously adaptable girl." When Colin looked over, the other man was paying careful attention to the side of the road. From the tone of his voice, he was just passing remarks—and when Colin didn't respond at first, he continued. "So many of your generation are, of course. You'd almost have to be, with the world changing as much as it has in your lifetime."

Colin had developed considerable self-control, so he was mostly beyond having to bite his cheek against the urge to laugh. Needing to do it now pointed as much to his unease as to the irony of Mr. Talbot-Jones's statement. "That could be," he said, careful to sound serious, "but maybe every generation thinks so about the one coming after."

Mr. Talbot-Jones shook his head. "When I was a boy," he said, "one couldn't get this far into the countryside by train or send a message across the country in minutes. I don't recall ever needing to keep up with as many developments as one does now. Fortunately," he added with a small smile, "I'm old enough to be excused for the most part."

"The trains do make a difference," said Colin, frowning down the length of the trail. The air had turned cooler—but the day was also rapidly moving toward evening. "My brother's estate is still a good fifty miles or so from the nearest station, and even the trains there don't run every day. It's quite a different place from the village here."

"Do you spend much time there?"

Colin shook his head, started to speak, and then held

up a hand. Behind the sound of the birds and squirrels, he could hear a faint trickling noise. "Water?" he asked, gesturing in the general direction of the sound.

Mr. Talbot-Jones shrugged, smiling. "Your hearing is a trifle sharper than mine, I daresay. I can't hear it—but it's likely. There's a creek on the property, and it's supposed to start at a spring somewhere in these woods. I'd always thought that I'd come out and find it one day, when we'd cleared the trails."

"I expect you'll have a chance, once we're finished," said Colin.

"I hope so. It would be a lovely place under normal circumstances." Now he did look at Colin. "And we're always glad of visitors, particularly family—I would very much like to have the forest to show them."

"Ah," said Colin, and he coughed. Reggie had said that her mother harbored expectations, and if Mr. Talbot-Jones hadn't come to his own conclusions, his wife might well have given him marching orders. No bad thing, given Colin's own inclinations—save for Reggie's request. "Yes," he said feebly. "Quite so."

Mr. Talbot-Jones's eyes narrowed, looking much like his daughter's when she was in a wary mood. "I think I should tell you—" he began, when, to Colin's great relief, a familiar voice called out a greeting, and they both turned to see Edmund on the trail just ahead.

"Good God," said Mr. Talbot-Jones. "How did you get here, Edmund? I thought you were taking care of business in the village."

"I was," said Edmund, while Colin mentally kicked

himself for being unobservant. He hadn't even heard the man approaching. "I took another path. They said you'd come out this way. The gamekeeper knows a shortcut."

"Helpful of him," said Colin, concluding that his earlier opinion of Hobb had been neither fair nor charitable. Anyone who sent Edmund out to save him from both the devil and the deep blue sea had certainly earned the right—retroactively, granted—to be suspicious of strange noises in his domain. "Feeling sensitive, I hope. We're at a loss."

"I can probably manage something," said Edmund. He didn't sound as hearty as usual, and though he stood in shadow, his face looked pale. "Colin," he said, "could I have a word?"

"Here?" Colin turned from Edmund to his father and then back, lifting his eyebrows. "Seems inconvenient."

"Are you all right, son?" Mr. Talbot-Jones peered at Edmund, sounding both touchingly worried and annoyingly suspicious. "What's happened?"

"Nothing. Nothing important. But it's urgent."

That combination suggested several possibilities to Colin, none of them pleasant—and none of them anything Edmund would necessarily want to discuss in front of his father. Mr. Talbot-Jones came to the same realization, for after a moment of thought, he sighed. "It's probably time I was heading back, at that," he said and shook his head preemptively as Colin started to speak. "I should fare well enough on my own. I'm going out, after all, not in—and that doesn't seem to cause as many problems."

"If you're certain," Colin began. Edmund made

no such protest. Was he that angry with his father, or simply that engrossed in whatever had sprung up?

Mr. Talbot-Jones nodded briskly. "Completely. Both of you be careful—ghosts aside, the ground is damnably tricky out here, and God knows what sort of obstacles there are, particularly after that storm. I'll see you."

"Back at the house," said Edmund.

"Yes, back at the house," Mr. Talbot-Jones repeated and walked off.

"Good Lord, have things been that bad?" Colin asked once Mr. Talbot-Jones was out of hearing distance. "I can't say I don't sympathize, but I thought he'd given up about the Heselton girl, at least."

"What?" Edmund shook his head. "No. It's not that. Let's keep going. I'll—I'll figure out how to put it along the way."

"Is this about Reggie?" Colin asked.

Again, Edmund looked dumbfounded for a second, as if he'd forgotten he even had a sister. "No. Not about Reggie," he said and started walking.

Colin followed. He of all people could probably stand to exercise a little patience.

Forty

WHATEVER NEWS EDMUND HAD GOTTEN IN THE VIL-
lage, he was in a much better mood walking back
to the house with Reggie than he had been while
brooding over lunch. She didn't ask—even with her
power, there were areas of a man's life that his sister
was much better off not knowing about—but was
simply glad that his mood had improved, even if that
meant he kept teasing her about her auto.

"Only three days until they can send a chap out to
fix the motor?" He whistled. "Modern convenience is
a wonderful thing."

"It is, in the city," said Reggie.

"You might have noticed that we're not."

"For my sins, yes," said Reggie, not entirely
sincerely. Whitehill and environs were very pretty,
with heaps of flowers and birds and things. A week
or two away from London, particularly at this time of
year, was nothing to sneeze at, at least in theory. The
devil, as always, lurked in the details. "If *you* want to
crowd yourself onto a train platform," she said to her
brother, "and then into a compartment with a lot of

rowdy children going back to school or old biddies who don't think women should travel or God knows what else, and be subject to the London and North Western's timetables, you can jolly well have the privilege. Not to mention riding back from the station along with whomever else came down, and having to try and make conversation with strangers before you've had dinner."

Edmund chuckled. "No, I'd *far* rather be shaken to bits, breathe a lot of dust and petrol and God knows what else, and arrive half-blind and nearly deaf—if I don't simply break down by the side of the road."

"That incident hardly counts," Reggie parried, "given how the horses acted up. It's probably a sign that I'm fated to walk everywhere. Can't imagine what I did to deserve *that*."

"Can't you?" Edmund asked, giving her a mock-doubtful look that earned him an elbow in the side.

"Only came down to rescue you from the clutches of a vicar's sister. I suppose that might have offended someone up there," said Reggie, glancing toward the clear blue sky above them.

"Any god who wants me to marry Amelia Heselton would run contrary to all sensible theology."

"Oh, well," said Reggie, laughing despite herself, "she wouldn't be nearly as bad if Pater hadn't egged her on. And—" She hesitated. If Colin couldn't say anything of their tentative agreement, she shouldn't. He could change his mind too. The thought made her insides go startlingly cold. "And you'll be going back to London soon."

"A tactical retreat, I think they call it," said Edmund.

"I just hope it's soon—and it's a pity. The country-side's marvelous. I was hoping I could get some hunting in." He glanced over at Reggie. "Our positions might be better next year."

Was he referring to his possible marriage, or her own? Was he hiding pleasure or resignation? Reggie couldn't tell and didn't have time to ask before the drive ended and deposited them at the front steps of Whitehill, which was, in the early evening, not anywhere near an ideal setting for sensitive conversations.

"For tonight, at least," she said, "you'd best take a brace. It's about time to dress for dinner."

Inside was the usual twilight hush. Downstairs, the kitchen would be buzzing with preparations. Upstairs, Mater and the other ladies would already be getting ready, but the front hall was empty and serene, bars of red-gold light coming through the windows and dancing on the parquet floor. Reggie was starting to ascend the stairs, absently removing her hat, when she heard her father's voice.

"Edmund?"

Although she wasn't the subject, Reggie turned anyhow, and saw her father standing flabbergasted in the doorway to the study. His hands hung limp at his sides, and he stared at Edmund, not believing some part of his senses. Reggie thought of the old saying, "He looked as though he'd seen a ghost," and the chill in her stomach reappeared, much stronger even though nothing was obviously wrong yet.

"Pater?" Edmund sounded puzzled, but not alarmed. "You didn't expect me back earlier, did you?"

"No. No." Mr. Talbot-Jones drew a hand slowly

across his mouth. "I don't see how you can be here at all. Not so quickly." He looked from Edmund to the door outside, then to Reggie. "And where's Mr. MacAlasdair?"

The chill began to radiate out from Reggie's stomach, sending icy tendrils into her veins. "I don't know," she said, speaking slowly and carefully, though she wasn't sure why. It seemed important to form every word correctly. If everyone could understand her, perhaps there would be some innocent, sensible explanation. "Didn't he go out to the forest with you?"

"Why, yes," said Pater, "of course. We walked a good ways too—I was quite surprised when you caught up with us, Edmund. I didn't know we had such a shortcut. Or"—his face, in the shadow of the doorway, almost matched the scattering of gray in his beard—"do we?"

"I wouldn't know," said Edmund, frowning. "I wasn't there. I've been down in the village for the last hour. There are half a dozen people who can say so. What are you talking about?"

Reggie thought of figures at the window: formless, then taking on human shape. She thought of the forest, where Janet Morgan had performed her unspeakable rites, and where she still lay—bound at the center of her power. Reggie had to moisten her lips before she could speak.

"He's talking about a trap," she said, and her voice seemed to echo in the hall.

Both men turned to stare at her. There was surprise in their faces, and horror, but not a trace of disbelief. Was this how prophets had felt in ancient days, delivering messages of doom?

Doom wasn't inevitable. Not yet.

"Where were you?" Reggie asked.

As her father answered, she listened closely, taking in every detail: the turns of the path, the fallen oak they'd passed, the time they'd taken. She listened, but she knew that what she was hearing wasn't completely accurate. Pater meant it to be, but it wasn't. Words got in the way of memory. Sometimes, words twisted it.

While he talked, she was stripping off her gloves. A few buttons popped off and fell to the floor, making little ticking sounds. Reggie dropped the gloves to lie beside them, once she'd managed to undo them, and stepped forward when her father reached the end of what he could say. In the silence, she held out one hand. "Remember where you were. Remember how you got there. And take my hand. Please."

Mr. Talbot-Jones stared back at her. The knowledge in his face had been buried under every conversation they'd had since Reggie's half-wild adolescence. Ghosts were one thing, and it was quite admirable for Russian immigrants and middle-class spinsters to be mediums, but a daughter who could read minds, even in a limited way, was more freak than asset. Because he loved her, he'd pretended not to know, pretended so hard that he'd even convinced himself. Because she loved him, and because her father's reaction was the least of what she could expect from the world, she'd learned to hide.

Now it wasn't just Reggie standing in front of him: it was all the truth he'd denied.

Edmund didn't move. Reggie didn't move, though she felt every breath and every second that passed. Then her father took hold of her hand.

He was old and human, and had none of Colin's training. The memories slamming into her head were barely coherent. Reggie saw the path away from the house, heard Colin's voice as if it was underwater, felt her father's interest in this young man who was so much more than he seemed, who had protected them all on at least one occasion and who had also taken an interest in his daughter. Gratitude and suspicion mingled. Colin was a nice young man who knew magic, but he was also a wealthy young man from an old family, and Pater was just worldly enough to be wary.

She saw and recognized a fallen tree and a patch of bright flowers. She felt her father wondering about Colin's connection to Edmund, and about Edmund himself—felt his sincere belief that Edmund would be happiest with a wife and children, mingled with Pater's own desire that his legacy live on, his fear that his son would be caught at—he wouldn't even think about the possibilities. Reggie wasn't the only one in the family who read newspapers. He'd followed the Wilde trial and thanked God that Edmund wasn't like that, in a talismanic way that was as much wishing as gratitude. He would never let himself know as much.

Pater and Colin stood talking on a section of the path by a stand of aspens. Reggie heard water running in the distance, and in the part of her mind that was still her own, she remembered her dream. It hadn't been just a dream. Some part of her mind had touched Janet's consciousness, a dead horror that still, in its own way, thought and dreamed. She knew that now, and knew that wherever they'd been, they were close.

Then Edmund's shape strolled out of nowhere,

Edmund's shape but not Edmund, and Reggie wanted to scream and throw herself into the memory. Her other hand came up, as if to reach out and drag Colin away, but it was no good. The past was past; she watched him walk off with the lying form, and as her father turned away in memory, she stepped back.

"Regina—" said Pater, stricken.

"I'm all right," she said, though her throat was thick and she didn't know whether she wanted more to cry or to be ill on the floor. Neither was an option. Her mind folded itself around the memories, accepting them as its own. "I can find him. Or I can find where you were."

"He's not a big man," said Edmund, clearing his throat on some remote planet off to the side, "but he'll have left tracks. I'll get my rifle."

"What good will bullets do against a ghost?" Reggie asked.

"Not much against a ghost. A damned lot against whatever poor creatures she sends at us. Wait here. I won't be five minutes."

He strode off, full of purpose and decision. Reggie, who had to wait, turned back to her father. "Thank you," she said, because she didn't know what else to say.

Mr. Talbot-Jones nodded absently and then frowned. "I should go," he said. "Not you."

"No," Reggie said, and her heart squeezed as she spoke the words. "I'm thirty years younger than you are. I'm stronger, and I'm quicker, even in skirts, and my eyes are sharper."

Also, if Colin had to change shape, she at least

wouldn't find it a shock. The other reasons held true, though. She wouldn't have mentioned them to her father's face if they weren't. She wouldn't have even let herself think them if the situation hadn't been dire, just as she'd tried not to notice the gray in his hair or the wrinkles near her mother's eyes.

Everyone hid things from themselves.

"Then for God's sake, take care," said her father, sounding as if he was angry at her. Reggie knew better. "I'll find Hobb and send him with you—"

"After us," said Reggie. To occupy herself, she pinned her hat back on. She suspected that the results were haphazard, but she didn't much care. "We can't wait that long. But send Hobb, and Miss Browne if she'll go, and anyone else you think might help. I've no idea what we're getting into."

"That's hardly reassuring," said her father.

"I know."

"How will we find you?"

"I'll make the trail as obvious as I can. Shouldn't be hard—I'm no great hand in the wilderness."

Edmund stepped through the door again, carrying a rifle. He stopped at Reggie's side, facing their father, and didn't speak.

Mr. Talbot-Jones didn't, either. Instead, he embraced each of them quickly, kissed Reggie on the forehead, and shook Edmund's hand. "We'll be waiting for you," he finally said. "Your mother and I in particular."

Forty-one

SOMETHING WAS BADLY WRONG.

Colin knew it before he'd followed Edmund for more than a few feet, even before they'd turned off the trail and onto what barely qualified as a path, just a line that was a bit less overgrown than the rest of the forest. Before, Edmund had moved with the sturdy grace of a young man used to an active outdoor life. Now there was a jerky, almost mechanical hitch to the way he walked, and when he looked anywhere but straight ahead, he paused for a second first.

"Are you sure you're all right?" Colin asked.

"Yes. Fine." Pause. "Thank you."

"Well—what did you want to talk to me about? Here seems as decent a place as any. No need to go farther along."

Edmund's head turned slowly. His eyes didn't narrow, nor did his lips thin, but Colin saw anger in his face, there for a second and then gone. It was like no anger Edmund had ever showed in the time Colin had known him. He was frank and open, and even his rages had passed quickly. The look he'd given Colin had held a long-lived emotion, and a poisonous one. There was a force to it, too, which made Colin want to step back, ridiculous as the idea was.

Then he shook his head. "I think I found something," he said. "I didn't want my father to see right away. Better if we tell him first. You know how he can be." Edmund smiled. "Old chap."

The stilted imitation of slang left Colin in no doubt. Whatever was speaking, it wasn't Edmund.

Green and gold, the forest blazed up around him. The birdsongs doubled their volume. Colin could hear the burble of water over rocks somewhere in the distance. He could smell pine and acorns, dirt and a small dead creature rotting. He saw every detail of Edmund, down to the faded aura whose edges now looked necrotic. Since his youth, this feeling had been familiar: the razor-sharp edge his senses took before a battle.

And yet there couldn't be a battle, he decided in a few seconds that seemed like hours. Not yet. Yes, he knew that Janet Morgan was speaking, not Edmund. He knew that she was almost certainly trying to lure him into the center of her power, there to kill him. But he also knew that she'd twice proved herself able to control living creatures. He'd thought she couldn't manage humans, but he'd been wrong, and he was paying now. And he didn't know how far that control went, or what happened when she released it.

Without a gun or a knife, without even a *body*, the ancient bitch had managed to take herself a hostage.

"Not the sort of thing a fellow in his sixties should encounter up close?" Colin asked. Any gentleman learned to conceal his feelings. He'd had more than a century to learn. Nobody, except Reggie, could have guessed that he felt anything more than concern for Mr. Talbot-Jones's state of mind. "I should have expected as much. Lead on—and I'll try not to faint when we come to the moment."

Edmund's throat produced a stunted little approximation of a chuckle. He started walking again. Colin followed, glad that the path restricted them to single file, trying to form a plan.

Odds were, Edmund couldn't catch him if he turned and ran—but then Edmund would be out here, *not* on his own. This wasn't good country for cliffs, thank God, but there were plenty of stones and sharp tree branches if Janet wanted to be spiteful, and Edmund might well be carrying a knife. Knives were so bloody *useful* for walking in the wilderness, after all.

Attacking Edmund, either physically or magically, might work better, except that Janet was in his mind. Colin didn't know what damage she could do there. She might only be able to pull the strings of Edmund's body, but it was just as likely that she could shatter his mind, leaving him mad for the rest of his life. Either way—

If I don't break his back at the first jump, he can still fight, he remembered reading, a line in some story he'd half skimmed on a train, *and if he fights—*

He was too fond of Edmund, *much* too fond of Edmund's sister, and he knew too little about what Janet Morgan was now, and what she could do. The only sound option was to play for time. She was, after all, taking him to the place that they'd all been trying to discover. There or on the way, he would almost certainly learn more.

One other consolation: if he knew too little, so did she. Whatever she was in death, Janet Morgan had only been a mortal magician during life. She might have been able to provoke the animals and to target them, but he doubted she'd seen out of the horses' eyes. She would expect Colin to fight like a man and to die like one. Others had made that mistake before.

"You're awfully quiet," said "Edmund," glancing back over his shoulder. He, too, looked and sounded only concerned. "Maybe I should ask if you're sure *you're* all right."

"Oh, yes," said Colin. "Just—bracing myself, you know. For what's likely to be ahead."

Satisfied that Colin wasn't removing a knife from his boot, "Edmund" looked back at the trail ahead of them. "Ah," he said, trying to sound sympathetic and getting about ten degrees off. Colin wanted to shudder and didn't let himself. "That's most likely a good idea."

Under the fake sympathy, Colin heard deep and malicious satisfaction. He walked on, his eyes on the back of his friend's body. With every foot, he hated the creature inside it more and more.

Before long, they reached the water Colin had heard: a stream, narrow but quite deep, running through the forest. The trees were shorter near it, the ground rockier, and here Colin didn't doubt his senses. Around him, the air felt more like March than August, and in his very bones there was a sense of wrongness, of dislocation, that hummed more strongly with every step he took.

He saw the cave before "Edmund" said anything. Ahead of them, a small hill rose, and in its side a hole opened, just barely big enough to admit a man like Edmund. The stream flowed from within, Colin saw, and his stomach made a slow, lazy turn as he realized it. This was where Janet had done her grisliest work, he had no question about that—looked at through mystic sight for a moment, the cave was a pestilent gray-black, like the face of a hanged man—and the stream had been flowing from there for hundreds of years, its water gradually pervading every part of the estate.

No wonder she had such a strong foothold.

"Interesting spot," he said, wiping his brow and catching his breath. He exaggerated both. Janet had seen too much to think he was feeble, but Colin would deny her no opportunity to underestimate him. "If I'd been a witch, I'd have used it."

"Witch," said the thing wearing Edmund's skin, with ill-disguised contempt. "Witches are peasant women fiddling about with herbs. She was more than that."

"As you like," said Colin. He took as close a look at "Edmund" as he dared, but saw nothing of use. The corruption of the place was overpowering, almost blinding. "We might go back to the house and tell the rest," he added.

Mrs. Osbourne might be able to help, or Mr. Heselton—or Colin himself, if he could get out of this miasma.

But Edmund shook his head. "We'd best see what's inside first."

That was the plan, then. Inside the cave Edmund would attack him, or there'd be a few of the local farm dogs, mysteriously "gone missing." Colin's blood would fall on the stone floor, and Janet would gain power from his death.

He hesitated, thinking perhaps it would be better to have the fight here—but just as Janet's power would be stronger in the place where she'd made her dedication, so it would be easier to break at the source. And if she turned to creatures with more natural weaponry than Edmund had, or brought them in on her side, her control might slip.

"All right," he said, "but you'd best go ahead of me. You're more likely to bring the whole place down, and it'd be no good for both of us to be trapped."

To his surprise and suspicion, Edmund just nodded and went forward, slipping into the cave with remarkably little disruption to the rocks. Janet must be very confident, Colin thought. But then, she assumed she'd be fighting a mortal with a few tricks. He still had a good hand.

He thought as much until he stepped into the cave and a wave of screaming force hit him in the middle of the back. Colin stumbled forward, tried to catch himself. He felt the rough wall slashing his palms and fell to his knees in the middle of the cold, dank cavern. Behind him, rocks roared downward, cutting off light.

In an instant, the transformation was on him. Lightning flashed inside his veins as his new form snapped into place, and he let out a roar as loud as the rockfall had been. Darkness was no obstacle to his eyes now, nor would a few piddling rocks keep him imprisoned. Colin snarled and looked around, seeking Edmund—and saw, instead, lines of green-black fire on the floor around him. They blazed their way between a ring of skulls, some animal and some, thankfully the older ones, *not*. Disgusted, Colin swatted at one of them with a huge claw and found himself paralyzed for a moment as waves of agony went through his body. The pain was like nothing he'd felt before. As soon as he could move again, he lashed out at the lines of fire with flame of his own, only to see it fade into the darkness.

He gathered himself in the silence, braced for pain, and then threw himself bodily forward, against one of the lines.

Pain followed. Escape did not. He'd hit a barrier more solid than any steel or stone he'd ever encountered.

Then, from the darkness around him, a figure walked forward. At first it looked like Edmund, but with blue eyes rather than brown. As it kept walking, the features sharpened, the body shrunk, and the hair turned long and pale. Colin recognized Janet Morgan from her portrait, but the resemblance wasn't complete, and not just because of age, or because this version of Janet was wearing a high-necked black dress and unpowdered hair. There was a blurriness about her features and a symmetry that wasn't quite human.

He remembered the white figure he and Reggie had seen, and cursed himself.

"Arrogant," said Janet, stopping in front of him. "So certain I wouldn't know. So certain you know best." She laughed. "So useful for me."

None of that was wrong. Colin held still, telling

himself he was saving his strength, truly horrified by how true her accusations were and how much harm was likely to result, and even more appalled by what he saw in Janet's face.

Evil was a given. It took a certain kind of mind to bargain with demons and sacrifice children and turn people into flesh puppets. Colin had expected malice and had seen enough in his time. But when Janet had laughed, her whole face had looked wrong. The mouth didn't move quite in line with the eyes.

She'd been able to pass quite convincingly for Edmund—but she'd been able to see the man himself. Trying to appear the way she had been, she succeeded in looking like a bad drawing.

You don't remember what you looked like, he said, talking silently as he often did in dragon form. He doubted she could hear, and it didn't matter.

In life, Janet Morgan had been a thoroughly loathsome human being. That had been one thing. The ghost before him didn't even remember how to be human anymore.

"I had heard about things like you," she said now, cocking her head to one side. "Freakish things. Neither one nor the other. Bastard blood. Mixed. Highly improper."

Colin watched her without moving. If she was trying to make him angry, she was in for a severe disappointment. He didn't give much weight to the opinion of a mad ghost. She was, however, worrying him badly, and not simply because he was trapped in her circle of dark magic.

As he sat there, he could feel power draining out of

him. It wasn't a great deal, and given time and food he'd recover, but he doubted he'd have either.

And where was the power going? And was Janet Morgan looking different as she went on talking? More…solid?

Colin was afraid that he knew the answer to both questions.

Forty-two

EVEN WITH DIRECTIONS AND HER FATHER'S MEMORIES to guide her, Reggie spent the first part of her far-too-long journey worrying that they were going the wrong way, that they'd missed a turn, or that they would at any moment do either. The forest was dark and dense, and there was far too much of it. Trees and undergrowth overshadowed paths, and the uneven ground meant that Reggie couldn't have run, even if she'd had time to change out of skirts and corset.

When all of this was over, she was never going anywhere more rural than Greenwich again.

If she found Colin alive, she would go wherever he wanted. Or she would go to a leper colony and do good deeds there. Reggie wasn't sure which she should promise. She wasn't sure who she was bargaining with, or what they'd prefer. She should have asked Mr. Heselton, she thought, and felt a manic laugh bubble up in her throat.

Edmund didn't look at her—he was attending too closely to the woods on either side of them, rifle firmly in his hands—but after the laugh, he said, "It'll likely come out all right, Reggie. You...know about Colin, he said."

"I know," she said. It was the first time they'd really spoken since they'd left the house. Between looking for the right path and not letting Janet Morgan catch them by surprise, neither one of them had much presence of mind left over for conversation. She wanted to stop talking when she sounded reassured, just as she thought Edmund had wanted to sound more reassuring, but he was a bad liar and she couldn't hold the words back. "But *she's* a ghost. And a demon."

"Might be a closer struggle than otherwise," Edmund agreed heavily. "But he does have us."

"Oh, good," said Reggie.

And a little voice in the back of her head asked her why they were even bothering to come out. If Janet's trap had worked, if Colin, the part-dragon, the magician with more than a century of life behind him, was actually in danger, what exactly did Reggie think two mortals and a few lead projectiles would accomplish?

She told the voice to remember fables about mice and lions and traps—or was that thorns?—that in setting her trap for large prey, Janet might have left smaller openings unguarded, that there had to be a reason mortals were running so much of the world. Then she told the voice to go to the devil. Then she wished she hadn't thought of the devil.

If Colin was fine, she'd feel like an idiot. Reggie had never thought she'd be so eager for that.

If he was in trouble or fighting, perhaps they'd arrive in time to make a difference, even if only as a distraction.

If he was dead—

Her heart lurched sickeningly.

—if he was dead, he'd be *dead*, and there would be nothing anyone could do about that. She couldn't think about any future beyond that possible point.

She wished she couldn't think at all.

"There's the fallen tree," she said and pointed, grateful for the distraction and simultaneously feeling her nerves sharpen even more. Now she knew they were getting closer.

Running would be bad. Running was not subtle, and it greatly diminished one's ability to notice anything, and she was likely to fall and break any number of bones, which would help exactly nobody. Reggie made herself walk and almost shook with the effort it took to hold back.

There on her left was the patch of flowers, fuchsia in the midst of the green and brown undergrowth. The air was colder here—the ghost, or night coming on? The sun had begun to sink in the west. Filtered through the leaves of the forest, the light looked almost bloody. She'd never been afraid of the dark, but the idea of walking through this place at night would have given her the shivers if she hadn't already been terrified.

How useful to know that there were limits to how scared she could get. Surely this would be immensely helpful in her life to come.

Reggie heard the sound of running water just before she saw the stand of aspens, and her stomach clenched at the normally pleasant noise. They were in the right spot—they were as far as Pater's memories could take them. Now, if Colin was in trouble, everything was up to her and Edmund.

"Should have brought a torch," Edmund said, kneeling down and squinting at the ground. "But I think—this way."

"Footprints?"

"One set," said Edmund, grimly.

He rose and they went on, as quickly as they could. It wasn't long before Edmund's eyes weren't their only guide. The air went frigid very quickly, and Reggie knew that it wasn't just fear knotting her stomach. With every few steps forward, she felt as if she was edging her way along a tightrope, one stretched over not just a void but an unspeakable mass of corruption. By the look on Edmund's face, his senses were telling him the same.

They were getting near Janet's sanctum. That meant they were going the right way. Hurrah.

"Are you all right?" Edmund asked once, when they were following the stream back to its source. This time he did look back, though only for a second.

Reggie managed a smile. "Been better. I'll hold up. You?"

"It's hardly Christmas morning," he said, "but I've a strong stomach. Years of food at Eton, you know— wait, have a look up there."

He gestured ahead of them, where they could now see a smallish hill. Light rock and summer grass covered most of it, but in the center, near the ground, a dark shapeless pile rose up. They went forward to look closer. Edmund held his rifle ready, and Reggie pulled a pin out of her hat. Whether there was any real magic about silver or not, a hat pin was at least both long and sharp.

Nothing attacked them as they ventured closer— nothing but the sheer wrongness of the place, which almost pulsed out of the ground—and they could see the pile of rocks resting against the hill's face. Edmund gestured to the muddy earth in front of them. "The prints stop here," he whispered. "Must be a cave behind all those stones."

Their next task was clear—but not easy. Neither Reggie nor Edmund had done much manual labor in their lives, and neither of them had *ever* tried to move large rocks while being quiet about it. After a hideous quarter of an hour, in which they expected to be heard and assaulted at any minute, they'd produced a small opening, through which neither of them could hear or see anything.

It wasn't quite man-sized, but it was big enough for Reggie.

"Turn around," she whispered. When Edmund gave her a blank look in response, she flapped a hand at him impatiently. "Around," she hissed, and this time she didn't wait. When she unfastened her skirt, he saw the light quickly enough and nearly spun. "You don't have a knife, do you?" Reggie asked, shucking petticoats. They'd gone in too much of a hurry—but time was of the essence.

"No."

"Damn." Fingers shaking only a little, she undid the buttons on her blouse and started on her corset hooks.

"What the devil—"

"I'm not climbing over a lot of rocks in a walking suit," Reggie said.

"You shouldn't go in at all," Edmund whispered back, not turning his head.

"One of us has to. I can go now, and I'll make less noise." Reggie dropped her corset to the ground and quickly refastened her blouse. She glanced at the dark opening of the cave, then took her hat pin from the ground again. Without a knife, that was likely the best she could do. "Move the rocks and follow when you can."

The hole was a tight fit, even for Reggie in her underclothes. She wiggled through as swiftly and as quietly as she could, sacrificing what felt like three layers of skin on her shoulders and knees in the process and tearing a strip off one leg of her drawers. She dropped a short way into darkness and stood still, blinking while her eyes adjusted.

Getting her bearings, she first saw the bulk of Colin's dragon form, crouched with the tip of his tail about a foot away from her. It lashed the air, but moved oddly in doing so, though Reggie at first couldn't see exactly how. The dim light didn't help, though there was more than she'd thought. The cave entrance let in a few rays of twilight behind her, while in front of her—

—she was abruptly very glad she'd stayed still.

Whatever it was that crawled across the stone floor in sickly lines of green-black light, it was as much outside Reggie's experience as ghosts or dragons had been a month ago. That didn't matter. She didn't need experience to know that anything that looked the way that light did was bound to be *extremely* unhealthy. When she discovered that the line nearest her ran between two skulls—one that might have belonged to a fox and one that was almost certainly human and also very small—she was even more certain.

She also wanted to be sick, but that wasn't an option.

Now she could hear a voice coming from the other side of Colin. It was female, sort of. It sounded more hollow than a human voice should, and while that might have just been the acoustics of the cave, Reggie doubted it.

"…as polluted as my brother left the bloodline, it was still *ours*," said the voice, almost conversationally. "You're of an old family yourself, and although it's freakish and deformed, it's evidently powerful enough to suit my purposes. And perhaps you can try to understand some of what I went through, seeing a jumped-up tradesman—"

Ah. Janet Morgan, playing with half a deck at most. Reggie didn't really need to listen anymore. Colin, if dragons' tails signified anything like cats' did, didn't want to be listening. So—why was he there?

Reggie looked up from the obscene light to Colin's tail. It snapped out with anger—and then seemed to hit some unseen barrier, directly above the green-black line. The huge body in front of her shuddered, and Reggie sealed her lips around a rather dragonish hiss of rage.

Getting angry wouldn't help.

Very well: he was trapped. The lines on the floor were the trap, like magic circles in stories. If Reggie remembered those stories correctly, and if *they* were right, then breaking the circle should free Colin. If she didn't and they weren't—well, it was still the only thing she could think of to do.

She tried to take a deep breath without making any noise.

Without chalk, how would one break a magic circle?

It couldn't just be physical. Colin could have put a foot through the lines or moved the skulls, if that was the only disruption necessary—or a stray rat could have done the same. Janet would probably have thought of that. What wouldn't she have thought of?

Something man-made.

Something metal.

Something silver.

Reggie swallowed and knelt down, the hairpin in one hand. She wished she could warn Colin. For the first time, she would have liked her power to work in two directions. She hoped that he'd be strong enough in this form to handle whatever happened next.

She braced herself, though she didn't know exactly what for.

Then she thrust the hat pin into the line of corruption.

Forty-three

POWER BURST IN THE DARKNESS LIKE A STRING OF grotesque firecrackers.

Colin, who'd felt Reggie's presence nearby and had spent the last few minutes trying to distract Janet, now saw the dark flame rush toward and into her. The not-radiance crawled over her now mostly solid body like a swarm of insects, seeking its source, maybe. Colin didn't have the time or the inclination to find out. He was simply thankful first that none of it had gone toward Reggie and then that it had stayed away from him as well.

He dared a glance behind him and saw that Reggie was standing. That was as much reassurance as he could allow his leaping heart. His head told him that she was a big girl and could take care of herself, and that he would help neither of them by ignoring their situation—and Colin attended to that judgment. Janet had been building herself a body, using his life force. When Reggie had severed that connection, Janet's power had rebounded on her in a way she couldn't have been expecting. Colin thought that she probably couldn't leave the body she'd made.

Now he didn't bother roaring—this was no time for either anger or braggadocio—but just spat fire toward Janet in a hissing red stream. The flame whipped out beyond where the barrier had once been and cracked across Janet's body.

She froze. She might even have flinched. But she didn't burn. Colin had turned his flame on men before. He knew how they smelled when on fire, and he knew the sounds they made. He knew that Janet should have fallen, shrieked, and died. Instead, the flame licked over her body, shone off the last remnants of the loathsome black light, and then died.

Behind him, he heard Reggie curse.

I'll see that sentiment, he thought in grim horror, *and raise it.*

Janet raised her head and looked at him.

Make that double, Colin thought.

She hadn't looked quite human before. Now she barely looked human at all. Whether she'd meant to construct her body this way, the energy returning to her had warped her still-developing form, or she'd shifted to a shape more suited to fighting a dragon, the blurring had become outright distortion.

A monster stood before him, not a woman: a thing with bleached-pale skin and no hair, with triangular eyes that were barely more than holes in its head, with a lipless maw where razor fangs clustered three deep. Outsized arms dangled, gorilla-like, from its sloping shoulders, with huge claws where hands once had been. The creature straightened or shifted further, and Colin saw with disorienting abruptness that it was almost his own size.

He'd never much enjoyed physical fights. He'd always left them to Judith and Stephen when he could. There were times, however, when the best way forward—or at least the only one with a chance of success—was the most straightforward.

Teeth bared, claws out, Colin went for the monster's throat.

For a second, its flesh gave, cold and gummy under his talons—he didn't get close enough to bite, and part of him was grateful for that, even as he snarled at the missed opportunity—and then it wriggled and threw him off, lashing at him with one giant, gnarled hand. The claws might have been bone or rock or pure magical force. Whatever the substance, it tore through the scales of Colin's side with alarming ease. The pain wasn't new or insurmountable, but the very fact of its existence was a very, *very* bad sign.

He might actually die here, he thought, though not for the first or hundredth time since he'd entered the cave. He'd had a quick moment of relief when the circle had broken, and now fear was right back, as persistent as Janet herself. She—it—was on him now, those damned claws digging into his sides, trying to get purchase and find a vital organ beneath the layers of scale and skin and flesh.

Colin snarled and shook, throwing off the thing's grip and knocking it into the cave wall. Stunned, it shook itself, then—as Colin lunged for it—sprang upward and over his head, ripping almost all the way through one of his wings. Agony went shrieking down through every pathway in his body. His claws sank into the stone floor as blood flowed over his side, steaming in the chilly air. From his back, the monster laughed at him.

One of the skulls hit it with a gelatinous *shlup*. Whether the impact hurt the creature or not, it stopped laughing, and Colin heard Reggie shout. "How funny was *that*, you bastard?"

Before it could respond, before—God forbid—it could set its sights on a new and far more vulnerable target, Colin whipped his head back over his neck and snapped his jaws together on the monster. He only got its shoulder, and the taste was as awful as he'd thought it would be, all mildew and slime; still, the thing screamed in a very satisfying way. He lashed his head back around and down, slamming the monster against the floor and making it cry out again.

Again.

As Colin went for a third time, the monster got a claw up and raked bloody gashes into his muzzle, making him roar with pain and loosening his jaws before he could override his body's automatic response. The creature dropped onto the floor. It wasn't bleeding, but Colin could see the marks of his teeth and claws. They lasted, and they went deep. That was encouraging.

But he was still bleeding. Profusely. He wasn't feeling weak or dizzy yet, but it might be only a matter of time. The veins in his wings were large, and there was the gash along his side too. And while he assessed the damage, the monster charged him again. Colin spun and slammed his tail into the cold white body, knocking the creature away, but it was a near thing. For a second, he could see his own blood on the thing's claws.

He really hadn't thought he'd die in a fight. Those few times he'd considered the issue, Colin had always thought he'd pass away like his father, fading quietly into another world when this one became too much of a burden. Then again, the world was full of surprises, even for his kind. He'd always said that, and the last fortnight would have convinced him even if he hadn't.

Reggie.

Battle kept him from paying much attention to her, but he knew she stood at the cave entrance, and dimly at times, he heard her shouting instructions to someone outside or screaming at the monster. "Bloody well *die* already, won't you?" had been one such exclamation. He knew she wouldn't run, not while she thought she could still do anything.

He wouldn't die in front of her. And he damned well wouldn't leave the monster that had been Janet alive to go after her and her family next.

It wasn't as though he'd been nonchalant about the fight before, but the thought of Reggie, the need to make sure she was safe, was like a cool drink of water to a man who'd been running for hours. Colin dug down and found the last strength left in his limbs, the last energy in his veins, and the will to push himself past agony, past the injury he knew he'd be doing himself.

The cave wasn't very high.

Then again, he couldn't get very high in his current condition.

He snapped his wings back behind him. The motion tore his wound deeper and he screamed, but even a scream of pain from a dragon was a forceful thing, and the monster hesitated, confused or intimidated, or both. That was all the time that Colin needed.

He gathered his muscles and leaped, arrowing himself straight up as far as the cave ceiling and his own strength would permit. Then, with another cascade of pain and the feeling of at least one wing bone snapping, he spread his wings as wide as they could go and dove like a hunting falcon onto the monster.

It raised its claws to defend itself, and they bit deeply into Colin's chest, but it didn't matter. He weighed more than a ton in this form. Dropping on the monster with all of his own strength and all the force of gravity behind him, he shook the whole cave when he hit. That his own claws went all the way through the thing, that his teeth snapped together on its neck, were almost minor developments.

Beneath him, he felt the monster fall apart, its body unraveling into air and force and whatever half-decayed matter Janet had used to make it. Her power began to disintegrate too—not that the cave or the forest nearby would be a wonderful picnic site for a generation or two, but the sense of corruption began to fade even as the creature dissolved in Colin's claws—and the energy she'd stolen from Colin flowed back into him.

Good, he thought as he lay on the floor. He suspected that he'd need everything he could get.

Forty-four

As Reggie rushed forward, the shape in front of her blurred and shrank. She couldn't follow the process and didn't think she wanted to. One minute a huge blue dragon was lying on the cave floor in a spreading pool of blood, and the next a slender young man was lying there in what now looked, relative to his body, like a *lake* of the stuff.

A person only had so much blood. She'd never been trained in nursing, the way Miss Heselton had, but she knew that, and by the time she reached Colin's side, her heart felt the size of a small raisin.

No, she thought. It was all she could think, a steady and arrhythmic chorus in her head: *no no, no no no, no*.

Edmund was behind her. He'd gotten into the cave during the quick, awful fight that had taken about a year, tried to aim his rifle at Janet Morgan's new form, and been unable to get off a shot without the risk of hitting Colin instead. Both creatures had been enormous, but they'd been so closely locked in their struggle that Reggie had barely found a chance to hit Janet with a skull, and had seen no further opportunity.

She'd stood on the side like the most useless of females in plays and novels. She might actually have wrung her hands. Now she knelt by Colin and tried not to think how much that image must resemble another from the stage: Woman by Her Dying Beloved.

At least Colin was breathing and his eyes were open. They focused on her as she drew closer, and he managed to lift an eyebrow. "Verra stylish, Miss Talbot-Jones."

"Hush up," she said, but he'd given her an idea. "Edmund, go grab my petticoats." The slash on his side didn't look too bad, in her extremely inexpert opinion. She couldn't see ribs or organs, and the flow of blood was relatively slow. "Should I help you turn over? Your back—"

"Back's fine. Wings dinna' translate across."

"Ah," she replied and said a prayer: quick, silent, and incoherent except for *thank you*. Now she only had to worry about the wound in his side and the blood he'd already lost, and the fact that, now she had time to notice anything but bleeding, both of his arms hung from their sockets at absolutely wrong angles. "Well—hang on."

With a visible effort of will, Colin smiled. "Dinna' worry yourself, lass," he said, and his speech was growing both more accented and more slurred. His eyes were glassier too. "I'll be all right. You're to thank for that. Knew there was a reason I love you."

"I—you—" Reggie shook her head. "No. You don't tell me that here. Not like this." There were too many of those plays in her memory, too many melancholy songs.

"However you want," said Colin, and then his eyes closed.

Reggie made an incoherent and extremely loud sound of alarm, and reached for him, but Edmund put a hand on her shoulder. "He's only gone under. Still breathing fine, see?" he said, handing her a petticoat which he'd already torn in two. "For the best—we'll have a job to do getting him home."

"Then let's get started," said Reggie.

∽

"You need to sit down, Regina," Pater said. "And you need to eat."

The drawing room was not far from Colin's door. It had been easy for Mr. Talbot-Jones to take his daughter by the wrist and draw her away from where she'd been wearing a hole in the carpets. He evidently hadn't acted out of impulse, for a covered tray sat on one of the tables, giving off an aroma of toast, and a cup of tea steamed beside it. There would, Reggie knew, be two lumps of sugar in it and exactly as much milk as she liked.

Eating felt impossible. She only knew she had a stomach because it felt so damned awful.

She sat, though.

"I'm all right," she said, as she'd been saying for the last hour. She'd said it to Mater in the middle of an embrace and a scolding. She'd said it to the Heseltons as they stared. She'd said it to the maids who had washed her and put her into a tea gown while she complied, boneless, with their directions. Say it enough and it would be true.

Physically, it was.

"Once you eat a little," Pater said, "you'll feel more inclined to go on."

He wasn't going to give up, and toast was not a difficult food. Reggie broke off a small piece, softened it in milk, and managed to swallow. The next bite was easier. She looked up at Pater and actually saw him for the first time since she'd come back. "How did you know?"

"My valet told me," he said with a faint smile, "when you were being born."

The thought of her father being nervous—too nervous even to eat—made Reggie smile herself, and either that or the toast and tea eased the taut wires of her nerves a little.

"Dr. Brant is very good," said Pater, "and so is Miss Heselton, though I fear she'll not be with us long."

"Oh?"

Mr. Talbot-Jones nodded. "She's only stayed this long because of her brother, really. We're too strange for her nerves or for her conception of the world, even if Edmund…well."

She wasn't the only one who worried. Reggie reached over and put a hand on her father's arm. "He'll be all right, Pater," she said, remembering her glimpse into his mind. "He's a sensible chap, though I'd never say it to his face. And he'll find his way."

"I hope so. You're both quite young, whether you realize it or not."

"Trust me," said Reggie "after this fortnight, I realize it."

A knock at the door made them both turn. Reggie's

stomach contracted again, and this time her lungs did too. Pater was the one to call out, "Come in."

Miss Heselton opened the door but didn't step inside. "Dr. Brant sent me," she said, "to say that Mr. MacAlasdair is asleep and in stable condition. He's lost blood, but fortunately the…cave-in…didn't damage any major organs."

"Oh, thank God." Reggie was already on her feet, toast in one hand.

"Dr. Brant also says he isn't to be disturbed," Miss Heselton said. "He'll check back in tomorrow and let us know when Mr. MacAlasdair can receive visitors."

Reggie sank back down. She couldn't be disappointed; she was too thankful. And, she realized now, she had no idea what she would have said in any case.

She heard Pater thanking Miss Heselton, and the other woman talking about finding her brother and having some tea to calm her nerves, and then the door shut again. Absently, Reggie lifted the toast back to her mouth.

"I'm not going to question your judgment," Pater said, once Reggie had taken a few more bites. "You know Mr. MacAlasdair well, and—and I can't deny that you have a certain facility for seeing beneath the surface of people. He seems an honorable man to me, and if you agree—"

"He's a good man," said Reggie.

Pater hesitated, then smiled. "I'm glad to hear it. Just be certain. You know your mother and I wish for a certain…continuity…regarding this house, and I can't deny that either, not now, but we also want you to be happy. Foremost, we want you to be happy." He sighed. "It's occurred to me that perhaps that hasn't been as evident as it should be."

"But I knew it," Reggie said and stood up to embrace her father.

❧

Two days later, after Mater had said several things about Reggie's state of dress and the questionable wisdom of running off into the forest and meant *I am so glad you're all right* by all of them; after a celebratory dinner of which Reggie had been able to eat very little and two nights when her exhausted body had taken over and dropped her into ten hours of dreamless darkness; two days later, she stood by Colin's door and chewed on her lip.

Reggie hadn't gone down the tree to visit him. Mostly, that had been because she was too tired, which she hadn't been able to understand. She hadn't done anything more strenuous than move rocks, and she couldn't see why she'd kept dozing off, or why her whole body felt rolled and ironed. "You've had a shock," said Miss Heselton, in one of her more human moods, when Reggie had brought it up.

Yes, Reggie thought. She'd had a number of them, and not all either physical or mental.

One of those shocks had played its part in keeping her out of Colin's room. True, she'd been tired. True, Dr. Brant had said Colin wasn't to be disturbed, and as he had more than a head injury to worry about, Reggie hadn't been able to justify violating that order. But adding up those two reasons didn't give her a whole.

You don't tell me that here. Not like this, she'd said.

She'd thought she was worried about tempting fate. Now that Colin was recovering, Reggie wondered if he'd actually *want* to repeat that particular sentiment to her, without relief and blood loss as factors.

The door to Colin's room swung open, and Dr. Brant stepped out. On his face, professional satisfaction mingled with the expression that had deepened more and more as he'd come to Whitehill: the one that said *I don't know what on earth is going on here, and I don't want to ask.*

He smiled at Reggie, though, and when he said, "I think Mr. MacAlasdair would appreciate your company—just for a little while, mind," his voice was positively avuncular.

That might have been a good sign. She would have read omens in the flights of birds, if there'd been any around—and if birds would ever seem completely innocent again.

"Much obliged," said Reggie.

She wouldn't ask Colin. She'd wrestle Janet Morgan herself before she brought up what he'd said and whether he'd meant it, or still did. She rubbed her hands against her skirt and stepped into the room.

"I'm here," she said as the door swung shut behind her. "Even properly dressed, for once."

"Pity," said Colin, and he grinned. He was sitting up already, wearing the same dressing gown he'd had on when they'd met. Oh, he was paler than he had been, and his eyes were shadowed, but a stranger would've seen no dramatic difference.

"It's indecent, you know," said Reggie, sitting

down in a chair by his side. Words came more easily than she'd feared. "Not me—you. You should at least look a little like you've almost died, not like you just got tiddly last night."

"I didn't have to," said Colin. "Morphine's a marvelous invention."

"Ha," said Reggie. Sitting near him, watching him smile and talk, she felt the iron bands that had been around her heart for two days loosen and fall away. "Trust you to enjoy dire injury. I suppose it's a new experience."

"I've had a few of those lately," said Colin. Wounded, he'd lost his unearthly speed. When he reached over and took Reggie's hand, she actually saw the motion. "And you've been worth all the others."

"Just because I saved your life—" said Reggie, reaching for a joke to steady herself, because she thought the chair was starting to float.

"No," he said and coughed. "Although perhaps I'm getting ahead of myself. I don't mean to, er, importune you with my feelings. If you don't share them, that is. No harm done."

The chair was definitely floating. That was all right. Reggie smiled and didn't think she'd be able to stop any time soon. "You really are a prize idiot," she said and leaned forward to cup his face in one hand. "Do you think I'd have gone tearing into a haunted cave—in my underthings, no less—for just *anyone*?"

"You?" he asked, his eyes shining like a summer evening. "Yes. Absolutely."

"Right. Hold still," said Reggie in, if not the

sternest voice, the sternest one she could manage just then.

Colin lifted an eyebrow and watched her stand up. "Why?"

"Because I don't want to kill you by accident," she said and bent down to kiss him, carefully and for a very long time. Despite her orders, he did move—cradling her head in his hands and stroking her hair. She wasn't inclined to complain, even when she broke off.

"I love you too," Reggie said. "And I think we're both very lucky that you heal fast."

She left the room laughing, not conscious of her feet on the carpet and only barely so of Edmund's knowing grin when he saw her face. One day soon, Colin would come out of the room with her; not long after that, their life together would begin. No matter how long that ended up being, Reggie knew it would be worth everything that had come before.

Read on for an excerpt from
the next book in Isabel Cooper's
Highland Dragons series:

Night of the
Highland Dragon

"LOCH ARANOCH?" THE GIRL SHRUGGED, FLIPPING A
straw-colored braid over her shoulder, and went on,
her accent almost too thick for William to understand.
"Aye. They're all queer up that way," she added, in
the just-for-your-information tone at which girls of
twelve seemed to excel in every place and generation.

Her brother elbowed her in the side. "No such
thing," he said to William, like a man attempting to
correct the foolishness of his juniors and womenfolk.
"It's only that 'tis a very small village, ye ken."

"And backward," said the girl, refusing to be
squelched. "Havena' even got the telegraph in."

"Have you gone there?" William asked.

The boy shook his head. "The farmers come in for
the market day, some of them. We're there with the
wool, so we've a chance to talk at times."

"Mostly with their daughters," said the girl, and she

received another elbow for the information—sharper, if her indignant squeal was any sign.

William smiled and reminded himself to be patient. Youth was youth in all corners of the world; shouting or snapping wouldn't get him the answers he wanted, and he would have found the bickering funny another time, if he hadn't been thinking about murder.

Neither of the youngsters knew his thoughts, any more than they knew about the body in the woods. William wanted to keep it that way as long as possible. With luck, he'd be long gone before they heard rumors about the dead boy. With more luck, nobody in Belholm would connect him or his questions with those rumors—at least, not where his quarry could hear.

He focused on the siblings again. Elsie and Tom Waddell lived at the edge of the forest, like all the poor-but-honest woodcutters in fairy tales. By local standards, they weren't poor—their father owned a healthy flock of sheep as well as his house and farm— but William hoped they were honest and that they knew the land well enough.

Under his gaze, they left off their argument. Tom, a few years older, had the grace to look embarrassed. "Sorry, sir. We're not very much acquainted with them up at the Loch, to tell the truth. I wouldna say anyone is much. But they're fine folk, I'm sure of it," he added with a glance at his sister. "Will you be wanting to go up that way?"

"Perhaps," said William, and he took a measuring look northwestward, where the mountains rose to meet the bright autumn sky. In theory, there was a lake somewhere beyond that line of hills, and a village nearby where "backward" people lived, "queer" individuals who were nonetheless "fine folk"…except that one of them might be a killer.

One of them might be a victim too. The dead boy might not have been local. By English standards, or at least by William's, Belholm was a small village, but it was big enough for the train to stop there twice a day, and there were plenty of farms on the outskirts where people kept to themselves. Nobody had reported a missing man, whether son, husband, brother, or farmhand, and William wasn't in a position to go making that sort of inquiry.

Even if he had been, he wouldn't have been able to give much information. The body he'd found had been almost unrecognizable. He'd made out sex, species, and rough age, but that had been all. Animals had done some of the damage—by the time William had arrived, the poor chap had been lying out for three days, in a forest full of scavengers—but the worst of it had come from human hands. The killer, whoever he or she was, had pulled the boy apart in a manner that called to mind the killings in Whitechapel a decade back, or the dissecting table.

…or a sacrifice.

Save when a mission called for it, William wasn't a gambling man, but he knew where he'd have put his money if he had been.

"Does the road lead anywhere else?" he asked and gestured toward the mountains. "Going that way, I mean?"

Elsie shook her head. "Who else would want to live up *there*?" she asked, wrinkling her freckled nose. "Bad enough to be this far away from everything, isn't it? At least here there's the train and the telegraph, and we're getting the papers from Aberdeen every day now. Up that way is just Loch Aranoch and the devil of a lot of forest."

"She's right," said Tom, albeit reluctantly. "If anyone else lives that way, they keep themselves to themselves even better than the folk of Aranoch. I suppose you'd get over the mountains eventually, but there's plenty easier ways to do that."

"And the people there are...strange? Backward?" William kept his voice light, sounding simply curious—if a shade tasteless—rather than as if he was fishing for information. So he hoped, at least: it had been a long few months.

"Ah, well," said Tom, with a more stoic shrug than his sister's, "they are a bit closed-mouthed, is the truth of it. And there are stories, of course, but that's just fancy," he added in the skeptical-man-of-the-world voice.

"Stories?"

"They *say*," said Elsie, eager to contribute where her brother was too embarrassed, "that people disappear up there."

Tom snorted.

Ignoring him, Elsie dropped her voice. "And I heard that the lady doesna' ever grow any older."

"The lady?" William asked.

"Lady MacAlasdair. She lives in the castle, and she's been there years, but she stays young and beautiful forever. And how would ye do that?"

"Hair dye," said Tom, "and rouge. And having *silly*

little girls tell romantic stories about people they've not seen once."

Ignoring Elsie's violent outburst at *silly little girls*, William chuckled. "I see," he said. "Have you met this young and beautiful lady?"

"Nay. She doesna' come out of Loch Aranoch much, 'tis true," said Tom, once he'd successfully dodged his sister's foot. "But the gi—the *people* I've talked to say she's in the village often enough. And they do say she's comely."

"And…people disappearing?"

"Stories," said Tom firmly. "Stories, and maybe old men who went hunting in their cups and broke their necks, or a man's wife running off with a peddler. There's no one bathin' in maiden's blood up at the Loch, sir—and none who should believe it, Elsie."

"Jolly good," said William, and he laughed again, as if he were just as skeptical as Tom. A bit hard on Elsie, of course, but there was more at stake here than the feelings of one youthful maybe-Cassandra. "People *do* go there and come back again, I assume."

"Oh, aye, of course. Not a terribly great many of 'em—"

"Who'd *want* to?" Elsie put in, sullen now.

"—but there was a painter came through the summer before last. He stopped here on the way back, and gave me sixpence for carrying his wee painting kit," Tom added in what might have been a hint.

"I think I can do a bit better," said William, and he dug two half-crowns out of his pocket.

Elsie squealed again, this time with delight. Tom

just grinned and bobbed his head. "Thank you, sir. Very much obliged."

"Think nothing of it," William said, wishing he had the power to make the polite saying into a command. "I shan't trouble you any further."

He could ask nothing else. Oh, he could *think* of things to ask, but the children probably wouldn't know the answers, and they might start wondering why he wanted to know.

A day or two from now, someone else—hunter, peddler, painter, or possibly but hopefully not another child out playing—would stumble over the body in the woods. Then the hue and cry would go up. Men would go around the houses and ask, and find out whether or not the poor soul had belonged to Belholm. They might even find out who he'd been. They *would* be Scots, those men, and they would have no connections to D Branch, nor prior encounters with the Consuasori, the Brotherhood of the Grey Duke, or any other of the mad and maddening cults that grew these days like mold after rain.

Nobody would be surprised at such an investigation, and the guilty party would take no particular alarm from it.

William couldn't afford to seem interested.

Watching the children leave—they kept to a polite walk as long as he was watching, but he knew they'd break into a run afterward, eager to get home or down to the shops with their windfall—he went over the facts he knew.

Item the first: the boy's ghost had managed to get itself to Miss Harbert, over in Edinburgh, before going on to whatever lay ahead. By the time the medium had been in position to receive, he'd been fading, but he remembered the essentials: the chloroform, the Latin, the sense of what Harbert and William knew was magical force, and, perhaps most importantly, the location. From what Harbert had said and William himself had encountered, remaining so long and so coherent when away from his body had taken both considerable strength from the ghost and some relaxation of certain boundaries from the other side.

Neither of those was a good sign.

Item the second: the killing itself. Chloroform argued that pain hadn't been a necessary component, but the killer had bled the boy thoroughly, then removed eyes, tongue, and hands. Symbolically, that probably meant sight, communication, and action—but William didn't know whether the killer had been enhancing his or her own faculties or restricting someone else's.

Item the third: tracks. There hadn't been many in the physical world. Even in good weather, a footprint wouldn't last for three days in the forest. William had a few resources most men didn't, though, especially when he was certain he wouldn't be seen. The equipment that let him look into the past—two silver chains, etched with runes and tipped at either end with onyx—was clunky and obvious, and the procedure not always reliable, but it had proved a godsend more than once in the last five years.

This time, the results had been mixed. As always, he saw the past through a thick haze, as bad as the worst of the London pea-soupers. While a clearer view would have been more *useful*, the blurred sort was often better for his peace of mind, as in this case: he'd seen the killer's form stooping over the boy's unconscious body and witnessed the slow process of the death, but the fog had hidden all details.

The killer was human, or human-shaped. He or she was tall for a woman, or middling-height for a man, and relatively thin, and moved like someone whose joints and muscles still obeyed them without a hitch. Otherwise, the murderer had only been a dark shape, and lost in more darkness soon after he or she had left the body.

Before the shape had vanished, it had headed up the road. It had gone up toward the mountains, where the children said there wasn't much but a reclusive village with a strangely young-looking lady, past a forest where men had been known to disappear.

Up the road, then, was William's destination too. If he left now, he might get there before sundown, but it didn't seem very likely.

He adjusted his bag—clothing, the silver chains, guns and ammunition, and a book for the train—on his shoulder, faced the road, and couldn't help but sigh.

He envied young Tom. He envied the boy's parents, who'd doubtless had some part in his hardheaded skepticism. He envied any man who could look down the road that faced him now and tell himself that this was practically the twentieth century, that he was in Scotland, not Darkest Transylvania, and that really and truly, nobody around here *was* bathing in maidens' blood or ever would.

Maidens' blood would be fairly mild—especially as

one could only go through so many maidens, even in a wholesome rural community.

As bad as the legends were, the truth would probably be worse. William had found that it generally worked that way.

⤞⤝

The restful thing about Agnes, Judith thought as she watched the other woman pour tea, wasn't that she didn't ask questions. She asked plenty: she was asking another one right now. "I canna think it's at all safe, can you? All of those wires right there in the house, and what if one of them breaks?"

That was the kind of question Agnes asked. That was the kind with which Judith could live very well.

"Then you die," said Judith. She broke open a muffin, still steaming hot—even looking human, she had certain advantages over those with only mortal blood in their veins—and reached for the butter. "Probably most unpleasantly. You'll remember I wasn't very enthusiastic about Colin's ideas."

Besides, she could see perfectly well in the dark, and she had no need to keep her servants up at all hours.

"You never are that," said Agnes.

"Not *never*. There's been an occasion or two. I like his wife well enough—that has to count for something, doesn't it?"

"More than many sisters would admit." Agnes smiled. "Will they be coming back soon, do you think?"

"I don't know," said Judith.

She knew that Agnes wouldn't ask *why* she didn't know, or how long Colin had been away before, or how old he was. Most people in Loch Aranoch wouldn't. Agnes was one of the few with whom Judith didn't always hear the unasked question, one of the few who dwelt comfortably with the answers she would never hear, and therefore one of the few mortals Judith could come close to calling a friend.

That was why she told herself that the gray in the other woman's hair was only shadows, and that she saw no lines at the corner of Agnes's eyes. Judith was decent at lying to herself, though not as good as she once had been.

"Aye, well," said Agnes, "it's been a great year for visitors, in any case. Your brothers, and that friend of the doctor's, and now Elspeth MacDougal's son's come back. I dinna know if you'd heard that."

Judith shook her head. Mrs. MacDougal had been housekeeper at MacAlasdair Keep for forty years, before old age had made her retire to a cottage with her daughter's family. She remembered the boy vaguely, as a towheaded youth running around the village; she thought he'd taken after the father, who she barely remembered more of.

"Come back for good?" she asked.

"He didna say. Not but what it would do them good to have another man about the house, with the third bairn on its way and the harvest coming in. But he's been living well down in London—"

Anywhere south of Aberdeen and west of Calais was *London* to Agnes. She knew the difference, Judith was sure. She just didn't care.

"—and there's few men who will want to give that up. His mother's that glad about it, though: I dinna think she'd more than three letters while he was away."

"Maybe he went to sea," said Judith, "and couldn't write regularly."

"Maybe," said Agnes, skeptically. "I'm just glad I've a daughter, that's all."

"Women go out into the world too, I hear." Judith smiled across the teacup. "More and more in this degenerate modern age."

"Aye, but fewer than the men, still. And they've more feeling for what they leave behind, I'm sure of it."

"Maybe," said Judith, and it was her turn to be dubious.

"You're here, aren't you? And your brothers all away?"

"Yes," said Judith, and she didn't add *for now*, or *after a hundred years or so*, or any of the other replies that might have sprung to her lips.

She was trying to think of a less revealing argument when the door opened a crack. "Mum?" Agnes's daughter Claire stuck her face through the opening. She was sixteen, all blithe blonde prettiness, and Judith still couldn't get used to it: in her mind, Claire was still a toddling girl with braids and a jam-covered face. "There's a man here looking for lodgings."

"You might be right," Judith said to Agnes. "Not about men and women—about this year."

"It's the railroads, I'm sure of it. Show him in, Claire," Agnes said. "We'll give him a cup of tea while we hear what he has to say. And," she added, lowering her voice as her daughter headed off to show the man in, "you might as well get a look at the man. He's likely to be the most excitement we have around here for a fortnight, unless someone's barn catches fire."

At first glance, the guest didn't *look* particularly exciting.

Oh, he was handsome: tall but not lanky, with broad shoulders and muscular legs and neatly cut hair the color of the turning leaves outside, graying just enough at the temples to lend him a distinguished air. Looking at him was a pleasant diversion. Judith, who'd diverted herself with handsome men a few times when she'd been younger and had more freedom, didn't think his presence was going to be the year's thrill for her.

Claire's sudden need to rearrange the parlor knick-knacks indicated that she felt otherwise, but that was sixteen for you.

Hat in hand, the visitor bowed smoothly. "I do hope I'm not disturbing you," he said in a voice thick with public school and university. His clothes were tweed, Judith noted, and practical, but good quality and—if she recalled her brothers' wardrobes correctly—the latest London fashion.

As he spoke, he looked around the parlor, his blue eyes taking in the deep red wallpaper and the stuffed horsehide chairs, the mahogany table and the damask cloth. In his face, Judith saw careful, if quick, evaluation, then satisfied confirmation. All was in order; he'd found what he'd expected in a place like this.

"Ach, no," said Agnes, giving him her warmest smile for prospective boarders. "Have yourself a seat and a wee bite. We've plenty to go around."

"I'm greatly obliged," said the man. "Do I have the privilege of addressing Mrs. Simon?"

Agnes smiled again. "Aye, you do. And this," she said with a gesture, "is Lady Judith MacAlasdair."

Already knowing what would happen, Judith saw the stranger's face freeze briefly in surprise. Where he was from, ladies didn't take tea with boardinghouse keepers. That had been true when Judith was young, and from everything she'd heard, the boundaries had only gotten firmer—Stephen's decision to marry a commoner out of the East End notwithstanding. She smiled into that startled expression, as blandly polite as she could manage. "A pleasure, sir."

Soon enough, and quicker than Judith would have expected, she saw the man recover himself, no doubt thinking that a tiny little Scottish village didn't operate by the same standards as civilized society. "The pleasure is mine, I assure you," he said. "I'm William Arundell."

Judith would have bet the castle and half a month's rent that he had at least two middle names, too, at least one of them along the lines of *Percival* or *Chauncey*.

In the back of her head, a voice very much like her brother Colin's said that it was deuced odd for the lady with the title and castle to be bristling about snobs. Judith told that voice to hush: Arundell wasn't just rich and educated. He was an outsider, for one thing, and for another...she didn't like the way he'd looked at the room, or at Agnes.

She certainly didn't like the way he was looking at her. It wasn't lust: she'd spent enough decades around soldiers and sailors that she wouldn't have batted an eye at mere lechery. No, Arundell's expression was gentlemanly enough, but underneath it she sensed the same evaluation he'd turned on the parlor, without— she was glad to see—the satisfaction.

What reason—never mind what *right*—did he have for sizing her and her friend and her village up like so many horses at auction, or so many freaks in a sideshow?

"What brings you up here?" she asked. "You don't have family in the village?"

Only politeness kept it a question rather than a statement. If Arundell had been anyone's relation, Judith would have known—unless he was a bastard who'd done incredibly well for himself. She was considering that possibility when Arundell shook his head.

"No, nothing of the sort," he said. "My physician recommended it. Not here specifically, of course, but getting away from city life, from crowds and smoke and so on, so I've been touring the countryside. One of the villagers in Belholm mentioned Loch Aranoch. It sounded like an excellent…well, retreat, if you will."

"I suppose we are that," said Agnes, laughing. "And you'll be wanting rooms, then?"

"For an indefinite time, if it could be managed."

"And gladly." Agnes got to her feet—still easily, Judith noticed and wished she could stop noticing such things—and put her cup down on the table. "Lady Judith, if you'll excuse us for a moment, we'll just be stepping into my office to settle the details."

Judith was glad to let them go.

Once again, the voice of self-reproach spoke up, wondering whether she was truly going to dislike the man because of a strangeness in the way he looked; once again she told it to be silent. If two centuries of life had taught her anything, it was to trust her instincts. Just at the moment, she couldn't act on this one—the man had done nothing overtly wrong—but she tucked the impression away, to turn over and look at later, from more angles and with better tools.

When Claire came over to nab a muffin, Judith thought she might have an idea where her distrust came from. A man who looked at Loch Aranoch as an interesting diversion might well look at its people the same way; Arundell wouldn't be the first man to decide that fresh things other than *air* would give him a new outlook on life. He was in his forties, if Judith was any judge, and Claire was sixteen. Agnes had probably told her a few home truths by now—Agnes hadn't had much time for men even before her husband had died—but that could hurt as much as help at Claire's age.

"Did you talk to Mr. Arundell much outside?" Judith asked as casually as she could manage.

"Well, no," said Claire, sighing, "not really. He said good afternoon, and I said aye, it was bidding fair to be grand, and could I be helping him with anything, and he asked was I the proprietor of this establishment, only in a joking sort of a way, ye ken—and he has a bonny smile, Lady Judith, you should see it—"

"I'm sure he does."

"And I laughed and said no," Claire went on. If she'd noticed the interruption, she gave no sign of it. Sixteen, Judith thought, was in certain ways the youngest age. Her own time in the valley of that particular shadow was a dim memory now, which went a good way toward arguing for the merciful nature of the universe. "And I asked did he want Mum, and did he want lodgings for a time, and he said he couldn't imagine leaving soon now that he'd seen how lovely the place was."

Judith made a neutral sound. It didn't sound, in fairness, as if Arundell had said anything outside the bounds of polite flattery. Not yet, at least.

"And then I showed him into the parlor. Do you think he'll stay for a while? Do you think he'll be at the fair?" Claire caught her breath at this evidently new idea. "I'll be having a new dress. Of course," she added, suddenly downcast, "it's bound to be out of style by now, and I'm sure he's used to very fashionable ladies."

"I'm sure he's used to *older* ones," said Judith. "And if he isn't, he should be, no matter how pretty you are. You're old enough to know what I'm saying, aren't you?"

She hoped so. Pure human girls were so damnably *fertile*, and the world wasn't kind to an unmarried woman with a baby. Loch Aranoch was small enough that everyone would talk, no matter what Judith did; bigger places had their own dangers.

Claire was nodding now, chewing on her lip and looking about to go into a fit of sulks.

"Besides, isn't the Stewart lad chasing after you these days? And haven't you been doing a good bit of chasing back?"

"Oh, aye," said Claire again. If she wasn't completely mollified, the mention of her beau still did seem to keep her from sinking completely into the doldrums. "But he's been all nervy lately. It's *tiring* for a girl," she added as the door to her mother's private office opened and Arundell followed Agnes into the parlor. "Just because a beast killed one of his old cows."

And at *that*, of all things, Judith saw Arundell's gaze sharpen.

Night of the Highland Dragon

by Isabel Cooper

— ❧ —

William Arundell is a detective working for a secret branch of the English government. When a young man is found dead, William's investigation leads him to a remote Highland village and the strangely youthful, intoxicatingly beautiful lady who rules MacAlasdair Castle. Nothing could have prepared him for the discovery that the charismatic Judith MacAlasdair is the only daughter in a long line of shape-changing dragons…or the fact that together they must put aside years of bad blood to save the British Islands from its deadliest foe…

— ❧ —

Praise for the Highland Dragons series:

"The mix of adventure and romance is just perfectly entertaining." —*Star-Crossed Romance*

"Magical, fantastic, and a great read for any dragon lover…" —*The Romance Reviews*

For more Isabel Cooper, visit:

www.sourcebooks.com

Legend of the Highland Dragon
by Isabel Cooper

He guards a ferocious secret

In Victorian England, gossip is as precious as gold. But if anyone found out what Highlander Stephen MacAlasdair really was, he'd be hunted down, murdered, his clan wiped out. As he's called to London for business, he'll have to be extra vigilant—especially between sunset and the appearance of the first evening star.

Mina wanted to find out more about the arrogant man who showed up in her employer's office, but she never thought he'd turn into a dragon right in front of her. Or that he'd then offer her an outrageous sum of money to serve as his personal secretary. Working together to track a dangerous enemy, Mina finds out that a man in love is more powerful and determined than any dragon.

"An outstanding read! A fast-paced, smartly written plot—fraught with danger and brimming with surprises—makes it impossible to put down."
—*RT Book Reviews* Top Pick, 4.5 Stars

"Mesmerizing, ingenious, slyly humorous, and wonderfully romantic."—*Library Journal*

For more Isabel Cooper, visit:

www.sourcebooks.com

About the Author

Isabel Cooper lives in Boston, in an apartment with two houseplants, an inordinate number of stairs, a silver sword, and a basket of sequined fruit. By day, she works as a theoretically mild-mannered legal editor; by night, she tries to sleep. Her family reunions don't generally involve ghosts, though snakes and alligators have been known to make themselves present. You can find out more at www.isabelcooper.org.